TURBULENT MAGIC

E.M. PETERSON

Turbulent Magic

ISBN 9798987569177 (ebook)
ISBN 9798987569153 (paperback)

The Flight Attendant

People said a lot of things the first time they rode on a dragon. Seeing one's town from above, recognizing important landmarks as they shrank into obscurity, and realizing that one's existence maybe wasn't as large as one thought, all had a way of changing one's perspective. The responses ranged from the indignant—*surely my roof doesn't have* that *many holes in it*—to the over-awed—*Arren bless and protect us*—to the theoretically profound but technically meaningless—*all our lives this was up here*.

Tal had heard them all. However, rather than focusing on the view, or the wrenching sensation each time the dragon beat its powerful wings, Tal was in the cabin making sure the passengers had fastened their seatbelts. The cabin was a clear glass shed, thirty feet long and twelve feet across. It wasn't particularly well-insulated, but was enough to divert the wind's direct assault, and would mostly catch unsecured passengers if they happened to hit turbulence—or worse—if the dragon experienced an unexpected sneeze.

"Excuse me, young man," a middle-aged woman said as he walked by. She sat very upright on the padded bench, as if ready to spring out the emergency exit at a moment's notice. "It's absolutely sweltering. Could you *please* turn the heat down in here, or will I be forced to speak with your supervisor about the flying conditions once we land?"

Tal had heard every conceivable reaction to flying for the first time, but he hadn't heard this one.

"I'm sorry to hear that," was Tal's automatic, if not necessarily sincere, response.

The woman adjusted the tall purple hat on her head as she continued: "I have on my fur-lined boots today—they wouldn't fit in my luggage, you know—and the scales are making my feet sweat terribly. I expected at least some modicum of comfort given the expense of my ticket."

The dragon had started his first bank turn as they reached cruising altitude, turning out to sea. The woman's fur-lined boots were positioned delicately on the scaly gray-red floor, which also happened to be the dragon's back.

"Just so I understand, the dragon who is currently carrying you safely to heights previously unthinkable for a human being, heights that wouldn't be possible without a landmark degree of interspecies cooperation, is too hot?" Tal asked. "And it's only your feet, which happen to be inside fur-lined boots, that are too hot."

"Precisely," the woman said. "Can you ask him to—I don't know—turn it down a little?"

It took every part of Tal to hold back a long, loud sigh.

"I'll see what I can do," Tal said.

He worked his way down the aisle on one side of the cabin. The dragon's spines ran through the center, with benches tied to the protruding spikes. Tal made sure everyone else was comfortably settled in before opening the rear door.

"Remember to ask him!" the woman in the purple hat said. He nodded halfheartedly and stepped out into the whipping wind.

Tal lowered his goggles and looped the hook of the tether that ran along the outside of the cabin to his harness. There wasn't much need for the harness today. Most dragons employed in aviation had broad, flat backs, and this dragon was a sure flyer when he wanted to be. Tal made his way up toward the dragon's head, his steps light. The first time he had walked on a dragon's back, he had found it unnerving how the scales gave ever so slightly under his feet, hinting at the softer flesh beneath.

The flight attendant's seat was tied onto the dragon's neck, close enough to his head that Tal could give directions if he needed to, and protected by a curved windscreen. Ronar's neck muscles flexed at Tal's presence. He bent back to look at Tal with one intelligent yellow eye.

"Looks like we're on course," Tal said as he sat. They were now several miles into the massive bay most locals called the Scythe. To their right ran the long mountain range that separated Eithlanel and Thelanel, the two provinces of the Unified Coast. On their left, on its own island deep in the bay, smoke rose from the volcano Hammer Top.

Ronar snorted as if to say, *Of course we are.*

"I know, I know, you've made this trip a thousand times." Tal switched his harness to the tether on the flight attendant's seat, but didn't bother with the buckle on the seat itself. The skies were clear, and they would likely have calm all the way across the bay. "I'll know the route as well as you soon. Varai knows I've flown it enough."

Ronar gave him a skeptical look.

"Hey, you might have thirty-plus years of commercial flying on me, but I have to deal with the passengers. That's gotta be worth at least time and a half."

The narrowing of Ronar's eyes told Tal exactly how compelling he found this argument.

"That reminds me," Tal said, "one of the passengers asked if you could . . . turn your heat down? Like the fire inside of you, I guess."

The next flap of Ronar's wings was so powerful, it jolted the cabin behind them. Ronar rocked his head backward and forward, letting out great belches of steam.

Well, at least someone found the situation funny.

When Tal next went back to the cabin, the latch on the rear door stuck as he tried to lift it. A real airline probably would have run safety checks to make sure the doors on the cabin were fully functional, but Tal's employer, Dragon Air, prided itself more on the cheapness of the ticket than making sure some critical piece of safety equipment—like the door that would need to be opened quickly in an emergency—was actually functional. Tal fiddled with the latch, feeling movement inside the door. Movement, then a loud *snap* as the entire latch came off in his hand.

Tal stared at the piece of metal. It had almost completely rusted out. He was actually surprised it had lasted as long as it did, given its state of decay. He stared at it for a long time, hoping no one had heard the sound. In contrast to the request for the dragon to cool his interior, Tal didn't think he could argue that passengers would be unreasonable to want their emergency door operational.

His first instinct was to apply a metalworking to the locking mechanism in order to get the door open, but he knew how that would end. The thought boiled inside him. He went off to the supply chest to find a crowbar and some twine.

With the door opened and tied in a half-open position with threadbare twine, Tal could let the woman with the purple hat know that, not only was it impossible for the dragon to make his scales colder, but the heat inside him actually provided some of the buoyancy necessary for his wings to keep them aloft. The woman looked down doubtfully at the ocean below, then at the rear door, which was rattling back and forth. A few masts from the shipwrecks that frequently occurred in the Scythe were visible from up here.

"This is unacceptable," the woman said. "You can be sure I won't be flying by dragon again any time soon, especially not with this sorry excuse for an airline. I must say, the quality of the customer service here makes me wonder if they provide any training whatsoever."

They didn't, though that was entirely beside the point. As he retreated, Tal surveyed the other faces in the cabin. No one appeared to be paying attention to the conversation. He did recognize the lined face and stooped frame of an older woman who appeared to be stifling a laugh. Despite her taking his flights at least twice a week, he'd never said more than a few words to her. In fact, he'd never said more than a few words to any passenger. The sooner they got to their destination, and with the least amount of griping, the better.

As Tal passed the old woman, she murmured, "You could offer to seat her outside. I'm sure her feet would be cooler out there."

That was almost enough for Tal to smile. Almost.

The truth was, Tal had a hard time smiling about anything related to his current circumstances.

In the distance rose the largest spires of Thelspoint. The capital of Thelanel appeared to emerge straight out of the bay, waves shattering against the solid granite seawall. He saw the city essentially once a day—either arriving at the city or leaving it, depending on the day—except for Sunday, his one day off, and the one day a week when he blessedly didn't have to see Thelspoint and all of its reminders of the person he no longer was.

He'd left for the city at thirteen, with ten years of training at Thelspoint University ahead of him. At the end of it, he would be a full-blown mage.

Thelspoint had become his home, particularly the streets and shops around the university. He'd studied for hours in his favorite tea shops, consumed more than a little mead at the taverns, and steeled himself against three-hour lectures on the impacts of humidity on metalworking magic. At the end of the day, he had retreated to his dorm room—private, if you didn't mind being able to hear your neighbor snore through the walls—and studied even more.

He desperately missed the energy of being surrounded by other talented students, learning complex and powerful magic. All of it had felt like he was on a path, like his future could be something great.

And here he was, flying a dragon who already knew where he was going, and making sure passengers who should know better didn't do anything stupid. A nearly exhaustive list of those stupid activities included: slipping and falling off the dragon, jumping and falling off the dragon, or Tal's all-time favorite of getting in a petty argument ending in fisticuffs that resulted in someone *else* falling off the dragon.

Two years since he'd left Thelspoint. Two years since he'd left the university. Two long, miserable years, each day a step further from his life as a mage.

Off to their right, a huge orange shape ripped through the air, traveling almost twice as fast as Ronar. This dragon was likely from the Heathermark Flight Group, which had dozens of flights a day to cities around the country. Their fleet was composed of majestic creatures whose backs could carry up to a hundred passengers, great Cernoths every last one, whose relatives ruled the kingdom of dragons far north and to the east, in the Claglands. By contrast, but not necessarily surprisingly, Dragon Air employed the smaller Eitnoth variety of dragon, like Ronar with his grizzled wings, his flaking scales, and body that bordered on scrawny by dragon standards.

The remainder of the flight passed smoothly. Tal visited the cabin a couple more times to make sure everyone was comfortable—sweaty feet aside—and to distribute cups of water from the tank at the back. All the while Thelspoint grew in size, soon becoming the entire horizon. Though its foundation was carved directly into the bedrock, the city's towers extended hundreds of feet in the air, marvels of magical engineering that had no right to stand as firm and as tall as they did. Tal had trained alongside mages who would go on to join the Architects Corps, who handled everything from magically enhancing building materials—with the use of metalworking, woodworking, and a half dozen others—to laying ley lines so the buildings knew exactly how to position themselves at all times. He knew just how much magic had been poured into Thelspoint's mere existence.

Ronar aimed toward the airfield just outside of town. In theory, one benefit of Ronar's relatively small size would've been a closer proximity landing pen, but Dragon Air had been unwilling to pay the modest extra cost of these pens, so they were stuck in a half-built enclosure well outside the city.

Scattered houses flitted below, the people going about their days between them undisturbed by the dragon's approach. Ronar glided, keeping his flapping and the resulting currents of air to a minimum until their flight path took them within fifty feet of the rooftops, and he had to break his momentum with a jarring extension of his wings. The whole cabin shuddered. Tal braced himself as the landing area grew beneath them. It never seemed quite large enough for the approach.

Landing was not Ronar's specialty. Tal had warned the passengers that the last few moments could be shaky, but even Tal found it unpleasant as Ronar dropped dozens of feet at a time, furling and unfurling his wings in an apparently random pattern to slow the descent. They lurched into the pen, Ronar's wing grazing one of the outbuildings and sending two attendants scurrying away. Then there was a massive *crunch* as his claws settled into the pen's rocky sand.

Ronar smiled, pleased with his performance, as Tal unstrapped himself and strode back to ferry the queasy passengers to safe ground.

He extended a ladder that was built into the cabin. Most passengers didn't have any trouble, but the older woman who had suggested putting the pesky passenger outside required a steadying hand as she carefully picked her way down each rung. He let her take her time, ignoring Ronar's impatience. When she settled back on the ground she was beaming at him.

"This time I didn't even have to ask you to help an old lady down this awful ladder," she said.

"I remembered from last time."

"And the time before that, presumably." The woman eyed the ladder with disdain. "That old thing is looking almost as rickety as I am."

The small part of Tal that still remembered what it was like to be a mage thought it might be nice to assure her that she was not in fact rickety.

Instead he said, "I'll make sure the ladder gets inspected."

"You didn't remember," she said, "that it's polite to ask the name of anyone you've helped down a ladder more than once."

Tal reddened. "Sorry. I'm Tal."

"I know."

"And you are?" Tal didn't mean it to sound skeptical, but any social graces beyond those absolutely necessary to complete his trips were as rusty as his magical theory.

"Enna. A pleasure." There was more than a touch of amusement in Enna's eyes. "Here, take this." She put out her hand, palm down.

"We're not allowed to take tips."

"It's not a tip, it's a gift."

Reluctantly, Tal extended his hand, and into it dropped something small, round, and very warm, as if Enna had been holding it the whole flight. It was a blue-green sphere with a fractal pattern dancing inside semi-translucent glass.

"See you next flight." She patted his shoulder and shuffled off.

Tal was tempted to toss the sphere aside, but something about the surface—which he was now convinced was glowing slightly—made him think it was infused with some weak magic. He stared after Enna, unsure exactly what to think about this turn of events.

Ronar shook himself restlessly as the attendants removed the cabin from his back. What he really wanted was food. Tal stuck the sphere in his pocket, and went off to find several hundred pounds of meat.

PROTESTS

These nights were the hardest for Tal. The three nights a week when Tal and Ronar stayed in Thelspoint, resting before the return trip to Upper Boden the following afternoon, somehow felt like a greater displacement than his actual home in the out of the way hamlet. The northern capital was all energy, ripe with the sounds and smells of nearly three million people in close proximity, and the energy of the resulting magic was overwhelming. There was a greater concentration of mages here than anywhere else, their spellwork coating the air wherever you went.

Every single one was a painful reminder.

The meat delivery had been on time, but when Tal rolled the massive cart in front of Ronar, dripping blood and chicken guts onto the ground, the dragon turned his nose up.

"Come on, Ro, this is the dinner we've got," Tal said.

The dragon flicked the pile of meat with his claw, dislodging what appeared to be the entire leg of a cow.

"Hey, I'm not the one who picks the menu," Tal said. "You get the staff meal, just like me. You want anything fancier, be my guest, but it'll come out of your paycheck."

Ronar licked tentatively at the leg, then bit down on it and heaved it aside with his mouth. He slurped down a few whole chickens, maintaining eye contact with Tal as he did.

"Your guilt tactics won't work on me."

Ronar harumphed, but the first round of feeding had revealed the next layer of meat, and suddenly there was a light in his eye. Tal looked down to see that his attention had caught on what appeared to be a large cut of short rib. It must have been thrown in accidentally, as it was a far higher grade than usual. Ronar's claw extended, pointing to the short rib. Then he pointed to Tal, and back to the short rib.

The bargain was clear. *I'll eat the rest of this garbage meat if you get me more of this.*

Tal sighed. He tried to avoid going into Thelspoint proper, but there was a not insignificant chance that Ronar would refuse to fly tomorrow if he didn't get what he wanted.

"Fine, you giant scaly baby," Tal said, "but I'm not springing for a marinated piece."

Ronar's spiny grin would have struck fear in most people. It just made Tal deeply annoyed. The dragon speared the short rib with his claw and delivered it delicately to his mouth. He chewed thoughtfully, closing his eyes.

Great, I'm stuck with the one gourmet dragon in existence, Tal thought, leaving the pen behind, and stepping out into the sprawling streets outside Thelspoint.

Tal likely could have found a butcher in the scramble of buildings outside the wall, but the outer wards had a bad reputation, especially if you didn't know where you were going. The outskirts of Thelspoint lived in the dangerous interstitial space between boring and seedy. Quiet, twisting roads between haphazard houses could just as easily hold nothing more than residents hurrying home to late evening meals, or a gang of muggers with knives already drawn. Tal let the looming shape of the outer wall guide him, every sound an alarm in his ears. He didn't have any desire to get robbed or stabbed while running errands for a temperamental Eitnoth dragon. Time was when he could have marched confidently through any part of the city or its outer wards, the slate gray of his mage robes the only deterrent he needed.

Once he neared the wall, the main road leading into the city widened, carrying straight through the chaos of Tanner's Row, and under the imposing stone overhang of Larchgate. A guard wearing the Thelspoint seal stopped him at the gate, inspecting his Dragon Air credentials before waving him into the city.

The city around him brimmed with life. Larchgate was the primary entry point for many of the city's imports, wagons lined up in orderly rows for inspection, while across the street the taverns that catered to traders were already full. Patrons spilled onto the street, mugs of mead clacking together and voices raised into the already loud evening. More than thirty inspection agents patrolled the area, poking at barrels filled with grain and surveying livestock.

Images of the gods were everywhere. In alcove shrines and the occasional standalone statue stood Varai, the god of discovery, whose raised right hand—extended as if reaching for an object beyond their grasp—was obvious regardless of whatever gender or age form they appeared in. Varai's partner at the top of the pantheon was Arren, and although occasional depictions of Arren were evident from their arms splayed to both sides at waist level, inviting and conciliatory to indicate they were the god of cooperation, there were far fewer of Arren's likenesses. Many of these Arren figurines could be found on necklaces worn by traders who had come north from Eithlanel, their shoulders wrapped in bundles of heavy chains meant to show the branching nature of consensus—as well, depending on who you asked, as its weight. Here in the north, despite official policy including both wings of the pantheon, Varai and their quest for discovery and knowledge reigned supreme.

Further up the road, Tal turned off into the Triangle. What from the outside appeared to be little more than an alleyway opened up onto a wide space—the shape of which was, of course, at least approximately triangular—with shops pressed shoulder to shoulder along the perimeter. He thought he remembered a butcher shop around here. Completing his mission without having to go too far into the city would keep him from having to step foot anywhere near the university. There were still traces of magic here, though. A potion shop's stately sign advertised all manner of tinctures, while next door a leatherworking mage offered animal skins spelled to provide extra protection from the cold.

Tal avoided any shop with a hint of magic.

The Triangle was a haven for higher end shops away from the hustle and bustle of the central business district. The shoppers here were dressed in the comfortable luxury of the discreetly wealthy, eschewing the magically animated shawls that dotted the trendier neighborhoods around Thelspoint in favor of topcoats and embroidered dresses in bright secondary colors. A fair number were obviously servants out on errands for their employers. Everyone was exceedingly polite, even the teenagers who had draped themselves across the four-level triangular statue in the center of the Triangle.

In the far corner, Tal came up short. What he had remembered being a butcher shop was now a bank specializing in small business loans and mage contracts. He looked around to see if the butcher had just moved down the row, but unless the high-end vegan grocery two doors down was wildly mislabeled, none of the stores around here sold short rib.

What was Tal doing? There was an entire street literally called Butcher's Row a few blocks from the university. His hesitation to go anywhere near it might be totally understandable, but that didn't mean he wasn't also being a coward.

Tal felt a pit growing deep in his stomach.

He tried to ignore that feeling as, thinking of Ronar and how difficult he would be if he didn't get the cut of meat he wanted, Tal trudged back to the main road and began climbing the hill toward the university.

One of the notable features of Thelspoint was how strictly they enforced the bans on private businesses on the central thoroughfares. Merchants and vendors were cordoned off into designated areas, allowing the roads to move with purpose. On one side, fenced off from the pedestrians, were railcars that you could ride up the hill. They cost a small fortune, and shot you upwards at a sickening rate. Tal had only taken them once during his time here, and afterwards had decided he would prefer a mode of transit where his lunch didn't end up in the nearest wastebasket.

The university's tallest buildings came into view just as Tal crossed the massive stone bridge that connected Outer Thelspoint with the inner district referred to as The City. Below flowed the artificial river that originated at the very top of Thelspoint. The water was pulled in from the sea, passing through a number of magical desalinizers and purifiers before flowing in a spiral down through the city.

Tal kept his gaze low, avoiding catching eyes with anyone who might be a student or professor. He had been a recognizable figure during his days at the university, and he doubted a Dragon Air flight uniform and a shorter haircut was going to be enough to prevent one of the younger students from identifying him.

Butcher's Row smelled how you would expect it to, though someone who worked as intimately with a dragon as Tal did couldn't possibly be a stranger to this particular stench. He found a butcher who advertised short ribs, and sidled inside.

Less than five minutes later, a bleeding stack of meat tied up in paper in his hand, Tal nearly ran into an old man as he exited the shop. He stopped midway through his apology. The knot in his stomach grew until it consumed his entire body. The man looked back through square glasses, wisps of white hair blowing around a face filled with recognition.

"Talarus, is that you?"

The most honest part of Tal wanted to put his packet of short ribs under his arm and sprint away. Tal was broader than he had been at the university, his hair cut shorter and his arms bulkier with the constant work of carrying equipment.

He could pretend not to be the same Tal this man knew. But he couldn't very well turn away from the man who had been his advisor and mentor for most of his time at school.

"Hi Nathan," Tal said, a sheepish grimace coming over his face as Nathan eyed his flying jacket, the Dragon Air insignia, and the obviously larger than human portion of meat in his hand.

Tal set the teacup down on the makeshift table on the balcony overlooking the landing pen. Ronar had retreated into the stable, munching happily on the short ribs. Nathan watched the dragon with passing interest. He looked demonstrably uncomfortable on his rickety—Dragon Air issue—wooden chair. Tal didn't have another chair to offer him. He sat on the top step.

"You always think a dragon is going to be majestic," Nathan said, "but really they're just apex carnivores who happen to breathe fire."

"And not all of them are even that convincing as apex predators," Tal said.

Tal had provided as many biographical updates as he felt comfortable giving as they walked back down the hill. Nathan had not reacted to his terse answers, had not questioned why it had been so long since he'd seen Tal.

"I'm sure your dragon has many great qualities," Nathan said, his voice unconvinced.

Tal took a deep breath. "How is your work coming?"

"Slower since you left. I have nearly completed my advanced textbook on languageworking as it relates to written words. Without your critical eye to examine it, I fear my writing may veer into the didactic too often, even for a textbook. I've had to rewrite several key chapters multiple times and still can't find other languageworkers capable of providing a real peer review."

"I'm sure it's fine," Tal said. Nathan's veiny hands on the teacup were painfully familiar from the days they had spent working magic over pieces of parchment, trying to induce written words to give up their exact meaning, rather than the multiple interpretations that a reader would project onto them. "And your studies with speech?"

Nathan shook his head. "There I've had only limited success. It seems to require a combination of a languageworking on the words themselves, as well as actively influencing them through a soundworking when they leave a speaker's mouth. I'm not quick enough to do it in real time. Your attempt in our final demonstration was as close as we've gotten."

Tal blanched. Their demonstration in front of the academic council had attempted to show that simple speech could be spelled so the speaker's true meaning would reach their listeners, regardless of the actual words. It had worked until about halfway through, when the listeners' heads had filled with an intense scream that hadn't stopped for close to an hour, courtesy of Tal's suddenly rogue magic.

Tal didn't like to think of that event. That wasn't the exact moment when he had decided to leave the university, but it was undoubtedly one of the many links in that chain.

"Everything I said before you left was true," Nathan said, leaning forward intensely, years seeming to shed from his narrow frame. "You still have immense potential. You belong back at the university."

"I'm not that person anymore," Tal said. "I haven't even heard the name Talarus in two years."

Nathan waved that off. "Names are meaningless. You're still that person."

"Am I?"

Tal opened himself completely, letting Nathan's magic tip itself forward and wrap itself around him. Magic had a magnetic pull, and Nathan's magic was stronger than most. But when Nathan's magic reached for Tal's own, it wrapped around a truth far too painful for Tal to say out loud.

There was nothing there. No magic remained in Tal.

Nathan gasped, then slapped a hand to his mouth as if to retroactively stuff the gasp back inside.

"It is exceedingly rare for a mage to lose their magic entirely," Nathan said when he had taken a moment to recover.

"Rare doesn't mean much to the rarity," Tal replied, bitterness coating every word.

"What happened?"

Tal shook his head. One day it had been there, and then one day it wasn't. There was nothing to tell. Yes, he had been nearly at the breaking point in his studies, every day and night filled with nothing but anxious nerves and an endless drive to be the best mage. But there was no climactic event, no burst of energy before the magelight that was his power flickered out.

"So you have been living as a layman?" Nathan asked.

"Without magic or purpose," Tal muttered. "You done with that?"

He picked up Nathan's empty teacup and brought it inside the multipurpose shed where landing attendants passed the time before their dragons arrived. He set it into the wash bucket, then gripped the sides of the bucket viciously. It creaked under his strong hands, hands that had once had the delicacy of someone who could do everything by magic. Spending half his day tying straps and steadying himself against dragon scales had imbued them with the raw strength of utility. Outside, the light was fading fast, the wall above Larchgate lit up in a hundred winking spots. It felt like a taunt, like a statement that, *Over here, all is light and warmth. Down there where you are, Tal, not so much.*

As he stepped back onto the porch, he started to tell Nathan that it was getting late. But Nathan stopped him.

"Talarus, I know who you are," he said. "Your magic may have left you, but it will not be gone for good. Come back, and we can work on it together."

Tal's smile, though rueful, was still genuine. "You always had a blind spot when it came to me. You always believed how much I could do. Even when my abilities didn't live up to that belief."

Nathan rose. As he started down the steps, he said, "Your magic can come back. But I promise it won't if you're off in the countryside, flying on some scrawny dragon."

Tal had only six passengers on the flight back the next day, and he snapped at half of them when they didn't fasten their seatbelts quickly enough. His mood was so foul that once they landed, a few of the passengers jumped off the ladder while only halfway to the ground in order to be away from him quicker.

His conversation with Nathan had unmoored him. Tal knew his magic was gone, yet it was uniquely devastating to have it confirmed by Nathan. This was the same Nathan who had discovered the secret to making two objects resonate in harmony so that, no matter how far apart they were, anything you did to one happened to the other. It worked particularly well with writing over long distances. Tal had once felt like he belonged in the company of people like this, people who were making discoveries that could help the world. He no longer felt this way.

There was a still deeper loss in Tal's heart. Once, Nathan had been the person Tal had gone to with any concern, any minor heartache, or just for a respite from the intensity of the university. Nathan had driven him on, yes, but he had also been the first to encourage Tal to take care of himself, or offer a strong cup of tea late at night. Tal had never been close with his father. For much of Tal's childhood he had worked as an itinerant mage, only returning for brief periods in which he was more interested in quizzing Tal on magical concepts than he was in any of the small and important developments of childhood. Tal's time with Nathan gave him a small taste of what having a father could be. Tal knew Nathan felt the same way. The professor had no family, having lost his wife years before Tal ever met him. This made the rift between them all the more acute.

The Upper Boden landing pen was really just a field near the center of town, with a fence separating it from a tree-lined lane.

This afternoon, there was someone standing just inside the gate. They obviously weren't a passenger, and they appeared to be yelling something.

Tal ignored them as he handed Ronar off to the attendants. The dragon had flown so well after eating short ribs that he was making a compelling—if vexing—case for a better diet.

Wearily making his way up the path toward the gate, Tal tried to ignore the shouting person. He could now see they were holding a sign.

Tal was successful most of the way, until it became increasingly apparent that the person was yelling at *him*.

He stopped and looked up. The sign read *Dragon Rights Now!* The person holding it was a woman a couple years younger than him.

"Your contracts are null and void!" the woman shouted. "Dragons can't legally sign anything!"

The woman wore light brown pants, tall boots, and a leather vest over a fine embroidered shirt. In fact, all of her clothes were obviously expensive, though they were caked in several days' worth of dust. She wore very round, very large glasses.

"Do you have nothing to say for yourself?" she yelled.

As he got closer, Tal said, "I'm an employee of Dragon Air, just like the dragon is."

"*The dragon.* Listen to how you talk about your supposed coworker!"

Tal sighed, ran his hands over eyes that were now feeling very tired, and looked at the woman dead-on.

"What is this, a protest?" he asked.

"That's right." The woman lowered her sign and raised another, which said: *Have a Safe and Immoral Flight.*

"If the purpose of this protest is to annoy someone who has literally zero say in anything you're protesting, you're doing a great job."

"And I will continue to annoy you until your dragons have the rights they deserve."

That was too much for Tal. He blew past her, slamming the gate shut behind him.

"You better not be here when we fly tomorrow," Tal called over his shoulder. He pointed to the attendants, who had finished lowering the cabin off Ronar's back, and were watching the exchange with amusement. "There's a special section of their training on *dealing with* this sort of thing."

Without another word, he turned toward home, the shouts of the lone protester ringing in his ears.

Cut Off

T al had not slept the night after his conversation with Nathan, and he was still awake at three o'clock the following night. One of many problems with his current profession was that it gave him too much time to think. He flew about three hours a day, then spent another hour or two making sure Ronar's needs were met. Beyond that, he was free to wallow.

And when the most present thoughts were about how his magic had deserted him, how he was completely cut off from that wellspring, there was plenty of wallowing to be done.

The place Tal called home had once been a covered wagon. The story around Upper Boden was that it had broken down not far from the center of town, and the angry mage it belonged to had used a strong woodworking to secure it in place while he went to look for a repairman. Ultimately deciding it wasn't worth the trouble, the mage had left it behind with the spell intact. Unable to move it, a succession of less well-off people in town had moved in, each replacing a different part of the wagon until it was as close to a permanent house as any other in the village. It was certainly less likely to get blown away by an errant storm, as the woodworking held to this day.

The limited space inside the old wagon suited Tal just fine. He had very few possessions when he was at the university, and most had remained behind when he left in the middle of the semester. By "left," he really meant, "snuck out in the middle of the night so as not to awaken anyone with the shame of having lost his power." But "left" was less of a mouthful.

He turned over the sphere Enna had given him back when they landed in Thelspoint. Its smooth surface still glowed dully. For the dozenth time he thought about tossing it outside, and found he couldn't. He got up and cleared out a glass bowl that had been filled with musty hardtack. Placing the sphere in the center of it, he set the bowl back on his writing desk. The sphere was barely bright enough to shine through the glass, but Tal liked the way the faint light rippled as his vantage point on it changed.

The sphere felt like something out of his university days, like one of the artifacts he had studied or the power sinks kept in the classroom to help demonstrate magical concepts. That made it both hard to look at and deeply comforting. On the border between a taunt and a reminder of how good things had been when magic coursed through him.

He had not always been powerful. He had arrived at the university the son of two working mages, showing enough promise to merit admission, but not enough to merit any special treatment. His first year in particular had been a slog. Everyone seemed to know the contours of magic better than him, especially those who had grown up in Thelspoint, soaking up magic with every breath. He passed his first year's exams through pure will and long hours in the library, doing well enough to place into one honors course, in languageworking.

He had worried that entire first summer about how hard the course would be. Instead, it had changed his life.

The professor of the honors languageworking class had a reputation as a strict grader and for making snide remarks about students' level of effort. An apprehensive Tal did his best during the first few weeks to avoid attention, but Nathan was having none of it. He regularly called Tal, and everyone else, to the front of the class to demonstrate core concepts. He would laugh at their blunders and wrong answers, wonder at the university's admissions process, and moan that no one had developed enough basic literacy to even read a text, much less perform a languageworking on one. Tal dreaded the class for the entire first month. He sat next to a fellow second-year named Meret. Meret had wild black hair and the early fringes of a mustache that would eventually give way to a perpetual five o'clock shadow. They happened to live in the same dorm, and more out of convenience than anything formed a miniature study group to combat their dismissive professor.

Spite had fueled Tal and Meret in those early days. If they worked hard enough, then maybe they could prove Nathan was wrong about them. Maybe Nathan would see that they not only belonged here, but could actually excel at languageworking if given the chance. Tal still remembered when Nathan had called them together into his office to tell them the results of their mid-year exam, an unreadable look on his face.

The two fifteen-year-old boys squirmed in their worn chairs. Meret ran his hands through his hair, sending dark curls cascading over his sweaty, acne-pocked forehead. Nathan slid two sets of papers across the desk. Each had a red circled "A" at the top.

"I want you to know that, as a rule, I don't give out As," Nathan said. "An honors class should test honors-level students, not provide them with a fancy class title to pad their future resumés. And yet the two of you have both received an A with, I might add, very similar answers on nearly every question."

"Are you suggesting we cheated, sir?" Tal asked, thinking that he'd never truly experienced fear until that moment.

Nathan actually laughed at that. "What I'm suggesting, Talarus, is that the two of you have clearly been conspiring. Conspiring to help each other succeed at a difficult subject." Nathan leaned forward. "And I love a good conspiracy."

That moment in Nathan's office had led to so many others. Research projects in Nathan's cutting-edge lab. Late nights with Tal and Meret bending their heads over languageworking texts. The seed of something powerful had germinated in Tal, and he almost couldn't help its fruits bleeding out of him.

He had shown himself worthy in the hardest subject. He could surely do well in the easiest ones as well.

So that's what he did. While Meret leaned into the specialization of languageworking, Tal applied himself to every subject at once. Plantworking and lightworking were his favorites, and he soon reached an honors level in each. He nearly ran himself into the ground with his late nights in the library and with extra credit assignments, but his success in Nathan's class had shown that the spring of his magic existed, and if only he could tap into it, he could succeed at anything.

Tal and Meret grew as friends, as sometime rivals, but always near the top of their class. Hard work was their badge of honor. Magic beyond their imagining their reward.

Those days in the university had not left a lot of time for quiet contemplation, but if they had, Tal might have been surprised by how much this intensity suited him. It was a far cry from his quiet upbringing in a small town a day's ride outside the city of Eith, one of the southernmost human majority settlements in the Unified Coast. His parents had always used magic in utilitarian ways, a means to make money or to fix things around the house. Nothing like the passion that burned in Tal during those university days.

And now it was all gone. Not just the magic itself, but all the hard work that lay beneath it. The triumphs, the friendships. He hadn't spoken to Meret since he left.

With the more present worry about his magic, Tal spared little time to think about his annoyance at the protester. Surely it was just a lark. A single protestor didn't mean anything. She would give up as soon as she saw that her efforts were in vain.

But the next day, when Tal arrived an hour before his flight to prep Ronar, the protester was there.

"Good morning," the protester said as Tal unlocked the gate to the landing pen. She had been waiting patiently outside, and tried to follow him in. He let the gate swing shut behind him, smacking her in the knee. She followed anyway.

"Ow. Given any thought to my demands? Drafted any memos to send to your employer?"

"Who should I say these 'demands' are from?"

"Well my name is Bex, and I represent an organization—"

"Bex," Tal cut in. "Are you delusional?"

"Not diagnosably."

"You're standing near a dangerous dragon, protesting by yourself, about a company that doesn't even have an office in this town."

Bex looked over at Ronar, who had just rolled out of his stable. He looked more sleepy than dangerous. He belched a puff of steam, then covered his mouth as if embarrassed.

"I'm on the dragon's side!" Bex said.

"Does he know that?"

Tal went about his business, cleaning any residue left over from the night of sleep off of Ronar's scales and wings. Dragons, and Ronar in particular, tended to produce a lot of unspecified buildup around their joints and in the folds of their wings. All the while Bex could be heard yelling slogans from thirty yards away. She had been bolder with her positioning this time, and was close enough that Tal had to hear every word.

"Can we get her out of here?" Tal asked one of the landing attendants when she showed up to excavate the cabin from the many layers of protective cloth that housed it overnight. The attendant, Leanne, was at least part gnome. She had a squat build and stood a head shorter than Tal.

Leanne looked at Bex doubtfully. "Employee handbook says we don't engage with protesters. We're supposed to shunt them to a cordon zone where they can do their protesting without getting in the way of company business."

The other attendant, a tall, silent man with a tower of curly green hair, had arrived. Preparations were well underway for the flight.

"A cordon zone, eh?" Tal asked. "As long as it's crucial Dragon Air business, I'd better get after it."

He made his way into the shed, where they kept the boards they used to patch the walls of the stable. Carrying a stack of boards and a toolbox, he skirted past Bex, to the edge of the landing pen. She eyed him suspiciously.

"Off to exploit some more creatures?" she asked as he passed.

"Thought I might con an Elthim out of his inheritance, as a start," he shot back.

"Elthim don't believe in private property," Bex said.

"That's what makes it so dastardly."

At the edge of the pen, Tal set to work. He didn't bother with craftmanship, bristling at the thought that a quick magical woodworking could've accomplished this task in a couple minutes. Every whack of the hammer was a reminder: *You! Whack! Don't! Whack! Have! Whack! Magic! Whack! Loser!* Tal almost tossed the hammer aside. Then he sighed, recognizing that the editorializing was in his head rather than in his hand.

A short while later he had built a roughly square fence surrounding a particularly spotty patch of grass. There was a narrow gap in the fence rather than a gate. He nailed a flat slat onto the post by the opening, and used a knife to carve in rough letters: *Protest Area.* He thought about it, then added: *Political demonstrations will not be tolerated outside the designated zone.* He then tossed the remainder of the unused boards unceremoniously into the middle of the new enclosure, and walked back to Bex.

"Ma'am, good news," he said. "We now have an official area for you to do your sad solo sign-waving in."

She followed him to the protest area, dragging half a dozen signs behind her. She looked at the fence critically.

"This is the worst protest area I've ever seen," she said. The boards were canted at a dangerous angle, and more than a few nails stuck out in the wrong direction.

"I'm a flight attendant, not a carpenter. Look, according to our rules, as long as you stay in the protest area, we can't force you to leave. Better for everyone if you just shout yourself hoarse from the dedicated zone rather than forcing a confrontation, no?"

Bex thought about it. "It'll do for now. But don't be surprised to find it gussied up a bit when you get back."

Tal groaned. "Ma'am, please don't renovate company property."

The flight took off without incident, the passengers seeming at most mildly amused at the protest. By the time they approached Thelspoint, Tal was beginning to feel a wave of relief at the thought that he wouldn't have to deal with any protests there.

They landed, and Tal felt further relief to see that only the landing pen attendants were waiting for them. Ronar, as if knowing this was the only place where his behavior would achieve any results, refused to eat until Tal went back to the butcher for short rib. This time Tal managed to avoid any run-ins with former mentors or other university contacts, though he did have to duck into an alley as a server from his favorite tea shop passed on the street.

Enna was on his flight back to Upper Boden the next day. She asked him to help her with her seatbelt—that particular buckle tended to get stuck closed.

"No more rude ladies with sweaty feet?" she asked. Tal had nearly forgotten the woman with the purple hat, and the reminder almost made him laugh.

"No, fortunately," he replied. "Just an Eitnoth dragon who has taken a sudden inexplicable liking to short rib and nothing else."

Enna nodded sagely. "Sounds just like my son."

Tal was tempted to jokingly ask if her son could also breathe fire. Instead, he grunted and pulled the strap tight across her lap.

"There you go," he said. "That should keep you from falling out of the sky."

When they landed, Enna once again asked for help getting down the ladder. And once again she dropped a dull glowing sphere into his hand when they reached solid ground. She winked at him, and then turned her attention to the shouting coming from the protest area. There were now three people inside the fence. Bex was still in front and yelling the loudest, with the short figures of two gnomes behind her. They repeated her slogans with more confusion than conviction.

"Well this is new," said Enna.

"Don't ask me."

"I'll ask them." Enna moved with impressive speed toward the protesters. Bex seemed all too happy to regale her with whatever talking points she could. Tal walked past them, intent on ignoring them as he held the gate open for the other passengers. But as he waited for Enna, he heard Bex clearly over the gnomes' half-baked shouts.

". . . it may sound a little obscure, but it's really a question of contractual rights. With any human contract, the negotiating parties have the opportunity to read and review the contract after it is written up, then amend it to negotiate a fair deal. Dragons can read and sign the contract, but because we can't communicate with them directly, there's no opportunity for them to provide their input and amendments. Therefore, any contracts they sign are void under our interpretation of the law."

Enna, obviously following, asked, "How do you propose to change that? None of us can speak with a dragon."

"There's a mage in Heathermark who has developed a device that will allow dragons to communicate with us. But the companies refuse to implement it because it's, in their words, 'prohibitively expensive.' Well, I say not using it is prohibitively unethical."

Tal asked from the gate: "Are you coming or not, Enna?"

"Don't worry about me," she replied. "I want to hear a bit more of what this interesting young lady has to say."

For the second time in as many days, Tal let the gate slam shut hard behind him.

Usually Tal would have been dreading his day off the next day, but with all the headaches his job had presented over the past few days, being forced to ruminate on his life was actually beginning to seem preferable to flying again. He ate a simple dinner of summer sausage and stale bread before heading to the one tavern in town. He always got there early enough on Saturday night to claim a table in the corner, where he would sit with his back to the room and drink ale in silence. He'd been doing this long enough by now that Mora, the bartender and daughter of the tavern's owner, kept a steady supply of ale coming without expecting him to say anything. He drank slowly, tipped well, and didn't cause any problems. A perfect patron, by some standards.

Even with his back to the room, Tal was still aware of everyone who entered as the evening wore on. He sipped the warm ale—he would've preferred mead, but they favored their beers down south—and listened for gossip. The tavern's regulars greeted Mora warmly, and dominated the space around the bar. A traveling bard had to be shooed away after it became apparent that he hadn't bothered to tune his lute before climbing onto stage and jumping into a screechy melody. A group of traders from the north were in town, having come all the way down the road through Lodefall. There was talk of trouble between the city-state under the mountain and the Unified Coast. That was potentially problematic for the country, but probably good for Tal's continuing employment, as the road through Lodefall and under the mountain pass was the safest land route connecting Eithlanel and Thelanel.

Tal peered over his shoulder to see a bearded man, tall and broad and with his hair shaved off completely, discussing the situation with his compatriots.

"I've never been through so many inspections in one day," the man was saying. "It's as if they expect every trader to be ferrying illegal goods through their city."

"To be fair, we *were* ferrying illegal goods," said the slender man next to him. His thinning blond hair sat flat against his scalp.

The bearded man rattled the table with his tankard. "Beside the point. They know we're good for the bribes, I've just never seen so many people concerned about what's coming through."

"I heard they're looking for dragonsbane," another man said. This one was too far to the side for Tal to see without looking obviously over his shoulder.

"Dragonsbane ain't real," the bearded man said.

"Then why would they be looking for it?" asked the man who was out of view.

Tal had had enough beer to laugh at that. The slender man waved at him.

"Oy, kid in the corner," he said. "You gonna eavesdrop, you gotta at least tell us what's so funny."

Tal searched the tavern's rafters, as if looking for an escape route. Then he swung his chair around.

"Dragonsbane is real," he said, "but it's highly volatile. It loses its properties—and tends to explode—within a few hours of brewing. There are no dragons within fifty miles of Lodefall. Why would anyone want to bring it through there, when it'll be useless by the time they can get close enough to kill a dragon?"

"Maybe they figured out how to unvolatilize it," said the bearded man. Tal marveled at how correctly he had pronounced his made-up word.

"That would make it not dragonsbane," Tal said.

The others nodded as if this made a great deal of sense. Tal turned back to his drink, feeling that he had slightly tipped his hand as a former student of magic. Tal's study of dragonsbane at the university had been rudimentary. Plantworkings focused more on plants with beneficial uses rather than poisons, and from what he understood, dragonsbane's volatile properties also made it resistant to most plantworkings. If someone was rumored to be transporting dragonsbane, they were either an incredibly powerful mage of a whole new variety, or the rumors weren't true. Tal would put his money on lies over unprecedented greatness every time.

"You said that so casually," said an ominously familiar voice nearby. Bex, the protester, had come in the back door, and was standing by the near corner of the bar waiting for a drink. "You say it could kill dragons the same way you would say a pesticide can kill ants."

Bex's eyes shone behind her thick glasses.

"I'm off-duty. Protesting at me won't get you anywhere," Tal said.

"I'm not protesting. I'm objecting to your callous speech."

"I don't see a difference."

Mora handed Bex a mug of ale, which she complemented with a suspicious gaze. Upper Boden was not known for welcoming newcomers.

"I'm just saying," Bex said, "you have a pretty messed up relationship with the one being you spend the most time with." She took a huge swig of her beer and made off into the crowd.

Tal stayed the rest of the night, managing to avoid any further run-ins with either traders or protesters. The energy rose until about midnight, at which point it slowly died down. Bex was still on the opposite side of the room until about one o'clock, chatting animatedly with a group of women from town. Tal wondered with dread if Monday would find some of those women joining the protests. He stayed late, drinking slowly enough to never get fully drunk, but quickly enough to avoid having to think too much.

There were only a few people left by the time he slouched out, paying his tab and tossing an extra handful of coins into the tip jar. He took the shortcut back home, which would take him through the center of town, back behind a chapel dedicated to Arren, and up the path that wound through an orchard. As he walked down the church alley, he saw a shape sprawled in a doorway. It was clearly alive, covered in dirty blankets and at least one sheaf of the local news bulletin.

Then he looked closer, and almost sprinted away. Lying asleep in the alley was Bex.

Just leave her there, he thought. *She's a grown woman, she can make her own decisions. She doesn't look like she's passed out from drinking.*

He bit down hard on his lip. He looked down the alley in both directions. There was no one else there. It was an early fall evening and the night grew cold. Not dangerously so, probably, but still not weather in which anyone should sleep outdoors.

Tal breathed deeply. Among the many things that weren't his problem, where this woman chose to sleep was at least in the top ten. He tiptoed up the alley, making for home. It wouldn't take long to warm up once he got a fire going. He tried not to feel guilty about that fact as he left Bex behind.

When he reached his cabin, the fire started eagerly. He relaxed into the comfortable threadbare chair near the fire. The buzz of alcohol was starting to fade, leaving behind a dreary emptiness. An entire day with nothing to do lay ahead of him. But tonight, at least he was tired enough to sink into sleep without facing his thoughts until morning.

Yet as it turned out, he couldn't sleep. As he lay beneath his heavy quilt, listening to the occasional pop of the fire behind the protective screen, he could only think of the woman sleeping in the alley. Most of the images in his head involved terrible things happening to her—her face frozen and blue after an improbable temperature drop, a bandit coming off the road and stealing all her possessions or worse—and he tried to reason that he didn't care.

Tal groaned as he sat up. Whatever tiredness he'd felt earlier was long gone. He'd be awake whether he helped Bex or not. He considered finding a book to read from the selection that lined the back wall, but he had read them all more than once. He also doubted he could focus on inert words with the thoughts racing in his head.

The room was so cozy, exactly enough space for one person, and for a fire to warm in just a few minutes. He had no desire to leave this comfort.

Varai damn me, Tal thought. Before he could think better of it, he was putting his boots on, slipping on his jacket, and heading back out into the cold.

With resentful step after resentful step, Tal tramped back down the hill to the alley.

When he reached Bex, he kept a careful distance. "Dragon rights lady? Are you okay?"

Bex woke with a start, uncurling glasses from her clenched fist. She groaned when she saw who it was.

"Are you coming to beat me up?" she asked. "Is this an act of corporate intimidation?"

Tal didn't dignify that with a response.

"You want somewhere warm to sleep?" he asked. "Come on, it's cold out here."

Bex rubbed her nose, which was at least three shades lighter than usual from the cold. Tal offered his hand to help her up. She stared at it as if it might be infected.

"Why should I trust you not to take me somewhere dangerous?" Bex asked.

"With this sleeping spot, you're basically trusting anyone who happens to come by already. Is trusting one person worse?"

Bex grumbled. She didn't take his hand, but she did gather her covers into a bundle and stand. "I guess if I'm going to get murdered, we can at least get this over with."

Tal led Bex wordlessly up the alley. He was finding that even a fairly low effort attempt to help this woman was making his tiredness return. His brain felt foggy as he walked Bex up the path through the orchard.

About halfway through the orchard, Tal realized Bex was no longer right behind him. When he turned, he saw her crouched by one of the apple trees, gathering a handful of soggy windfall apples from the dewy grass. She set them in the center of her blankets, which she began folding into a makeshift bag.

"So you have enough money to drink at the tavern, but not enough to buy apples that aren't filled with worms?" Tal asked.

The night was dark, but not dark enough to hide Bex's indignation. "I'm a reasonably attractive woman in the ass end of Eithlanel. I've never once paid for my own drink."

To be honest, everything about Bex had so annoyed him that he hadn't bothered to gauge whether she was attractive. With her thick glasses and rumpled clothes, she could've been outright unattractive, but Tal found that wasn't the case. If it wasn't directed at him, he probably would have found her passion for her cause—however ludicrous that cause was—at least mildly endearing. Bex squinted at him.

"Okay, that does seem a reasonable solution for the whole alcohol thing," Tal said. "But ale isn't dinner."

Bex snorted, finding one more apple in the grass and inspecting it closely before biting into it. "Neither is an apple, but beggars can't be choosers."

"You don't have any money," Tal said. It sounded harsh and a little rude coming out of his mouth.

"Fuck no," Bex said, immediately making Tal feel better about his rudeness. "Wouldn't really be doing the whole starving protester thing right if I did, you know?"

They continued up the path, Bex slowing every so often to secure her apple haul.

"I guess Upper Boden is as good a place to be without money as anywhere else," Tal said.

"Especially when there are irascible dragon flight attendants around to help," Bex said.

Tal grunted. "Irascible is good. I like irascible."

"Are they less irascible down in Lower Boden?"

"I can't really recommend Lower Boden," Tal said.

"Why not?"

"It fell into the ocean a hundred and fifty years ago."

As they emerged from the orchard, Tal's wagon came into view, inviting wisps of smoke curling out of the chimney. Bex looked at it doubtfully. Her expression became even more doubtful as he unlatched the front door to let her inside.

"I know I'm not really one to talk, given the whole sleeping in an alley thing, but this is the smallest house I've ever seen."

"And I suppose you came from some grand estate," Tal shot back.

Bex grimaced, the flickering light from inside casting a shadow across her face. That wasn't a grimace of annoyance. Tal faced her, and the grimace turned into a sheepish smile.

"Bloody hell," Tal groaned. "You actually came from some grand estate."

"It's definitely an estate, although I don't know if it's considered 'grand,' at least not by Heathermark standards. It's called Braisecroft."

"Your estate is so big it has a name?" The name itself did nothing for Tal, but he did know that the outskirts of Heathermark were filled with many of the wealthiest families in Eithlanel, their estates taking up enough land for a whole town apiece.

"What the hell are you doing out here, then?" Tal asked.

"I'm cut off, obviously. My parents didn't like me protesting for dragon rights. They're devastatingly unreasonable people."

"Didn't know rich Heathermark merchants cared so much about dragon contracts."

"They don't. But my parents aren't so much rich merchants as they are the owners of Heathermark Flight Group."

They *owned* Heathermark Flight Group? The company was so impossibly large, such a monolith of the air travel industry, that it hadn't crossed Tal's mind that any single family could actually own it.

Bex registered the shock on Tal's face, and seemed to think it prudent to change the subject. "In any case, I do know that we're not both sleeping in there. We're not doing the whole 'there's only one bed so we have to both sleep in it, me insisting we sleep far apart at first, but slowly moving closer and closer in the night until we're spooning by morning' thing."

Tal laughed. "I've never liked that trope. Don't worry, I won't be sleeping here. I'll just show you where everything is and be on my way."

"So you're going to sleep in the street?"

"I'm not sleeping in the street. My buddy Ronar has a spot in his stable."

Bex's confusion peeled away to reveal a smile. "You know, you might be the first man who's ever chosen to sleep with a dragon rather than me."

Tal reddened, and stepped back out into the cold.

Good Deeds

Dragons snore. Tal knew this, of course, but in practice the volume and consistency of that snoring always shocked him. With the complex system of membranes in their noses—which snapped shut to prevent damage to their nasal lining when they breathed fire—there was simply a lot of *stuff* between a dragon's lungs and the open air. That stuff created a low rumble as it opened, and a fleshy *snap* as it closed. Tal couldn't imagine how loud this noise would've been had Ronar been a great Cernoth with a snout three times as large.

Tal slept as far from the dragon as he could, but Ronar's wings sprawled so far out into the hay that there was only a tiny corner available. Ronar's heat was enough to keep the uninsulated space warm, and Tal laid his jacket across the hay to prevent it from poking into him. It kind of worked.

If he noticed Tal's presence, Ronar showed no sign. Despite the legends about dragons sleeping with one eye open to guard their treasure against bold fortune seekers, dragons were in reality incredibly heavy sleepers. It turned out, having thick scales covering your entire body meant you could afford to sleep deeply, without much fear of anyone ambushing you in the night.

The last time Tal had slept with Ronar was when the dragon had suffered a bad infection around the scales where they usually attached the cabin to his back. Tal had to apply a salve to the flaking scales every hour to prevent Ronar from roaring in pain.

At the very least Ronar's snoring tonight was of the healthy variety. That still didn't make it quiet enough for human sleeping.

When early morning light hit the stable's far wall, Tal could still remember most of the night. But as the light seeped in, he finally rolled over and slept solidly.

That is, until a giant talon slipped under his arm, and twisted it upward. Tal let out a shriek of surprise. Ronar stood over him, gently knocking against his arm.

The dragon wore a toothy grin that couldn't mean anything besides, *Get up, sleepy head.*

"Alright alright," Tal said. Ronar scooped beneath Tal's side with another jab of his talon, sending Tal sprawling into the prickly hay. "I'm up, you menace!"

Ronar opened his mouth, filling the air with a spray of steam. It precipitated down over Tal, cooling to an extremely unpleasant mist in the chill morning air.

"I get it, you want breakfast. Wait literally two seconds and I'll get it for you."

The dragon didn't seem to think that was good enough, letting out a clicking croak of displeasure.

"And before I get back here and you get all pissy," Tal said, finding his feet and looking for his boots, which had somehow disappeared into the hay, "there is no short rib in Upper Boden, so don't even ask."

Ronar pushed the stable door open, stretching like a giant scaly cat as the daylight hit his face. The process of lacing up his boots gave Tal just enough time to think about how "there is no short rib in Upper Boden" would actually be a pretty good motto for the town as a whole, before he ran off to the stable's meat locker.

Starting as it did with the disruption to his routine, Tal was surprised to find that the day passed quickly. It was nearly two o'clock in the afternoon by the time he had fed and bathed Ronar. The full wing massage Tal gave him wasn't strictly necessary, but as he approached what could be referred to as "dragon middle age," Ronar appreciated Tal's efforts to keep his wings from growing stiff on a day that he wouldn't be flying.

When he could no longer pretend Ronar required anything more from him, Tal began the too-short walk back home. He walked all the way through the center of town rather than taking the shortcut through the orchard. There was almost no one out in downtown Upper Boden, since when one referred to a "downtown" in Upper Boden, one was really referring to exactly one tavern, a blacksmith (opening days Thursday and sometimes Monday if they were in the mood), and a town square where half a dozen cows chewed through scrubby grass. It wasn't much to take in, but Tal took his time, his steps loud against the packed dirt, apprehension in his chest.

Tal was taken aback to find the cabin door latched. He actually wasn't sure how Bex would've done that as she left, unless . . . He felt a pit grow in his stomach as he considered the possibility that Bex might still be there, asleep in his bed.

The door creaked open on its uneven hinges, revealing a completely empty room. Tal stepped in carefully, inspecting every corner for signs of unexpected grime or missing items. His possessions were undisturbed, the books on the shelves remaining in their straight lines, his exactly two dishes clean and on the drying rack, the glass bowl with the two spheres still sitting on his desk next to the usual stack of miscellaneous papers. The papers were far straighter than they had been the night before, and Tal's nerves churned at the thought that Bex might've gone through them. They contained not only his blank application for readmittance to the university—which he hadn't even been able to look at—but also the very short rejection letter from Heathermark Flight Group that, Tal remembered with further horror, featured the signatures of the owners of Heathermark Flight Group. Bex's own parents.

Tal felt like crying.

Next to the papers was a scrap of parchment cut from a mostly blank page of the Dragon Air flight manual. There was a note scrawled on it, in a cursive so vertically cramped that it appeared to have just jumped up from the line below. The note read:

Thank you for the warm bed. It reminded me of sleeping in the servant's quarters at the ostentatious castle where I usually live. Or maybe the quarters for the servants responsible for serving the servants. Seriously, have you ever considered renovating and adding at least another two square feet of floor space?

Anyway, I straightened up your desk because it was bothering me, but don't worry, I didn't read any of your VERY IMPORTANT documents. I did however make your bed for the first time in its existence. Your sheets asked if they could come with me, but I lied and told them you'd treat them with more respect in the future. Thanks again.

Cheers,

Bex

P.S. See you at the PROTEST AREA tomorrow.

Tal held the note, considering whether to toss it into the hearth. Instead he folded it and tucked it in with his now very organized stack of papers. He turned to his bed and found that Bex had not only made it with a military precision, but had also fluffed the pillows, swapping the pillowcases so the cleaner and better-fitting ones were on top. Tal did his best to see this tidying as a kind gesture rather than an indictment of his lifestyle.

Then he took a closer look at his bookshelf and nearly threw up.

The many tomes there, most concerning magic with a few famous works of literature sprinkled in, were in an entirely different order. His system of classification, which started with subject and proceeded alphabetically by author or editor, had been completely overrun. Instead, the books now ran along the shelves in order of color, with like colors next to each other, and the in-between shades merged seamlessly into a gradient.

Tal stared at the shelves in shock. How would he ever find anything in this color-coordinated mess?

As he worked his bookshelves back into some semblance of usable order, each title that passed through Tal's hands was a reminder of a class or project. His languageworking textbook from his fifth year, a treatise on the fundamental properties of bioworking, even a copy of a study Nathan had published featuring Tal and Meret's names in the acknowledgements.

Tal had proudly brandished this study in one of the first meetings of the club the two young mages had founded. It was still so new that they didn't even have a name—they were just a collection of seven top-tier students with a loose goal of working together to further their academic success. Over time the group had grown, taking on the name the Completists.

Tal tucked the copy of Nathan's study next to a longer text Nathan had authored, and paused. He had avoided thinking about the Completists since his exile, for the same reason he avoided thinking about anything related to the university. In some ways, the Completists had been the height of his achievement, every bit as much as being named the Preeminent Mage in year seven. As the goals of the organization solidified and their membership expanded, they took on the aspect of a secret society, meeting in darkened rooms in tucked-away corners of campus, swearing members to never share what they learned, and even at times veering into sillier behaviors like bespoke greeting spells for individual members. In Tal's sixth year, a member of the Completists had occupied all but one of the top ten slots in the academic rankings, and they were meeting to share not just the most intriguing concepts they had learned in their classes, but also new discoveries made in their individual research.

As much as the Completists were a power center of the best and brightest in the university, they were not without their points of tension. Tal and Meret fought constantly—good-naturedly and less good-naturedly—about the direction the organization should take. Meret insisted that they only allow the best student from each discipline to join. The Completists were meant to represent the entire spectrum of magic, so why would they want overlap in their areas of study? Tal insisted that the best students should be admitted, regardless of whether someone in the organization already specialized in their chosen area. The result was an unproductive mishmash of both membership philosophies, and a group that was largely divided based on whether they agreed with Tal or Meret.

Tal had heard rumors that the group had collapsed under Meret's leadership, but he was far enough outside the university gossip grapevine that he couldn't confirm why.

By the next morning Tal had almost managed to return his books to a working order. He had spent the entire first hour cursing Bex, until he realized he hadn't revisited his classification system in some time, and that he had been conflating several subcategories of different disciplines incorrectly.

He spent so much time directing annoyed thoughts at the woman that it was startling to see her in the flesh, holding a sign in the protest area as promised.

"The innkeeper!" she said, jabbing a sign that read *Dragons Have Long Memories* in his direction.

"I guess it wasn't a good enough stay to warrant a second night," Tal said. He'd conducted a cursory sweep through town the night before, but had found no evidence of Bex sleeping in public. He still wasn't sure why he'd felt this was his responsibility.

"I'm on credit at the actual inn now," Bex said. "I just gave them a necklace as collateral. Who knew a family heirloom might be worth actual money? Apparently it was encrusted with jewels that are considered 'precious' or something."

"You continue to astound me."

Enna had appeared at the gate. Tal stepped up to let her inside, and stamped her ticket. As soon as he did, Enna moved not toward the waiting dragon, but toward Bex.

"Enna, where are you . . ."

Tal gaped as Enna strode into the protest area. Bex handed her a sign.

"Another convert!" Bex said with triumph.

"No hard feelings," Enna said, giving Tal a sympathetic look. "It's just that she made some good points, and I do so enjoy dragon travel. I want to make sure it's as ethical as possible."

Tal rubbed his brow so hard that a few eyebrow hairs came away in his hand.

"So you bought a ticket just to protest the same airline you've been flying on for years?"

"I didn't think you noticed how often I fly, that's so sweet," Enna said. However sweet it was, it didn't stop her from brandishing the sign. "But I bought the ticket so I could get on the flight. There's still plenty of protesting time before our scheduled departure."

"Dragon rights now!" Bex shouted. Enna's weathered voice joined in.

The next few people to arrive were not passengers. Tal recognized them from the bar, and his heart sank as they started chanting even before they stepped inside.

He opened the gate to let them into the protest area.

The group had grown to seven at this point, with a steady stream of people arriving at the gate to catch their flight, join the protest, or just see what the hullaballoo was about. Even a Trug appeared. Trugs tended to live in the dumping grounds outside of town, using the orifices on the bottoms of their gelatinous bodies to consume and process waste. Though they, like dragons, lacked the ability to communicate verbally with humans, they were known to have human or greater intelligence. Behind the Trug stalked a gnome. Though they had far from human intelligence, gnomes could speak, which sort of grandfathered them into human society as well. Tal opened the gate for both, the Trug squelching its way inside, the gnome tromping behind it.

"Where do you find these people?" Tal asked Bex.

The gnome looked annoyed at having been called "people." She was just under five feet tall but built so thick across the chest that she could have lifted Tal easily over her shoulder.

"Me and Janice go way back," Bex said, draping an arm around the gnome's shoulder. Janice smiled, revealing three delicate tusks protruding from her bottom row of teeth.

"Bex got me out of a tight spot involving a misunderstanding about some 'requisitioned' goods."

"The misunderstanding being that they were in any way acquired legally," Bex said, pounding Janice's knotty shoulder with a fist. "I'm still proud of that one. Talking the police into giving me back the bail money after their delinquent gnome had skipped town was one of my finer moments. Especially since I was the one who helped her escape."

"Some truly anarchist shit," Janice croaked, searching through the pile of signs until she found one that was suitably uppercase.

"What about the Trug?" Tal asked. "You bail him out of prison too?"

Bex shot a sidelong glance as the Trug squelched unhurriedly around the edge of the enclosure. "I truly have no idea who that is. To be honest, I'm a little scared."

"They do eat garbage," Janice said. "So yeah, you should be worried."

That earned Janice another solid sock on the arm.

"Well, enjoy your protest," Tal said. "I'm going to do my job."

The protesters booed Tal good-naturedly as he made his way back to Ronar.

Tal busied himself with preparations, ultimately deciding to break regulations and just leave the landing pen gate open so he didn't have to keep letting people in. He worked with Leanne, the half-gnome attendant, to do a final safety check on the redundant straps holding the cabin in place. He kept glancing back at the protest area. Someone had brought a massive, steaming jug, and the smell of coffee wafted clear across the landing pen as cups were filled and passed from hand to hand. Tal's hands were stiff on the cabin's leather straps in the chill morning air. Part of him wished he could warm them around one of the cups. A clump of protesters had formed around the coffee, their tones modulating from the outrage of those brandishing signs to the friendly chatter of people sharing a hot drink. It made Tal queasy.

"Where do you find these people?" Leanne asked Tal. The fact that he was suddenly associated with the protesters in her mind was more than a little troubling.

"I think we're beyond people at this point," Tal replied. "Who knew Trugs cared about dragon rights?"

"They're very fair-minded creatures, Trugs. If you're able to tell what's going on under all that goo."

There was a commotion as one of the protesters from the tavern was expelled from the cordon zone. Apparently they had thought they were joining an anti-dragon protest, and it had taken until now to realize they had been chanting the wrong slogans. For some reason, the protester was allowed to keep their mug of coffee as they slunk away.

"What's it all about, anyway?" Leanne asked.

Tal sighed and did his best to explain what he remembered of Bex's description, positive he was butchering it. But when he had finished, Leanne's round nose and cheeks were turned down in a scowl.

"That's it, it's really all very silly and semantic," Tal said.

"Doesn't sound semantic to me." Leanne stared hard at the protesters, then took the strap she had been tying and shoved it against Tal's chest. "Here, hold onto this."

"What for?"

"I'm joining the protest, of course!"

Tal had been doing far too much gaping recently, but he did so once again as he watched Leanne, still wearing her blue Dragon Air jumpsuit, slide into the increasingly crowded protest area. Ronar looked back over his shoulder with amusement.

"What, don't tell me you're going to join the protests too," Tal said.

Ronar's throat rumbled. He shook his head, yellow eyes narrowing to slits. Then he blinked twice. To Tal, it seemed to suggest that he agreed with the protesters in principle, but wasn't a fan of chanting slogans or holding signs. Or simply that he couldn't be bothered to think about contracts when there was a beautiful short rib waiting for him in Thelspoint.

Thelspoint was starting to seem like a really good place to be, now that Upper Boden had proven itself reliably protesty.

Tal and the silent attendant with green hair, whose name he still did not know, continued to work, taking over Leanne's jobs as best they could. They were able to depart more or less on time in the end, though there was a decent delay as Tal went back to collect Enna, extricating her from the protest area and helping her up onto the dragon's back.

Strangely, once they were airborne it was one of the smoothest flights Tal had ever flown with Ronar. In the air, Tal could finally breathe. The protesters hadn't aimed any particular bile at him personally, but there was still an obvious implication that he was a willing cog in an unjust machine.

"That was quite the ordeal," Tal said to Enna as he passed out cups of water to the passengers. Most had looked more amused by the protests than concerned, and Enna still had a mug of coffee.

"Oh yes, it was great fun," Enna replied. "That Bex is a real firecracker." That was decidedly not what Tal wanted to hear.

Enna continued: "I heard she slept in your bed the other night." That was *also* decidedly not what he wanted to hear.

"It was a gesture of charity, nothing more," Tal said. "I slept in the stable with Ronar."

"You didn't have to do that."

"I sure as hell wasn't going to let her sleep in my bed with me in it!"

"That wasn't what I meant," Enna said, smiling wide at having forced Tal into innuendo. "You didn't have to offer her your bed, period."

Tal scratched his head. He felt like Enna was going to give him another sphere at the end of this trip, and the thought annoyed him. If she gave him two at once, he might have to get a different job. He wasn't sure he could handle that level of kindness from a sweet old lady, even if the exact function of the spheres was still a mystery.

"Now you have a choice about whether to continue your generosity," Enna said. She didn't seem to mind the one-sided nature of their conversations. "The Dragon Air offices are in Thelspoint. You could swing by and see if they'd be amenable to the protesters' demands."

"I cannot begin to describe how much horror I feel at the thought of even considering doing that."

"Bex said there's a device that could allow dragons to speak to us. Don't you want to hear what Ronar has to say?"

Tal pondered this the rest of the way to Thelspoint. He considered Ronar a friend more than a colleague or—regrettable though the classification was—some kind of vehicle. He also felt that they communicated effectively as it was. Tal had never had a problem identifying Ronar's needs. He had a remarkably expressive face, and an impish sense of humor that Tal didn't think he would've been able to identify unless they had some sort of understanding.

Tal's stream of thought stopped as, on the way back into the cabin to check on the passengers, he heard a young couple discussing the protesters.

"They've got a point, you know," said the shorter of the two. She was wearing fingerless gloves and crocheting a scarf at a remarkable rate given the constant motion on Ronar's back.

"They do, I'll grant you." The other was taller and built more sturdily. Her shock of pink hair stood up on top and was buzzed on the sides. "But what do you want me to do about it? Take a caravan three weeks back to Thelspoint?"

"With a little planning . . ."

"So three weeks by caravan," the woman with pink hair continued, "just in time for your mother's birthday, then three weeks back? Should we do it all again when your brother's wedding comes around?"

The crocheter's eyes never left her work. "I'm not saying we have to give up flying entirely. I'm just saying, they've got a point is all. Maybe when we get back, we protest ourselves. That way maybe the dragons will start being treated well by the time we have to go back for my cousin's friend's yet to be born child's ceremony to receive Arren's blessing."

The taller woman slapped her forehead so hard that Tal winced. "I completely forgot about that fucking thing."

"Don't let me forget to buy our tickets."

Tal slipped away before he had to hear anything more being said in support of the protesters. He was just trying to get through his work . . . but was it unfair that Ronar could never speak for himself? Tal set the thought aside. The idea of marching into the office of his employer and making demands, when he had no actual power in the company and was obviously replaceable, was laughable.

Regardless of what Enna said, once they got to Thelspoint it wouldn't matter. The protesters were far behind in Upper Boden. He almost breathed a sigh of relief as they began to come down in their landing pen outside of town.

That is, until they actually landed, and Tal saw the brand-new fence around a small section of the landing pen. Three people stood inside. Tal squinted his eyes to see that a painted white sign hung from the front of the enclosure, with the words *Protest Area* marked in neat letters.

He didn't know how, but Tal was absolutely certain Bex was behind this. He was beginning to wish he'd stolen her blankets as she slept in the alley rather than offering her a warm bed.

He helped Enna down to the ground, and was rewarded with exactly one sphere.

"Don't Invite a Wyvern into Your Pavilion" – Anonymous (probably)

The protests continued to grow at a steady pace at each destination. The residents of Upper Boden and Thelspoint figured out that they only needed to drop by for a few minutes each day as the dragon flight arrived or departed, and could otherwise go about their business. Tal argued with Leanne until they finally reached a compromise that allowed her to join the protesters only after the initial setup was finished, which meant the flights wouldn't actually be late, but Leanne could voice her protest even as she continued to collect a paycheck from the organization she was protesting against.

The crowd in Upper Boden fell into an almost comfortable rhythm. Tal could usually identify who would be showing him a ticket and who he would need to point in the direction of the protest area. This distinction was made far easier on the day when Tal arrived to find that more than half of the protesters had begun wearing orange vests with a giant Dragon Air logo on the front, a red X crossing through the misshapen image.

Tal leaned over the fence near Bex, taking in the garish garments. Bex's vest was at least two sizes too big, and hung down well below her waist.

"Good to see that protesting doesn't preclude you from participating in high fashion," Tal said. Bex was pouring a cup of coffee, intent on ignoring him. He was about to walk away, but then, to his surprise, Bex extended the fresh cup to him.

"You look undercaffeinated," she said. "And joke all you want, we know we look fantastic."

Tal stared at the cup. Bex's hands around it were snuggled into a set of fingerless gloves. Tal thought absently that taking this cup might in fact immediately invalidate his employment contract with the airline.

He took it. Bex's fingers were warm as they brushed against his. The cup of coffee was even warmer.

"This does not constitute an endorsement," Tal said. Bex gave a *that's a likely story* huff before pouring coffee for a gnome who had come up behind her.

Tal sipped, expecting the coffee to taste like dirty portable coffee carafes and betrayal. Instead it tasted like some of the best damn coffee he'd ever had. He narrowly avoided sighing audibly, but Bex had already registered the appreciation on his face.

"One of the gnomes in our group runs a smuggling operation that siphons off the best beans from the coffee trade up the coast," Bex said brightly. "I won't tell you which one."

The gnome standing next to her winked at Tal. With the size and dampness of gnomish eyes, the action generated a spray that came disconcertingly close to splashing into Tal's beverage.

"I've got work to do," Tal said. He looked back as he made his way to Ronar. He realized he had not even thanked her. That didn't stop a gleeful expression from spreading across Bex's face.

Each morning, from that point forward, there was a cup of coffee waiting for Tal as he walked into the enclosure. He would trade a few barbs with Bex and the others before taking the cup with mumbled thanks.

He did complain when he walked up to the enclosure one day to find that overnight it had grown up into a full-on pavilion, complete with a roof, at least two permanent walls, and—for reasons he could not fathom—a massive candelabra with lightworkings hanging from each arm. These cast a bright glow over the interior, very much at odds with the grass and dirt floor.

"Are you kidding me?" Tal asked as he and Leanne walked by the structure. It was a far cry from the hasty fence Tal had put together a week and a half ago.

The boards from that project had been stacked carefully next to the pavilion with a note reading: *Thanks for letting us borrow these!* tied to it.

Leanne looked sheepishly at the pavilion.

"Did you know about this?"

"I had a bit of time after I clocked out last night," Leanne replied.

Tal's stomach sank. He was so perturbed by the new structure that he'd almost forgotten to collect his coffee. There it was, sitting on a newly constructed countertop at the edge of the pavilion, close enough that he could reach it from the outside.

"And what exactly did you do with this extra time?"

Leanne gravely met his eyes. "I think you know."

Tal sighed, the sound turning from pain to something much more appreciative as he took the first sip of his coffee. It was, somehow, better than ever.

"Well you're clearly much better at construction than I am," Tal said, patting the half-gnome on the shoulder. "I just hope they compensated you adequately."

"A good deed well-performed is its own reward," Leanne said. If Tal hadn't been holding such good coffee, this comment might have sent him over the edge into despair.

The growth of the protests was mostly well orchestrated, with Bex turning the protesters into a permanent, persistent presence. But not every step was perfectly thought out.

Somehow, Bex had recruited a wyvern to join the protests in Upper Boden.

Wyverns were the smallest breed of dragon, the largest of them able to support only a single rider. This was not the largest. That didn't mean it was an entirely safe companion in an enclosed space.

Tal had been prepping the interior of Ronar's cabin, finding himself straightening the benches so everyone would have enough legroom—a detail he probably would've found unthinkable to concern himself with even a couple weeks ago—when Bex came running across the pen.

"Are you by any chance good with dragons?" Bex asked breathlessly as Tal descended the rear ladder. "It's a bit urgent."

Tal thought he could hear Ronar laughing as he followed the obviously flustered Bex back toward the pavilion.

Her urgent tone was warranted. Something had set the wyvern off, and it was now thrashing around the pavilion, sending protesters scurrying to the corners and scattering the floor with cups and furniture.

As Tal entered, the wyvern lashed out, narrowly missing him.

"Watch out!" came a belated shout from one of the protesters trapped in the corner.

Tal assessed the wyvern's body language. Obvious fear ran down every inch of its scaly frame. It had flared its wings, an unconscious stress response that prepared dragonkind to quickly take to the air. What could be stressing this wyvern out so acutely?

Tal stepped forward, trying to project calm. The wyvern ignored him completely. It wasn't interested in any of the humans, gnomes, or Trugs, Tal realized. Its attention was on the room generally, and more specifically on the candelabra hanging from the ceiling. A couple times its long tail had almost hit it, but the structure was too tall for the tail to reach, and there wasn't enough space within the pavilion for the wyvern to fly up to it.

"Does that lightworking have a switch?" Tal asked Bex, pointing at the candelabra.

"There's a box under that counter. It's tethered to the lightworking."

Tal dodged another swish of the wyvern's tail, ducking behind the counter where the protesters usually served drinks. He found the wooden box. It was equipped with a simple mechanism, a wire running between a piece of metal at one end that would have a counterpart in the candelabra, and a power source at the other end. Tal simply disconnected the wire.

The candelabra flashed off.

There was a scream as the wyvern gave one last violent spin, before coming to rest in the middle of the pavilion. Tal scooted out from behind the counter. The wyvern was breathing raggedly, its eyes half-closed.

A voice in Tal's head wondered how he had so easily identified that the wyvern was bothered by the light. He didn't have time to consider this voice as he looked down at the wyvern, hoping this was more than a momentary calm.

"Is it okay?" Bex asked. "Is it going to light us on fire or try to chop us in half with its tail again?"

She needn't have worried. The wyvern wasn't just calm. It was asleep.

Incidents with light-sensitive wyverns aside, the protests continued with amiable consistency. Tal soon began to find the protesters' presence almost comforting. It was not just the coffee. It was the consistency of showing up to a place and seeing familiar faces. Bex liked to refer to him as a "betrayer of dragonkind" as he walked in, but if such an epithet could be an endearment, it was when it came from Bex.

That was not to say they let Tal off the hook. Around town he would see faces from the protests and not know whether he was about to receive a hearty hello or a cold and disapproving shoulder. Pro-dragon slogans were not limited to the protest areas. A couple protesters who were also regulars at the tavern had taken to sending Tal orders of pickles after overhearing that they "weren't his favorite." He was quickly growing to like them after eating so many for free.

During this time, Enna continued to give Tal a sphere from her seemingly endless supply every time she flew. Tal's collection had grown to over a dozen, though they glowed no more brightly than a single one had.

He was on the way home after a late-night flight one evening, bouncing his new sphere in his palm, when he noticed an unfamiliar shape against the tree outside his house. Startled, he brought up his lantern. The shape turned out to be many shapes—a collection of signs, many of which were familiar from the protests. In case there was any doubt that the signs were targeted at him, the one in front said, *There's Blood on Your Tal-ons!*

The menacing effect of all of this was somewhat undercut by the fact that, when he reached his porch, there was a massive gift basket sitting there, complete with a note in Bex's handwriting inviting him to enjoy an unspeakable amount of delicious muffins and the crushing weight of his own shame.

Tal briefly considered that the muffins might have been tampered with, but when he broke into the first one, a light citrusy pastry with crystallized sugar on top, he decided that even if it was filled with deadly poison, it was probably worth it.

A Compelling Case for Doing Something

After a string of good weather, a flight halfway to Thelspoint was interrupted by a sudden storm blowing in from the sea that turned the Scythe into a boiling cauldron. Shipwrecks rattled in the waves below. The wind knocked the cabin and Tal's seat from side to side. They had been caught dead in the center of the bay, with no sight of land in any direction.

Tal's goggles streaked with rain, his riding clothes drenched within seconds. The windscreen in front of him did nothing to stop the water spinning in from all directions. He considered turning back, but this far into the bay he could no more see the mountain chain that separated Thelanel from Eithlanel than he could Thelspoint in front of him. He checked his compass, wiping away water in order to read it, then gave Ronar a tug on the steering mechanism to guide him onto course. The dragon kept his head bent against the rain, eyes narrowed to slits.

The cabin was likely mayhem, but as long as the glass didn't break, the straps didn't snap off, and they didn't crash, the passengers should be safe. Provided they had strapped themselves in. Too late to check now.

They dove, trying to find any visibility. Climbing above the clouds might be a surer way of improving their sightline, but with the thinning air, Tal and the passengers would likely pass out. Ronar would be fine, but bringing home a load of asphyxiated passengers was a bad look for all involved.

Tal could see nothing. Ronar's wings battled the wind, sending him juddering from side to side. Lightning shrieked past. For a second, Tal was completely blind. Then the thunder came, and the force of it knocked him back into his chair. Lightning strikes were rare on dragons given the insulation lining every layer of scales, but they weren't impossible. More lightning volleyed around them, far too close for comfort.

Ronar leveled off and roared. His vision was far better than Tal's, so it took a moment to register what he had seen. The spires of Thelspoint rose amid the clouds. They were close.

The next few minutes were frantic, with updrafts pushing Ronar skyward and the dragon angling himself to stay below the clouds. At one point Ronar folded his wings for close to thirty seconds, falling fast. Tal could almost feel the screams coming from the cabin. To the untrained eye this probably looked like a very bad idea, but Ronar knew exactly how low to dive before extending his wings and leveling out on the next updraft. Something in Ronar's body language, or maybe the glint in his eyes, told Tal: *I've got this.*

Tal's voice was useless against the whipping wind. He scratched Ronar along his scales, affirming his trust.

Ronar refused to break as the storm continued. Soon they were swooping low over the outskirts of Thelspoint. The wind had died slightly, but rain continued to bludgeon them. Just as they were about to spiral toward their usual landing pen, a serpentine shape appeared in the air in front of them.

The creature was a wyvern, with a lone man on its back, part of the Thelspoint fleet used for official business. The man waved a lit signal rod at him. Tal found his own signal rod tucked in the holster under his seat, activating the red crystals inside by smacking it against the side of the chair. He indicated with the rod that he would follow.

The wyvern led them into a wide bank turn, taking them out of the flight path of any dragons coming directly toward the inner landing areas. It was far enough ahead that Tal had to squint to see even a trace of the lit rod. As the turn continued, Tal realized they were aiming much closer to the city wall than usual. The wyvern guided them down toward the huge fields that were usually reserved for Heathermark Flight Group landings. They were just a short walk from the city wall, and with how much space must cost here, only Heathermark Flight Group could afford to land their dragons so close.

The landing area was chaos. A half dozen dragons thrashed on the ground as teams of attendants struggled to remove drenched harnesses. It took a team of horses to pull the Heathermark cabins, and two cabins were stuck in the mud on the dirt track leading to shelter. Meanwhile, two massive Cernoth dragons circled overhead, unable to land.

Tal followed the signal rod down to the one open spot. It was a tight fit, even for Ronar. Ronar bellowed as he aimed for it. Even Tal, used to Ronar's less than smooth landings, let out a yelp as Ronar jerked from side to side, grazing a brick wall, almost colliding with the dragon next to them, and eventually coming to rest in a squelch of mud and dislodged grass.

The wyvern landed by Ronar's head—much more gracefully, and with an imperious look that conveyed exactly what it thought of Ronar's performance—bringing the man on its back near enough to yell over the rain. He wore a slate blue flight suit and helmet. His thick blue gloves appeared to be fused to the wyvern's reins. The circular insignia on his chest marked him as a lieutenant in the Thelspoint Air Patrol, the aerial unit of the city's police force.

"You from Dragon Air?" the lieutenant asked.

"Yeah, we usually don't land this close."

"You do now. Your landing pen is currently on fire, along with two of the other smaller landing pens. The whole skies are a mess."

Tal's clothes had long ago become more water than fabric. He shivered, hoping it wasn't a sign of hypothermia. It didn't seem like ideal conditions for anything to burn.

"They think it was a lightning strike," the lieutenant said. "Working theory, anyway."

Tal unbuckled himself, and got up to check on his passengers. "Thanks for the assist."

"Clear out as soon as you can. We need that landing spot ten minutes ago."

The lieutenant whistled to his wyvern, and spurred him skyward. Ronar shook his head, trying to clear the water out of his eyes.

"Don't worry, Ro," Tal said, patting his side. "We'll be dry soon. You did great." Tal looked around, but there was no sign of the attendants who were usually stationed at his landing pen. All the other teams were busy with their own dragons. One of the larger Heathermark fliers had obviously had a crash landing, splintering one side of its multi-level cabin. Attendants scrambled to clear debris as a team of medics carried injured people away.

The storm was bad enough, but how had a lightning strike torched three landing pens at once? The pens and the stables attached to them were vulnerable to fire, given that their floors were wood covered in hay, and they housed creatures that were essentially living furnaces. Still, three pens at once . . .

Tal held his breath as he opened the cabin door, expecting the worst.

"Is everyone okay?" Tal asked.

"Just some bumps and bruises," said a short woman with a no-nonsense face and a maroon leather jacket. Tal thought she was a regular passenger, but couldn't remember her name. She had been the first to stand and attend to the others.

The others murmured their agreement. Tal approached the middle-aged man who appeared to be the worst off. His leg had banged along the side of the bench during the turbulence. A nasty bruise ran the length of his shin. The man's brother looked on with grave concern.

All flight attendants were trained in at least minimal first aid—and even *minimal* was probably ambitious for Dragon Air—but Tal's university instruction had involved extensive medical training. Though it had been primarily of the magical variety, the concepts were the same. He was rusty, but the man didn't appear to have lost any range of motion, so Tal didn't think anything was broken. He most likely didn't require immediate intervention. Tal told him as much, and the man and his brother thanked him.

Water still splashed against the cabin roof. It would almost have been pleasant if not for the accompanying wails of distressed dragons.

"I hate to ask this, but I need help getting the cabin off the dragon," Tal said to the group. "It's a mess out there, and they really need us to get clear—is there anyone strong who can help me? I know it's not super reassuring to hear at this point, but the cabin is really just several pieces strapped together, so one volunteer will do the trick."

The overwhelmed faces of people who had just been through an ordeal and were now being asked to help with something that was decidedly not their job stared back at him. But the woman in the leather jacket, calm as ever, immediately volunteered.

"Thank you. We can, I don't know, comp your ticket or something?" Tal had no idea if that was something he was allowed to offer, but the situation seemed dire enough to warrant it.

With a scoff, she said, "No need. My flights are on my employer's tab anyway." She introduced herself as Claret. Her strong handshake reassured Tal that she'd be more than capable of handling the weight of the cabin.

It didn't take long to unload the passengers, the brother of the injured man helping him limp to safe ground. As the rain slowed, a swarm of onlookers had come out to watch the chaos at the landing pen, meaning that the unlucky passengers had to push through a crowd on their way out. Tal turned to the work of disassembling the cabin. Ronar grew more restless with each passing minute. Claret followed Tal's instructions to the letter, approaching each maneuver with a care that suggested she worried a wrong move might hurt Ronar.

"I think I'm getting the knack of this," Claret said as they extended the wheels attached to the back portion of the cabin. She had asymmetrical, chin-length silver hair that she kept pushing back from her eyes as she worked. Free of his restraints, Ronar began to sway toward the stable. He had to skirt around the medical cart being loaded with the injured passengers from the crashed flight, and dive out of the way as an Eitnoth dragon came in for a sidelong landing. The storm had picked up again, and these dragons looked the worse for wear. The wings of the one that had almost crashed into Ronar must have come up against a terrible shearing wind, because they had a nasty rip across them.

"You know, Dragon Air is always hiring," Tal said.

"Afraid that might be a bit of a step down compensation-wise." Claret grimaced. "Sorry, I just put my foot squarely in my mouth. I meant no offense."

"None taken. What is it you actually do?"

"I do freelance questing for the Thelspoint government. Lucrative, fun, and dangerous."

Tal grunted as the wheels stuck in the mud. They strained against them together. "So you like, what, investigate crimes?"

"Sometimes," Claret replied. "There's an awful lot of going into abandoned shrines, tripping booby traps, and slaying draugrs."

Tal didn't say what he was thinking, which was that Claret might be the single coolest person he'd ever met. Instead he said, "That probably has better benefits than Dragon Air anyway."

Claret laughed, sending Tal's brain into an alternate reality where he not only knew biographical information about his passengers, but could actually laugh with them.

Over the next several minutes, as they dragged the pieces of the cabin into a storeroom and made the long walk around the edge of the churning landing pen, Claret told him about her questing work. They checked in on Ronar, who had found a comfortable patch of hay and was already asleep, as Claret described her most recent quest. An orphan child had started showing signs of demonic possession, but when Claret went to destroy the essence of the demon, she found that the child had actually created the demon, and was in fact a powerful mage who had shrunk himself down into the body of a little girl, and in the process had lost any memory of being a mage.

"What did you do with them?" Tal asked in horror.

"Only thing we could do. Put them in a school for troubled children. Never mind that he's a sixty-year-old running around in a six-year-old's body."

Tal supposed this was probably the best that could be hoped for. He thought how nice it would be to find a bed, or even just somewhere indoors with a warm hearth. The stables, despite smelling of injured dragon, were already a welcome respite. But outside, the chaos was only increasing, and surely they needed anyone with knowledge of dragons to help. He couldn't do magic, but he could at least try to make himself useful.

"It looks like Ronar is all set," Tal said. "I'm going to see if they need me anywhere else. It still looked bad out there. You're free to go, you've done more than enough."

Claret's maroon jacket showed no sign of the downpour—likely the result of an expensive leatherworking—and its shoulders rose as she shrugged.

"Guess there's still helping to be done," she said.

The rest of the evening was a blur. They joined in wherever they could, assisting the crews pulling the huge cabins from the backs of the Cernoth dragons, bringing the injured dragons food or salves, and guiding passengers through the muddy landing field to the exits. There wasn't much time for talking, but with each strap they pulled together, each mixture of sweat and rain wiped from their brows, Tal felt a spark of kinship with Claret. He almost let himself admit that being useful could have its perks.

Tal checked in on Ronar one last time once Claret left. He was still fast asleep. Tal now took the time to inspect every inch of his back, making sure his scales hadn't sustained any damage. As he ran his hand along the rough surface of Ronar's leg, his fingers lingered over a spot that was hotter than the others. Dragons were always warm, but a truly hot area usually meant some kind of abrasion. The usually gray-red scale was bright red around the edges, the membrane chafed raw. Tal winced in sympathy. Moisture always made the straps that secured the cabin to Ronar's back move around more, which was a sure recipe for exactly this kind of irritation. He went off in search of a salve.

In the far corner, near a storeroom he hoped would have tubs of dragon tonics, Tal found himself the only human in a hallway that ran along the side of the stable. Thick slats separated him from the warmth of the dragons inside, but there were enough gaps in the wood that he could see the shapes of three large Cernoths grouped together, apparently in communication but completely silent save for the movement of air in and out of the powerful lungs that fueled their seventy-foot bodies. They hadn't seen Tal. An instinct told him to stay out of sight. He kept behind the barrier wall near the storeroom, watching the dragons through the space between slats.

Just as with Ronar, he could infer some of their meaning through their gestures. The largest of the dragons was grumbling about the rain, and the presence of Eitnoth dragons who they usually didn't have to share a stable with.

It's regrettable, but temporary, another seemed to say.

When the largest dragon growled again, Tal found that he could understand it almost as well as if it was speaking in a human tongue: *For the record, I was against torching the other landing pens. It was Journak who wanted to send the message.*

I believe the message was sent, said the smaller dragon. The words drifted to Tal as if on the intuitive level of a dream. Like words in a dream, their meaning arrived long after the words themselves. *I do not know that it will be enough.*

We know humans are prone to overreaction, the largest replied. *Their treatment of us will only worsen. This accommodation itself could be seen as a slight amongst the older dragons.*

The third dragon, who had not spoken yet, was an unusually bright green color. Tal blinked as this dragon's words drifted out of mist in his mind. *And some even believe humans will use dragonsbane against us.*

The largest dragon grunted something that to Tal sounded an awful lot like, *Even better*, shifting his massive weight deeper into the straw.

Dread built inside Tal. Surely he was projecting these words onto the dragons rather than actually understanding them. It had been a trying day, and his mind was playing tricks on him. Even with the hard wood of the fence against his hand, his perception felt oddly disassociated, as if this reality was happening to someone else.

The storeroom door shrieked open, and an attendant stepped out, oblivious of the dragons meeting just feet away.

We will continue this discussion at a later time, the large dragon said.

As if the idiot can understand us, the green dragon snorted.

Tal snapped back into himself, seizing this opportunity to rush toward the end of the hall, turning so it looked like he and the man had been walking to the storeroom together. The man looked confused, but held the door open for him, and Tal slipped inside.

He searched for the salve, finding the stuff in a giant vat that was mostly empty after the evening's events. His thoughts ran in so many directions, he almost dropped the flask he was decanting the salve into. He wasn't sure what was more upsetting, the fact there seemed to be a conspiracy among the dragons, or that he had apparently been able to understand enough dragon speech to come to this conclusion. There was a threat beneath the dragons' words, one that wasn't quite clear to him, even if he believed he could understand them. A conspiracy, but one that seemed to rely on how the humans reacted to the dragons' behavior. His mind still buzzed, unable to pin itself back to a firm reality. He closed the salve inside the flask, and went to tend to Ronar.

Bad Management

Enna and Bex had been trying to convince Tal to visit the Dragon Air office about the protesters' demands for the last couple weeks, but there were several reasons why he hadn't.

First, he didn't want to.

Second, making requests on behalf of the protesters would feel like caving to their strategy of persistently annoying the shit out of him. He didn't want to encourage that type of behavior.

Second part B was that it felt like bending to Bex specifically, and just thinking about allowing her to win at anything made him a little angry.

Third, Dragon Air's management was widely known to be reactionary, impetuous, and needlessly cruel. And that was when they weren't too busy being relentlessly incompetent.

All of this made the walk to their office in Thelspoint's business district quite a long one. The business district made up a large portion of Thelspoint's inner ring, and was fortunately far enough from the university that his chances of running into anyone he knew were low. Low, not zero.

Tal's thoughts bounced back and forth between images of destruction, confusion over what he'd really heard the previous night, and dreading an encounter with Meret or anyone else from the Completists. Tal's loss of magic had never been publicized, as far as he knew, but people talked. And Preeminent Mages didn't just disappear for no reason. Surely they had theories—the group had always loved theorizing about anything even obliquely magical, and Tal couldn't bear the thought of himself as their subject.

Most buildings in the district were at least four stories, orange brick the primary building material. The center of the district featured high-rises, most still orange, but with larger windows and some possessing the brilliant sheen of a stoneworking. In order for such tall buildings to be practical, mages would have supplied moving platforms to travel between floors, an enormous expense both in materials costs and in labor for a university-trained mage.

Dragon Air's offices, of course, were not in the center of the business district. They were at the far end, in a two-story brick building that had once been a hideout for elements of Thelspoint's criminal underworld. The office had been the site of a raid that resulted in the deaths of eight gang members, injuries to almost a dozen constables, and scorch marks from offensive magic that had never fully been scrubbed away. Dragon Air had been able to purchase the offices at a deep discount.

One would think this would free up funds to renovate the office. One would think incorrectly.

A gnome sat behind the welcome desk, which Tal knew for a fact contained hooks for the crossbows that the gang had kept to hand in case of a raid. Tal hoped these hooks were empty. Despite appearances—the round heads, deceptively soft skin, and beards that looked more like the fur of an ermine than human hair—gnomes were by and large excellent shots.

"I'm here to see Pieter," Tal said.

The gnome scanned a piece of paper in front of her, then squinted at Tal. "And who are you?"

"My name is Tal. I'm a flight attendant for the company."

The gnome gave no indication that this rang a bell.

"You interviewed me?" Tal said. Nothing. "It doesn't matter. Is Pieter in? There's something I need to ask him."

"Do you have an appointment?" the gnome asked.

Tal tried to hide a scoff. "This is Dragon Air. Appointments, like on-time arrivals, aren't really in our repertoire."

"Oh, so you do work here." The gnome stood. "Right this way."

She led him down a dingy hallway stuffed with so much company memorabilia there was barely space to walk. A dozen commemorative plaques lined the walls, next to models of dragons with improbable cabins strapped to their backs. Most gave far too much credit both to the size of the dragon and the workmanship of the cabins.

"Fair warning, Pieter may just be waking up from his mid-morning nap," the receptionist said. Tal's foot sunk so far into the rug, he feared the floor would give way entirely. "He gets very cranky when he's woken up."

They stopped at a door with a wooden sign hanging above the lintel. The sign, which Tal had to tilt his head to read because one of the nails holding it in place had come unstuck, said *Head of Operations*.

"Any advice?" Tal had never spoken to the Head of Operations before, and still wasn't sure his nerves were up to the task.

"Make sure you're not waking him up from his mid-morning nap," the gnome said, already edging away from him. Tal thought he could hear the sound of snoring from within.

He knocked on the closed door. There was a long silence. He knocked again. More silence.

Tal turned questioningly toward the receptionist, but she was already halfway down the hall.

"Well, are you coming in or what?" boomed a voice from behind the door.

Tal took a deep breath that did little to calm him, and entered.

The Head of Operations's office was cramped by any measure, but was made considerably more so by the fact that the boxes of files along the walls turned inward at the top, threatening to topple over. In the chair, his feet up on a desk strewn with paper and quills, was the Head of Operations himself. He didn't sit up any straighter, just drummed on his ample stomach as Tal stepped inside.

"Pieter, thank you for seeing me," Tal said.

"Good timing, I've got a few minutes before my mid-morning nap."

There was no discernible place for Tal to sit. He stood awkwardly in front of Pieter's desk, hands clasped behind his back.

"I have a somewhat unusual request," Tal said, embarrassment already coursing damply through him. "You see, there have been some protests at our landing pens, both in Upper Boden and here in Thelspoint."

"You're looking for clearance to rough 'em up a little?"

"No, no, nothing like that," Tal said quickly. "They're making some very reasonable demands, and I thought . . ."

"Did I just hear the word 'reasonable' before the word 'demands'? You must not have been in the airline business long, kid."

Tal bit his lip, trying not to let his nerves turn into frustration. "It's one small thing, which I don't think would even require that much from us."

"'That much' is still some," Pieter said. He kicked his feet down onto the floor, dislodging one of the larger stacks of paper from his desk. The very thought of more work seemed to have agitated him.

"Basically all they want is to use this new technology. It's a device that allows people to talk to dragons."

"*Talk to dragons,*" Pieter spluttered. "Whatever could you want to do that for?"

"They want to get the dragons to approve their employment contract. I think? I wasn't exactly clear on the process."

Tal felt more than a little unimpressive. If he'd spent the last couple weeks preparing his argument rather than actively rejecting the idea outright, maybe he'd be having more success.

"As far as we're concerned, the contracts are signed and set in stone. Everything was done by the book and one hundred percent legally."

"The protesters are concerned that the legal process might not be ethical."

Pieter closed his eyes in exasperation. "Have you told these people that they have better things to do than splitting ethical hairs?"

"Not in so many words," Tal said, with each passing moment feeling his initial assessment that this was a bad idea becoming more and more correct. "Obviously I wouldn't argue we buy the translator device, that's too expensive. I'm just asking, if they were to somehow get ahold of the device, would the company say we're amenable to using it? If I tell them that, it would get them off our backs. Send them off on a wild goose chase while we appear more reasonable than we actually are."

Tal's phrasing didn't trip Pieter up at all, which was a minor miracle. "You said this device is expensive?"

"Extremely."

"And these protesters, are they people of means?"

"Not at present, no."

Pieter checked the clock on the wall. Tal wondered how far he'd encroached on his scheduled nap. "That's not good enough."

"Of course, there's always the other outcome to consider," Tal said hurriedly. "We've been assuming dragons want to be paid like any other employee, in addition to their substantial room and board. But that was only ever an assumption. It's just as possible that dragons don't need coin, and would be just as happy with alternative compensation."

"Alternative compensation?"

"Like longer grooming sessions, or slightly more specific meal selections. All of which I'm sure an astute businessman like yourself could arrange at a wholesale discount."

Pieter's eyes took on a faraway glaze, as if he was already imagining how he could rip off the new groomers he would hire with the dragons' recouped wages.

"Fine," Pieter blurted. "Tell the protesters that if they can get their hands on the device, we'll use it."

"Thank you, sir. That'll make my life so much easier."

Pieter waved his hand for Tal to leave. But before he did, Pieter intoned, "Just one clarification. If we use this device and are forced to make any monetary concessions on the contracts, I'll know exactly who to fire."

68

Card Games

"You realize this is a horrible deal, right?" Bex asked. "The device is expensive for a company. No person will be able to afford it."

"That's the best I could do," Tal said. He'd invited Bex to the tavern to fill her in. She adjusted her glasses back and forth as she thought.

"It's better than nothing," she said. "Barely."

Tal's stomach sank at that, and then sank again as he realized the initial sinking feeling meant he actually cared. "So the mage in Heathermark, the one who created the device, they wouldn't be willing to loan it out? Or even rent it?"

The noise of the tavern bubbled around them. Traders had been in and out all week, and the locals were present in full force, as if asserting themselves over the rowdier out-of-towners.

"She's been firm on that. She can make so much money selling it to the government, allowing them to communicate with the wild dragons out in the Claglands, that it doesn't make sense for her to risk it on rentals. Bit of a stingy lady, given the potential for her device to do good. I guess that's true of most university mages, though."

Tal nearly choked on his ale. For the millionth time he wished it was mead, and that they were in Thelspoint rather than what had recently been described to him as the ass end of Eithlanel.

"Do you know this mage's name? I have some connections in the university."

"Nirza."

Tal slumped back against his chair. He really shouldn't have said anything.

"What, you know her?" Bex asked.

"I've only met her once," Tal said quietly, "but my old advisor was a student of hers."

"Your advisor?"

At Bex's confusion, Tal was forced to tell her about his past life as a student, about his studies under Nathan, and about Nathan's relationship with Nirza. Nirza had been department head for languageworking all the way back when Nathan was a student. That meant Nirza had been close to one hundred and twenty years old when Tal met her at a ceremony honoring her service to the university. Tal tried to skirt around as many details as possible, but Bex asked probing questions at every pause, forcing Tal into memories he would rather not relive.

"I'm sorry you went through that," Bex said.

"I know what you're going to ask, and the answer is no."

Bex laughed. "What did you think I was going to ask?"

"To ask my old advisor if he'd talk to Nirza, to see if he'd vouch for us."

Bex studied him. Her ale had been forgotten throughout the conversation and was far fuller than his. Today she wore a long wool jacket over a flowing blouse. Her thick glasses were square rather than round. Tal found himself charmed by the fact that she had multiple pairs.

"I wouldn't have asked you to do that," Bex said. "It sounds like seeing him again almost gave you a heart attack."

"The attack was more of the panic than heart variety, but yeah. Right idea."

"You must think I'm a pushy monster."

"You're not pushy?" Tal asked.

"Within reason."

"When I think of reasonable, I don't usually think of organizing protests in multiple cities about a cause that has nothing to do with me."

Bex faked a simpering grin. "I love it when men compliment me."

"Not to mention making my job way harder when there's nothing I can do about it."

"So your inconvenience is more important than the rights of intelligent beings?" Bex picked her mug up to take her first drink in about ten minutes, but set it down again before it reached her lips. "I can tell that you think I don't believe in what I'm doing. Like this is all a whim, or to piss off my rich parents."

Tal's stare must've given him away, because Bex looked furious.

"Okay, I get you," Bex said. "And maybe it's fair for you to think that. But know that I *do* believe in what I'm doing. I grew up around dragons. Every day after school, I would meet my father at the stables. He was still doing his own inspections back then. Watching a dragon fly is one thing, but there's something about seeing the mundane details of their lives—how much food they need to eat, how they get picky about certain kinds of meat, how gentle they are around the people who care for them—that not many people understand. When you're around an intelligent creature like them on a daily basis, you begin to feel they're almost . . ."

". . . human?" Tal asked.

"Definitely not," Bex said. "But the sentiment is right. They're kind. They're powerful. They're funny. Their brains work differently, but they're just as conscious, just as worthy as any human. So yeah, this contract thing might be the wrong approach, or maybe I'm getting hung up on something insignificant, but as soon as we start glossing over the worthiness of beings just because they can't speak like humans, we're discounting the beauty of every other kind of intelligence."

Tal felt the power behind her words, the animating force of conviction. More than that, though, he felt their truth as someone who had spent the last two years around a dragon. Despite sometimes driving him crazy, there was no other individual, human or dragon, who Tal was as comfortable around in this iteration of his life. Even if he couldn't respond with words, Ronar communicated as well as any friend. Tal did not allow himself to consider that Ronar's inability to communicate with words might not be as clear-cut as he had previously thought, if he was anything like the dragons in the stable back in Thelspoint.

"Sorry, got a little carried away there," Bex said, covering up the awkward silence that had begun to stretch on. In that silence, the noise of the tavern reasserted itself. A man had fallen off a stool at one of the center tables, and the burlier of Mora's bartenders was calmly inviting him to find a different establishment to sober up in. Bex finally took a sip of her ale.

"No, don't apologize. I just wish . . ." Don't say it. He shouldn't say it. He *couldn't* say it, not if he was going to retain any sense of his own dignity. He said it anyway. "I just wish there was anything in my life I cared about as much as you care about this."

Bex, to Tal's shock, started to laugh. It wasn't a derisive laugh, or even one that sounded particularly amused. Instead it was a laugh of wonder, of awe at how ridiculous the world was.

"Not that long ago, we knew next to nothing about each other," Bex said. "We were on the opposite side of a literal protest cordon zone."

"I did build said cordon zone."

"The original version. The quality of the workmanship wouldn't let me forget that. Yet here we are, and you're sharing something I can't imagine was easy for you to say."

"I can already tell it was a bad idea."

"Your secret is safe with me. If there's one thing I'm good at, it's keeping people's insecurities to myself after they reveal them at an awkwardly early juncture in our relationship."

"A *really* bad idea."

He couldn't tell why, but the more Bex smiled, the more he felt the creases of his own mouth wanting to do the same. They hadn't done that much recently.

"I won't force you to help me," Bex said finally. "I feel we've both put our cards on the table. We know what we're doing is in good faith. Even if you are hiding behind the bullshit excuse of inconvenience."

Tal had to smile at that. "Cards on the table, we both know that's not what it's about."

"Good." Bex got up, raised a mug that had to be at least half full still, and drained it in a single swig. "See you on the picket lines tomorrow, Tal."

His name felt like a punch coming out of her mouth. A shocking but somehow pleasant punch.

T al's eyes were watering as he made his way home, and he didn't know why. The conversation had stirred something in him, something he would much rather have continued to bury under routine and the occasional wash of slightly too much ale.

He had every right to feel exhausted, having recently been through a powerful storm and helping half a dozen dragons in distress. The exhaustion had followed him back to Upper Boden. So had the knowledge that there were dragons out there with the singular goal of causing mayhem in the human world.

But this exhaustion ran deeper. It was the exhaustion of having denied a part of himself for too long, and finally facing it long enough to realize how badly he'd missed it. This part had come alive in the landing pen as he'd helped unhook cabins, guided passengers to safety amid thrashing tails of panicked dragons, and did whatever he could to be part of quelling the chaos around him. It was the same part that had jumped at any chance to help younger mages in the university. Anyone in the Completists had enjoyed near-unlimited access to Tal's abilities, whether that meant helping with a plantworking assignment, or simply relighting someone's lamp in the library. Students would show up at his dorm room door, at his table in the dining hall, anywhere in all of Thelspoint, and he had helped them without a second thought. To be needed like this, to know that his mere presence benefited others, was a gift he hadn't realized he'd lost.

When Tal reached his home, someone was sitting on his doorstep. A cloak's cowl covered their face. Tal wondered if Pieter had changed his mind, and this was a Dragon Air-hired thug sent to beat him up. But when the figure stood, Tal recognized her crooked posture.

"Enna?"

"I didn't know we were neighbors," Enna said. "I live just up the road, past the tanner's and over the hill."

"I didn't know we were neighbors either. How did you find out we were neighbors?"

Instead, Enna held up a linen drawstring bag. It was lumpy, a soft glow piercing the fabric.

"My spheres always know where their brothers are," Enna said, hefting the bag in her withered hand. "Aren't you going to invite me inside for tea?"

Faced with no other choice besides telling an old woman to shove off, Tal unlatched his cabin's door and let Enna into the cramped space. She said nothing as he busied himself making a fire and drawing water from the well out back. Her eyes took in everything from where she sat in his only chair. Surely she must see the empty cabinet Tal had left open, the two dishes stacked in the washbasin. The dust that coated each book that had come back with him from the university. There was no criticism in Enna's expression. When the tea had steeped, Tal handed his only teacup to Enna, and poured himself tea in a bowl that was just narrow enough to pass as a cup if you didn't look at it too closely.

"So, how are my spheres doing?" Enna asked. "Have they started glowing yet?"

Tal nearly overturned his tea bowl as he sat on his bed. He looked over to his growing collection of spheres in the glass bowl on the table. The light coming off them was different today. Slightly whiter and definitely brighter, enough that his desk looked oddly spectral.

"I suppose they are," Enna said, following his gaze. She removed a single sphere from her own bag. It blazed a brilliant white.

"I think that's new," said Tal. "They didn't look like that earlier today."

Now that he thought about it, he hadn't been paying much attention to the color of the spheres with everything on his mind recently.

"Interesting," Enna said. She returned her sphere to the bag.

"If you don't mind me asking, what exactly are these? I've studied all sorts of magical artifacts and never come across anything quite like them."

"Probably not surprising." Enna sipped her tea, and set her cup down on top of the stack of books Tal hadn't finished organizing. "They've been out of fashion for a while. Back in the old days, the government would use them as a means of identifying potential mages."

That made sense. Before the boom in magic over the past hundred years, service as a mage was required as a duty to the realm, not elective. Without a way to tell who had that power, there could be no way of enforcing mandatory service.

"Every child was given at least a dozen of these spheres," Enna continued. "If they started glowing—the spheres, not the child, hopefully—then they would make the long journey to Thelspoint. No dragons to ride back then."

"So you basically did the same thing to me?" Tal tried to add some suggestion of anger into his voice, but found he was mostly curious.

"The spheres have a significant flaw. They only tell you if their owner has magic actively radiating from their body, not whether they possess the potential for magic. A lot of future mages were missed because the power was dormant."

"My power is dormant, too," Tal said regretfully.

"Don't be thick!" Enna gesticulated so wildly toward the glass bowl that she rattled her teacup nearly off the stack of books. "You own these spheres, and they only glow at all when their owner's power is active. You want to tell me these aren't glowing?"

Tal stared at them. "I suppose they are sort of glowing."

"Which means there's some power in you."

"The spheres are wrong. My power is long gone. I can't even do a simple fireworking to get a fire going, or a waterworking to make the pot boil faster."

Enna was leaning forward, as if preparing to shoot to her feet. "You can't do any magic you're used to doing. That doesn't mean your magic has deserted you altogether." She leaned back, seeming to relax.

"I don't know what to tell you. I can't feel anything."

"I knew I made a good decision giving these to you," Enna said. "Only time will tell exactly why."

When Enna left, Tal slammed the door behind her much harder than could possibly have been considered polite. He stared at the spheres, eyes narrowed against their glow. He considered throwing them out, glass bowl and all, and got as far as picking them up and holding them above the wastebasket. He paused, standing over the reek of yesterday's chicken bones and a loamy pile of spoiled cabbage.

Tal set the bowl of spheres back on the counter. He eyed the remnants of some soapy water that had splashed onto the counter when he washed Enna's mug. Lightworking had always been among the easiest of the magical disciplines for Tal. Manipulating the flow of light through a substance, like the sparkling bubbles on the counter, always felt more like tricking one's own eyes than extending one's will into the physical world. Light already danced through the water, and Tal allowed himself ten long seconds of trying to trick his eyes into making it dance more.

He gritted his teeth. A flash of blue. A flare of red. Any movement at all would have been enough, would've assured him that the potential within the spheres was not a lie.

The light did not change.

Tal swept his hand across the counter, wiping the water back into the washbasin and sending spheres scattering into every corner of the kitchen.

His magic might not have abandoned him entirely, but why then could he not feel it within himself? At the university, it had run through his veins every time he used it. It was a hum he believed was synonymous with being alive. Until it had left him.

And yet, as he got on his hands and knees to pick them up from where they had fallen, the spheres glowed.

An Embarrassment of Mentorship

Tal was going back to Thelspoint, as he often did. That was what he locked onto, the routine of it. The view as they approached the city was the same. The deadly sweep of the Scythe and the smoking peak of Hammer Top were the same. Even the landing zone would be the same, a temporary replacement pen having been erected where the previous one had burned down.

What would not be the same was that as soon as he landed, he would be heading deep into Thelspoint and marching into the university he had flamed out of two years ago.

He thought about spheres, and it made him confused.

He thought about lost magic, and it made him sad.

He thought about asking Nathan for a favor, and it made him want to throw up.

Bex was on the flight, having apparently found a little money and set aside her qualms about flying on the back of a dragon with an unethical contract. Tal did at least get some satisfaction from her look of amazement as she stared out the cabin's glass wall. She had of course flown before, but all those flights had been on Heathermark's massive Cernoth dragons. With a smaller dragon like Ronar, the passengers sat much closer to his flank, providing a far more direct view out the side.

Bex's constant affirmations that he was doing a good thing did nothing to make Tal less nervous about what he was about to do. She wouldn't accompany him to the university—he had to draw a line somewhere—but had come to gauge any interest in their cause from the dragons housed in the stables here in Thelspoint. She still couldn't go to Heathermark. Her stated reason was that Heathermark dragons were more brainwashed, and therefore less likely to support her. Tal wondered if the personal nature of her rebellion against her parents was just as relevant. Thus far she had avoided a direct showdown, and Tal couldn't blame her for wanting to push this confrontation back as long as possible.

They parted ways at the bridge between Outer Thelspoint and The City. Bex's lively chatter had helped Tal ignore his impending arrival at the university, but once she was gone, disappearing into the underpass beneath the artificial river, Tal was alone with his fear. Well, not entirely alone. It was impossible to be truly alone in Thelspoint. Traffic continued at a businesslike pace in both directions across the bridge into The City.

The cluster of buildings collectively referred to as Thelspoint University was not its own separate entity as such. It bled indiscriminately into the city around it, and it wasn't uncommon for a private residence to be surrounded by three or four buildings owned by the school. But the sensation of stepping on campus was still terribly distinct. Students—ranging from their early teens to well into their twenties—passed by with confident strides. Tal passed two of the grandest academic buildings on either side of College Street. The Hall of the Elements was ornate, with heavy marble columns that spoke of an imposing and powerful history. Opposite the hall was the Research Center, a marvel of bulbous glass, dozens of classrooms visible from street level and buzzing with activity.

The square in front of the Hall of the Elements was dominated by an animated statue of Varai. He appeared in his male form, arm slightly bent as he plumbed the sky for knowledge. The god of discovery was a fitting symbol of the university's research. His partner Arren occupied a similar position on the façade of the Assembly Hall just a mile away, where she appeared in her female form and reminded the Unified Coast's government that their job was to create cooperation—both within the provinces and with their neighbors to the north and south. When he first arrived, Tal had been surprised by the omnipresence of Varai around the university. The work of academia seemed so separate from any religious practice. Yet he had come to appreciate that most of Varai's devotees saw the god as a symbolic representation of the value of knowledge and discovery, not a literal being. This was at odds with how Arren's disciples practiced, particularly further south in Eithlanel. In the great city of Eith, those who invoked Arren's name during a negotiation were thought to be encircled with Arren's breath, filling them with a powerful sense of compromise.

Nathan's office was in the languageworking annex, in the warren of connected buildings that had sprung up behind the Hall of the Elements. The annex was every bit as tatty as the entrance was grand. If Tal were still a student, he would use the main entrance, taking in the vaulted ceilings of the grand foyer. Hanging from the ceiling were hundreds of statues carved of pure crystal, enacting a long-ago magical battle. From time to time, a burst of fire or ice would fly from one of the statues. Tal didn't think he could withstand such a direct interaction with the school's majesty today, instead finding the little-used back entrance to the annex, off an alley where bins labelled as experiments in compost acceleration nearly blocked the way. Each step further onto university property added another sliver of apprehension in Tal. His breaths further shortened with each stride over uniform cobblestones.

No one questioned Tal on his way in. The university had an open-door policy with the city, the implication being that if one had an inclination to cause mischief at a school filled with powerful mages, one was more than welcome to try.

Tal paused at the bottom of the stairs. These would lead up to the floor that housed the faculty of languageworking and their smaller seminar classrooms. He recognized this faux marble stair with every fiber of his being, the way it twisted upward, grooves worn deep into the center of every step with the passing of thousands of feet. It could so easily be an early fall day, and he could be on his way to have his advisor sign a course change form, or to pick up a syllabus from a lecturer's office. For a moment, Tal did not feel so separate from that life.

He gritted his teeth and climbed the stairs.

Nathan's office door was open, but there was no sign of him. Tal checked the clock on the wall, then the schedule posted on the professor's door. Office hours slots, course schedules. Nathan was currently wrapping up a lecture down in the auditorium the languageworking department shared with historiography. Tal could wait for him here.

And yet he felt a stray impulse come over him. He hadn't stepped foot in a university lecture hall in two years.

He knew the way to the auditorium by heart. He also knew the hall was large enough to slip into unnoticed. In fact, when he arrived, the door was propped open to help ventilate the stuffy room, and Tal ducked through before he could think better of it.

Only a couple in the back row—who seemed more interested in whispered flirtations than the lecture—looked up. He sat quietly on one of the benches at the rear, the stadium seating giving him a high vantage above the lecturer. It was so odd to sit in this room without opening a notebook or unstopping an inkwell. Nathan was in fine form today. Even his large lectures relied on hands-on demonstrations, and a student currently stood by the podium, his hands on a piece of parchment covered in exaggeratedly large text.

"Remember that the text's meaning doesn't come from you," Nathan was saying. He stood a few paces away from the student, speaking to the class. "It comes from the text itself. As such, what we are doing is not an act of creation, but one of *revelation*. The meaning already exists, we simply allow it to flow through a different medium. Now, prepare your languageworking—repeat your anchor phrases at least three times—and begin to trace the words with your hand."

The demonstrating student ran his fingers along the massive letters. It was probably the same parchment Tal had used in a long-ago lecture, though he couldn't remember what it said.

Which was unfortunate, because what this student was doing was unlikely to give him any clues.

A voice rose from the parchment, a high, raspy voice that sounded almost confused. This exercise should be projecting the written words into sound loud enough to fill the auditorium, but what came out instead was a garbled mess. Tal thought he caught the word *orcanistration*, which both wasn't a word, and certainly wasn't on the parchment. The class laughed.

Nathan took it in stride. "Did anyone else hear, 'We took our time going up the hill, but when we tripped, we came down in a hurry'? My hearing isn't what it used to be." The student who had drawn the hideous sound out of the parchment looked grateful, if a little sheepish. "You might not think Mr. Copper did much, but the fact is, in order for the magic to work at all, it must recognize that whatever it is acting upon has semantic content. This parchment is no more than a piece of paper with ink thrown over it, yet he told the magic that the ink had meaning. In my experience, that is half the battle in languageworking, recognizing that things have meaning to be acted upon—whether translated, read aloud, or otherwise transmitted—and are not merely inert objects."

Nathan waved for the student to return to his seat.

"That's all for today. For next week, read *Peregrine* chapters six through eight, and come ready to tell me the historical ramifications of audible projection. And anyone who can manage their own projection will receive two bonus points on the next exam!"

The students filed out, barely giving Tal a look. One grumbled that two bonus points was terribly stingy given that Nathan's exams tended to have over a hundred questions. Tal laughed to himself.

Nathan threw a languageworking over the blackboard to erase the chalk. Even the scrawled arrows on his diagrams disappeared.

"I wasn't expecting a new student today," Nathan said, no surprise in his voice.

"I promise I'm just auditing," Tal said. The acoustics in the auditorium were wonderful, and Tal didn't have to raise his voice to be heard all the way at the podium. "I remember this exact lecture. I think I was just a second year."

Nathan rolled the parchment lovingly. "It wouldn't surprise me. Usually the practical courses don't start until third year, but you and Meret were always throwing off my timing. Now, are you going to make an old man walk up all those stairs, or are you going to come down here?"

Tal picked his careful way down the steep steps, reminded of the hundreds of times he had been called to the front of this very classroom. Many of those demonstrations had gone about as well as the student he had just witnessed, but many more had pushed Tal to show something extraordinary. Something that had surprised even himself, and convinced him that Nathan knew better than he did how to pull out his magic.

Nathan sat on one of the cushioned benches in the front row, which probably hadn't felt the press of a student butt in the last decade. Tal sat at a respectful distance beside him, feeling the weight of the magic present in the room.

"Have you reconsidered my proposal?" Nathan asked. His offer to help Tal rediscover his magic had never been far from Tal's mind. Neither had the shame of what it would mean if he failed.

"Thoroughly. Thoroughly enough to know it's a horrible idea."

Nathan stuck out his lower lip in a way that seemed to say, *I suppose I must allow you to have your own opinion, even when it's incorrect.*

"I did have something important to talk with you about," Tal said. "It concerns languageworking. And dragons."

At that, Nathan's eyes lit up. "Two of my favorite subjects."

Tal briefly filled Nathan in on the situation with the dragons, the device they needed from Nirza, and the amorphous threat of rogue dragons. He skipped around the conversation he had overheard between the dragons in the Heathermark Flight Group stable. He had thought it through, and even if he *could* understand them, it wouldn't help. There was little enough hope that a representative of the airline would believe the translation from a neutral device, but if it came directly from a person? They could easily say he was making it up. The bigger question of what it meant if he could actually understand dragons felt easier to bury under the more immediate logistical concerns.

"You've gotten yourself involved in a bit of a controversy, eh?" Nathan said. "Just like your university days."

"It was entirely unintentional. I did, like, *one* person a harmless favor, and now all of sudden everyone expects me to solve their problems."

"The way all great men find the quest that defines their purpose, Talarus."

Tal was glad Nathan felt comfortable ribbing him. It meant he didn't believe Tal only deserved pity.

"Speaking of controversy, have you seen Meret yet?" Nathan asked. "You were always two extremely competitive peas in a magically flaming pod."

"Is he struggling without his favorite academic rival? I'd hope his dedication wasn't contingent on having me to compete against."

"Oh, his academics are fine. Not Preeminent Mage levels, but he's doing things in languageworking that I've never seen a student even try. I was talking more about the dissolution of your little club."

"The Completists are done?"

Nathan nodded. "Meret is many things, but a unifying leader is not one of them. He started to expel members if someone else with the same specialization joined. He would apparently make them routinely compete for their own spots. People like being in a secret society, not having to constantly prove they belong in it."

"He always took the hard line on what it meant to have a complete array of mages in the group," Tal said, shaking his head.

"The idea of having a complete collection only works as long as elements of that collection continue to remain in—well—the collection."

Tal smiled ruefully. Even though he had predicted this outcome, sadness still stung as he considered that the group he'd poured so much effort into over the years had fallen apart.

Nathan waved his hand, dismissing the subject. "What is it you actually need from me?"

Tal took a deep breath. "I need you to convince Nirza to give us access to the device, just temporarily. None of us have much money, certainly not enough to buy it or even rent it at the standard rate."

"Nirza is one of the most stubborn people I know."

"Her stubbornness might lead to something terrible." Tal was increasingly inclined to believe what he had overheard the dragons discussing the night of the fire. Everything had pointed to dragons creating further chaos. For what purpose, it was still hard to say, but when it came to beasts whose fire could level cities, the motive didn't really matter.

"Does she still listen to you?" Tal's nerves grew shakier just thinking about the dragons. "Would she hear how important this is if it came from you?"

Nathan considered. "If you could convince her that what's happening with the dragons is enough of a threat, then yes, maybe. She won't give it to you only if you tell her it's the ethical thing to do."

"She doesn't care about ethics?"

"She cares about greatness. Those are two very different things. If she can do the great thing by saving us from an actual threat, she will. If she is forced to do the mundane, she will charge you an exorbitant sum for it. She is a devotee of Varai, through and through. Knowledge above all else."

This wasn't going as well as Tal hoped. "What evidence would she need?"

"You said the landing pens burned. That's a start." Nathan set his hands squarely on his knees, with an air of finality. "Nirza may be the one you need to convince, but that doesn't mean she's the only one with stipulations."

"Stipulations?"

"Conditions. Terms. All of that good stuff." Tal felt his stomach drop. Nathan continued: "If I help you with this, you will obviously owe me."

"This is blackmail." Tal meant it as a joke, but was so afraid of what he knew Nathan was about to say that it came out bitter.

"What's a little light blackmail between mentor and mentee? If I make an introduction to Nirza, if you get access to the device, I won't make you return to the university. But I will kindly request that you help me with one project. A simple research project. The subject of which is: where have your powers gone, and what can we do to get them back?"

Tal buried his face in his hands. It wasn't the first time he'd done that in this exact classroom. This felt far worse, however, than forgetting the answer to an easy exam question.

"Okay," Tal said. "I'll think about it. I'll have a good cry about it, then I'll think some more, then maybe cry a little more. Then I'll let you know."

"That's all I ask."

"So why exactly are you behaving like a sad cow about this?" Bex asked. She had somehow secured them guest passes to the student dining hall, and was loading her plate with crusty rolls, potatoes, and an entire rack of pork ribs.

"I don't want Nathan's charity," Tal said. By Varai, he had missed dining hall food. He had aimed to take a reasonable amount, but his own plate was overflowing as well.

"All I hear is 'moooooo.' Come on, progress is progress. Thelspoint wasn't built in a day."

They found a pair of seats at the end of one long table. It was peak lunch hour, and the hall was full of students, forming groups that flowed into each other, shifting as students left for their next class and new arrivals joined. The buffet lines moved rapidly, foodworkings ensuring that all the dishes remained perfectly warm all the way back to your table, a dozen minor metalworkings allowing the serving implements to scoop perfect portions and have their handles remain clean even when they fell into the mashed potatoes. Overhead, a chandelier shaped like a dragon periodically roared and spouted real fire.

Bex dug into her bread with a ferocity that suggested she hadn't eaten properly in weeks, spreading slabs of butter large enough to singlehandedly keep the dairy industry in business.

"I don't get it, if everything goes well, you end up back with Nathan figuring out how to get your magic back," Bex said. "Isn't that what you want?"

"Of course that's what I want. That's not the point."

"Tell me what the point is."

Tal groaned. "You don't get it."

"That's because you don't explain things well."

Loud expletives were frowned upon in the dining hall, but Tal was no longer a student, and found himself very close to making an exception. A group of seventh- and eighth-year students walked by, whispering to each other as they passed Tal. His hair was now cut short rather than grown in the traditional shoulder-length style worn by boys at the university, and his face was far tanner and more weather-beaten from his time flying. But still, he should have expected to be recognized.

"Those people weren't even our age and this place is huge," Bex said. "Did they actually know who you were?"

Tal had to steel himself for what he was about to say. "Probably. The face of the Preeminent Mage gets smeared just about everywhere."

"And that's like, what, class president?"

"Best mage in the university," Tal said.

Bex raised an eyebrow. "Wow, I'm sitting across from the Preemptive Mage."

"Preeminent. And no, that's not me anymore."

"Don't you want to like, you know, get your big, fancy title back?"

"You don't understand!"

Tal found he had no more appetite. The roasted vegetables on his plate steamed tauntingly.

"I was the best in the school," Tal said. "Everyone came to me for advice, about every kind of magic. I was the person who set an example, who showed everyone what magic could be. Then one day, my magic was just gone. It was gone, and the entire person I'd been, the one who was the best, in a place where even the least talented student is still a genius, was gone. Can you understand what would happen if I tried, really tried, and wasn't able to become that person again?"

"So you're scared," Bex said. Her nonchalant tone, and the nonchalant way she bit into the ribs on her plate, was a razor of ice against his throat.

"Yes, I'm scared. And I think I have every right to be after what happened to me."

Bex shrugged. "That's an opinion."

"It's not an opinion, it's fact."

"Let me ask you this, though. When you were here, what did you love more: actually doing magic, or being the person who was the best at doing magic?"

Tal had had enough. "You're talking about things you know nothing about. You don't have a speck of magic in you, what right do you have to lecture me? You think you know everything just because you grew up on a giant estate and your parents owned a fleet of dragons?"

Bex wiped her mouth calmly, but behind her glasses, her eyes were pure rage. "You know, it's probably good that you had a chance to experience what it's like to not be the best. That way you can feel what it's like to be a piece of shit like the rest of us."

With a screech, Bex's chair slid back. She took her plate with her as she stormed out.

Before she had even disappeared out the dining hall's wide doors, a hand slapped down on the table, rattling Tal's plate. He looked up into familiar eyes.

Meret had aged firmly into adulthood in the last two years. The perpetual five o'clock shadow that had shaded his jaw was now a close-cropped black beard, and his eyes, always intelligent, now glistened with obvious power. His hair still fell in its usual messy curls, but now it imbued him with an almost frightening wildness. He was every bit the powerful mage, only months from graduation.

"This is an unexpected treat," Meret said, no hint of pleasure in his voice. His eyes ran to the empty seat across from Tal, as if registering Bex's absence. Then he bent and slid into it.

"Good to see you, Meret," Tal said. Potatoes were congealing on the end of his knife, but he didn't dare scrape them off because he feared his hand would shake.

"Did you come back to gloat? Maybe dance a little on the grave of the Completists?"

"I was really sorry to hear the group broke up," Tal said. "Truly."

Meret reached across the table and pulled a single pea off of Tal's plate. He studied it for a moment before tossing it into his mouth. He chewed for what seemed like an inordinately long time for one pea.

"I'm sure you're *so* sorry that the group you abandoned came to a swift end," Meret said. "I'm sure it doesn't *at all* feel like a big, fat 'I told you so.'"

"What the hell are you talking about?"

"You abandon us. You leave me in charge. And the group dies. So Tal's philosophy was right all along, eh? Tal, who is always right, the Preeminent Mage, the golden child of every single department, vindicated one last time."

Tal considered getting up, but then considered how much worse it would be if Meret followed him all the way across the dining hall. He knew it had been a bad idea to eat here.

"You have nothing to say?" Meret asked. "Please, tell me how you didn't abandon us."

"I lost my magic, Meret," Tal said in a hushed voice.

"You still could have stayed. We needed you as a leader, not as a mage."

That took Tal aback. He had always assumed his contributions to the Completists came from his primacy in all things magical. He'd never really thought about leadership as its own thing, only as an extension of his spellwork.

"I couldn't stay," Tal said.

"You could've. You could've asked for help." Meret's voice softened, but only briefly. "But I forgot. Tal never, ever, ever asks for help."

Meret rose, a grim smile on his lips. The anger, the hurt, the disappointment in his eyes and voice, all were too real, too blunt, too overwhelming.

"See you around, Tal," Meret said. "I'll let you know if I hear about any other organizations you can destroy."

Meret slouched out of the hall, a cloud of power around him.

Circumstance, Ale, Evidence

After his fifth ale, Tal decided to do some investigative work. He reasoned that searching for evidence of the dragons' plot did not in itself count as helping either Bex or Nathan. In fact, the sooner he confirmed that no such evidence existed, the sooner he would be free of any obligation—coerced or otherwise—to involve himself further.

The majority of the rubble from the fire was stacked in the scrap heap near the rebuilt landing pen. Tal imagined he looked quite a sight stumbling through the rickety gate leading to the pile of garbage, sliding over composting vegetables and chicken bones as he made his way up to the pile of burned wood. There was little left of the old landing pen. The fire had burned remarkably quickly given that it had been raining.

"If I was a piece of incriminating evidence, where would I hide?" Tal asked the empty air.

The empty air didn't respond, and Tal started sifting through burned boards and melted nails. He had a cheap lamp with him, enchanted with a mediocre lightworking that cast a glow composed of more shadow than light. It was just enough to see what he was looking for. Which was . . . well, he wasn't entirely sure what, but he assumed he'd know it when he found it. Or at the very least could honestly say he hadn't found anything once he'd trawled the whole pile.

With each passing drink, Tal had tried to stop thinking about his argument with Bex that afternoon, and his confrontation with Meret. This, of course, had made him think even more about both.

He hadn't said anything untrue in his argument with Bex, but with the benefit of time and the slightly dissociating effects of alcohol, he did have to admit that the truth made him feel like an ass. It was hard to imagine his past self seeing him like this, so lacking in confidence that he hadn't been able to choose his words carefully, or stand up to Meret.

Tal tried to turn his attention back to the dragons. For some reason, the thought of what very well could be some kind of dragon uprising was easier to stomach than his own failings. What did he know? The dragons had not been seen in the proximity of the landing pens on the night of the fire. The pens that had burned were all adjacent to each other, forming a roughly equilateral triangle and served by a central stable, which had also burned. His thoughts felt foggy, but he knew they were heading somewhere.

"Find anything yet?" came a voice from the entrance. Tal whirled, slipping in the rubble and falling hard on his butt. Bex leaned over the gate. She'd changed clothes, rolling up the sleeves of a gray jumpsuit that looked an awful lot like the ones the municipal garbagemen wore.

"What's with the get-up?" Tal asked, trying to rise gracefully, but slipping a few more times as the rubble shifted under him.

"Do you like it?" Bex asked. "Please tell me you like it, your approval is *so* important to me."

Okay, he deserved that. "I'm mainly wondering if you had to mug a garbage-man for it. They're city employees, that's probably a felony."

"I'm not *that* much of a villain. You'd be surprised what you can find at a Thelspoint thrift shop."

"Well, you do look quite dapper," Tal said. "Very garbage-core. Want to help me look? I've found exactly zero evidence."

Bex opened the gate and picked her way toward him with much less difficulty than he'd had earlier.

They didn't talk much, other than going over what meager facts they knew. Bex added the important insight that the pens hadn't burned simultaneously.

The fires were reported in three separate waves at least ten minutes apart, which the constables had assumed meant it spread from one pen to the other as the crews struggled to put the first fire out. It could also mean three fires set separately.

"But the fire couldn't have crossed from one to the other," Tal said, pulling a nearly intact board off the top of the pile, inspecting it, and tossing it to the side. "The only point where they actually make contact is through the stable in the center. If it had passed through there, the other two would have gone up at the same time. That stable is like a tinderbox."

"And it was raining much too hard for sparks to pass the distance between the pens," Bex said, finishing his thought. He wasn't sure why, but his thoughts felt stronger and more polished when she helped him complete them.

They searched for the next couple hours, the lamp casting spectral shadows around the stinking pit. Tal hadn't apologized to Bex, but hoped his cooperation was an acknowledgement of remorse. Even if he couldn't—wouldn't—put it into words. Bex was more than willing to get dirty, putting the jumpsuit to good use as she climbed over the rubble, flinging boards aside with no regard for the filth around them. She had brought two pairs of gloves, which came in handy as they handled the sharper debris. How she had known to bring two pairs, Tal didn't ask. Bex was still obviously fuming, and the withering looks she shot Tal every few minutes were enough to keep his questions to a minimum.

Long after Tal had given up any hope of finding anything useful, Bex unearthed something that looked like a giant snake. On closer inspection, it was a section of tube made out of a rubbery material. It had compressed significantly in the heap, but broken apart it was close to a foot in diameter.

"This some kind of flying gear?" Bex asked, tossing it to Tal. Tal staggered under its weight as he caught it.

"Not that I'm aware of." Tal studied the tube. There was something familiar about it, but the familiarity was incomplete, a small part of a usually much larger picture.

Bex sighed. "Well, I'm about ready to call it a night. I've got a big day of protesting tomorrow."

Tal was too busy trying to remember why the tube felt familiar to think of a response. He'd worked with a material like this before . . .

"Oh my," he said.

"'Oh my'? I swear, you've been spending too much time with Enna."

"'Oh my' as in, holy shit I just figured out what this is."

Bex slid down the rubble pile, pulling level with Tal. Her hair was up in a ponytail that it wasn't quite long enough to maintain, and almost a third had escaped, spraying out like a mane around her head. It matched her intent eyes.

"Have you ever seen dragon fire?" Tal asked. Bex shook her head. It was a rare thing in a world where dragons were seldom a threat. "Dragon fire is typically widely dispersed. They don't have lips, so they can't direct the air into a narrow stream as it comes out. That means their fire is more of a wide spray. The fire can travel decent distances—maybe fifty to a hundred yards—but if they put enough power in it to carry that range, the spray ends up almost as wide as it is long. Not great if you're trying to hit a specific target."

"A whole landing pen is a pretty big target."

"Not in a dense area like this."

Bex narrowed her eyes. "The tube?"

"Dragon Air doesn't fly many flights in the extreme cold. That's more common on the long-haul routes Heathermark covers. But on some of those flights, they'll actually harness the dragon's fire breathing to keep the cabin warm. They concentrate the fire through a mask the dragon wears—which seems super uncomfortable—and run an insulated tube all the way back around to the cabin."

"So this is a warming tube."

Tal bobbed his head between a shake and a nod. "The dragon doesn't blow continuously into it. It'll just blow a directed stream of fire, enough to light various heat sinks in the cabin's walls." Tal held the tube up, peering inside.

"With a tube like this, a dragon could easily have blown fire from a long enough distance to stay hidden."

Bex stared at the tube, then wrapped one arm around Tal's shoulder. The half-hug was more chummy than anything else, but Tal still felt an unexpected dip in his stomach at the contact between them.

"See?" she said. "Who needs magic, or to not be a dick, when you know about tubes?"

Tal released a tense laugh, trying to focus on her arm against his shoulder rather than her words. He lightly pushed against her grip. But he found he didn't want to push away too hard.

Tal had to spend the morning preparing for his flight back to Upper Boden while Bex made herself busy at the rubble heap. Knowing exactly what she was looking for, she came away with three more sections of tube, although not the mask that would've attached to the dragon's mouth. The last scrap of tube, however, all but made the lack of a mask irrelevant. Where the others had been broken, pulled apart by falling wood or crushed under the wheels of the fire brigade's water carts, the final one had three slashes in the middle. Three slashes that were obviously inflicted by the claws of a large dragon.

The tube was a symbol of his good faith effort to help, and while he could feel a hint of forgiveness from her, Tal understood that Bex was not one to forgive easily. Everything in her world was black and white, good and evil. Tal found himself yearning for her forgiveness nonetheless.

The flight back was full of familiar faces, including Bex, Enna, and Claret. Claret's leather jacket was purple today, and she wore a short sword across her back. Usually weapons weren't allowed on dragon transports, but since Dragon Air was unwilling to pay for actual security, Tal decided they didn't have to know about the adventurer's sword.

Claret and Bex were talking animatedly as Tal helped Enna down off Ronar's back upon their arrival in Upper Boden. The adventurer seemed to think Bex's focus on dragon contracts was too narrow, and that they should question the ethics of the entire dragon flight industry. This left Bex speechless. Few things left Bex speechless.

Enna slipped a sphere into Tal's palm. Its color faded as soon as it touched his hand, but not quite as much as when Enna had last given him one. She smiled mischievously, forcing Tal to shoo her off to prevent her making a comment about his burgeoning magic. She walked with Bex up the lane to town.

Claret was waiting for Tal as he passed out of the gate. He held the pile of tubes awkwardly in his arms.

"Your sphere is glowing," Claret said.

"I hadn't noticed."

"Not glowing much, of course."

Tal gave her a withering look. Claret just smiled back at him, swishing a lock of her wispy silver hair out of her face.

"You don't want to see mine?" she asked. With a flourish, she removed a single sphere from its own pouch at her waist. It shone a fluorescent white.

"Can you turn that thing down?" Tal asked, shielding his eyes. Claret laughed. Magic was rare in Upper Boden, though if it came from anyone, he should've expected it from a freelance quester. "Is that your party trick? Showing everyone you're ridiculously powerful by blinding them with the evidence of your magic?"

"I assure you, it's strictly practical," Claret said, tucking the sphere back into the pouch. "If I look at that sphere, I know instantly how my power is holding up. In my line of work, keeping track of your magic is important." Claret pointed to the tubes. "Are you running some sort of experiment?"

Tal hesitated. He didn't know her that well, despite having spent a chaotic evening helping corral dragon equipment with her. Could there be any risk to telling her about the threat, about Nirza and the possibility of understanding dragons?

He opted for an abbreviated version. In every ellipsis, Tal was positive that Claret could fill in her own meaning.

She stuck out her lower lip. "It sounds like you've got yourself a bit of an adventure cooking."

"Probably not all that exciting by your standards."

"Adventures have a way of surprising you. Tell you what, if there's ever any coin involved, or at the very least an opportunity to throw some spells around, I'm your gal, alright?"

"Of course," Tal said. Claret patted him on the shoulder, then strode off toward the center of town, leaving Tal alone with his new glowing sphere and an unwieldy pile of tubes.

Rental Discounts

After tossing and turning for multiple nights, Tal decided not to deliver his response to Nathan in person. Instead, feeling the exact opposite of courageous, he mailed a terse letter letting Nathan know that he'd found evidence for Nirza, and that he would very much appreciate Nathan putting in a good word. He mentioned nothing about the other side of the agreement, that he would come back and work on a project with Nathan.

When the response came, it came enchanted with a languageworking that read the note aloud. Nathan's voice was full of laughter:

Talarus,

I am pleased you have decided to accept our bargain, and will look forward to seeing you next week. Say, 6pm sharp in my office on Monday evening?

Yours,

Professor Nathan

P.S. I have alerted Nirza to your coming. She will be expecting you, and said something along the lines of "I hope the little bugger has something damn good for me, otherwise I'm charging him double." Best of luck with that.

Tal tossed the note into the hearth. As if in anticipation of this response, Nathan had also spelled it to be resistant to burning, so it took close to an hour before it finally caught fire, sitting in the coals and periodically giggling at Tal.

Tal awoke on Sunday morning to the sound of a horse neighing outside. There were no clocks in the tiny space, but the light streaming in through the sole window was far too dull for it to be much past six o'clock. The horse noises were followed by the sound of boots on gravel, and an inevitable and cranium-shattering knock on the door.

Crisp air streamed in as the door opened, revealing Bex, looking like she had been up for at least two hours. She had put on makeup and washed and combed her hair. Her glasses were polished so thoroughly that Tal couldn't see even a suggestion of his own reflection.

"Ready to go?" Bex asked, pointing to a simple, uncovered horse-drawn wagon. "I only have this guy for the day, so we have to make it back by tonight."

They hadn't discussed when they would go to Heathermark to see Nirza. Bex looked Tal up and down disapprovingly, from the shirt with one sleeve still crumpled and folded up around the elbow, to the shorts that had obviously just been slept in.

"Is that what you're wearing?"

Bex gave Tal a generous fifteen minutes to get ready, just enough time to rinse his hair with cold water and shape it into something other than one giant cowlick, and put on the one set of clothes he still owned that wasn't tailored specifically for flying. His boots were still obviously flight boots, sporting metal grooves that could latch onto a flight seat. He tossed the pile of tubes into the back of the wagon, and they were off.

Bex pushed the horse at a breakneck pace. She steered deftly, taking the narrow corners of the dirt-packed road hard and only once sending them into a skid that nearly sent them over the edge.

"You sure you don't want to drive?" Bex asked. "There's no way this is harder than steering a dragon."

"You'd be surprised how little actual steering is involved," Tal said, holding onto the armrest of the wooden seat for dear life. "It's more like having a very one-sided conversation and hoping they follow your instructions."

"So you agree that it's one-sided."

Tal rolled his eyes. "I'm helping you out. Don't make me regret it."

Bex squinted at him. "If you're not really steering the dragon, what's the point of you being there?"

"It's mainly so they can pay me," Tal said. "But I suppose there's some value in having a human in charge while we're in the air. Occasionally we'll have to invoke Sky Protocols and take charge if a passenger gets too rowdy."

"You were in charge during the flight? I never would have guessed."

"Sky Protocols are a real thing. Look it up."

Bex muttered to herself. Tal thought he heard the words "pompous goofassery" somewhere in the mutterings.

As they descended from Upper Boden to the flatlands to the north, the road widened out and became straighter. Through the next few towns, with full daylight coming up, there were more and more people out on the road. Carts and wagon trains passed in the opposite direction. They had to swerve several times to avoid carts and people moving at more reasonable speeds. It had been a long time since Tal had traveled by cart. His mind went back to the most recent trip, the return from the university. He hadn't taken in many of the sights, as he had been curled in the back with the luggage, wishing he could disappear from the world. The cart had belonged to a gnome, who had unfortunately overstated the extent to which he actually owned the cart. When its owners had finally caught up with them and repossessed the cart, throwing the gnome off about thirty miles north of Lodefall, they had been so startled to find a depressed former mage among the luggage that they'd allowed him to stay for the rest of the trip.

The air warmed as the morning progressed, the hood that had been keeping his ears warm against the chill coming off, the sun cradling the right side of his face as they traveled north. The region between Upper Boden and Heathermark was the breadbasket of Eithlanel, wheat and corn fields stretching as far as they could see. The stalks of wheat glowed yellow under skies populated by only a few puffy clouds. Beneath them, the wagon's wheels were a steady rattle. The horse's hooves clopped gently against packed dirt.

They stopped for a late breakfast at a roadside stand, and were treated to freshly baked bread, soft cheese, and slices of cured meat with a dollop of fresh honey. Bex insisted on paying.

"I thought your parents cut you off," Tal said as he licked a smear of honey off his pinky.

"They did. Fortunately, with a staff as large as Braisecroft's, you can't trust everyone not to let a rogue daughter reclaim a small part of her fortune."

"You bribed someone to give you access to your money, didn't you."

"Never bribing!" Bex said, her face somewhere between amusement and genuine outrage. "Most of the staff like me a lot more than my parents, so it was just a simple matter of diverting funds—"

"—stealing—"

"—funds that were already *mine*, thank you very much, into a new account that doesn't have parental controls over it."

"Won't your parents notice the money is missing?" Tal asked.

"I'm only siphoning off the interest," Bex said.

Tal didn't bother pointing out that the interest alone on her account appeared to be more than most people's income from working an actual job.

With the fortifying weight of breakfast in their stomachs, the last several miles to Heathermark passed quickly. The entry into the city felt much more gradual than arriving in Thelspoint. While Thelspoint had been built vertically to accommodate its place between sea and cliff, Heathermark spread indiscriminately into the inviting countryside around it. What looked at first like villages were revealed to be the outlying suburbs, and primarily residential areas would be interspersed with more farms and even a couple of wooded areas before the buildings finally grew into consistent rows. In keeping with its horizontal theme, no building in Heathermark was more than four stories tall. Heathermark also lacked any wall or defensive fortifications, so they could take whatever track they liked as they moved east toward Nirza's address. Tal would have liked to visit central Heathermark, which was renowned for its parks and gardens, but the mage lived almost three miles from the city center, so instead they found themselves traveling down a pleasant residential lane. The people were relatively well-off, and their well-tended lawns, gardens, and thatched roofs reflected this. In contrast to Thelspoint, there were few with magical abilities. The city lacked the hum of magic, relying instead on its agricultural wealth and lack of any borders that required defending.

Amid all the ordinariness, Nirza's three-story wooden house was a shocking sight. The wood was an almost burned black, and each floor was anywhere between thirty and forty-five degrees misaligned from the one below it, making it appear as if the top floor was about to spin off into the sky. Vines cascaded over the wrought iron fence encircling the property, overflowing with wildflowers that Tal suspected were magical in nature. This suspicion was confirmed when the flowers started hissing as the wagon pulled up out front.

Tal stepped down off the wagon and approached the iron gate, which loomed over eight feet tall above them. The garden on the other side was so overgrown he could barely make out the front door.

"Do we just, like, knock?" Bex asked.

"Knock where?"

There was no knocker or even a discernible handle on this side of the gate. The flowers floated at the ends of the vines, watching the intruders suspiciously. The house reminded Tal of a monster waiting in ambush.

"Well, that was a nice trip," Tal said. "We should have time to see the parks before we head back." He turned as if to return to the wagon. Bex's firm grip held him at her side.

"Don't wimp out on me now, mageling," Bex said. "I need you to explain the tubes, remember?"

"You did make it very clear that my primary role is that of 'tube explainer.'"

"*What are these tubes that need explaining?*" came a deep voice. It seemed to emanate from the flowers on the fence.

Tal took an instinctive step back. Even in his time at the forefront of languageworking and plantworking, he had never been able to endow living plants with the appearance of speech.

"I'm Nathan's former student," Tal said. "He said Nirza would be expecting us."

The flowers eyed them.

"We brought proof that the dragons are plotting something." Nerves threw an uncharacteristic quaver into Bex's voice. She hadn't had nearly as much exposure to this sort of magic as Tal. And even Tal felt anxious under the flowers' watchful gaze. One of the vines extended over their heads, positioning a flower to peer down at the wagon's contents. The flowers' colors changed from a streaky orange to bright red.

"*Please tell me you have brought more than this,*" said the disembodied voice.

"We can explain," Tal said. "Nathan wouldn't waste your time, would he?"

There was a deep sigh. "*I suppose not. Very well, bring your 'proof' inside and we can have a chat.*"

Bex looked simultaneously giddy and like she would rather be running back to Upper Boden. Tal felt much the same. He collected the tubes from the back of the wagon, sending up a plume of ash. He arranged them in a loose loop over one shoulder as the gate creaked open. Plants peeled themselves back just far enough to create a narrow walkway. They stepped carefully over weeds and roots. The door to the house was ajar, its red paint chipped where it met the walkway.

Tal and Bex looked at each other. Then Bex shrugged, and pushed it open.

Magical spaces were as diverse as mages, and Tal had never seen a space quite like this. The entire first floor appeared to be some kind of workshop, with clockwork apparatuses covering every wall and surface. Sounds of whirring and hammering filled the air. One device looked like an ordinary clock, yet ticked off an entire day on a single hand. Another pointed to different weather conditions, its hand locked emphatically in the sunshine position. Spelled candles burned in chandeliers, but did not drip. Abstract frescoes stretched across the ceiling.

"Go on, have a gawk," said a voice from the spiral staircase in the center of the room. A face peered out from between the slats in the banister. The face was upside-down. "But it's much more comfortable upstairs."

Bex led Tal up the stairs, tubes trailing behind. The stairs were steep, and there were far more of them than the space could possibly hold without magic. They were struggling for breath by the time they reached the next floor and came to an abrupt halt. The floor in front of them was rotating. What had been a sightline down a hallway became first a bare wall, then a room. The movement stopped with a grating sound, and they stood, disoriented, in front of a cozy sitting room with three cushioned chairs.

A wiry woman sat in one of the chairs, one short leg crossed over the other. She wore dark pants and a dark blouse, with sleeves rolled up to reveal strong, tattooed forearms. It wasn't easy to distinguish between dirt and the natural color of her hair, but the stern expression on her pointed features was not hard to interpret. She gave off an intimidating impression of quiet power. Nirza's green eyes surveyed them, particular attention falling on the tubes that Tal began to feel might in fact be some kind of badge of stupidity.

"I remember you," Nirza said, indicating Bex rather than Tal. "You're the daughter of the owners of Heathermark Flight Group. I went to some high-toned function at your manor house."

"You'll have to be more specific," Bex said. "Braisecroft has seen hundreds of those awful things."

Nirza's laugh was the crack of a whip, sharp and over just as quickly. "Sit. You can leave your tubes on the floor."

As Tal and Bex sank into the chairs, which let out a *whumpf* of air, Nirza lifted a hollowed-out gourd from the end table next to her. She took a long sip of whatever was inside through a wooden straw. Even from a few feet away, the beverage's bitter smell was overpowering.

"I must admit, I'm having a bit of difficulty with your parents," Nirza continued. "You know of course about my device. They seem to think the price I'm asking for its use is unreasonable."

"I'm having a bit of difficulty with my parents too," Bex said.

"We came to see if you would be able to bend on your price, for a good cause," Tal said. Bex's disapproving look suggested he'd jumped in too quickly, but Nirza was unfazed.

"Nathan said as much. How is the young man?"

"The loss of one of his favorite students hasn't slowed him down too much," Tal replied. The mention of their relative ages prompted a closer look at Nirza. Even with skin that was leathery from sun exposure, she still didn't look much older than sixty.

"Right, your little performance issue," Nirza said. Bex stifled a laugh. "Now now, losing one's powers is nothing to be ashamed of. I've always thought mages cared too much about their magic. Always trying to hold onto their power even after it's outlived its usefulness."

"You're doing amazing things with your magic," Bex said.

Nirza sighed, as if deciding whether to tell her off for the fawning remark. "I am, above all else, a utilitarian. My magic has allowed me to live a long time and make a great deal of money. If it left me tomorrow, however, I do believe it would come as a relief. Magic is an extraordinary responsibility."

"It also lets you do extraordinary things," Tal said.

"Yes. And it is those things that matter, not the magic itself. Take your mentor, for example. When he discovered the secrets of mirrored languageworkings, he employed magic no more powerful than what is already used by students, and yet he created a world where you can be in one place, and write easily on a piece of parchment in another."

It was true. Tal had been early on in his time at the university when Nathan unlocked the arcane series of workings that allowed a languageworker to create mirrored objects, where words written on one of the objects would appear on the other. Even at his young age, Tal had understood it was a combination of seven or eight different simple workings rather than a truly new magic. As Nathan was one of the only people ever to master this technique, the innovation hadn't yet been widely adopted, but it was clear to anyone how transformative it could be.

If Bex was as taken aback by the way this conversation had started as Tal was, she didn't show it. She straightened her glasses.

"We need your help," Bex said. "You know that already. And you know all about the moral question of the dragons' input into the contracts that bind them to their employers. What you don't know is that Tal has gotten Dragon Air to allow him to use the device, so long as they don't have to pay for it."

"The discount airline?" Nirza asked. "I've always thought flying on one of their dragons was the sign of a poorly repressed death wish."

"We all might have more to worry about than their safety record soon," Tal said. He filled Nirza in briefly on his suspicions about the dragons torching the landing pens, and explained how the tubes would have allowed them to do so from some distance away. Again he skirted around the actual dragon conversation he had overheard. Every time he approached it, Nirza looked at him more suspiciously.

"We believe that if we're able to start using the device to help some of the dragons, then we have a shot at avoiding any more incidents like this," Bex said. "They're angry. Understandably so. We need to act before that anger gets out of hand."

Nirza uncrossed her legs and rose from her chair. She took her gourd with her, sipping contemplatively as she stared out the round windows onto the garden below.

"I have access to some money," Bex said. "Nothing like what you're asking, but if you're willing to rent us the device rather than selling it . . ."

"And what if I don't want to stop the dragons?" Nirza asked, her voice far away. "What if I believe that the dragons are justified in their actions, and letting some human towns burn would be a kind of justice?"

Nirza had not offered them anything to drink, but if she had, Tal would have choked on it.

"What?" he spluttered.

Nirza turned back to them, a glint of mischief in her green eyes. "It's not such a bad argument. The dragons have been horribly mistreated, pressed into military service whenever conflict strikes the human world. While being employed to help us travel might be more humane, it's still far shy of letting them roam free."

"Unbound dragons flying wild throughout the Unified Coast was the exact problem that dragon employment was meant to prevent," Tal said. "They're massive carnivores who can easily burn an entire town. There have to be some rules keeping them in check."

"By the yoke of literally flying us on their backs?" Nirza asked.

Bex's eyes shone. "You want to create some kind of dragon society, don't you? Outside of human control."

Nirza nodded. "It's the least bad option. The dragons here in the west were cast out of the Claglands by their own people. I suspect many of them are outcasts for nothing more than slights on another dragon's honor. Regardless, we're stuck with them. I suspect, and this is a strong assumption, that if we were to finally use the device, this solution would be presented."

"So this was the goal of the device all along?" Tal asked. "It's not about fair practices, it's about dismantling the entire system?"

"If that is what they choose, then yes." Nirza took another sip, and frowned at her empty gourd. "You will want a moment to process this. Just know that if you use the device, this outcome is a possibility."

"You make it sound like that would be a good thing," Bex said.

Nirza shrugged. "I can't deny that the thought has crossed my mind. Unlike gnomes or Trugs, dragons are inherently incompatible with a human world. In their homeland dragons hunt vast herds of antelope and caribou, ones that humans would no doubt try to domesticate or slaughter. They are not designed for a static world of agriculture and cities. They are predators, who exist in complex communities based on honor, strength, and family.

"Those who would like the outcast dragons to create their own society understand that humans and dragons were never meant to coexist in proximity. They believe that humans will only ever use dragons, not incorporate them as equal members of society. And as soon as the fragile alliance between the species is no longer favorable to humankind, humans will hunt them by whatever means necessary. So they walk a tightrope, trying to convince their brethren that humans are not worth coexisting with. They must cause enough destruction that humans react and reveal themselves to be the heartless monsters these dragons believe they are, yet not so much that human society decides they need to be eradicated rather than relocated."

Tal took a moment to process this. "So you're saying that all of the chaos dragons are sowing, it's really just about provoking a reaction from the humans?"

"Humans are nothing if not reactionary." Nirza sighed, straightening and softening. "The dragons are right not to trust us. I was a young mage when I was tasked with facilitating the relocation of gnomes out of Eithlanel after the founding of the Unified Coast. We were told that this was necessary, that it would ensure peace between us and the Gnome Kingdom. The settlers we were relocating, they knew nothing of kingdoms or treaties. All they knew was that we were ripping away their homes. I never heard a compelling reason why the gnomes should be sent away, beyond their leaders agreeing the lands of Eithlanel were to be ruled by humans, and governing the gnomes would be easier back in their own kingdom. In all the years since, I have never heard a better reason."

Tal and Bex exchanged a look.

"The only reason that makes sense to me is spite," Nirza said, moving back toward them and holding up her empty gourd. "A reaction against people they didn't like. How much worse would the reaction be to a creature torching their cities?"

Then she was gone, disappearing into the circular hallway at the other end of the room.

Tal got up and paced the edges of the green rug. It had an abstract floral pattern, splashes of yellow and orange curling as if wilting. Somewhere far off in the house, there was the sound of a kettle lid being lifted, water running.

"We should go," Tal said. "This is way more than I bargained for."

Bex had crossed her legs under her on the chair, looking at him intently. "Dragon Air doesn't have to know any of this."

"Come on, Bex, you're basically asking me to undermine both of our livelihoods."

"You can find another job. Maybe Nathan will succeed in making you a mage again."

The thought of doing anything with Nathan made him sick. Tal did not particularly like his job as a flight attendant, but it was at least something he could actually do. It was solid, stable. And if everything transpired as Bex and Nirza wanted, it might be gone.

"You obviously have a connection with Ronar," Bex said. "Don't you want what's best for him? If you actually care about him, his voice needs to be heard."

"And what happens if he decides to use his new voice to quit? There's no dragon utopia out there right now, as much as she might wish it."

"He could help create one."

Tal groaned. "In all my time flying with Ronar, he's never given me any indication he's unhappy. I don't want to give him false hope and then pull that out from under him."

"How could you know whether he's unhappy?" Bex asked. Suddenly Nirza was in the doorway, a steaming gourd in one hand, a metal orb in the other.

"I do believe your friend has been lying to you," Nirza said. She sat again, setting the orb unacknowledged on the table. "That's the second time he's directly referred to what a dragon was thinking or saying. You don't think I missed your little gap with the Heathermark dragons? You clearly overheard their conversation. That's how you knew they were responsible for burning down the landing pens, how you knew to look for evidence in the first place."

"Tal, what is she talking about?"

"It is obvious, my dear, that Tal can understand dragon speech."

TEST RUN

T he ride back to Upper Boden was uncomfortable enough that Tal felt fortunate Bex hadn't yet made him get out and walk. Even the device tucked underneath the bench, poking out of its carrying case just enough to catch the afternoon light, couldn't brighten the mood.

Nirza had given them use of the device free of charge, asking only for a large security deposit, which Bex had arranged through her bank in Heathermark. Though it should have felt like a victory, Bex was obviously in no mood to celebrate.

"If it helps, I didn't believe I could actually understand them," Tal said. "I still don't."

"It worked well enough for you to understand that the dragons were responsible for burning down the landing pens."

The reins were wrapped so tightly around Bex's fingers that her knuckles had turned white. She stared unflinchingly ahead.

"I don't see why this is such a big deal," Tal said. "We have the device."

"All I've wanted since I understood how my parents' business operated was to ask the dragons for their input, to understand what they feel. And now I find out you've had the ability to ask them this whole time?"

"I haven't always had it."

Was that even true, though? He couldn't remember the first time he had intuited something Ronar meant. He'd always believed he could just read gestures, that it was like looking at a person's face and understanding their emotions. Yet at some point, he knew deep down, he had crossed a line into understanding actual dragon speech.

"If you had told me, we could have asked Ronar first before going on this wild goose chase," Bex said.

There was a deeper truth beneath those words. If dragons didn't mind their employment, it wasn't just the trip to get the device that was for nothing. Everything Bex had done to advocate on their behalf would be proven meaningless as well.

The trip back felt incredibly long, and the last part of it, up the narrow roads leading to Upper Boden, was well after dark. Rain had threatened all evening and was now spitting down. They pulled up hoods, their eyes down, as Bex navigated around the muddy ruts in the road.

When they reached Tal's home, he said, "First thing tomorrow, before my flight to Thelspoint, we use the device to ask Ronar some questions?"

"Sure." Bex's boots squelched as she stepped down from the cart to tighten one of the horse's straps before the last leg of her trip.

"I was thinking I could compare whatever the device says to my understanding. You know, if I might have some kind of gift with the dragons, it's worth figuring out how well it works." He took a deep breath, feeling Bex's anger roll over him. "Maybe if I can confirm it actually does work, then I can do more. The device makes everything official, but more informal conversations with the dragons will let us know where to focus our efforts."

"Our efforts?" Bex's raised eyebrow, while amused, was somehow also incriminating.

Tal sighed. "Don't make me repeat it. I'm offering to help, however I can while not also running my life into the ground."

"You're so annoying," Bex said, climbing back behind the horse. "See you tomorrow, Dragon Whisperer."

As disparaging nicknames went, Tal supposed Dragon Whisperer wasn't the worst Bex had called him. He set the device down on his desk, next to the glass bowl. There were now eleven spheres in the bowl, glowing faintly. He didn't light a lamp as he got ready for bed. The spheres still weren't really enough to see by, but while before they had symbolized something arbitrary, elusive, he was beginning to suspect he understood the magic they were pointing him toward. Tomorrow would prove if that assessment was correct.

He lay in bed, the weight of sleep descending. Just once, he opened his eyes to check on the spheres and confirm they were still glowing. They cast traces of light over the device, turning its surface into a shimmering mirror. He dozed off before he could consider that he hadn't once in the past twelve hours lamented that he was no longer at Thelspoint University.

Ronar was in a rare mood the next morning. Their flight was usually not until at least midday, and the dragon had objected to being woken up by his flight attendant and the person who usually yelled slogans from outside his pen. He scooped up hay from the floor of the stable, tossing it in the air. He sent a couple stools and buckets flying—Tal winced at the thought that Dragon Air would likely take the cost of the replacements out of his paycheck—and turned away from the entrance, flopping his tail so they would have to step over it.

"What is with you, Ro?" Tal asked. He stroked Ronar's tail gently. The tail squirmed. Ronar obviously didn't want to hurt them. More than a few airline attendants had been injured by a dragon's tail, and Tal was grateful for the hundredth time that Ronar cared for his safety.

His hunched shoulders seemed to say, *What is she doing here?*

Or maybe it was more than his hunched shoulders.

"We have something we want to try out, but only if you're willing," Tal said. "If you'd prefer, she'll leave and it'll just be me."

Ronar's canted smirk made it obvious that it was somewhat presumptuous of Tal to think he was such preferable company. Ronar stared the two humans down, then unwound his tail and turned toward them. He eyed Bex with a level of intent that would've scared anyone who wasn't as used to dragons as Bex was. She raised her hands in a supplicating gesture.

With a deep sigh, Ronar settled into a crouch, reaching a talon to pick up the stools he had knocked aside. He set one—the only one still intact enough to sit on—in front of him. Tal set the device on the stool, feeling Ronar's eyes on him. Though the device was mostly round, it had striated edges that could cut you if you weren't careful. Ronar barked nervously as Tal unwrapped it.

"It can't hurt you," Tal said. "It contains a powerful languageworking. When we turn it on, it should allow us to understand everything you say."

Ronar gave a *let's get this over with* dart of his head.

To turn the device on, as Nirza had instructed, Tal rotated a circular section at the top of the device. A tiny rod popped up, which he pumped several times. As he did, a larger rod on the side of the device appeared. Bex had to help him when his fingers kept slipping on the pump. Her hands were just as sweaty as his.

Then, with a deep hum, the larger rod began to glow a deep white.

Bex's breathing beside him was ragged. "Is it working, Ronar?" she asked.

"*How can we tell?*" came a rumbling voice from the device. Ronar started, and Bex nearly shrieked with glee.

"I have no clue how it works," Tal said, "but it should translate any dragon speech."

"*Dragons do not speak. We communicate.*" The second thing a dragon had ever said to a human, and it might have revealed one of the deepest truths about the creatures.

"I can't believe it," Bex said, both hands folded on top of her head. "I can't believe it."

"*She is odd,*" Ronar said, "*but she is obviously comfortable around dragons. Does she also work for the airlines?*" His mouth didn't move, and yet Ronar's voice boomed in Tal's head, as well as out of the device. This close it felt like the speech was grabbing hold of his brain and shaking it.

"Varai help us, no," Tal said. "She thinks the airlines are unethical."

"*Do you?*"

Tal found himself caught completely off guard. Though Ronar often communicated things Tal could understand, this was much more direct. Tal wondered if Ronar usually didn't bother putting his thoughts into speech—communication—because he thought nobody would understand.

"I think Bex has raised some valid concerns," Tal replied. Bex's look of victory made him want to throw something. At the same time, just at the edges, it warmed his heart ever so slightly. "Ultimately it should be up to the dragons. Do you have any problems with your employment? I can't guarantee Dragon Air will listen, but we can try to change the contracts."

"*If I wanted to leave, I would leave. My contract is a piece of paper, nothing more. I agreed to the bargain, but I do not hold it sacred.*"

"But would you change anything?" Bex pressed.

Ronar shrugged. "*Not at this time.*"

Throughout the conversation, Tal had been trying to compare the device's output to his own understanding of Ronar's words. It was hard to do in real-time, but he thought the two lined up very closely. If anything, the device's translations were slightly more formal than his own. He wondered why the two forms of magic would produce different results.

Tal looked over at Bex, whose expression was pure panic. Ronar noticed it too, and curled one gentle wing around their backs. It created a pocket of warmth.

"*Don't worry, young one. I am but one dragon. Before I had this job, my life had little purpose or meaning. That is not true for all of us.*"

"Which others do you think need the most help?" Bex asked.

Ronar considered this. *"I do not have much contact with others of my kind, but when I said my contract was just a piece of paper, I know that is not true for all contracts. The—and I mean no offense to either myself or to you, Tal—better airlines spell their contracts. They're nearly unbreakable, from what I understand. They are also incredibly long, complicated, and difficult to read. And no dragon I've ever heard of has legal counsel."*

Bex's eyes gleamed. "Better airlines, like Heathermark Flight Group?"

"Exactly."

"I knew it," Bex said. "Thanks Ronar." She collected the device, switching it off and waving before she left man and dragon behind.

What an excitable little creature, Ronar said to himself. *She has a good heart, though.*

Tal grimaced. He had understood every word, even without the device.

"Ro," he said. "There's something I need to tell you."

A Very Mature First-Year

T he excitement of that morning's conversation with Ronar had given Tal little time to dread his meeting with Nathan that evening. Now, apprehension flooded him. He didn't know exactly what his old mentor had in store for him, but the process of pulling magic out of someone who had lost it could hardly be pleasant. With his ability to understand Ronar now out in the open, Tal thought the dragon would talk his ear off. Instead, he spent most of the flight saying passive-aggressive asides at a low volume to see if Tal could hear.

"Yes, Ro, I have actually had a conversation with someone who isn't a passenger or actively protesting against my employer in the last twelve months," Tal said in response to one of these jibes. Ronar rumbled a laugh. "You're not exactly one to talk. I've never seen you speak with another dragon."

We dragons are solitary creatures. You humans are needy creatures. With needy needs.

It hadn't been Tal's goal to find more people who could annoy him on a daily basis, but apparently that was exactly what he'd done by learning to understand Ronar. Well, if Ronar continued to behave like this, he was definitely *not* getting his short rib tonight.

W hen they landed, Tal had just enough time to find Ronar a massive cut of short rib before meeting with Nathan.

Ronar was soon pushed from Tal's mind as he ascended to the university. It was a gray night, the kind of night Tal had almost preferred as a student, since it made sequestering oneself indoors to study feel easier. The sky made even the marble columns on the Hall of the Elements look dull. He still used the side entrance. His trip to the dining hall with Bex had given him more than his fill of recognition by fellow students.

Nathan was waiting in his office.

"Talarus, come in, come in," Nathan said. "And shut the door."

Nathan's conspiratorial tone rang alarm bells, even as Tal did as instructed. "Safe flight in?"

"My dragon is a terrible lander, but other than that, nothing exciting to report." Tal looked across the desk as he sat down. Nathan's fingers looked like they were playing two separate flutes in mid-air. "What in Varai's name are you so worked up about?"

Nathan smiled giddily. "You've been holding out on me, Talarus. Your new . . . power."

Perhaps it had been too much to hope that Nirza wouldn't tell Nathan about his ability to understand dragons. But he had hoped it, too much or not.

"I don't know how it works, but yes, I can . . . interpret dragon speech. That's the only sign of any magic I've exhibited since I left the university—if it even counts as magic."

"In my admittedly very knowledgeable opinion, I believe it to be some kind of automatic languageworking," Nathan replied. "Worry not, we shall get to the root of it. You've laid out our starting course of study very clearly."

The clock on Nathan's wall whined. Tal thought the boxy design looked familiar. He wondered if it was one of Nirza's contraptions and, if so, if it had any hidden magical properties.

"I know it's strange being back," Nathan said, "but why aren't you excited to be here? You look like you're being frog-marched by the constabulary."

"I told you I've shown no other magic. Dragon speech or not, I'm not really a mage if I can only do one thing. One unconscious thing, at that."

"Don't be silly! You've only exhibited one thing *so far*. The fact of the matter is, this proves there is still magic in you. It's still under the surface, working its . . ." Nathan paused, clearly trying to find another word other than *magic* to describe what his magic was doing.

"That's exactly the problem," Tal said, his voice harsh. "I can't feel it under the surface. You've probably been a mage too long to remember this, but there's a massive difference between how you feel with magic and without it. Magic is like this pleasant ringing in your ears at all times. When that disappears, you're left with silence. And that silence is *loud*."

Nathan's kind eyes met his from across his desk. Tal had always loved that when you spoke to Nathan, he gave you his full attention. He didn't shift papers on his desk, didn't check the time. The entire force of his empathy was on you. Today, Tal chafed under that gaze.

"We can start small," Nathan said.

That word—*start*—was so loaded. Because starting was one thing, but beyond the start was the actual result. The actual success and failure. Tal breathed deeply, feeling a hum of anxiety that was anything but magical. He nodded, feeling like that nod was as binding as the scratch of a dragon's claw on their employment contracts with the airlines.

Nathan was obviously doing his best to hide out-and-out glee. He rose from his desk, joints and chair creaking. His office window was really a collection of smaller rectangular windows, each of which opened inward with its own tiny latch. Nathan opened just one with a satisfying click, and stretched his hand outside. He pulled at something. He kept pulling. A thin piece of string had been tied to the window frame, and Nathan was tugging whatever was at the end of it back inside.

"I did mean *small* literally," Nathan said as he unhooked the string, cradling something in his cupped hands.

In his palm was a tiny reptile. Its head was no thicker than a couple of Enna's spheres stuck together, its entire body a thin curl of scales that seemed to be in perpetual motion. It unfurled tiny wings, flapping to stay aloft a few inches above Nathan's hand.

"A snapdragon?" Tal asked. He'd never actually seen one before. They were far more common in Nomtir, the country to the south of the Unified Coast. Many gnomes kept them as pets, which worked well as long as you weren't too concerned about the occasional spurts of sparks they would shoot when agitated.

"Dragons, wyverns, snapdragons—all of these share a common evolutionary ancestor. It is very possible they share some aspect of language as well."

Tal's apprehension was slowly being offset by something else. He was genuinely curious if his ability would work on this very small, likely far less intelligent variant of dragon. The snapdragon squeaked and flew in a circle. Nathan tied the tether tighter around his finger. With his other hand, he laid out a fresh sheet of parchment and marked it with *Dragon Speech Observations – Day 1.*

"How should we start?" Nathan asked.

"I guess . . ." Tal paused. "I guess we ask it a question."

He leaned forward until he was eye-level with the snapdragon. It continued to fly, adjusting its flight so it never came too close to Tal's face. From what he knew of their behavior as pets, snapdragons generally liked humanoids, and were rarely aggressive unless provoked.

"Hey, little guy," Tal said, feeling immensely silly. "How are you doing today?"

The snapdragon switched from spinning to bobbing from side to side. It looked at Tal—at least he thought it did. Its eyes were so small and flighty that it was difficult to tell where its attention actually was.

Fly! Fly! Fly! came a high-pitched voice in Tal's head. *I like to fly!*

Tal laughed. "I'll bet you do. It looks really fun."

It is! You should try it!

"I don't know if I have the right equipment for that."

No wings! The snapdragon did a cheerful flip, and emitted a chittering laugh. The laugh came through as sound rather than whatever languageworking allowed Tal to understand it. Nathan watched in fascination.

"I'm Tal. What is your name?"

Pear! Hi!

"Hi, Pear." Tal couldn't help smiling. "Are all snapdragons named after fruit?"

Whatever we eat first! That's the name! Pear! Pear! Pear! My brothers and sisters are also named Pear!

Tal paused to translate the conversation so far—with fewer exclamation points—as Nathan scribbled furiously on his parchment.

"This is wonderful," Nathan said. "We've just confirmed something about snapdragon sociology that is probably only known to a handful of people."

"We also know that they share speech with dragons," Tal said.

"Or your abilities are expanding."

Tal shot down Nathan's smile with a wry look. Yes, his mentor's comment had been patronizing, but that wasn't what caused him to protest. It was that Tal was almost certain that the bits of meaning from snapdragons were exactly the same as those from the dragon.

"Where do we go from here?" Tal asked.

Nathan pulled out a whole sheaf of parchment. "I couldn't help but come up with a system. It's a list of questions, designed to assess the limits of your abilities, and to start creating a codex for understanding snapdragon gestures as they relate to meaning." Of course.

The parchment was covered from beginning to end in numbered questions, many accompanied by labelled flowcharts with follow-up questions.

Before Tal dived into the questions, he asked, "Pear, you don't mind me asking you a few questions, do you? If you'd prefer to be off flying somewhere, I don't want to stop you."

Talking to human! Flying can wait!

Well, that certainly settled it. Tal grasped the parchment in both hands, and started running through the questions.

Bex had been despondent when she found out the Heathermark Flight Group contracts were magically *and* legally binding. She became even more so when, through communicating with dragons using the device, she realized that one of the contract's stipulations meant neither party could discuss it or show copies to anyone other than legal counsel. And as the now familiar refrain went, dragons didn't have lawyers.

Tal didn't see her much over the next few days. The protest area was about half full, the pavilion lacking much of its animation without Bex's leadership. The protesters knew Tal was working on their behalf, and greeted him cordially with a freshly poured mug of coffee whenever he arrived. It did make one wonder why they bothered showing up, though given the quality of the coffee, Tal wasn't complaining. Ronar found the sign that read *Ronar is an outlier!* particularly funny.

Tal only found out where Bex had been the following week, after his second session with Nathan. For all his excitement, his mentor had been willing to take things slow.

"Think of it like being a first-year again," Nathan said. "You aren't expected to know anything yet."

"I'd like to think I'm a very mature first-year, at least," Tal replied. "Albeit an unusually untalented one."

The next session involved two more snapdragons as Tal and Nathan attempted to understand how they communicated with each other. Interestingly, Tal found this much harder. Their communication flowed together, overlapping and intertwining, and Tal kept having to ask them to stop or slow down so he could catch up. Snapdragons were so good-natured that they didn't mind the interruptions, but they were also so easily distracted that every few seconds their conversation would become a manic heap of exclamations once again.

Nathan spent the entire session scribbling away on his parchment. He'd been trying to match the meanings with gestures made by the snapdragons, speculating that part of Tal's ability was an instinctive grasp of how dragons would position themselves to convey certain phrases or ideas. This had been Tal's assumption about understanding Ronar, that it wasn't so much true speech as it was a way of *showing* words through bodily movements. Like a less clear version of sign language. Which made it startling when Nathan threw his pen down in the middle of their second session. He told Tal that he'd found not a single consistent gesture. The snapdragons would often say the same things while waving their wings in different ways, or use the same gesture as they said totally opposite things. Either Tal's translation was unreliable—which Nathan doubted more than Tal did—or movement didn't create meaning.

Tal felt a swell of hope at this revelation. This meant the explanation he hadn't dared allow himself to believe was becoming the most likely one. He was in fact operating a languageworking. Magic still flowed in him, even if he couldn't feel it.

He was still floating on this sensation when an unexpected figure appeared from the crowd in the main university courtyard and grabbed him by the shoulder.

It took him a second to realize that he wasn't being mugged in broad daylight. Unless Bex had embarked on a new career. She smiled as she yanked him out of the flow of traffic.

"How were magic lessons?" she asked.

"Actually, really good," he said.

The Bex who had been despairing about the state of the dragon contracts was now entirely gone. Pure excitement gleamed from her features. It looked really good on her.

"You and me are going out for a drink," Bex said.

"What if I have plans? I could have a date with a fellow university dropout."

Bex's appraising look was one part scrutiny, one part joke. "You? A date?"

Tal didn't want to admit that this stung a bit, coming from Bex.

Bex concluded: "I suppose if you can get past the smell of dragon, there's a version of Tal that would—after a pretty significant day spent exclusively on bathing—be somewhat a little bit attractive."

Tal also didn't want to admit that this made him feel unaccountably good. If anyone else had said this, he would've tried to summon a fireworking to light their jacket on fire.

"How come you're in such a good mood?" Tal asked. "I want to know what I'm getting myself into."

"The one thing that reliably makes me smile." Her smile turned slightly menacing. "I have come up with a scheme."

Rather than head to one of the taverns that catered to university students, they walked to the Brushworks, a neighborhood that had originally been almost exclusively home to artists living in shabby converted warehouses and stables. As time went on and the city became more affluent, and the neighborhood more trendy, it had transformed into a popular nightlife spot for the city's young professionals, the area's former real squalor now an affected, self-conscious one.

It was still one of the most fun areas of the city at night. They found themselves at a bar that looked like a paint shop from the street. Inside, past easels where canvases dried, a back door led into a courtyard. The courtyard was strung with lights, layers of balconies on every side, stretching at least six stories up the buildings around it. There was a bar at every level, and a dance floor on the ground floor. Each bar was technically a different establishment, resulting in a constant flow of diverse customers. Bex and Tal leaned over the railing—which of course had miniature tables that extended from it, if you knew where to press—on the third level, looking out over a sea of dancing people.

"I came here once when I was a fifth-year," Tal said. "They were having a themed party where everyone had to dress up as their favorite opera hero."

"Who'd you dress up as?" Bex sipped a dark drink that smelled of whiskey and ginger.

"I did what half the crowd ended up doing: I went as William Shackleburg." Shackleburg had written and directed the last five winners of the award for best opera, and was known for a distinctive style of dress that was easy for a university student to emulate. It mostly consisted of wearing as little clothing as possible.

Bex snorted. "That must've been quite a sight."

"It was half people in tiny skirts, half people dressed as dramatic heroines in ball gowns. Oh, and at least a quarter as the grand champion from his last play."

"Seems like you should have stayed at the university for the math classes, at least," Bex said. Tal smiled as he sipped his own drink, which had at least a quarter cup of mint floating in it. It tasted like honey, and strawberry, and summer. On this chill fall night, it tasted faintly of nostalgia, like being slightly out of step from his position in time.

"So what's this scheme you've come up with?" Tal asked.

"It's still an amorphous type of scheme, which is honestly the most fun stage of scheme. But I've been doing some research into the Heathermark contracts, and I think I know where they are."

Tal swirled his drink, pressing into the railing as a group of young women sidled past, the makeup around their eyes a visor of silver.

"I sort of assumed they were just in the corporate office," Tal said.

"That's what I would've guessed too, but then I thought about how Heathermark actually operates. About how my *parents* actually operate. Heathermark Tower, their headquarters in Thelspoint, is where everything happens, where my dad spends most of his time. But it's also where he puts on his most legitimate face, where he insists on everyone wearing uniforms and has strict rules about haircuts. Something this obviously unethical wouldn't be kept there. He'd want this close, which is why I'm not thinking Heathermark Tower. I'm thinking Braisecroft."

"You're guessing they're at your family's estate?" Tal heard the doubt in his own voice.

"I'm not guessing." Bex's eyes shone even brighter. She pulled out a sheet of paper covered in an elaborate floorplan. "Did you know that by Heathermark law, if you're listed as a resident of an address, you can pull all the records for that building? Well, I took a little trip up to the records office."

She laid the paper out as best she could on the railing. The floorplan showed every room of Braisecroft, extending onto multiple pages to account for all the different floors, wings, and outbuildings. They were labelled in minute detail.

"Did you know that you grew up in a very small, very normal house?" Tal asked.

"I smacked the last person who told me that with this very floorplan."

"It's so thick, I imagine they're still in the hospital."

Bex's attention fixed on a specific point in the plans: a room that was significantly smaller than most. It also didn't appear to be connected to anything, except by a single long passage leading back to the main part of the estate.

"Look here," she said. "I've never seen this room. I never even knew it existed. But I pulled construction records from when it was being built—dozens of filing cabinets, dividers, a couple of drafting desks. Just as importantly, there are orders for tons of locks, a security door a foot thick, and at least twenty registered metalworkings."

Tal nodded. While it was possible to get metalworkers willing to work under the table, any reputable metalworker, especially one with university credentials, would insist their work be documented. Bex's parents had constructed this room by the book. It had a suspicious amount of security, by the book or not.

"I'd bet anything the contracts are there," Bex said. The way she said it made it impossible not to believe her.

"This is some first-class sleuthing," Tal said, "but I'm not hearing a scheme yet."

"That's the problem. I still don't know how we get into that room. It's likely spelled against unauthorized entry, and the only way in—unless we were the size of a mouse or something—is through the main passage. Which would obviously be guarded."

Bex raised her glass, apparently unconcerned with this impasse. Tal raised his as well, and together they toasted to "figuring it out somehow."

They got a second drink, speculating without much progress on how they could get into the records office. Their plans got sillier and sillier, involving more and more complicated contraptions to the point where accessing the records would require that they first invent, perfect, and then successfully implement teleportation.

"Hey, it could be done," Bex said. "You get a dragon going fast enough . . ."

". . . and Heathermark will force it to sign an unethical contract?"

Bex gave him a mock scowl, but it didn't stay on her face long. As the darkness deepened, the lights strung across the courtyard had changed color, softening to a warm orange. They threw bright spirals across the reflection on Bex's glasses, glistening over the damp streak her drink had left on her upper lip.

"There are two things I know about you," Bex said after a moment. "That you fly dragons, and that you used to be the Prevalent Mage." Tal didn't correct her. "Tell me a third thing. It takes at least three different *things* to know a person."

"That's potentially a low estimation of what comprises humanity," Tal said. Bex just watched him, smiling to indicate that didn't count as an answer. He had to think for a moment. There was plenty in his past that made him who he was, but much of it he wanted to forget. There was the estrangement from his parents, who were both working mages and had assumed he would be as well. There was the divorce between parents who had been too similar—in their need to dominate the family as well as their personalities. Then there were the minutiae of his life at the university, the friendships he'd made and all the daily rituals that didn't involve studying. All of these things, though, felt tied up in his struggle over losing his magic. They didn't feel like him. They felt like things that had happened to him.

"I can talk to anyone," Tal said finally. "If I'm in a room with one person, it doesn't matter who it is. I can talk to them for hours upon hours. Back when I was at the university, I found every single person I came across interesting."

"You don't find people interesting now?"

"Only some people." Their gazes locked. "The shitty part of that time was that 'interesting' didn't always mean 'worth talking to.' Everything was filtered through that value judgement of trying to be the best, and what this person could do to help me achieve it. I feel scummy just thinking about it."

"You're beating yourself for acting the same way as everyone else," Bex said.

Something softened in Tal at that. "If I'm with anyone, I can talk to them for three, four hours, and never get bored. Learning about their life, how they see the world, it's endlessly fascinating. But here's the catch. The minute there are more than two of us, I lose track of the individual people in the conversation. Like they just turn into part of a group rather than their own person. People who have only seen me in groups think I'm this taciturn guy, when in reality I'm just struggling to remember that a circle of six people is actually just six different people standing in a circle."

Bex laughed. "Have you considered that they just can't understand you because you use words like 'taciturn'?"

Tal shrugged and sipped his drink.

"I think you're interesting to talk to," Bex said, "though I have to admit I did agree with the folks with the limited vocabularies when I first met you. You were very, very grumpy at me."

"Well, in all fairness, you were really fucking annoying."

Bex's laugh almost made her spit her drink over the railing. Tal thought about how much trust it took for the dancers below to believe they wouldn't have an errant drink dropped or spit up on them from above. He also thought how beautiful Bex looked when she laughed.

"So that's my third thing," Tal said. "That officially make me human?"

"I'll allow it."

"But now it's your turn." Bex looked panicked, but Tal pressed on. "I know you have wealthy parents who no longer support you because of your decisions, and I know you're wildly passionate about helping creatures who can't speak for themselves. What's your third thing?"

Bex swished her drink in her mouth, as if the taste of alcohol might help her think. Then she took an overwhelmed gulp.

"Wow, look how nervous this question is making you!" Tal said, putting a hand on her arm. "You don't have to answer if you don't want. My thing was pretty dumb anyway."

Bex leaned into his touch, and Tal felt warmth spreading through his chest that was definitely not just from alcohol.

"Can we agree that third things have to be dumb?" she asked. "Because yours definitely was, and I want to make sure we acknowledge that fact before I say my thing."

"This is gonna be good, I can tell."

"Stop!" Bex smacked his arm.

"Yes, dumb is perfect."

"Okay." Bex braced herself, as if preparing to share terrible news. "I love to dance."

She eyed him sharply, like she was expecting him to suddenly announce that it was getting very late and he'd better be getting to bed. Tal returned her gaze, hoping his smile revealed his actual reaction rather than looking overly gleeful. Because the truth was, this revelation was *adorable*.

"I'm going," Tal said, "to require some more explanation."

Bex slurped her drink furiously before saying, "Ever since I was little. Doesn't matter the type. I've done tap, ballet, even a little bit of the experimental variety that's so popular in the operas here in Thelspoint."

"They don't call it the Shackleburg Shuffle for nothing."

"It doesn't matter what kind of dance it is, as long as there's music, an open place to move, and a rhythm to move with."

"Do you by any chance have a professional career as an experimental dancer you're not telling me about? If so, it would put you in the list of at least the top three most interesting people I've ever met."

"Only top three?" Bex smiled mischievously. "I don't have a secret dancing career, but I wish I did. Maybe that's the dumbest secret of all."

Tal's first impulse was to make a joke, but he could also tell that revealing this had taken a great deal of courage.

"So? You think I'm the biggest dork now or what?" Bex asked.

Tal shrugged. "I think you're really cool. The only thing is, now that I know you'd rather be dancing than talking to me, I have to insist that we end this conversation."

Bex's eyes widened.

"Because now we simply must dance," Tal said, taking her by the hand. They climbed down the flights of stairs, weaving their way through the rowdy crowd, and down to the bright lights of the dance floor. A few people protested as they pushed past, but their expressions as they watched Tal and Bex, seeing them as a pair, a single unit, sent a little thrill through Tal.

Bodies packed together, music coming from a band in one corner, a soundworking projecting the music. The bright and up-tempo music featured multiple fiddles locked in a friendly duel. Tal and Bex made for the center, finding a pocket of space next to a group of university-aged men dancing so vigorously that sweat sprayed from their long hair.

Tal was a terrible dancer. But importantly, he knew he was a terrible dancer, and never let his limbs get out of control the way an oblivious terrible dancer might. The woman across from him, it was clear from the first swaying movement of her body, was not a terrible dancer. He couldn't identify any particular style, but no matter how the tempo shifted or the instrumentation changed, Bex was always exactly in step with it, every movement perfectly natural and suited to the music.

Bex laughed as she straightened her blouse, which had come untucked within seconds. She let its edges hang, more concerned with freedom of movement. They danced together. Bex didn't remark on Tal's lack of style. He sensed that someone being here with her was all she needed. Quality was secondary to enjoyment of this simple act. Occasionally she would take his hand and make him twirl her, or slide into a chassé from side to side, but for the most part their dances were their own.

The dance floor was tight enough that bumping into others was inevitable. Every time she did, Bex incorporated any loss of balance into the dance. A couple times she even made passing friends with people who had just run into her because they did the same.

They danced for close to two hours, pausing only to grab another drink, continuing to dance as waves of people passed in and out. As the night wore on, the clientele skewed younger, the crowd rowdier. The band obliged, playing ever faster and louder.

On the way back from one of the trips to the bar, Tal looked down from the balcony. He had to catch his breath—flying dragons required a very different kind of physical exertion. He stopped at the top of the steps leading back into the crowd, and caught sight of Bex, who had continued to dance without him. A tall man in an expensive vest had approached her, and she followed his lead, blundering through a half waltz that was completely out of sync with the song. Tal almost laughed. Every time the man tried to force a movement that didn't make sense for the music, Bex would wince. Tal's stomach was telling him it felt something about seeing Bex dance with another man, but it wasn't sure exactly what. He took his time heading back through the dancers, careful not to spill their drinks, bobbing in time with the crowd as he focused on keeping his balance.

Bex was mid-spin when Tal reached her.

She did the following in order: she smiled at Tal, told the man "My date is here," took the drink from Tal, and completed her spin. The man left, bearing an expression of good-natured disappointment.

"I'm your date now?" Tal asked.

"I don't let anyone who's not my date buy me more than one drink. So yes, by definition."

"I bought it with money you gave me . . ."

"Congratulations on becoming my date. I'm sure everyone is super proud of you."

"It's my greatest achievement. Far greater than becoming the Preventative Mage."

Bex was so in shock at Tal having mimicked her joke of mislabeling his old title that she actually stopped dancing for a second. Just a second, but it was enough.

The music slowed a couple minutes later, and it wasn't long before a large group left the dance floor to wait for a faster song. Bex reached for Tal's hand and positioned it at her waist. She leaned against him, eyes straight ahead. She was at least four inches shorter than him, so meeting his eyes would have required a probably overly intimate look up. As they swayed, Bex leading, Tal couldn't help wishing she *would* look up. He wasn't sure he would've been able to maintain eye contact, though.

Bex didn't overcomplicate things, allowing Tal to dance at a comfortable pace. The sensation of her against him was all warmth, all energy. Again, he wished she would look up.

Then she looked up.

Her glasses didn't at all dampen the intensity in her dark brown eyes. Tal looked back, dipping his chin. A smile danced over Bex's lips.

"You're not a bad dancer," she said. "You just don't know what to do with your feet."

"Isn't that kind of the whole idea?"

She shook her head, sending her hair smacking against his chest. "Dancing is a mentality."

In that moment, listening to Bex spout an aphorism that was either profound or utter nonsense, any part of him still resisting her broke with a laugh. It left his whole being open to what he actually wanted. And what he actually wanted was her.

Tal was almost whispering when he said, "I'm glad you told me about your third thing."

Bex leaned her head fully into his chest, and Tal's insides shattered.

The music stopped moments later. Tal was tempted to kidnap the band so they would keep playing forever.

"Sorry folks, there's a noise ordinance," said a voice over the soundworking. "You don't have to go home, and you *can* stay here. Just no more music."

There was a mass exodus from the dance floor and the first level, but many in the balconies stayed put. Bex gave Tal a questioning look.

"Can I show you something?" he asked. "It's a bit of a walk, but I promise it's worth it."

"As long as it's not a secret evil lair," Bex said. "I promised I'd never date a guy with one of those again."

"Shit, guess we should just call it a night then."

Bex laughed and followed him out into the night. The streets quieted as they wound back toward the university. It was a Monday night, after all, so any students still awake were either studying hard or actively neglecting their studies.

The building Tal led them toward was not the tallest on campus, but it did sit on the hill overlooking the center of the university. It had an odd design, almost like an upside-down pyramid, with a narrow base and a wide, flat top. Tal led Bex to the service staircase. He'd been this way many times since he first volunteered for the plantworking faculty. He loved the calm of the fields and greenhouses on the building's roof. They began to climb the narrow staircase.

"Are you sure it's not an evil lair?" Bex asked, winded. "Evil lairs usually have this many stairs."

"Aren't the stairs usually going in the opposite direction?" Tal was also winded.

"I don't know, some of the best lairs are sky lairs."

"I suppose it would be fitting, given that I'm a dragon rider."

For a second, the door to the roof wouldn't budge, and Tal feared that someone had finally done the sensible thing and locked it. But then it gave with a creak, and they were transported to an improbable meadow.

It was dark and smelled green and alive. Tal led the way, skirting around beds where plantworking students cultivated experimental crops, and passing a greenhouse that would've glowed a metallic blue during the day. Tal had spent many hours cleaning that greenhouse's glass to allow more light for the finicky plants inside, some of which had been carnivorous and tried to bite off his arm.

They came to a small bluff. Tal found the exact point at its top where three boulders converged, each large enough for both of them to stand on. He helped Bex up onto one, reveling in her curiosity. The curiosity quickly turned to wonder as she saw what was before her. From here they could see straight down into central Thelspoint. The city was alive with light, pockets of revelry mixed with the lights of shops that were open late, and lightworkings bathing the streets. From this vantage point, though, the most assertive presence was the manmade river.

The river began in the spire jutting out from the next building over, beginning its spiral flow in the canal directly below. It gave the sense that the river was flowing out from beneath their feet, as if they were falling into it, plummeting inexorably down into the rapid current as it curved its way around the university, before circling back into the city proper.

"Wow," Bex breathed. "I feel like I'm on a ship that's simultaneously sailing and flying."

Tal smiled. That wasn't even half of what he wanted to show her.

"Wait there," he said, leaping to the next rock. It was possible the lightworking he had placed here during his university days was gone. He'd spent dozens of hours on it, carving the magic so narrowly that only someone standing on one precise spot could see it. His feet instinctively found two nearly invisible grooves that marked where to stand. He felt the unbidden sting of tears. The lightworking was still there. It was painful to be confronted with something his old self had created. Especially when it was this splendid.

"Okay," Tal said, feigning nonchalance as he stepped away and the lightworking vanished. "Just come over here, and find the grooves." Bex let Tal guide her to the correct point, and Tal felt a thrill at being so close to her, not to mention the wonderful sweep of the back of her neck. "Right . . . there."

Bex gasped, reaching a hand back to grab his. She was too distracted by the view to notice her hand closing awkwardly over three of his fingers. If Tal stood with his toes almost touching her heels, he could see what she did. Amazement seeped through her.

Through Tal's lightworking, the view of Thelspoint had been transformed. It was still the same buildings, the same lights, the same river. Yet every element burned brighter, so that even the shadowed sections were cast in the light of day, the brightest lights shimmering with a fractal radiance.

And the river. In Tal's original lightworking, he had only wanted to transform the river, so he'd spent the most time refracting the light that reflected off of it. As a result, the entire river appeared to be made of silver flame. Every twisting bank was as sharp as a knife. Every splash was a cascade of silver drops. The current was a roiling, burning force. A couple crafts floated against the current, looking as if at any moment they would be sucked down into flame. Instead, they hovered above the water, improbably, immune to the silver around them.

"Tal, did you . . ."

"It took a while," he said. "Water is tough to do lightworkings with because it doesn't reflect the same color all the time."

Bex's speechlessness told him that she understood. What they were witnessing was not just something beautiful he had created. It was a window into what his world could be. It could have felt like a window into a world that was lost, but with Bex there, with Nathan's insistence that he still had magic in him ringing in his head, it didn't feel that way.

He didn't register Bex turning around until her arms were wrapped around his waist. Didn't realize she was tipping her face up toward him until she was inches away. They kissed then, the silver of the blazing river pouring over them. All thought, all loss, all hope, every bit of it disappeared from Tal's mind as the kiss consumed him completely.

A Scheme Takes Shape

When Tal woke Ronar the next morning, the dragon sniffed him deeply.

"Damn Ro, it's a good thing we're friends," Tal said. "I don't let just any flying lizard sniff me like that."

You smell sweet. Like rain among gingkoes.

"Are all dragons poets?"

You smell like desire.

Tal whacked the dragon across the nose with the butt of the pitchfork he'd been using to distribute a fresh bale of hay. "Just because I can understand you now doesn't give you license to invade my personal life."

And just because you can understand me doesn't mean you should forget the relative wisdom of provoking a vicious dragon.

Dragon speech—from dragons rather than snapdragons—was so deep as to be almost monotone, making it very hard to interpret intent. Tal stared Ronar down, for the briefest instant imagining what it would be like if Ronar did finally take offense and decide that he made a better lunch than he did a flight attendant.

Then Ronar laughed.

"You're a menace," Tal said. "A flying, scaly menace."

Don't forget it.

Once they were airborne, on their way to Upper Boden, Tal made the walk back to the cabin. He stopped and sat at the end of the bench next to Claret.

Ronar's wingbeats gave the cabin a brief floating sensation with each powerful stroke.

"You smell like you're up to something," Claret said as he sat down. Her leather jacket was orange today, flared at the collar so it could've easily served as a gorget in a pinch.

"Why does everyone feel the need to comment on how I smell today? Keep your noses to yourselves." Claret seemed content to let him spin himself out. Tal relented: "As a matter of fact, there is indeed a bit of scheming afoot."

He told her about the mission to break into the Braisecroft records office to retrieve the contracts. Claret's eyes shone, the shine of a dedicated heister getting their hands on a new job.

"Look, this sounds illegal, and I won't get involved," Claret said, lowering her voice, "but I'm happy to serve as an informal advisor."

"As an informal advisor, how would you advise we get into the office?"

"Very informally." As Tal rolled his eyes, Claret said, "Sorry, couldn't help myself. The main thing to keep in mind is that security in these kinds of places is oriented toward humans. Guards at any entrance a human could fit through, spells to detect when people enter. So my advice is to avoid the human."

"Can you give an example?"

"When we do our work, which definitely doesn't *ever* involve going into cities up in Mithlein in order to steal military secrets, even when those secrets could potentially avert a future war. Just saying as a hypothetical."

"Right . . ."

"In this definitely hypothetical and not at all based on my most recent mission scenario, we've used tiny metal 'creatures' no larger than a cockroach. These creatures are really just complex metalworkings, spelled so we can see through their eyes and control them from afar."

That did sound useful. "Where, hypothetically, would a person get their hands on one of these creatures?"

"Unfortunately I can't, even hypothetically, help you there," Claret said. "There are only three such creatures in existence, and all three of them are locked away in a vault in Thelspoint. A vault that only a handful of high-ranking officials have access to."

"I take it that breaking into that vault would be harder than the original problem."

"It would also be considered treason." Claret nodded matter-of-factly. Her demeanor suggested nothing was truly off the table as long as one was also aware of the consequences.

"I think if we're going to come up with a good scheme, one of my top criteria would be that it not involve treason."

Claret nodded again. "Might be at a bit of an impasse then."

Tal felt slightly defeated as Claret bid him farewell after the flight, and he started making his way back up the hill to town. The feeling didn't last long, as his thoughts turned to the previous night, and to Bex. A fluttery feeling that was one part anxiety, one part excitement, and one part not knowing what the hell was going to happen or what he wanted to happen, had taken up residence in his upper chest. It might have been easier not to think about it, but his mind kept returning to the light on Bex's face on top of the greenhouse, the way her lips had felt against his.

He slouched into his wagon home, mind churning but not resolving anything. Before he could flop down on the bed, his eyes caught the spheres on his desk. He didn't feel any different, still didn't feel the throb of magic in him. Yet the spheres were inescapably brighter than the day before.

Tal had hazy dreams that night, most involving a vague research project with Nathan. In them, hundreds of snapdragons swarmed around them, and Tal tried desperately to convince them to stop. There were simply too many of the creatures to understand, and when he did tap into one's speech, they were as grumpy and stubborn as Ronar. The dream ended with the swarm becoming denser and denser, threatening to consume him.

Tal sat upright in bed. The room seemed almost daylit under the spheres' glow. And a wild idea for how they could break into Braisecroft began to take shape.

140

CHAMOMILE

Nathan was elated when Tal entered his office and told him he wanted to figure out how to give snapdragons commands.

"Just the kind of innovative thinking we need more of here at the university," Nathan said. Tal didn't say, for the millionth time, that he wasn't part of the university and wasn't likely to be anytime soon.

Pear could obviously tell something was up when he came in through the window, bouncing around on his tether and looking excitedly at Tal.

Tal wasn't exactly sure how to start.

Another lesson! Pear said. *Good to be back!*

"Thanks for coming," Tal said. "How are you with following directions?"

North, south, east and west!

"Not those kinds of directions. If I asked you to fly up to the ceiling, then from one side of the room to the other, would you be able to do that?"

Nathan unclipped the hook that was keeping Pear's tether in place. Pear shot upward, grazing the ceiling's wooden beam in precisely the center of the room, and flying in a gentle spiral. He only went a couple inches before stopping.

Other side now!

Nathan watched Pear skeptically, but Tal thought he might know the reason for the odd behavior.

"Pear, did you just divide the room into two sides, and then fly from one to the other?"

Pear's *screech* meant that was exactly what he had done. Interesting. So he could follow instructions, but had interpreted them in his own literal way.

"Could you please fly to the wall nearest the door, and then to the opposite wall? Staying near the ceiling the whole time."

The snapdragon obliged.

"Great. Now, could you please do that again, but as quietly as you can?"

As Pear streaked across the ceiling one more time, Tal noted how quietly his wings fluttered, how if you weren't looking closely he appeared more like a darting shadow than a dragon. This could work.

They spent the entire evening teaching Pear commands. A few things became apparent: first, Pear required very specific instructions, otherwise he would either execute his own version of the command or freeze up entirely; second, he seemed to be having more fun with each passing challenge; and finally, he could function in another room or out in the hallway without direct supervision, again as long as he had a specific instruction.

During their final training exercise, which sent Pear to steal a pen from the office next door, an unwelcome face peered in the door.

"Why is there a snapdragon in Professor Rhys's office?" Meret asked Nathan, taking a second to register who was sitting in the chair across from him. His face twisted into a cruel smile. "Varai be praised, the Preeminent Mage!"

"Meret, how are you?" Nathan asked. "I have a visitor helping me with some research."

"A visitor . . ." Meret seemed about to say something snide about Tal's current status with respect to the university, but instead stepped forward into the room. "Seems like very important research if it involves the least of the dragon family."

Found it, found it! Pear said from the other room.

Nice work, Tal said, struggling to split his focus between the snapdragon's quiet voice in his head and Meret. *Now bring it back to me.*

But there's a wall between us.

"It is indeed very important research," Nathan said as Tal's blood pressure rose in response to Pear's inability to follow the exact same route he had just taken. "Small examples often enable understanding of much larger concepts."

Meret studied Tal. "I'm surprised he can help with any research anymore."

"Believe me, I'm here under protest," Tal replied. He instructed Pear, in agonizing detail, how to navigate back into the hallway, then into Nathan's office.

Meret had to duck as Pear careened in, a pen dangling from his claws. He dropped the pen into Tal's lap and took a few more chaotic laps around the room before coming to rest on the bookshelf, Meret's eyes on him the whole time.

"Did that snapdragon just steal a pen for you?"

"It would appear so," Tal said.

Steal! Steal! Pear's high voice rattled in Tal's mind.

"You are sworn to secrecy," Nathan said with a conspiratorial smile. "Tal's research is a bit more specialized than anything I've done before."

"I didn't know 'specialized' meant the same thing as 'not even capable of a basic languageworking.'"

Nathan ignored Tal's look of discomfort as he pressed on: "Tal has recently developed the ability to communicate with dragons, and we are simply studying the mechanics of that communication."

Meret's eyes widened, a frustrated hand running through his dark hair.

"Alright, I understand when I'm being told to fuck off," Meret said. "Enjoy your snapdragon training."

He hustled out, obviously so discomfited he had forgotten whatever question he'd originally intended to ask Nathan. Nathan's smile held all of its usual mischief.

"A brilliant mind," Nathan said, still chuckling.

Tal wondered how long it would take Meret to realize that Nathan had been dead serious about his abilities. "This is only going to make him hate me more."

"That's between the two of you." Nathan mimed washing his hands. "I'm not involved."

At the end of the session, Tal asked Nathan if he might take Pear along with him, so they could practice more than just once a week. He might as well have asked if Nathan wanted a giant slice of cake and a foot massage.

"We will have to arrange some type of padded box," Nathan said, poking around his office for something suitable. As he searched, he tossed the detritus of half a dozen forgotten experiments behind him, sending forth a cascade of alembics and half-filled notebooks. "You don't want him bouncing around when you're in the air. Food won't be an issue, as long as you don't keep your home too clean."

"Too clean?"

"They're not picky, though they do prefer bugs to fruit. Might be worth letting the dishes pile up for a few days."

Having lived the last two years next to an orchard where swarms of flies and wasps constantly buzzed around the remains of fallen fruit, Tal didn't think access to bugs would be an issue. The stream of tossed objects stopped, and Nathan straightened. He held a tiny box with sliding slats along one side.

Tal thought there was more to the triumph in Nathan's eyes than merely having located an appropriate box. He tossed the box to Tal. Tal inspected it. It looked small, even for Pear, but he was already flitting around it.

This will work! Safe inside! Without further delay, Pear dove inside the box, somehow pulling the slats shut behind him.

"Suitable indeed," Nathan said, sighing back into his chair. "Why the sudden interest in giving instructions?"

There was no way Tal was telling him it was for a minor heist. "It's sort of the natural extension of what we've been doing, right? Communication is about conveying meaning, of course, and meaning only matters if there's some tangible outcome from understanding the meaning."

Tal couldn't be sure, but he thought he heard the sound of snoring coming from the box.

"Some would argue that being able to communicate your thoughts and feelings is just as important as getting someone to do what you want," Nathan said with a wry smile.

"Point taken."

"I am thrilled you're actually enjoying our studies together. Seeing that light back on your face—it's every professor's dream for their students."

"It's finally something I can do," Tal said. "Even if I might not know how it works."

Nathan hesitated, as if he wasn't sure whether he should say what he was about to. Pear was now without a doubt snoring in the little box. Every few seconds steam puffed out between the slats.

"There have been some whispered conversations among the faculty," Nathan said. "Just a few of us, nothing official you understand."

Tal's stomach dropped.

"Some of us think there could be a path to reinstate you at the university," Nathan continued. Tal's stomach fell further, did a backflip, and then smashed itself to pieces on the floor.

"Students are required to cover at least three areas of magic in their studies," Tal said.

Nathan's hand waved dismissively. "There are some among the faculty who believe these requirements to be overly restrictive. Yes, we hope mages will be well-rounded magically, but what if a student displays prodigious talent in a single area? Would we reject that student and all they could offer?"

"It's so rare to only possess a single area of magic," Tal said. "The distinctions between the different branches are artificial, you've always said that."

"All the more reason not to be so narrow in our definitions." Tal could feel his mentor winning the argument. "Maybe if you demonstrated your newfound ability to the provosts, we could make a case."

"You know I would do almost anything to be a student again," Tal said. "But being put on display like that, not knowing if they'll find my magic worthy . . . I don't have that in me."

Tal's tone had tipped over from agitation to panic. Nathan reached across the desk to place a hand on his forearm.

"We will do nothing you're uncomfortable with," Nathan said.

Tal wiped away a tear of frustration. "It's not that I don't want to. The last time I lost my magic, it was under the pressure of exams and assignments. I don't trust myself not to have the same thing happen if the stakes are that high."

Nathan's hand was warm and slightly tacky from the humid room. He kept it where it was as he said, "I think you underestimate yourself."

There was no response Tal could formulate that wouldn't result in him choking up. He couldn't even manage a conversation about a test to reenter the university. How could he expect to handle the test itself?

Nathan didn't push further. Instead, he suggested they take a walk down to one of the tea houses just outside the university. Tal agreed gratefully, tucking Pear's box under his arm. The snapdragon didn't wake as they took the stairs down to the street, jostled their way through a courtyard filled with students on their way to the dining hall, and into the narrow tea house. It had a bead curtain rather than a front door, and much of its furniture was in need of urgent repairs—not to mention a good cleaning—but it served the best chamomile in the city.

Sitting across the table from his mentor, Tal let silence wrap around them. When the tea came, the waiter poured two steaming cups. Tal remarked on the quality of the tea as he sipped, otherwise not saying much. Though it was late, the shop was still mostly full. Students pored over textbooks or class notes, their precious work dangerously close to the magical heat sinks that kept their tea warm. Tal could pick out half a dozen specific aromas—black tea, peppermint, and spiced ginger among them—but the most notable was the deep one that clung to the furniture, to the rafters, and even to the employees themselves. It was the powerful amalgamation of a hundred different teas, lacking a specific flavor yet somehow its own smell.

When Nathan did finally speak, it was not to persuade Tal of anything, or even to remark on the day's success. He began to talk about life at the school, which second-years were excelling and which were driving him crazy. Most of the news amounted to little more than gossip. It was exactly what Tal wanted to hear. There were no stakes to any of it, only the insular and ultimately inconsequential goings-on of a talented student body that was far too interested in what everyone else was doing.

"What has Meret been up to since the Completists fell apart?" Tal asked.

"He does a lot of work with me, as you would expect," Nathan said. "He truly is a great languageworker. He's already received offers to work on the faculty once he graduates, but I suspect he has something grander in mind. Maybe private practice, maybe a lucrative research job for a large corporation."

Nathan looked Tal directly in the eyes, as if trying to gauge whether he would be jealous of his old friend and rival's continued success. And how couldn't he be? Meret had been able to continue his academic success while Tal had been stuck down in Upper Boden.

"He was always better than me in that one discipline," Tal said. "I could always pretty much crush him at anything else."

"There was never any competition between you, of course."

"Of course not."

Nathan, thoroughly unconvinced, continued: "Truth is, Meret hasn't been the same since you left. People like him, they thrive on having someone to compare themselves against. They need someone to feel by turns jealous of and superior to. You were always that person for him."

"That's a stupid thing to need."

"Is it? We all compare ourselves to those around us. It's how we gauge our place in the world. He just latched onto one person, one person who happened to be you. And when you left, he found that, well, there's no one quite like you."

"You're gonna make me cry," Tal said. He'd been going for sarcastic, but the sting in the corners of his eyes ruined the effect.

Thankfully, at that point the slats on Pear's box slid open, and the snapdragon poked his head out. He sniffed suspiciously.

"Guess you've never been in a tea house, eh?" Tal asked, grateful for the opportunity to change the subject. He slid his cup across the tabletop, then picked up the pot that the waiter had left on the table and filled the cup to the brim. "Be careful, it's hot."

Heat, it turned out, was not a problem for a creature who could breathe fire. Pear curled his long neck, lowering his head down to the cup. With a great slurp, he drained almost half the tea. With a second, the rest was gone as well.

Nathan and Tal looked on in horror.

That's good!

As Tal began to pour more, the snapdragon started gulping directly from the stream coming out of the pot.

Tal stopped and said, "I suppose there are some things I need to teach you about tea."

Teach me everything!

Tal began explaining the ritual around tea and how one should drink it. Whether these rules could be applied to snapdragons, it wasn't clear. With each passing second Pear became more and more excited. His eyes had widened from their usual slits, revealing fully dilated pupils.

Just as Tal was telling him how you had to wait while tea steeped, Pear screeched and flew into the air. He streaked from one side of the tea shop to the other, sending papers scattering and people scrambling. The formerly tranquil tea shop descended into pandemonium. Menus flew everywhere, and at least three bunches of tea that had been drying from the rafters came tumbling down. A group of younger students stood on their stools as Pear zipped between the legs of their table as if attempting to encircle them with an invisible string. Pear didn't seem to mind slamming into the dividers between the tables, denting the intricate wood and probably himself in the process.

"It appears," Nathan said, after apologizing to a young woman who now had a fireball-sized hole in the middle of a page of notes, "that some of the calming effects of chamomile tea that are observed in humans may have somewhat the opposite impact on snapdragons."

Tal needed another cup of chamomile after that.

Tal took his time working with Pear. He only trusted his own ability to explain tasks so far, and knew there might be danger if the snapdragon was caught spying at Braisecroft. It was as illegal to hurt a snapdragon as it was to hurt a Trug—very—but the rules probably didn't apply to an intruder in a secret records room.

After a week, Pear was improving at making his own decisions based on Tal's loose instructions. The key was that Tal had to specifically tell Pear that he could exercise his own judgement. Tal couldn't delay telling Bex about his plan any longer.

"This is insanity," Bex said once he told her. They sat on the front steps of Tal's wagon home. He would've made tea for them, but all he had was chamomile and he wanted to avoid riling Pear up. The snapdragon slept on his desk, a wing hanging halfway out of his box.

"I knew it was a bad idea," Tal said.

"No, it's a fantastic idea. Using a snapdragon as your own personal miniature thief. It's completely and utterly brilliant and insane."

A glow began in Tal's chest. "We don't know if it will work. They could have security measures that work on reptiles. He could be too big to fit through whatever hole we can find."

"Or the contracts could be in a locked box."

Tal had thought about that. He hadn't come up with a solution besides hoping they were in such a secure room that Bex's parents hadn't bothered to lock them up. He had also thought to test whether Pear could read, and was shocked to find that he could, though his vocabulary was mostly limited to words for various fruit and bugs.

"Do snapdragons breathe fire?" Bex asked.

"Yeah, it's more of a concentrated beam than a ball, but they're still dragons."

"Easy. He melts the locks."

Tal was doubtful, both because he wasn't sure if melting a lock would actually make it open, and because using fire on a container that housed very flammable documents seemed like a good way to call attention to their presence, or make the whole exercise moot by burning up the documents—and Braisecroft.

"Easy," Tal repeated. They sat at an awkward in-between distance, not quite close enough to touch, but much closer than if they were just two friends sharing a stoop.

"Remember a couple weeks ago, when you thought my whole campaign for dragon rights was a crock of shit?" Bex asked so suddenly that Tal's laugh burst forth of its own accord.

"How do you know I don't still think that?"

"Because instead of telling me to shove off, you came up with a brilliant plan to retrieve the contracts. To help the cause."

"I'm not entirely sure I'm doing this for the cause. It might have a little more to do with who's leading the cause."

Bex's cheeks were a rapidly ripening strawberry. "So you do like me."

"Of course I like you," Tal said. "I wouldn't train a snapdragon for just anyone. They're a huge pain in the ass."

There was no conscious impression that it was happening, and yet suddenly the space between them had closed. Their legs pressed against each other, and their faces were together just as quickly. This kiss was slower, more tentative, than the one they'd shared on the roof of the greenhouse. But it also lacked the frenzy of alcohol, of having danced so close together in a sweaty tavern in the Brushworks. It felt gentler, and somehow more real.

The kiss progressed quickly, pulling them back inside his house—Pear fluttering off to give them privacy as soon as it became apparent what was happening—and onto his bed. They moved against each other, no amount of closeness seeming enough, no depth of kiss quite satisfying their desire. At some point Tal's shirt had come off.

There still remained a layer of fabric between them. Tal's hand searched around the hem of Bex's blouse. She gently redirected his hands up to her breasts, still over her shirt. Even through the blouse, Tal could feel their satisfying heaviness, the way they gave ever so slightly under his touch. A new sprig of desire sprouted in him.

"Don't look now, but you seem to have lost your shirt," Bex said through a laugh.

Tal looked down at himself, feigning surprise and outrage. "But my haberdasher assured me this was the peak of style."

Bex kissed him again, nipping ever so slightly at his lip. "This is nice."

"It is."

"Just so we're clear, I don't want to go any farther than this. I know myself, and ..."

Bex trailed off. She'd set her glasses by the faintly glowing spheres on the desk. Her face, so familiar to him already, looked different without the thick lenses. There was something private and vulnerable about her without them, as if the glasses were part of the persona she projected to the world.

"And what?" Tal asked gently.

"And I don't have an easy time separating this ..." She trailed off again, this time waving a hand vaguely between them, with particular emphasis on Tal's shirtless chest.

"I understand," Tal said.

"The feelings follow the physical, whether I want them to or not."

"I understand," Tal said again. "We won't do anything you're not comfortable with."

Bex's smile lit Tal up. When she spoke again, her voice was a low whisper that sent a shiver through him. "It's not that I'm not comfortable. I just don't want to fall for you any faster than I am already."

Things Going Exactly to Plan and Not in Any Way Violently Off the Rails

Bex had managed to borrow the exact same wagon they'd taken the last time they went to Heathermark. This ride, however, was much more pleasant. An ease had established itself between them, and Tal found himself laughing without either of them having told a joke, as if any conversation with Bex brought lightness into him. Pear was free to fly around, but after circling the cart a few times, he came back and slept on top of his box, which Tal had set on the seat between him and Bex.

They took back roads as they neared Heathermark. Bex's parents lived in a sprawling enclave over two hours by foot outside the city. Trees had been planted at intentional intervals, hiding the mansions from view. Evenly spaced evergreens towered high over a road that had been recently cleared of pine needles, which collected in damp ditches on either side. Everything had a planned feel, like they were traveling through a simulacrum of a real forest. The road was hard packed dirt, but far better maintained even than the main road to Heathermark. Through the trees, Tal glimpsed ornate entryways, and more than one carriage house that could have easily housed a family of ten. Bex eyed each house warily from beneath the hood of her cloak. It shielded her face and hair, but Tal could tell she still felt exposed.

"How long has it been since you were back?" Tal asked. Dappled shadows passed over their heads, making the snapdragon seem to disappear and reappear.

"Almost two years since I came on my own. About a year since their guards dragged me back in order to have a 'little chat' about my behavior, and let me know I was being cut off."

Tal hadn't seen his own parents for close to a year, either. "Well, hopefully there will be no 'little chats' today."

"They always find a way to surprise me with new ways of making my life difficult. My dad especially. If it was just up to my mom, we'd probably still be a real family. A real family who never discusses anything important or addresses how much we all despise each other, but a real family nonetheless."

"Is she as involved with the business?" Tal asked.

"Trying to decide how culpable she is? When Pear finds the dragons' contracts, we may well find out." Bex's eyes met his for a long moment. "In my mind she's just as culpable, but honestly much less involved. Technically she's on the board of Heathermark, but she's more of a rubber stamp for my dad. She doesn't have any interest in the daily operations. I'd be surprised if she even travels to the offices in Thelspoint more than once a year. Much better to hang out at Braisecroft and not think about what her husband is doing to their dragons."

"Willful ignorance can sometimes be the happiest way to get through life."

Bex tried to gauge if he was joking, then shrugged in agreement and glanced at Pear, who had seemed content to ignore their conversation. "Speaking of ignorance, is your little spy really up to this?"

"I've given him his detail already. I just hope I was clear enough."

Tal had spent long enough practicing with Pear that he felt confident in how he needed to phrase instructions. But they simply couldn't account for what was actually inside the records room. Tal had a nagging fear that his inability to give specifics might cause Pear to freeze up when he got inside. He pressed this fear down, trying to convince himself to trust the snapdragon's intelligence.

They parked the cart in a wooded lot bordering the estate. It had been partially cleared for what Bex revealed had originally been planned as a private home for just her and however many servants she wanted. After her falling out with her parents, the work had stopped in its early stages, leaving a cleared area of forest with a couple years of growth on it. The vegetation was enough to hide their cart from curious eyes passing on the road. They were careful to stay away from the overgrown path that led to Braisecroft proper, at the end of which they could see one corner of the horse stables. Their own horse, who Bex had tied up to a tree nearby and was now feeding, seemed intrigued at the smell of others of his kind, yet remained mercifully quiet.

Tal went through the plan with Pear one more time: He would enter through a vent that allowed air into the subterranean section of the house. According to the floor plans, they should be just large enough for him to squeeze through. Snapdragons had a snakelike ability to compress their bodies, so it was possible he could simply slip under the door into the records room—unless it was crafted true enough that there *was* no space under the door.

Too much uncertainty. Tal would be glad when this was over.

Pear, on the other hand, displayed no anxiety at all. In fact, his excitement had been growing consistently as they neared the estate, and Tal had to keep calling him back from where he was doing little spirals in the air.

Finally, Tal was satisfied that Pear was ready and let him fly off into the trees. He disappeared into the densest stretch of forest, blending in perfectly.

Silence fell over the woods. It was the silence of a half-domesticated forest—birds chirping happily away, squirrels darting here and there—a forest that was alive and growing, yet somehow dampened by the presence of humans. Somewhere a bullfrog sang his fall ballad. Their horse snorted contentedly in the corner of the clearing. There were bugs everywhere.

"How long do you think he'll take?" Bex asked. She'd been anxiously looking around, focusing most of her attention on the path, as if at any moment Pear was about to fly back down it. That or a team of armed guards. Bex had said there were likely at least a few stationed at the end of the path.

"It depends on too many things," Tal said. He put his feet up on the front of the cart.

"Don't pretend you're not nervous," Bex said.

"I figure if I act like I'm not nervous, maybe my brain will take the hint from my body and chill out."

Bex laughed dryly. "It's worth a shot. I was gonna go for some anxious pacing myself."

"It would certainly be a promising way for your parents to see you for the first time in a year, if we're discovered."

"In all honesty," Bex said, "if I see them, I'm more worried about projectile vomiting everywhere."

"As a man of science, I would find that fascinating," Tal said, before adding: "As someone with more than a passing romantic interest in you, I'm really hoping we don't see your parents."

Instead of pacing, Bex settled for sitting on the cart with one leg propped in front of her, knee bouncing wildly.

Time was hard to gauge in the woods. The creak of the wooden boards under Bex's shaking boot mingled with the chorus of nature. Some almost industrial sounds reached them, which Bex attributed to construction on one of the estate buildings. Tal tried to allow his excitement at the potential of discovery to push down the guilt at having sent Pear into a dangerous situation. He knew he had no right to ask the snapdragon to do this. It was all for a greater good though, right? If they had access to the contracts, they could determine exactly how Heathermark had screwed over the dragons, and could start to right those wrongs. Perhaps more importantly, resolving the contract issue would serve as an olive branch to the rogue dragons bent on causing more chaos. It was maybe their best hope for preventing future escalation of the fire-breathing variety.

Still, they waited.

As the sun passed well below its zenith, casting the weeds and grass into shadow, a breeze blew over the clearing. It felt warm, almost sickly in fall air that should've been crisp and clean. Tal and Bex exchanged a look.

Help me, came a quiet voice over the wind.

"Did you hear that?" Tal asked.

"Hear what?"

I'm inside. I need direction. The voice spoke directly into his mind. It belonged to Pear. It was a small relief that he didn't sound frightened.

"Pear's asking for guidance," Tal said. He tried to respond, to ask what the snapdragon needed, but he'd never communicated over such a distance. The space between him and the records room was a solid wall preventing Tal from projecting dragon speech. "I think I need to get closer."

He started to get down off the wagon, but Bex grabbed his arm. "There are almost certainly guards at the end of that path. If they find you, they find me."

"If I get caught, you can take the wagon and make a break for it."

Bex's breath hissed out as she relented. "No, I'm not running. We'll go together. If you're caught on your own, they can arrest you as a trespasser. If it's both of us . . . well, I won't technically be trespassing, and I can say you're my servant or something."

"Charming."

"Beats me telling them you're the former Prevaricated Mage who's spying on them via snapdragon."

"For so many reasons. Are you sure?"

Wordlessly, Bex swung her legs down. Together they crept down the path toward the estate, grass swishing under their boots.

In his former life, a lightworking might have focused Tal's vision to better make out guards among the patchwork of light and shadow beneath the trees, or he could have performed a windworking to bring sound more clearly to his ears. Instead, he walked forward with only his human senses for security.

Pine needles cushioned the path, occasionally interrupted by sticks or the odd branch. The going was quiet on the soft, newly fallen needles. Any scuff against the roots, or even the creak of their leather boots, felt magnified. All the while, Pear's gentle prodding for assistance came to Tal out of the ether. Tal tried repeatedly to answer, but his replies were still too weak.

Another gust of warm air swept past. The pines rattled above them. Tal had feared there would be a guard, or perhaps a stable hand in the stable at the end of the path. They found only three horses, quietly chewing on their feed under the open structure, completely unbothered by the intruders.

Bex and Tal kept to the shadows at the edge of the stable. They had a better view of Braisecroft from here. The main house was still some ways off to their left, on a hill with winding paths leading up it. Fountains sprayed ostentatiously into the air on the main grounds. There seemed to be rather a lot of fountains for a single family, some of which stood at the center of massive areas paved with colored bricks, areas that could only comfortably be described as plazas.

"Nice place," Tal whispered. "Which of the plazas the size of a town square was your favorite as a child?"

"It's a tossup between the one with the fountain of the Smartass Mage and the one with the World's Worst Flight Attendant."

The estate was abuzz with activity. Workers unfolded chairs and unfurled a tent in one of the plazas, while others erected scaffolding on a carriage house be-hind the main house. There were few armed guards, most of them concentrated by the house, with just a few standing at the brick armory off to their right. The armory was right above the records room, at the top of a clearly manmade hill. The whole estate had an artificial feel, from the rigorously planted flowerbeds blooming to the exact same height, to the grass mown in checkerboard patterns that complemented the paved spaces. Bex's parents must spend a fortune on their grounds crew. Or maybe they exploited them just like they exploited the dragons.

"This way," Bex said, leading him out from under the stable's eaves. They circled along a shaded path around the edge of the estate, paved with green brick that blended into the grass framing it. Tal tried again to contact Pear, but the connection remained one-way. How close would they have to get? The path led its winding way toward the armory. Much closer and they would come within sight of the guards at its entrance.

There was another gust of hot air. And suddenly the guards had far more to worry about than two human intruders.

The dragon flying overhead was a huge, bulky Cernoth. This one had no harness or passengers. It roared low over the buildings, scattering the panicked servants and work crews in all directions. It dove, catching some of the mist off the fountains, before launching itself in the air again. Shouts came from the armory as a couple dozen guards emerged, crossbows in hand.

As the Cernoth streaked low again, crossbow bolts rattled off its scales. The bolts couldn't possibly hurt the dragon, the small tears they might make in the creature's wings more like annoying bee stings.

The dragon was undeterred. It swooped down, letting its tail lash across the grounds, smashing several fountains to bits. Water spurted out of the gashes left behind.

Groundskeepers who had been weeding the gardens at the edges of the plazas ran for cover, dodging a hail of stone. Other servants rushed toward the main house and the scant protection it might provide.

"What in Arren's name is it doing?" Bex yelled over the sounds of smashing rock and terrified screams. Tal couldn't say for sure, but the pit in his stomach told him they were witnessing the continuation of whatever had started with the torching of his landing pen. Only this attack was far more direct.

The dragon unleashed a fireball, scattering the guards around the armory. Fire scorched the brick and blackened the grass around it, but did little more than that. Contrary to some of the worst fears about a dragon attack, dragons only breathed fire, not fiery missiles, so anything that wasn't flammable wouldn't burn for more than a few seconds. It was a statement of intent, though, and the guards responded in kind.

A hatch opened on the side of the armory. A massive contraption rolled out on metal wheels. It looked like a cannon, resting on a system of gyroscopes that a guard cranked to rotate. A conveyer belt fed shot into the machine. The rumble of cannon fire soon mixed with the rush of the dragon's flight. Fist-sized cannonballs shot skyward, far faster than any crossbow. Several struck true, making a sound like metal pans being slammed together.

The dragon roared in pain.

Bex and Tal continued around the fringes of the grounds, Bex's steps manic with the horror of seeing a Cernoth attack her family home. They came around the backside of the armory, in full view of the guards. The guards, their eyes on the sky, completely ignored them.

Even here, on the opposite side of the estate from the main house and the under-construction carriage house, they could still see clearly as the dragon bellowed in rage and drove its body down into the carriage house, taking its roof and a large chunk of the top floor with it.

The dragon spiraled upward, bricks and ceiling tiles hailing around it. For a second Tal thought it might be about to leave, its point having been made and the cannon obviously a threat. He took advantage of the moment to try contacting Pear again.

Two things became clear: First, that Pear was still out of range, and second, that the dragon was far from done.

It broke out of its spiral and streaked downward. The cannon fired almost once a second, rattling streaks of crimson into the afternoon. The dragon ignored the shots, even as cannonballs clattered off its scales, even as some struck so true that brown blood plumed from its belly. It headed straight for the cannon.

The guards operating the device got in a few last shots while the dragon continued toward them. But by the time fire once again streamed from the beast's muzzle, the guards were already fleeing, abandoning the gun as they sprinted around the other side of the armory.

A torrent of fire broke over the cannon. Metal wouldn't burn, and it likely contained at least a few metalworkings to prevent it from melting, but there was no protection as the explosive gunpowder that powered the gun ignited all at once. A tremendous explosion shook the air, sending guards scattering, brick into the air, and Tal and Bex to their knees.

"Look!" Bex yelled. Tal's ears were still ringing. It was hard to focus on anything, but he followed the direction Bex was pointing.

The side of the armory had been blown wide open by the force of the blast. If they made a break for it . . .

Tal's stomach fell. Five guards appeared from around the corner of the armory, some with obvious signs of burns on their heavy jackets. Tal and Bex froze as the men ran directly toward them. One even had a loaded crossbow, which made Tal feel stupid for not asking Bex if her parents happened to have a shoot on sight policy when it came to intruders.

Tal braced either to be tackled or for the thud of a bolt through his chest.

The guards clearly saw them. One's face even registered recognition at the sight of Bex. They didn't break stride as they streaked around the intruders as if Tal and Bex weren't there, making for the relative safety of the woods—assuming the dragon didn't decide to move on from estate bashing to starting forest fires—and disappearing from view amongst the trees.

"Cowards!" Bex shouted after them. Tal was too relieved to argue. There was probably a fair argument that, in the face of a fire-breathing Cernoth, running away was the most prudent choice.

Ignoring this voice of wisdom in his head, he followed Bex toward the armory, and the gap created by the exploding cannon.

The dragon had turned its attention to the boathouse abutting the small manmade lake on the far side of the grounds. It methodically peeled off the stucco shingles, sending a clatter over the fleet of unused rowboats on the shore. The few guards who had stayed to face the dragon ran down toward the lake. It wasn't clear exactly what they intended to do now that their one effective weapon against the beast had been destroyed. By their panicked shouts, it seemed the guards themselves weren't sure either.

Inside the gutted main floor of the armory, Tal and Bex picked their way through the charred remains of the wall and furniture that lay in shattered heaps in the rubble. The room had been decorated with small portraits that might have, when intact, depicted the guards' families. Even if the protection was minimal given the state of the armory, there was something comforting about at least having one wall to muffle the sounds of destruction.

A staircase led down into the passages beneath Braisecroft. Tal felt a tingle in his mind every time he tried to contact Pear now. They were close. At the bottom of the stairs, engulfed in near-complete darkness, the tingle became a spark. Tal said, *I'm here. What do you need?*

The only light came from under the door at the far end of the hallway, nearly a hundred yards away. The magelights on the walls and ceiling had gone out with the explosion. There was no response from Pear. Bex studied him uncertainly.

After a long period of time, made longer by the cacophony of the entire boathouse being torn apart filtering down to them, a response finally came: *Thanks! Instructions, please!*

Tal gave Bex a thumbs up and asked Pear what he needed. The snapdragon had gotten stuck with the latch mechanism on the cabinet he thought housed the contracts. They consulted back and forth for a minute, but Pear didn't have the vocabulary to describe what he was seeing, any more than Tal could interpret his increasingly desperate attempts to describe what probably amounted to little more than a hinge.

Going nowhere! How about I show you!

Show me? Tal responded.

Worth a try!

Tal had no say in what happened next. There was no sensation of being pulled out of himself, no sense of movement at all. Yet suddenly his mind's eye was in one place, while his body was in another.

His sight flitted about in a dim room. Tiny wings beat frantically at the corners of his vision as he looked down at a wooden cabinet. He was looking out of the snapdragon's eyes and yet, even as he did so, he also looked out of his own. He was simultaneously in the hallway with Bex *and* in the locked room, above a box of contracts. His brain felt split in two, just as his perception was. Bex eyed him with concern. Tal found he couldn't speak while maintaining his split awareness.

He saw at once what had tripped the snapdragon up. The cabinet had no exterior handle or lock, making the technique they had practiced for targeting metal weak points with a concentrated beam of fire useless. To his credit, Pear hadn't tried to burn through the heavy wood. Tal focused his snapdragon eyes on the cabinet. It was locked with an unobtrusive mechanism that would click open when pressure was applied to one corner. He instructed Pear to press against each corner in turn, until the bottom right gave slightly, then popped open. Tal's vision blurred as Pear spun in a celebratory circle. Pear didn't need further instruction. The drawer was filled with nearly identical pages, each a contract between a dragon and Heathermark Flight Group. They'd done it.

There was still the small matter of the dragon who was actively ransacking the estate, however.

With a feeling like missing three steps at once, Tal's awareness returned fully to his own mind. He thought he might be sick. He felt Bex's hands on his shoulders, holding him up.

"What was that?" Bex asked.

"Pear just let me into his head. I was somehow able to see out of his eyes. It was . . . kind of incredible."

"You look like you're about to pass out."

"I'm lucky I haven't. Come on, let's get out of here. Pear found the contracts."

They ascended once more into bright afternoon light. Through the broken armory wall, they saw that the dragon had finished demolishing the boathouse, and now ignited huge swaths of grass as it glided unhurriedly toward the main house. Tal turned toward the trees as they crawled out of the rubble, only to find that Bex had stopped, looking across a field of ash and ruin at her home.

Surely she wasn't sentimental. She'd been kicked out of this home, by parents who exploited the dragons who worked for them. If anything, this had the odd ring of justice to it.

"Come on!" Tal said, urging Bex down the hill.

But she wouldn't move. When he ran up beside her and followed her gaze, Tal saw why. In the largest windows of the main house, windows blown out by the sheer noise of the dragon's rampage, two figures looked out over the destruction.

"It's them." Her voice held no emotion.

The dragon had seen Bex's parents, too, and now landed on the berm that ran down the center of the estate, between the armory and the main house. It tramped, unhurried, along the berm, breathing spouts of fire and steam into the air, shaking the earth with bellow after bellow, and shattering any remaining windows on the grounds.

Before, the dragon had taken pains not to harm more guards than it had to. Now, its intentional stride indicated that Bex's parents were the exception.

Then it spoke: *Powerful leaders of Heathermark. If only you had the foresight to ward your home against dragon fire. I'm going to enjoy watching you burn.*

There was no question in Tal's mind that this dragon was about to torch the entire estate house along with whoever was inside.

No one but Tal could understand the dragon, of course. Bex's face was stricken. Instead of gauging the dragon's progress, instead of charting their escape, Tal just watched Bex's eyes. The growing horror in them told him everything. Bex wanted to beat her parents, to force them to change her ways, but she certainly didn't want *this*.

With a sensation just as jarring as the one he had experienced when leaping into the snapdragon's perception, Tal's legs began carrying him down the hill, onto the path that ran parallel to the berm. He sprinted along a brick walkway that would take him directly in front of the dragon.

Bex shouted after him. She followed, with a hesitation that betrayed a much more reasonable fear of dragons than Tal was currently displaying.

The path took Tal past the dragon's tail, forcing him to duck as the barbed mass twitched from side to side. The air above Braisecroft was now so hazy with steam and ash that it was difficult to see the sky.

I wonder what you will taste like, the dragon mused. *Probably corruption.*

Tal's legs were a whirlwind beneath him. In several places the path's bricks were so torn up that he had to leap over piles of them, or run onto the equally chewed up grass. The dragon's claws dug into the berm. It hurled clawfuls of debris toward the house, rattling the siding and sending scattered earth over the grounds.

You don't want to do this! Tal said to the dragon as he ran. The dragon didn't acknowledge him. It flicked a picnic table dismissively off the berm, sending it directly over Tal's head. His knees cried out as he skidded to the ground. He pressed painfully back to his feet.

Between the dragon and the house was a patio that would've seemed large if not for its proximity to the multiple plazas that formed the rest of Braisecroft. A long table draped in a linen tablecloth had been half set for a meal, chairs scattered around it. Tal ran to the table, acutely aware he was now directly between the dragon and its prey. He jumped onto the table, his muddy boots scraping against the fine linen.

The dragon frowned down at him. It had a striking ridged jawline that formed into an unusual webbed pattern under its chin. Its singular appearance wouldn't significantly affect how it felt to be eaten by it. The dragon didn't say anything as it swished its head from side to side. It clearly didn't want to kill him, but not wanting to and not being willing to were two different things.

You don't want to do this, Tal repeated. Surprise crawled over the dragon's face.

A boy with the tongue of a dragon. How intriguing.

This Cernoth dragon was dark brown, and the high ridges around its eyelids matched its jaw. They made its yellow-green eyes appear both somewhat startled and more than a little murderous.

I have no quarrel with you, it said. *Step aside, and let these swindlers meet their fate.*

I can't do that, Tal said.

Then I shall go through you.

You would really kill one who speaks as you do? This was more of a bluff than Tal would've liked. Yet he sensed a strange deference from the dragon, as if Tal's gift made him its kin in some respect.

He wished Ronar was here with him, even though his dragon was less than a third the size of this monstrosity.

In response the dragon reared back, then released a fireball fifteen yards wide. It struck the ground in front of Tal, shooting sparks up toward his face and obliterating the wooden chairs.

Tal stood strong, his boots braced against the tabletop, his arm held out to shield his eyes. He couldn't have said where this courage came from. Maybe it was a final recognition that a life of anonymity and passivity in Upper Boden would mean allowing people to burn. Or maybe it was the fact that Bex was there with him, watching from the edge of the path leading up to the patio. She seemed to understand this was an encounter that had to happen between him, the dragon, and his newfound powers.

What is it you actually want? Tal asked.

I want these swindlers to die.

I don't believe you.

The dragon sat back on its haunches, a look of haughty anger on its face. *I want my freedom. I want Heathermark to tear up my flight papers. I want no more humans on my back. I want to create a new home with my kin, wherever we may.*

Tal turned on the table, and waved to the two figures who were still watching from the window above him.

"Yes?" said a man with a trim beard, leaning out the window. His rich voice was tempered only slightly by fear.

"Would you consider releasing this dragon from its employment if it allows you to live?"

"We don't respond to blackmail!" the man shouted.

Tal could see Bex rolling her eyes, even at this distance.

"How's this: either you start responding to blackmail, or you get incinerated!" Tal shouted back.

"Another dragon will be right behind this one, blackmailing us again if word gets out."

We are wasting time, the dragon said.

Tal glanced over his shoulder. Heat grew in the air between him and the dragon as it charged up its next blast of fire. Tal's mind snapped unwillingly to the thought of just how unpleasant a death by dragon fire would be.

If you are released from your contract, will you promise not to incite any more violence or grievance toward humans amongst the dragon folk? Tal asked. There was something about a dragon's eyes—perhaps the size, perhaps the way they narrowed into horizontal slits, perhaps the dangerous intellect within them—that made him want to look away. But he met them now, and found that he could speak to the dragon on a deeper level than even the telepathic words that usually comprised dragon speech. The creature's eyes narrowed further, and Tal understood everything.

He understood that the dragon had been coerced into service without fully understanding what he was signing up for.

He understood that this dragon was a father, whose family waited in the northeast, in the ancestral dragon homeland that humans called the Claglands.

He understood that he could never return there, but could still imagine a new home outside the reign of humans.

And he understood that this dragon's pride had been deeply damaged by being used as a means of transport.

Tal yelled up to the window one more time, asking Bex's father to release the dragon from service, and insisting that he would take no further action against the company.

There was a long silence, the only sound the low crackle of fire consuming the boathouse down the hill and across the lake. Parts of the boathouse had begun to fall off into the water, sending even more steam into the thick air.

"Fine," came the voice from upstairs. Then the blinds snapped shut behind the paneless window frame.

Tal sighed. So much for a grand agreement between dragons and humans. *How do I know he will keep his word?* the dragon asked.

There was a sudden flash of light, followed by a sound like thunder being deconstructed and spread out over several different octaves. The dragon stumbled on the berm, his claws scraping for purchase.

Tal could only hope this was not some new attack. He let his hope deepen as the dragon smiled. Tal smiled as well. Witnessing a magical contract breaking had a terrible beauty to it.

The dragon didn't speak. He spread his wings wide. He swelled his stomach out, and with two crushing beats of his wings, he was aloft. He roared as he streaked into the evening air. Tal half slid and half stumbled off the table. Adrenaline was leaving him now. Bex arrived at his side before he could rise, helping him to his feet. Somehow they were both unhurt.

With a *snap*, the blinds opened once again. "Bex? What are you doing here?" This time the voice belonged to Bex's mother.

"Just thought I'd stop by to see if there happened to be a fire-breathing lizard tearing up Braisecroft," Bex said.

"Who is this person?" Bex's mother asked. "And what in the world has he done to my tablecloth?" Tal thought some form of thanks would've been more appropriate.

"Don't you dare answer that," Bex said. Tal looked down at the tablecloth, which was covered not only in mud from his boots, but also what appeared to be an entire tureen's worth of gravy and brown goo that must be congealing soup.

"I'm sorry," Tal said. "At the very least the dragon is gone, though. He won't trouble you any further."

"I suppose that's some consolation," Bex's mother said. Bex's face was red with fury, and her grip was painfully firm as she led Tal by the shoulder, away from the house and back out onto the grounds. Bex's mother's cries for them to come back lacked feeling.

With the immediate threat gone, they had time to take in the damage. Some buildings on the outskirts—the stables among them, fortunately for the horses—had escaped the dragon's wrath. The armory would need to be completely rebuilt, and more than a dozen fountains replaced. The boathouse was down to little more than its foundation. Bex's eyes raged as they took it all in. He couldn't read her as well as a dragon, but he thought her anger was directed more at her parents than the creature who had hit her childhood home with the force of a fiery tornado.

They picked their way through rubble, back down the path toward their waiting wagon. Halfway along it, they met Pear, who struggled to stay aloft as he grasped a packet of papers twice his size in his spindly claws.

Relief washed over them. At the very least they'd achieved their primary objective.

"Well done, Pear," Bex said, taking the documents from the snapdragon. He gave an exhausted sigh before darting down to settle on Tal's shoulders and circling his wings around the back of Tal's head.

I found them! Pear said. *Right where we looked!*

"You did good," Tal said, patting his tiny friend on the snout.

LEGALESE

"**I** don't understand any of this," Bex said. She flipped the last few pages of the contract over, then dropped the entire packet heavily on the table. It rattled the ale mugs that had accumulated around them. She had spent the entire ride back to Upper Boden reading the documents, some of them aloud, but had come no closer to understanding what they actually contained. "It's like they're trying to be intentionally confusing."

"I mean, that might actually be the case," Tal said. He slid his empty mug to the side. Mora the bartender appeared at his shoulder with another. She'd always provided great service, but she reached a whole new level of hospitality when Bex was there. A certain magnetism made it easy to do things for Bex. At least, that was how Tal felt.

"Do you know any lawyers from your university days?" Bex asked.

Tal shook his head. "The School of Law is separate from Thelspoint University. There are some associations with languageworking, but for the most part the students don't interact. University mages aren't supposed to study law."

On the small stage at the far end of the tavern, a musical competition was well underway. Three different musicians had already played three different instruments in turn—first a solid lute, second a passable lyre, and third a flute that was so screechy Tal wouldn't have been able to discern the variety of instrument if he hadn't seen the bearded man blowing with all his might into the complaining instrument.

"You mean a formal education at a magic school might not adequately prepare you for the real world? Shocking."

"It certainly didn't prepare me," Tal said.

He had meant it as a joke, but Bex's expression only held concern.

"You know, due to me losing my magic and becoming completely useless?" Tal said.

Bex's brow furrowed. She took a sip of ale, keeping eye contact with Tal the whole time. As she set her mug down, her stare edged into a glare. He tried to match her gaze, but looked away before long.

"Good, glad that's understood," Bex said.

Tal wasn't exactly sure what he was supposed to have understood, but he did intend to reconsider making jokes at his own expense in the future. The flautist left the stage to rousing applause, which was clearly meant to show appreciation for the man's departure rather than his musical talent.

They returned to poring over the contract. Bex had scooted her chair around to the end of the table so they were shoulder-to-shoulder. Being this close still sent a thrill through Tal, making it difficult to focus on the words rather than Bex's warmth and the soft rush of her breath.

"If I wasn't worried about third-wheeling, I might be offended that you didn't think to ask your official adventure consultant for advice," came an abrupt voice from behind them. Tal spun to see Claret with two mugs of ale in hand. Her leather jacket was a deep forest green, and she'd dyed the longest strands of her hair to match. The rest remained silver.

"I sort of thought you were more into, like, slaying goblins and retrieving treasure than legal stuff," Tal said.

Tal briefly wondered if Claret was here with someone—hence the second mug of ale—but as she spoke, she alternated sips between the two separate mugs, keeping the exact same level of liquid in each.

"You have no idea how much paperwork is required before going on a sanctioned quest," Claret said. "You get used to amending and signing a lot of boring forms meant to fleece you out of treasure. It's just part of the job."

If being a professional quester involved alternating between paperwork and risking death by goblin spear, Tal wasn't sure he saw the appeal. But he was glad for Claret's presence.

"And now I hear that your adventures involved not only infiltrating the estate owned by the esteemed operators of Heathermark Flight Group, but also staring down a Cernoth dragon," Claret said. "I probably would've recommended a stealthier approach, for the record."

Claret broke off to shoot a critical eye toward the stage. A new lutist had entered the competition, and for the first time Tal understood why anyone had bothered making this instrument in the first place. The crowd leaned toward the young woman playing a rapid tune. Conversation dulled to a rumble. Claret nodded her approval before turning back to them.

"The trip to Braisecroft was a lot less stealthy than we intended," Tal said.

"And involved a lot more saving of the very people you're allegedly fighting against," Claret said, pointedly. "May I?"

"By all means," Tal said, handing the contract over. "We can't make snout nor wing of it."

Claret cleared a space between her mugs. She skimmed with almost mechanical speed, not stopping her pattern of sipping from both ales equally.

Tal and Bex leaned back in their chairs, taking in the tavern crowd. It was just over half capacity, it being Sunday night. They were having a special on fried meatballs drenched in a sweet and spicy sauce. Nearly every table had either a plate piled with meatballs—each with a little stick impaled through it—or the demolished remnants of one. Tal hadn't yet seen any of the meatballs pelt a musician for their poor performance, but the threat in serving them on the same night as the contest was implicit.

The talented lutist stopped playing. She wore a thick hood, and seemed to be emerging from a trance as she raised her head to take in the cheers from the audience. She shuffled off the stage, accepting a tankard of ale offered by a smiling Mora.

"This is sick stuff," Claret said, snapping the cover back over the contract.

"Sick in a good way?" Bex asked. She gave Tal a shrug as if to say, *Why not?*

"In a gross way. There's a lot of stuff about what services will be rendered, the condition of equipment, flight crews and all that. The most interesting section, though, is at the end."

"That's the part Tal didn't get," Bex said, poking an elbow into his ribs.

"There are several addenda that were obviously added much later," Claret continued. "The way this contract is structured, the company has almost un-limited ability to add whatever clauses they'd like, as long as it can plausibly be considered necessary for the operation of the company. Functionally, they can put whatever they want in here."

"How are they allowed to structure it like that?"

"Because it's a bad contract, and Heathermark was obviously negotiating in bad faith, due to the fact that they're evil people who only care about profit." Claret shot a regretful look over to Bex.

"It's not news to me." The same fire that had burned in Bex's eyes that afternoon at Braisecroft had returned, less guarded after a couple of drinks.

"There's also some recently added language in here saying that, if Heather-mark goes bankrupt, they can use the dragon contracts as collateral for loans to keep them afloat. This part's a bit beyond me, accounting-wise, but it comes up several times."

"Why include that? These people have ungodly amounts of money," Bex said.

Claret shrugged. "It certainly raises the question of who they would even sell the contracts off to."

"There's something else we need to know," Tal said, not wanting to go too far down this rabbit hole. "Given my current . . . situation in regard to magic, I can't tell if this contract is sealed with a languageworking."

"You want to know if it's magically enforced?" Claret asked. "I can tell you, but it's gonna cost you."

"The old finances are a bit thin at the moment," Bex said. "You know, the whole being cut off thing?"

Claret eyed her two mugs. She lifted one in her right hand, then poured its contents into the other. The ale rose precisely to the top of the mug. She waved the now-empty mug at Tal.

"A refill would suffice," Claret said.

As Tal flagged down Mora—who first had to deliver an order of over two hundred meatballs to a group of gnomes occupying the long tables in the center of the tavern—Claret put a hand over the contract and closed her eyes. Even if she felt magic there, there was no guarantee she would be able to identify what type of magic it was. Magical signatures varied greatly, but usually the more powerful the magic, the more obvious its signature, and the clearer it would be. Unless whoever had cast the languageworking had been powerful enough to place the languageworking and cover its signature at the same time.

"It's not super obvious," Claret said after thanking Mora for delivering her payment. She began to sip from the new ale, and then from the old one. "I'm not the most magically-inclined individual. I know how you university folks like to shit on us self-taught mages."

"I believe I once heard a professor say that a self-taught mage was a contradiction in terms," Tal said.

"I hope you slapped him," Bex said.

"I'm pretty sure I asked him to be my advisor. Have I mentioned that the university didn't make me a better person?"

"I'm strongly considering upping my price to include meatballs as well," Claret said, breaking out in a smile. Within it, Tal saw an understanding of the gulf between who he had been then and who he was now. "Take this with a grain of salt—I'm fairly certain this contract does contain a languageworking."

"Does it magically enforce the terms?" Tal asked. That type of working was pretty common.

"Not exactly," Claret replied. "What the languageworking does is lay out a framework for magical enforcement. Basically, at any point Heathermark can start forcing every dragon to do what's outlined in the contract if they weren't before."

Tal's head spun. "I don't get it, why not just use the simpler binding?"

"Because they can also amend the contract," Bex said.

It took Tal a second to see the connection. When he did, he groaned.

"This is some messed up shit," Claret said. "No offense, Bex."

"Once again, I am not responsible for my parents' actions," Bex volleyed back. Tal put a gentle hand on Bex's elbow. She let her weight fall against him.

"I'm trying to wrap my head around what this means," Tal said, "because at the end of the day all contracts are essentially a way of getting people to do things."

"This is far beyond that," Bex said. "It's combining enforceability with malleability."

That helped. The understanding that had been eluding Tal snapped into place.

"Okay, just so I have this straight," he said, "they could amend the contract without the dragons knowing it, but let whatever provisions they've added remain unenforced. Then at a whim they can decide to start magically enforcing them."

"That's the size of it," Claret said, brushing her green hair out of her eyes. "Activate their dragon army whenever they want. At least, that's what I would do."

"Have I mentioned that being a professional quester doesn't make you a better person either?" Tal asked.

Claret grinned, revealing that two of her teeth on one side had been replaced with gold.

Bex was frowning. "I think it's more likely they would just lock the dragons into a more favorable business relationship. My parents are businesspeople, not conquerors."

"Not always a huge difference between those," Claret said.

"Thank you for explaining all this," Tal said. "At least we know what we're up against now."

"And that you're more than a little bit screwed," Claret said. She rose from the table. "Though you don't seem all that broken up about that fact." She let her gaze dance between them. Something about the way this validated his relationship with Bex made Tal's heart dance. Claret disappeared into the crowd, taking her two mugs of ale with her.

"Well this is certainly bleak," Tal said. His fingers drummed an erratic beat on the contract's vellum cover.

Bex bit her lip and stared into space in a way she sometimes did when she had an insistent thought she was trying to set aside. "Well, even if it is legally gnarly, it's far less traumatic than what happened today. I realized I never thanked you."

"For?"

"For preventing my parents from being burned to a crisp. Facing down a live dragon. All that good stuff."

"I sort of thought you were mad at me for that."

"No, no, I was mad at them. They created this situation. It's their responsibility, their actions that put you there. That's what I was mad about. Of course I wanted you to save them."

"It was more of an instinct than anything, to be honest." Tal was still trying to piece together the afternoon's events. "After I saw through Pear's eyes, I felt like I was just following an instinct toward the next dragon. I don't know how to explain it."

"I think I know what you mean." Bex smiled at him. "Doesn't matter why you did it, it was the right and kind thing to do."

Bex continued to look at him. Then without warning, she scooted her chair forward and planted a kiss on Tal's cheek. It left behind a faint stickiness of ale residue on his warming skin. The tenderness of that kiss set something twirling in his heart. And made him want more.

A rumble of excitement went up from the crowd near the stage. Tal did a double-take as Claret climbed up onto the stage. She put her mugs down at its edge, instructing a random gnome in the front row to guard them for her. She started assembling a complex set of wood and metal that didn't look like any instrument Tal had ever seen.

"So about you not wanting to have your parents burn to a crisp. Does this mean you could forgive them?" His tone betrayed the fact that he didn't find this likely.

Bex's eyes lit with a dangerous spark. "I don't want them to die. That's as far as it goes, Tal. Look at these contracts. They're evil people. If you spend your time forgiving evil people, you only allow their evil to continue."

In this statement Tal saw the truth of Bex. She was all conviction. And when it came to the people around her, she was absolute. Once forgiven, always forgiven. Once cast aside, never returned.

Claret finally finished assembling her instrument. It turned out to be a zither, connected through a complex mesh of strings to a drum set by her foot. Using a set of pedals, she could either bang the drum or pluck the additional strings. The result was an odd mélange of bending sound and rhythm. After a few seconds adjusting to its strangeness, the audience was rapt.

Tal and Bex didn't discuss further what they should do with the newfound information, recognizing that what they had experienced today warranted a break from worrying about dragon-related matters. Instead, they listened to the strange sounds coming from Claret, Bex comparing it to the best performances she'd heard from the traveling caravans that came out of Lodefall. Bex loved the city under the mountain, a city containing just as many multitudes as Thelspoint, but with a bent more toward the gritty—mining, trade in ore—and the artistic—primarily drama and sculpture—and a deep suspicion of magic of any kind. Their traveling shows were legendary, but according to Bex, they paled in comparison to the immersive shows at the Granite Stage, where performances unfolded in a multi-level amphitheater carved deep into the mountain's rock.

The audience roared as Claret hit a final bending note. No one had mentioned the rules of the musical competition, but if applause was a factor, Claret had clearly won.

Bex kissed Tal goodnight as he left the tavern. He wound his way back up through the orchard, trying to let the giddiness of being with her block out thoughts of work the next day.

Back at his converted wagon, there was yet another distraction. A creature larger than his house rested beside it, half a dozen lanterns held aloft by a company of cloaked figures illuminating its gray-brown scales. The creature was a grayling, one of the smallest varieties of dragon that could still hold passengers—no more than three or four. The retinue turned toward him. There were at least eight of them, one shape in particular catching Tal's attention.

The shortest figure did not hold a lantern. The others showed the older man a great deal of deference. Even through the shadows, Nathan's face was instantly recognizable. Seeing his mentor in Upper Boden gave Tal the sense that he'd suddenly fallen into a dream.

"Talarus, apologies for dropping in unannounced," Nathan said.

"I've done the same to you," Tal said.

"Glad to continue the tradition. I usually don't like to fly, but when Heathermark Flight Group dispatches a dragon with a personal message, well, it seemed unwise not to take the opportunity for a free trip."

One of the other figures stepped forward. He was dressed in the finest traveling cloak Tal had ever seen. It took Tal a moment to recognize his bearded face from earlier that day. It was Bex's father.

"Nathan is beating around the bush, as usual," the man said. "We haven't been formally introduced. My name is Theo. I believe you know my daughter."

I kissed your daughter like ten minutes ago, Tal thought as Theo extended a hand and Tal forced himself to take it. *Your daughter who hates you.*

"As Nathan said, we're sorry for dropping in unannounced," Theo said, "but we thought your actions today required a swift response."

Tal looked between Theo's and Nathan's expectant faces, then to the faces of the people in their party. Most appeared to be guards, one with the flying boots of a flight attendant. The flight attendant would've had to make the roundtrip to and from Thelspoint to collect Nathan in the time Tal and Bex had spent traveling back from Heathermark and debating the contents of the contract. His dragon would be ragged after such a quick flight.

"Are you going to burn down my house in exchange for what happened to Braisecroft?" Tal asked. "Apologies in advance, I don't think the monetary value is proportionate."

"Not that kind of response," Nathan said, wearing a grin that filled Tal with a keen sense of dread.

"You saved my life, my wife's life," Theo said. "This is more of an 'in what way can we reward you for your help' kind of conversation."

Tal didn't reply. A reward? The long shadows cast by the cloaked figures' lanterns made his house appear to be moving, jostling along as it had in its last life as a wagon.

"I'll let Nathan give you the details," Theo said.

Nathan had been looking like he might blurt out the details anyway. "Theo and his wife Marjory have agreed to sponsor your return to the university. You may resume your studies as a special adjunct, free from the restrictions on taking classes in multiple areas of magic. You could study only what your abilities allow."

Tal didn't respond. He couldn't let himself believe this was real.

"I know this is a weighty decision," Nathan continued. "I would ordinarily want you to think on it. However, we're nearing the deadline for the current term. Theo has long been a benefactor of the university, and his influence allowed us to push this through. It took more than a few favors."

"We have always taken an interest in the goings-on at the university," Theo said. "We never know what Preeminent Mage might go on to do valuable work for Heathermark Flight Group after they graduate."

"Can I have a few days?" Tal asked, weakly. "This is so generous. I just . . ."

"They held a special session of the university's board before the new semester," Nathan jutted in. "The votes are available to make this exemption, but if you don't take this now, the board is unlikely to approve it again next year."

"They'd change their mind that quickly?"

"They'd change their members that quickly." Theo's soft voice was a stark contrast to the amount of power he obviously wielded. Nathan's eyes, on the other hand, were almost pleading. "The board only keeps half its members each year—it's a duty rather than a privilege—and this semester's board is more . . . friendly than previous years."

Nathan's eyes were desperate.

"We were heartbroken to hear you were forced to drop out," Theo said. "As thanks, we wanted to offer you a way back in."

The only sound was the grayling dragon scratching impatiently in the dirt. No one had bothered to remove its harness. The poor beast's scales must be chafing terribly. The feeling of disassociation created by Nathan's presence had only grown alongside the strange sensation that nothing he did or said in this moment mattered. Like in a dream, this scene would happen without him.

But this was no dream, and his mentor was offering him the exact thing he had yearned for over the last two years.

"I've taken the liberty of drawing up a contract," Theo said, offering him a leatherbound sheaf of papers that was much thinner, but made out of the exact same materials as the dragon contracts Pear had pilfered. "Bring the signed documents to Nathan when you fly to Thelspoint tomorrow, and we can make sure that's the last flight you ever have to crew."

A Betrayer Comes Home

There was little Tal could rightly say to defend himself. He knew exactly who Theo was, who both of Bex's parents were. He had seen the contracts himself and understood just how exploitative they were. He even knew that his new contract might well contain language just as restrictive and controlling. These were bad people.

Yet that knowledge felt small in the face of what these bad people offered.

Pear raced quiet laps around the ceiling all night. Tal's eyes and mind followed him on his continuous revolutions.

There were other considerations besides the source of the offer. He still had to face the embarrassment of returning to a school where magic was status, and where he had little of either. Hopefully having a special place carved out for him meant he wouldn't have to show his lack of magic on a regular basis, but fear nagged at him.

All of these considerations were important. Tal knew that. But the single truth that his decision actually rested on was much simpler: If he accepted the offer, more than likely Bex would never speak to him again.

There were a million rational arguments, of both head and heart, why Tal should turn down the offer. As he gazed up into his ceiling, watching Pear flit past cracks that let in gentle drabs of moonlight, and which had on more than one occasion let in a stream of rainwater, he knew those rational arguments couldn't defeat the basic facts of his identity.

Nathan's voice permeated every thought. For some reason, Tal thought less about the profound lectures or moments of triumph than he did about one lesson during his second year. The class had been assigned a combined light- and languageworking that would take the text from a page and project it in colored lights in the air. From the languageworking perspective it was actually pretty simple, since they were working only with the actual written words rather than implied meanings, yet of the four students who had tried so far, none had come close to presenting the words correctly. The fifth student was a shaggy-haired boy named Larit, who had outpaced Tal in most languageworking tasks. Watching him try the exercise, though, made it clear that Larit couldn't figure out how to put the two schools of magic together. Blazing lights flashed above the paper, but they were nothing like words. Tal had raised his hand in a way that would've felt rude if not for the fact that, by this point in the class's collective failure, most students were either shouting unsolicited advice, or openly doing homework for other classes.

"Yes, Talarus?" Nathan said.

Tal's fifteen-year-old body was still getting used to his last growth spurt, and as a result he rattled his desk with a wayward knee as he stood.

"Can we try it together?" Tal asked. "There are two areas of magic required, so maybe right now we need two mages."

Nathan studied Tal with eyes that could either have been suspicious or intrigued. He gestured for Tal to join Larit at the lectern.

"Thanks for the assist," Larit said, spraying another smattering of sparks. "I'm dying up here."

"No promises. Just follow my lead."

Tal stared down at the paper. It was a single sentence, chosen at random from one of their textbooks. Tal looked hard enough that he could have recited the boring words from memory. Then he dug deep into his languageworking, laying out the words in his mind. He laid this image over a simple plantworking focused on the lectern's grainy wood. Larit started as the wood bent, the words transcribing themselves into the wood exactly as they were on the paper. Larit was puzzled, but a breath from Nathan told him he was on the right track.

"Now, take your focus off the page," Tal said. "You're a strong enough lightworker to mirror something as basic as shapes in wood, right?"

Larit continued to stare. The classroom had gone quiet. Then Larit's shaggy hair was bobbing as he nodded. He put his concentration toward the wood.

Then, in the air, the single sentence chosen at random from their textbook projected itself in blue light. At least one student gasped.

"Why in the name of Varai did that work?" Larit asked.

Nathan was smiling broadly. Tal could have tried to give an explanation, but Nathan would explain it better than he ever could.

"Talarus cut the languageworking out of the equation," Nathan said, speaking to the whole classroom, whose attention had returned now that it was clear the assigned task was possible. "Every single one of you saw that sentence not as words on a page, but as a sentence of text, with its own meanings and associations. Talarus's minor act of vandalism presented the reality that, yes, they are words on a page, but the words are also a collection of shapes—not prefixes or suffixes, or even letters. They are as much ink as they are meaning. All Talarus did was demonstrate that."

Larit nodded, understanding blooming. Tal smiled.

That was the thing that was so hard to describe about magic. A lot of times it wasn't about what you could do, not really. Mostly it was about a minor insight, a spark of understanding about the way the world worked. A moment of recognition. This was what Nathan had shown him in nearly every lesson, that the world could be understood at the most minute level, figured out and offered up to others by way of magic.

In every thought about his future, the fact remained that this way of viewing the world, the way of seeing and understanding that Nathan had kindled within him, was still part of Tal. His magic may have left him, but Tal was still a mage.

He had chosen the mage's life long ago, and it was worth giving up everything to reclaim it.

Even Bex.

Tal's racing mind was no longer the reason he couldn't sleep. Now he couldn't sleep because of the tears stinging his eyes.

When Tal arrived at work the following morning, he had three large bags with him. Claret, who had just as many bags, eyed them suspiciously as Tal secured the luggage in the compartment near Ronar's tail.

He hadn't seen Bex before he left. She would be working out a way to use the dragon speech device to override the contracts, or at the very least determining if such a device was possible to use under the contracts. She wouldn't know he had gone for good until she received the letter that Tal spent most of the flight composing in his head. At a certain point the dozens of potential apologies became so overwhelming that he abruptly got up from his flight attendant's seat and walked back to the cabin.

Thankfully, Enna was on this flight. Beside her, its gelatinous form somehow strapped into the seat, was the Trug who had joined the protests weeks ago.

"Tal, this is Simon," Enna said, indicating the Trug. "He doesn't speak, of course, but I've been getting to know him in my own way."

"Good to meet you, Simon." The Trug extended a piece of its gray body, morphing until it almost looked like a human hand. It was the same metamorphosis the Trug had used in order to hand Tal its ticket. The Trug waved.

"Do you mind if I join you?" Tal asked.

He sat next to Enna, with Simon on her opposite side.

"It's getting cold out there," Enna said. "The first nips of winter in the air, especially up here."

"Yeah, it's much better inside." Compared to the sometimes oppressive heat of the dragon's back in the summer, now the cabin was comfortably warm.

"I noticed you brought along quite a lot of bags," Enna said. "Are you going on vacation?"

"As nice as a vacation sounds, I've actually had an opportunity to go back to the university."

Enna's face betrayed an edge of disappointment as she said, "Oh Tal, that's wonderful. So the spheres I gave you are glowing, I presume?"

Tal reached into his pocket and took out one of the spheres. He'd kept all of them with him, despite the fact that they were heavy and had no immediate use. The sphere glowed. Not brightly, but enough. There was magic in Tal, whether it manifested in one way or a hundred. That glow felt like fate. Enna looked satisfied. Satisfied, and still disappointed.

"Well, I suppose they'll have to find a new flight attendant," she said.

"I'm sure they can find one who actually likes flying."

"But not likely one who can talk to dragons," Enna noted.

"You never know."

Enna gave him a look that dismissed any possibility of him being anything but one of a kind. Tal found himself unsurprised that Enna knew his secret. Comprehension of things she had no business knowing covered this woman like scales on a dragon.

"I'll miss seeing you on my weekly flights," Enna said. "When you get to my age, you start valuing the friendly faces."

The sting in Tal's chest struck him as slightly unreasonable. "I'll be sure to catch a flight the next time I need to come back to Upper Boden."

"Ronar must be even sadder than the rest of us," Enna said.

Oh boy. Tal stared forward through the glass at the front of the cabin. He could just make out the tips of Ronar's horns, undulating as the dragon pumped his wings. He hadn't told Ronar, and the idea that he should have made that unreasonable sting feel even stronger. Enna didn't comment on Tal's sheepish expression. There was a definite downside to befriending older women, especially if one was looking to avoid accountability.

"Well, I guess I'd better be having a conversation with a dragon," Tal said through a sigh. The Trug gurgled encouragingly. Of course the blob was on Enna's side.

"I think that would be wise," Enna replied sweetly. "You wouldn't want him to be upset. I've heard dragons hold a grudge like no other creature. That, and they have very large teeth."

Tal rose. "I'll do it out of respect for the teeth."

He took his time navigating back to Ronar's head, double-checking the clips on his safety harness the way he had the first time he flew, before the interchange of clips became so second nature that he didn't bother making sure the next one was attached before the previous one unclasped. His thoughts of Bex made his hands clumsy, his steps along Ronar's back unsure. He already missed her.

The Scythe stretched wide below them. Hammer Top was smokier than usual, and Tal wondered if they were due for an eruption. If so, it would be twilight in Thelspoint for weeks, depending on the wind's whims.

Thelspoint. For the first time in ages, the thought of the city conjured an image untainted by dread and regret. Its silver spires now seemed to suggest that he could climb as high as he wished.

He was going home.

"Hey Ro," Tal said as he took his seat. "Turbulence not too bad?"

There had been storms in the area, but thus far there hadn't been any wind gusts powerful enough to cause more than a small bump during the flight.

I have compensated appropriately when I feel a disturbance, Ronar said. *I am a professional, after all.*

Tal snorted. "I sort of have something I need to tell you, related to that."

Ronar waited. There was more tension than Tal would've expected in his posture.

"I'm leaving, Ro. I'm going back to the university."

The dragon said nothing.

"I needed to tell you that this will be our last flight together."

Ronar still hadn't responded when the cabin shuddered. A wave of turbulence bounced Ronar several feet upward before he could steady himself.

See what happens when you break a professional's concentration? Ronar asked.

"I'm sorry, Ro, I really am."

An opportunity is an opportunity. I will be sorry to have to take on a new flight attendant. You were kinder than most. His use of the past tense tore through Tal.

"You've been an incredible partner. At times you were the only person I could talk to."

Even before I could talk back. Ronar barked a laugh. Tal ran his hand along the scales next to the seat. They softened beneath his palm.

"Even then," Tal said. "Maybe especially then. Sorry I was such a sad sack."

Does that imply that you are now a happy sack?

Whatever he was feeling, from the anticipation, to the pain of what his decision meant, a dragon's corny humor certainly helped. "I promise I'll get you one last short rib meal before I go. How about that?"

Ronar nodded his massive head. For the first time since Tal had known him, he actually breathed a spout of fire. Gasps of surprise sounded from the cabin. Fire streamed below them, eventually burning itself out and leaving only a wisp of smoke behind. They fell a few feet as the buoyancy of Ronar's body changed.

"I feel the same way," Tal said with a smile.

Know that one more kind gesture doesn't mean you aren't abandoning me to what will likely be a future of being flown by an incompetent rider. You are well-versed in kind gestures, but there are other forms of kindness. I will not lecture you on how these differ.

Tal wished he didn't feel an indictment in these words, one that went beyond the fact that Ronar would now have to suffer a new flight attendant.

There is more. To learn our speech and cross the mind bridge of dragon communication means that you are no longer only human. You are a dragon thing.

A dragon thing, every bit as much as a snapdragon or a wyvern. Maybe more so because of your slightly higher intelligence. Ronar chuckled, shaking the straps on Tal's harness. *I believe you are akin to a hatchling, and I would expect that your words will hold more weight with dragon kind than most other humans, even if they are the words of a newborn.*

Tal nodded. Against the age, wisdom, and power of even the smallest dragon, he did feel every bit a newborn.

"Thank you, Ro, for everything." He stroked Ronar's scales one more time.

T he approach to Thelspoint felt like a fated return. Ronar did his part, swinging wide for the best possible view of the city. How had Tal not noticed how warm each building looked, how the very thrum of magic coming off the streets was an invitation? How had he ever blanched at this beautiful sight?

As Tal helped Enna down off Ronar's back—the Trug had disembarked first, sliding down Ronar's leg and landing with a squelch in the dirt—she handed him one last sphere. This one was perhaps three times as broad as the others, and shaded red.

"I thought your magic might return," Enna said. "It's always hard to tell what form it will take. This will help show you the form."

Tal took the sphere into hopeful hands. Enna's spheres had been one of the only things that allowed him to believe in his own magic, such as it was.

"This reminds me of a device the university gave to first-year students," Tal said. "It resonated when you used the type of working you were best suited for."

Enna smiled. "Come, you didn't expect me to actually tell you how it worked, did you?"

"No, that's never been your style."

"Exactly. I must remain helpful but unclear even as we go our separate ways."

At the mention of going their separate ways, Tal felt an unexpected pang of loss. He had half a mind to ask Enna for her address so he could write to her, but there was still at least a shred of professionalism in him, which felt like a last wall against this type of intimacy.

"Don't look rueful," Enna said. "You have to follow your path to know where it ends up."

With that, she pointed to the large sphere—which had taken on a slightly greener tinge in Tal's hands—nodded deeply, and turned to go.

Tal watched the gate close behind the passengers. The excitement of his reentry into the university had been joined by a deep hollowness. He set about his business, helping to unbridle and wash Ronar for the last time. It was a task both easy and familiar, leaving far too much room for thoughts of Bex to creep in. He looped the driver's harness onto its holder against the wall of the stable, and thought about Bex's passion, likely now turning to anger directed his way. He dumped out a bucket of graying, sudsy water, and thought about how it wasn't too late to decline Theo's offer. He filed Ronar's nails, knowing none of these thoughts could derail him from the path before him. The path he should have been on all along.

Before he could return to the university, Tal had to go into the Dragon Air office to submit his formal resignation. It was wildly short notice, but Tal had been assured that Theo had written ahead to inform Pieter and the rest of Dragon Air's management of the circumstances. Perhaps most relevant, Heathermark Flight Group had already paid out the remainder of Tal's contract, as well as two weeks' worth of lost revenue from the flights Tal would've helmed.

They'll probably just cancel the entire route and not even bother replacing me, Tal thought. Dragon Air had an allergy to training new hires, often allowing empty roles to go unfilled until flights were missed or bridles snapped. *I guess that's their choice. All we're doing is flying people thousands of feet in the air on top of scaly beasts. Who are we to expect that process be well-maintained?*

The Dragon Air office was just as dingy as it had been the last time he visited. At some point in the interim there had been a staff party, and the remains of a pile of chocolate cookies—likely seconds from the local baker if their irregular shapes were any indication—were strewn on nearly every surface. Tal picked one up, finding it rock hard. He was surprised none of them had molded, although Tal supposed it was unlikely that pastries as desiccated as these could grow much of anything.

He found Pieter in his office. The manager had obviously been waiting for him, as he waved Tal in before he could knock. His pinched face scrutinized Tal, nostrils flaring and collapsing as if trying to smell his employee's alleged magic.

"I hear you're abandoning us," Pieter said. As usual there was nowhere to sit. Now that he was no longer in need of this man's approval, Tal found himself standing straighter.

"You received the letter from Heathermark Flight Group?"

"The letter from the enemy? Yes, I seem to recall that one." Pieter sneered. "They paid through the nose to get you out of your contract. I always knew they had no sense of how to handle a budget, but the sum strikes me as extraordinary, even by their standards."

"Glad to be valued."

Pieter scoffed. "Overvalued."

"So I'm released from my contract?"

"Of course. You're paid out. You never have to step foot on a dragon again."

There was something else he needed to address before he could go. He could still try to help Bex's cause, even as he left her behind.

"I have one proposition for you, before I go," Tal said, unclasping his hands and running them through his hair. "Really more of a suggestion to improve the business."

"With the money Heathermark gave me, you could suggest we shut down operations entirely and I'd listen," Pieter said.

"Don't do that." Tal forced a smile. "It's about the contracts. We managed to get access to the device that allows humans to speak with dragons."

Seeing Pieter's face darken, Tal quickly continued: "We talked to Ronar, and he has no problem with the current contract. It seems unlikely you'd have to make many concessions if you allowed the dragons to speak their mind."

Pieter chewed this over.

"Not only that," Tal said, "but we learned some very interesting things about Heathermark's contracts."

"Those contracts are secret, kept under lock and key," Pieter shot back.

"They are, unless you have someone on the inside who can show them to you. And let's just say that you have the opportunity to cast yourselves as the most dragon-friendly airline in operation."

Pieter stared at him blankly. It took Tal three deep breaths to prevent himself from saying anything he would regret. Instead, he said: "If you use the device, and quietly leak rumors that Heathermark is so restrictive that no dragon in their right mind would want to sign up, you'd have first pick of any dragon. You would not just have access to the best talent, the best flyers. You could also cut your rates since Heathermark will have to pay a huge premium to lure in any new dragons with their current practices."

Pieter's eyes glowed at the mention of this cost-saving measure.

"What," he asked carefully, "are the exact practices Heathermark has been engaging in?"

By one measure, Tal had done right by Bex. Pieter had agreed to expand use of the device as long as he didn't have to pay for it, and would begin spreading word of Heathermark's dangerous contracts throughout the dragon employment networks. By another measure, Tal had given Pieter the exact blueprint he could use to further exploit the dragons, just as Heathermark had. Tal found this darker scenario unlikely, not least because the workings required for the Heathermark contracts had required a mage of great skill. And where there was great skill, there was usually a large fee, and where there was a large fee, Dragon Air was rarely to be found.

The approach to the university made the entire decision to leave Upper Boden worth it. It was the first truly cold evening of fall. He had stopped in one of the expensive shops in the Triangle to buy a new sweater—navy blue, with leather shoulders and the high neck that was in style this season—and felt for the first time in a long time like he belonged in Thelspoint. This feeling only increased when not just Nathan, but a whole group of faculty and students met him at the main entrance to the university.

Tal recognized some of the faculty. Maeve was primarily part of the languageworking faculty but also taught parttime in lightworking. Warbus was not much shy of four feet tall, and had given Tal an A+ in bioworking in his fourth year. Tal was also introduced to a new professor named Helena, who specialized in fireworkings. The students were all new to Tal, at most vaguely familiar from the blur of underclassmen during his last couple years there. Each professor had collected the best and brightest from their respective departments to meet him. Nathan was certainly pulling out all the stops.

"An independent study, I can't believe it," said a student named Clem after they'd been introduced. She had rosy cheeks and spoke so quickly that she ran out of breath. "I applied for one in fireworking last year, but they said I would have to complete my distribution requirements instead, like everyone else."

"I've been told I'm a special case," Tal said, trying to avoid mentioning his lack of other magic, and only too late realizing that his obfuscations primarily served to make him sound incredibly entitled. He changed course. "They realized if they wanted me to do my research, they'd have to find a solution that didn't require me to fail three other classes."

"Talarus is being modest," Nathan said, leading the unwieldy pack past the entrance to the Symposium Hall, and up to the Head of School's office. "He aced every class he took during his first stint as a student."

Tal didn't think this was helpful. He also didn't particularly want to risk the students starting to call him Talarus.

Soon he had something more pressing to worry about, in the shape of Meret stepping out from a stairway as they turned onto the Head of School's corridor.

"Ah good, the final member of our group," Nathan said with forced brightness.

Meret fell into step with an expression that suggested he'd rather be anywhere else.

"You're signed on for this independent study nonsense?" Tal asked.

"Don't gloat," Meret shot back, not bothering to keep his voice down, so the rest of the group surely heard every word despite the clacking of their shoes against the stone floors. "You have apparently stumbled across a once in a generation gift. If it has anything to do with languageworking, I'd be foolish not to claim at least some of the plaudits."

Tal restrained himself from rolling his eyes.

"If only we all had such an admirable commitment to our academics," Nathan said dryly, effectively—and thankfully—ending the conversation.

There was paperwork to sign in the Head of School's office. The group of twelve fit easily inside the vast, mostly unfurnished room. The Head of School was an old mage named Bonnett, whose office contained dozens of improbably large indoor trees that were just as withered as he was. No one was really sure why he hadn't retired, as he had long since lost his hearing and the ability to remember names. He mostly relied on his assistants to put the correct papers in front of him. As a result, it was extremely difficult to get any new policy approved, as the trustees wouldn't allow anything in front of him without their consent. This made the fact that Bex's parents and Nathan had managed to get Tal's return approved all the more impressive.

Bonnett didn't make much of an occasion out of the paperwork signing, but as Tal scrawled his full name over the final sheet of parchment, the gathered crowd clapped, with Meret's sarcastic claps ringing long after everyone else's.

Bonnett didn't ask for clarification, despite the look of confusion on his face. Instead, he said: "Thelspoint University is committed to occupying the cutting edge of magical research. The ability you have demonstrated to speak with dragons may prove to be a watershed moment for relations between our species. Understanding dragon speech, and ultimately determining how to share this ability, is your sole reason for being here. I hope you will be able to retain your focus, even as the typical students go about very different lives around you."

There was an edge to Bonnett's words, a sharpness that suggested he knew more than he let on.

"The students and faculty we have gathered here today hope to be the first to share this knowledge," Nathan said. "They all recognize just how important this moment could be."

"Yes, both in terms of relations between humans and dragons and the academic career of the person responsible for bringing this talent forth," Bonnett said, examining the papers one last time. Satisfied, he closed them into a drawer on his desk.

Nathan didn't respond to the barb. He clapped Tal on the back in a way that managed to be collegial rather than overly informal. "Welcome back to the university."

Despite the gathered audience, despite the grave words, and despite what he had left behind in Upper Boden, Tal felt the happy sting of tears. Someone in the back of the group spoke, and a moment later Clem was passing something forward. Tal took it. It was a handkerchief to wipe his eyes.

A Dubious
Transmutation

Fortunately, Tal managed to keep his emotional outbursts limited to the one moment in the Head of School's office that evening. Insisting that he must be tired, Nathan shooed away the rest of the . . . what to even call them? Acolytes? Sycophants? No matter what he called them, Tal was crestfallen to find that Meret was responsible for leading him to his new room in the upperclassmen apartments. Only students in their last few years, most of whom were well into their twenties, lived in these apartments. His was actually three connected rooms sprawling over close to eight-hundred square feet, between a bedroom, a joint living and dining room, and a washroom with a bath so deep he could've stood up in it and kept his shoulders underwater.

Meret was strained as he led Tal through the dorm, halfheartedly noting as they passed his own room. The festivities and attention Tal was receiving seemed to have deflated him. As Meret showed Tal his room and tossed him a set of keys, Tal paused in the doorway.

"Meret, can I ask you a question?"

"Of course." Meret's black hair was roughly parted in the middle and fell to his shoulders. His habit of running his hands through it was even more pronounced than usual.

"What has everyone been told, you know, about me? About my abilities?"

"We were told you had somehow experienced a transmutation of your powers. That your ordinary magic has been changed—how exactly they didn't tell us—into an ability to understand dragon speech."

A transmutation. Nathan had always known how to spin a narrative, especially in an academic setting. This explanation would go a long way toward preventing awkward questions about his missing magic.

"That's exactly right, I'm glad that was made clear," Tal said. "Thank you, Meret."

Meret smiled at Tal's relief. "It's what we've been told." The smile sharpened into something cruel and unforgiving. "Whether it's what we believe is another matter."

Tal shut the door as quickly as he could.

Tal felt as if he'd stumbled into a dream. Given what Tal's dreams were usually like, this typically would've entailed some horrible threat that he could only stop with the use of simple magic. The threat would then inevitably eat, maim, or slowly suffocate him as his magic failed to protect him. This, however, was another type of dream altogether, one he hadn't allowed himself to dream—in his waking hours or his sleeping ones—since he had left the university. It was the dream of once again demonstrating something no one had believed possible, of making magic come alive in himself and others.

He sank into the four-poster bed that had been made up for him. The last two years on Ronar's back already felt like a distant memory. The university's dorms were never as silent as nights in Upper Boden, yet in the warmth of the magic around him, Tal fell asleep easily.

When he did dream, it was of Bex's face, suspended above a lake. Reflected in the dark water were hundreds and hundreds of dragons.

The next morning the same group as before met in Nathan's classroom an hour before the regular start of classes. Nathan laid out his intentions.

"The students and faculty gathered here represent the best across every discipline that has potential overlap with dragon speech. I have collected others from languageworking—thank you for joining us, Maeve—who obviously have an interest in any kind of speech. I asked Warbus to bring his bioworking expertise to bear, as the biology of dragons surely dictates how their speech functions. Just as we have vocal cords, there must be a speaking apparatus that can be defined once we understand what dragons are saying. And finally, Helena is from the fireworking faculty. I must admit that this connection is somewhat more tenuous, since we don't know how dragon fire would be involved in their speech. We cannot, however, rule out any avenue of inquiry."

"I also have more experience than most with dragons," Helena interjected from the third row. She had a thick, harsh accent. It sounded northern, perhaps as far north as the neighboring country of Mithlein, the Ts and Rs almost guttural and the vowels seeming to stretch on forever. "I spent eight years in the Claglands while I completed my research."

It was strange to see professors sitting at the desks around the semi-circular lecture hall as if they were students. Though Helena couldn't be more than a decade older than a student, despite the time she'd spent with the dragons, it was still rather like seeing an adult sit in a rocking chair designed for a six-year-old.

"Thank you for that clarification, Helena," Nathan continued. "In her new research, Helena has advanced a theory that dragons' fire, rather than a biological process, is actually a function of a complex system of fireworkings. Truly cutting-edge stuff. I thought it prudent to avail ourselves of her expertise."

Tal noted that Warbus had bristled at the mention of Helena's study. Helena's theory had probably caused some unpleasant ripples in the community of bioworking scholars. Tal almost laughed. He'd spent little time missing the academic rivalries between high-profile scholars at the university, yet now he found them almost comforting.

"The goal is for Talarus to introduce each of us to his dragon speech abilities in whatever way he can," Nathan said. "I will ask him to schedule time with each of you—faculty and students together from each department, if possible—to see how your discipline might overlap with his. He has no curriculum for this independent study, so I expect him to use these regular meetings with you to guide his inquiry. Should it be deemed that one area of study is more relevant than others, he may decide to spend more time with the students and faculty from that department. Or to drop one discipline altogether."

"Nathan's students always remark on his ability to provide rigid structure," Tal said.

Nathan laughed. "The ability to provide *the structure they need*, not structure for structure's sake."

"Truly, thank you for setting this up," Tal said. All attention turned toward him. Tal's legs decided of their own accord that it was an appropriate time to stand. "I want to thank you all for being here as well. I know how busy university life can be. Squeezing in one more project must seem a near impossibility for many of you. I promise I won't take up more of your time or effort than I absolutely need to."

"It's no burden!" said Clem, who looked very comfortable in the front row. Murmurs of agreement bounced around the auditorium. Meret did not join in.

Tal continued: "The truth is, there's no textbook for understanding dragon speech, no theoretical basis for why it's even possible. We will do our best to create that understanding. I do need to be honest, though. I myself have no idea how any of this works, even after communicating with several different dragons. I fully expect our first flailing attempts to make minimal progress. But if we achieve even a shred of understanding, I think it will have been worth it."

"Thank you, Talarus, for the reminder," Nathan said. "Because of the unusual circumstances, also know that no grades will be given. We do what we do for the good of mankind and for the promise of furthering our knowledge. As such, effective collaboration is its own reward."

A wide, self-satisfied smile grew across Helena's face. She obviously understood, just as Bonnett had said, that the reward for being part of such a landmark study went far beyond any academic grade or credit.

All of Tal's previous work was in a classroom setting, or as Nathan's assistant. Did conducting your own research into something important always feel this free, this disorganized, this exhilarating?

"Unless anyone has any questions, we can start scheduling the recurring sessions," Nathan said.

The next twenty minutes were lost to logistics as they jockeyed for the precise times that would work for all involved. At the end of it, Tal had a weekly schedule on a piece of parchment. He was reminded of the excitement he'd felt at the beginning of each term when he received his schedule, comparing it among friends to see who had been placed in the same sessions, working out how to get between classes in time and identifying which free blocks could be used for extracurricular activities and which would need to be saved for studying.

As the others filed out on the way to their first classes of the day, Nathan stayed behind, leaning over Tal's desk.

"Is this the grand return you imagined?" Nathan asked.

"Mostly I just wanted *a* return. I wasn't really expecting it to involve cutting-edge research."

"I hope you don't feel I'm being hyperbolic," Nathan said. "It is important work that no one has ever done before. However, the world will continue to turn even if we fail."

Tal thought about this, then pictured the dragon scorching his way across Braisecroft. What would happen if the dragons decided all humans were to blame for their treatment, not just a select few?

"How are you settling in?" Nathan asked. "Any culture shock?"

"It's strange. Most of the faculty are the same, as well as many of the students. Between those who have graduated, and everyone else getting older, it's like it's entirely the same place, only populated by different people. Even stranger is that some of the younger students, ones who I could never have possibly met, remind me of the students that came before them. It's like there are molds for the people here, they just get swapped out with different individuals."

"The recurring cycle every teacher experiences," Nathan replied. "I see how it could be jarring at first. The essence of the place stays the same, even as the individuals within it change."

"It's enough to make you wonder if one person being here actually matters." Tal wasn't precisely sure what he meant by this. "Don't listen to me, I'm still just feeling a little displaced."

Nathan patted his arm fondly. "A little displacement isn't such a bad thing, as long as you know deep down that you are where you belong."

Tal nodded, feeling the truth, and the betrayal, in those words.

Research and Capabilities

T al began each of his collaborative research sessions with the distinct sense that he had no idea what he was doing. It didn't help that students and faculty alike followed his lead on how the sessions should be formatted, how they should endeavor to connect dragon speech with their areas of study. Under Tal's guidance, the connections made amounted to exactly the same number of insights they'd had before the project had begun. The only consolation was that they hadn't actually erased any knowledge from human understanding, even if the looks Meret shot him during their sessions indicated otherwise.

The fireworking lab was a rectangular room constructed entirely out of stone and thick mortar. Every object in the room was either made out of non-flammable material, or had been fireworked to resist burning. Today Helena, Clem, and two younger male students stood around a lit brazier in the center of the room. There was no obvious fuel source.

"So, what shall we do today, Tal who speaks to dragons?" Helena asked.

"I'm open to suggestions," Tal said. "This morning with Warbus we spent most of the time looking at a dragon skeleton." He didn't add that they'd gotten precisely nowhere.

"A dead dragon isn't likely to reveal many secrets," Helena said. "They are beings of enormous magic. Even if they do have a habit of building their spires out of the bones of their dead, when they die, their magic leaves them, just as it leaves us when we die."

"That's why we're exploring fireworking," Clem said. "Dragon speech could very well be a product of their magic." The way she jumped to back up her teacher told Tal a great deal about their dynamic. They introduced the two younger students, who were research assistants assigned to the lab.

"There's always the possibility that it's part of their magic, but that the magic doesn't involve fireworking," Tal said.

"Failure is always a possibility," Helena said with a confidence that indicated this was a true statement in general, but not one that need apply to her in particular.

"I stayed up until three o'clock this morning coming up with research plans," Clem volunteered. "Your arrival was so sudden, I would've liked more time to prepare."

"Let's use one of those plans, then," Tal said. "You're clearly more prepared than I am."

Clem beamed. She had a plainly pretty, inquisitive face. Her jaw-length brown hair looked like it had been cut by someone with a crick in their neck.

Tal wouldn't have thought to try the initial test, which involved Helena, Clem, the assistants, or some combination of all four whipping fire into specific configurations, and asking Tal to identify if there was anything like dragon speech coming from it.

"We want to see whether fireworking itself is the language." Clem smiled as she explained things, as if magical research was the most exciting thing one could possibly be doing on a Wednesday afternoon.

"I do not expect this to work, to be clear," Helena said.

Helena's doubts did nothing to perturb her student. "I doubt it will work, either! But you have to cover the basics before you can move on to more complex topics."

Tal concentrated on the heat in front of him. Clem shaped the fire from the brazier into a rough sphere, which turned gently over itself in a tight circle. It was strange trying to interpret language from a ball of fire. In truth, Tal wasn't used to needing to concentrate hard to interpret dragon speech. It just came to him, whether he wanted to understand or not.

As a result, this line of research felt uniquely pointless. He stared into the flames until his eyes watered, until deep afterimages burned in his vision. The others manipulated the flames into multiple spheres at once, into curling vines, even into the shape of a miniature dragon.

Neither Helena nor Clem showed any obvious concern that Tal had no reaction to the flames. Clem struck down notes in shorthand while maintaining control over the fireworkings. The flames came as naturally to her as any magic had ever come to Tal.

It was hard to think about magic coming easily now. Now it was just like any other unpredictable force. At least the fireworking classroom was equipped with dozens of sheets of fireweave, a thick fabric that could encase a person in a fireworked barrier that would temporarily protect them from flame. Tal had once seen a first-year student coated in the stuff. They looked like they'd been turned into stone, stuck inside the tough weave until someone pried it off them. Tal would've preferred to control the fire itself rather than relying on emergency magical items.

"I don't know how much you remember from your fireworking training, but we often think about the heart of the flame," Helena said. "We think of it not as a physical heart, but an actual spark of consciousness at the center of the fire. Fire has a will, much like a living creature."

"Like a dragon's will."

"Precisely. My research suggests that the will of the fire and the will of the dragon are intertwined, that the ability of the dragon to translate its will into flame form is what gives them the ability to breathe fire and survive the inferno in their chest."

"Let me see if I've got this right," Tal said. "This may be factually completely incorrect, but my abilities encompass not just dragons, but also snapdragons, wyverns, any direct relative of a dragon. I'm going to try to interpret the fire as their relative as well."

Tal couldn't tell if Clem's gape was horror or excitement at a new theoretical possibility. Helena's narrow eyes were so intimidating that Tal wasn't surprised she'd spent years staring down dragons.

Once again the assistants shaped the fire, this time bouncing a single ball from side to side. Tal removed his focus from its physical location, trying to focus instead on its trajectory. The fire was acting on the will of the two assistants, their joint input telling the flames which way to move. Within this motion there must be some semblance of the flame's own intent.

There. At the end point of each turn, there was a moment where the flame seemed to pause. It gathered its momentum, and then rocketed back in the other direction. In reality the flame hadn't stopped for more than a millisecond. Yet he was sure the intention within the flames was pausing.

Tal recoiled. Clem clapped her hands together.

"You felt something, didn't you?" she asked.

Tal nodded, not ready to put it into words.

It was possible that he'd felt something dragonish within the fire. It was also possible that his other magical powers were returning.

Tal wrapped himself in a mental layer of fireweave to protect himself from ruminating on what he'd felt in the fireworking session. Instead of thinking, he dove into the next day's languageworking with Nathan and Meret. Meret had already familiarized himself with the tests they'd run on Pear and the other snapdragons. In contrast to Clem's sharp, eager presence, Meret was always calm in his studies. He approached his work with the coldness of someone fully in charge of his power, with no need to go out of his way to show it off.

"The challenge, as I understand it, is that we have no means of translating the components of dragon speech into the components of human speech," Nathan said. "This means that we cannot construct a reliable codex to translate between them. Even if we did, the components would be recognizable only to someone like Tal, who can already understand the speech itself, making such a codex redundant."

"So the whole venture is pointless?" Tal asked.

"If we discover nothing about how the power works, then yes," Meret retorted.

"You might have a little too much faith in me," Tal said.

"I have faith in giving things a shot rather than giving up."

Nathan smiled, and so did Tal. Meret had obviously come to replace Tal as Nathan's protégé within languageworking. Tal thought that was as far as it went. He saw nothing like the warmth Nathan often showed Tal. For his part, Meret gave no signs of worry at Tal's return. It made sense. In Meret's mind, excellence with languageworking was all that mattered. Because Tal had his own separate abilities, they could complement each other rather than competing. The coldness of that calculation might benefit Tal at the moment. Fully trusting his former partner in magic, however, was another matter.

Many of their first attempts at translations mirrored those Nathan and Tal had already tried. All failed without fanfare. Pear once again played the role of the dragon, and his dancing words soon felt as much a part of Tal's thoughts as his own internal monologue.

Deep into the session, which had already run past the two-hour mark, Meret frowned.

"I believe we are reaching the line, Nathan," he said.

Tal was tired and frustrated by this point. There was a tinge of something sharp in his voice as he said, "What line would that be?"

"The line where an avenue of research should pause," Nathan said, "at the line between thoroughness and futility."

"I believe anyone who has studied languageworking for long is well-acquainted with that line," Meret said.

"We've certainly at least been introduced," Tal said. "I can tell it's close because the backs of my eyes feel like they're about to fall out and slide back into my brain."

"I'd let the bioworking faculty take a look at that," Nathan said.

"Because it's not remotely how eyes work?" Meret asked.

Nathan stood abruptly. "Punchiness is a strong indication that the line was crossed a long time ago, and we'd be better served with a warm cup of something caffeinated. Tea?"

They agreed, Meret saying that he didn't have any more classes that day, and they made for the teahouse together. This was such a normal occurrence in the university that it filled Tal's heart with warmth. Hours spent on academic study, minds growing tired together, the obvious solution an informal trip to one of the cozy teahouses around campus. They walked to the closest shop, which was tucked on a side street near the lightworking faculty's building, a square monstrosity that this time of year was still slate gray, but which would be slowly decorated by its students throughout the year as they manipulated its surface to reflect light in different patterns. After every graduation ceremony, it was wiped clean so that the next class could make its mark.

The three of them huddled into the back room of the teahouse around a steaming blue pot. The tea was an infused blend of black and herbal, with a smoky bite offset by a bright, sweet aftertaste. As was traditional, they talked about anything besides the research. Instead they gossiped about which faculty were fighting each other over grant money, what students in the languageworking discipline were "secretly" dating, and what outlandish article had been published in the *Thelspoint News Inquirer* that morning.

Usually the nature of the conversation would have allowed Tal to relax, but with a little space, everything in the teahouse reminded him of Bex. The server could be Mora delivering a pot to Bex's table. The tap of feet on the planks behind him could be announcing her arrival. Or a bespectacled face appearing in the doorway might shine, for a moment, like hers did.

Even though their research had been fruitless thus far, Nathan accepted Tal implicitly back in the university milieu. Meret, on the other hand, spent a little too much time taking jabs at Tal's persistent lack of magic. Every failure to further discern dragon speech was just another opportunity for Meret to gripe. He turned the conversation back to their research as steam rose from his teacup.

"I suppose what I keep coming back to is the ability for every kind of working to be explained," Meret said to Nathan, with a scholarly tone that elided the fact that the subject of their study was sitting at the table beside him. "Take bioworking, for example. You talk to any bioworker, and they will tell you that within their magic they can sense at the very least the organs of whatever being they're working on, and in some cases even the individual cells. The way Tal describes dragon speech lacks any such framework."

"An instinctive understanding is still an understanding," Nathan said.

In their occasional spats, Nathan usually took Tal's side. He apparently felt, however, that it was within Meret's right to have reservations about the research itself. Even when those reservations implied a lack of confidence in Tal.

"Sure, but it lacks rigor," Meret said. "Sorry Tal, but it does."

"I mean, I agree with you," Tal said.

Nathan flashed Tal a disapproving look. "You are referring to research with clearly defined parameters and measurements. Exploratory research is different. What we do now is generating hypotheses, not divining solutions."

"So we're not going to actually come to any conclusions?" Meret asked. "We're just going to stroke each other's egos while not actually solving any-thing?"

"This is the process," Nathan said. "You may not like it, but I don't need you to like it. I just need you to shut up and follow it."

Tal bit his lip, suppressing a laugh. Though Nathan was clearly as frustrated by the lack of progress as Meret was, this was a rather entertaining way for that frustration to manifest.

Nathan wasn't done: "The reason a bioworker can describe how their magic impacts an organism at a cellular level is that they have a vocabulary for those systems. It took a lot of research—like the research we're doing now—to create that vocabulary. Comparing a new field to an existing one, with existing language, frameworks, theories, and accepted truths, is simply shortsighted."

Meret held up his hands, conceding. "I just hope we show some sort of progress soon. That's all."

"I agree," Tal said. Then he did something that surprised even himself. He gave Meret a reassuring pat on the shoulder. Every single person at the table looked confused. And nobody addressed it.

As Tal walked back to his dorm, his boots scraping over cobblestones chilled by the autumn air, his collar pulled high against the breeze, he felt a peace he hadn't experienced in years.

Tal ensconced himself in the library, searching for any scrap of information about dragon communication. There was scant usable research on the subject. Since no one on record had ever been able to communicate with a dragon, previous scholars had approached the subject from an anthropological—dracopological?—lens. That meant there was plenty of information, including the studies published by Helena, about dragon rituals and the way their societies and family units were constructed, while there was very little about actual methods of communication. Some early scholars had even speculated that dragons possessed no speech at all. Tal made a note of these books and articles, and flagged them for the librarians to review. He had once kept a running tally of all the erroneous sources he had sent to be reviewed—not for removal, but to include a librarian's note within the source indicating the information was deemed incorrect or out of date. It felt powerful to once again be part of this ongoing conversation around the knowledge students consumed, the truth represented by the "official" sources.

Tal stayed at the library deep into the night. The huge space never closed, and there were always students about at all hours of the day and night, studying at the carrels in the honeycomb of the lower levels, or at the desks that ran along the edge of the rotunda. Tal preferred the rotunda seats, and would often look up into the frescos on the interior of the dome, which cast shimmering lights on the entryway six stories below. The lights changed depending on the day. This evening they bathed the whole ground floor in an aquatic glow. The frescos mostly depicted Varai in their various incarnations, many with head thrown back, mouth open as if receiving a morsel of pure knowledge from the sky. With the light dancing off Varai's robes, the god appeared to be walking straight off the ceiling and into the library.

Tal had temporarily set aside his books in order to do something he had been putting off for too long: composing a letter to Bex. He'd fed the first three drafts into the fireplace in the wall behind him. They had started out sappy, veered into self-righteous, and then took a turn into terse and boring. With the fourth draft, he thought he was close:

Dear Bex,

I am sorry for disappearing so suddenly. I wanted to explain what happened, though by now I would guess Enna has filled you in on everything. I understand the Dragon Air passenger/protester whisper network keeps all of you informed of my activities at all times. I don't think I ever really appreciated how your presences grounded me, at a time when my only real companion was a dragon (even if, for some reason, I could understand that dragon).

After the incident at Braisecroft, your parents made me an incredibly generous offer, to sponsor my return to the university as a student, with a special status to accommodate my "situation." I wanted with every fiber of my being to turn it down. I know you see them as the enemy, and of course I still do too. They have behaved in incredibly immoral ways, and clearly care nothing for the dragons who work for them. Yet in giving me this sponsorship, they have restored me to the life I always wanted. As soon as I returned to the university, I felt like myself again, fulfilled in a way I never was in Upper Boden. I trust you know me well enough to understand how much this change means to me.

I hope you can forgive me for taking this step. I am still in your corner when it comes to your work with the dragons, and I will do anything I can to further your cause. I think that my studies here, which concern dragon speech and the mechanisms that make it possible, may be of use in this regard. Time will tell.

Most of all, I would like to see you. You are welcome to visit the university any time. My new schedule is surprisingly full, but I could probably manage to visit Upper Boden if you are still there, and if you don't hate me so much that you never want to see me again.

Yours,

Tal

PS: Did you hear from Pieter about using the device to speak with the Dragon Air dragons? I believe I was able to convince him it was in everyone's (read: his) best interests.

Tal frowned down at the parchment. He thought about removing the phrase about her hating him, but decided better of it. It was a true sentiment. A couple quick tweaks to wording later, he was rolling the parchment up and stuffing it into a postal tube to send off to Upper Boden. Even after he stowed the tube under the desk, he kept picking it back up, opening it to pull the paper out, and then closing it again. He found having the tube with him so distracting that eventually he left all his belongings behind—theft was unheard of in the university—and went down to the mailroom off the first floor of the library.

The gnome behind the desk had been sleeping, and wasn't thrilled to be taking his mail at two o'clock in the morning. Tal had to repeat the address twice before the gnome could locate it in the file full of addresses and their relevant postal codes. Eventually he deposited it in a box marked "Express – Upper Boden." The express postage had cost extra, but Tal thought it as good a use as any for the stipend Bex's parents had given him. He would feel better when that note was in Bex's hands. And more importantly, when Bex finally sent him a reply.

If she sent him a reply.

Meret found Tal at his desk about half an hour later, and insisted on walking him back to their dorm.

"There's no test tomorrow," Meret said. "At least not for you. If you burn yourself out, we'll never discover anything worthwhile."

Tal didn't have the energy to protest. His mind wandered as Meret told him about his metalworking test the next day, about how his professor was such a stickler that a minor spelling mistake could result in a failing answer. Dim lights illuminated the roads leading back to the dorm. The chill in the air whispered of the first days of winter. At some point Meret stopped talking, leaving them to walk in an almost amiable silence.

Even though he knew the letter hadn't been mailed yet, part of Tal wanted to rush back to the post office to check if Bex's response had arrived. Most student mail was delivered directly to their rooms. He knew he would be at the post office every day anyway.

"You still with me, Tal?" Meret asked during a long silence in which Tal's face must have been showing his stricken, imagined reaction to receiving the news that Bex had branded him as her mortal enemy, and would not only no longer be speaking to him, but would also be working to destroy him and everything he held dear.

"Oh yeah, fine. Just a little tired. I think I overdid it with the studying. Attempting to understand dragon speech is hard even when there's a dragon involved, but when you're grasping at straws like we are, it's even more so. I'll be fine."

"Have a little faith," Meret said. "The rest of us are still mages, even if you're not."

"Thanks," Tal replied. "You're a beacon of joy as usual."

After the minimal progress of the first few days, Tal was surprised to find himself enjoying the repeated failing attempts to pull any meaning out of the other disciplines. The second weekend he was there, he went out to one of the student taverns with Meret and Clem. Meret had softened somewhat toward Tal. Tal suspected this mostly had to do with the fact that Tal was showing some signs of an exceptional form of magic in his ability to talk to dragons. If there was one thing Meret could connect with in a person, it was magical ability.

The only real breakthrough was the hint of fire speaking in the previous fireworking session, and it was hard to even classify it as a breakthrough. It was more like a suggestion of progress rather than progress itself.

In his free time, Tal tried his own basic fireworkings to see if he had indeed rekindled some of his previous aptitude. He tried to provoke the smallest change in an existing fire, which even first-year students could do without much trouble. He failed spectacularly. As much as it was a disappointment for Tal's personal magic, it was an encouraging sign that they were onto something when it came to the relationship between fireworking and dragon speech. In fact, Tal soon found that he could hear no hint of language in fire that wasn't actively undergoing a fireworking. Those limited meanings echoing within the flames must come from the fireworking's volitional action—in the conversation between human and fire.

That was as far as they'd gotten. They had no similar breakthroughs in bioworking, and the languageworking research was still stuck trying to pull consistent meanings from a single snapdragon phrase.

For all that, Tal found himself settling into comfortable rhythms, never dreading even the sessions he knew would go nowhere. The routine itself was enough. The university itself was enough.

The only urgency he felt was for a response from Bex. When a week had passed, he began to suspect there would never be one. He went to the post office every day, enduring constant jibes from the gnome behind the counter, who assured him that there couldn't possibly be anything so unimportant that someone would bother not sending him mail about it every day.

Because of this, Tal was feeling ready to throw something when Nathan called him into his office one day after a particularly unproductive language-working session. Meret's notes were scattered across his desk, a few badly crumpled, as if Nathan had taken out his frustration about the research on . . . well . . . the research.

"These damned snapdragons," Nathan said. Pear, who preferred Nathan's office to Tal's room, was zigzagging from beam to beam, ignoring Nathan's outburst.

"Do you need me to take him for a few days?" Tal asked.

"It's not his presence. Or I should say, it's not anything he's doing while he's present. It's what he's *not* doing. And maybe more importantly, the thing that he is not."

"The what?"

"He's not a dragon!" Nathan snapped. Pear stopped darting about long enough to give Nathan a withering look, before twisting into more flying loops.

"I think he knows that," Tal said.

"He doesn't know much of anything, including how to speak in full sentences. He is also completely unqualified when it comes to being a firebreather."

In response, Pear unleashed a tiny fireball. It blinked out into smoke in an instant.

"See what I mean?" Nathan's hair stood on end the way it did when he'd been running his hands compulsively through it. "If this line of inquiry with fireworking is real, we need the genuine article, a real dragon who can breathe fire, not a pale and very tiny imitation."

I'm tiny! Pear said.

"Yes you are," Tal replied without thinking. Then to Nathan: "I agree that it would be helpful to work with an actual dragon, but in case you forgot, I'm no longer a flight attendant. I don't have such ready access to dragons anymore."

"Maybe Helena does," Nathan suggested. "Though I believe her dragon 'friends' are mostly still in the Claglands. What if we tried some dragons a little closer to home?"

"Such as?"

"Your sponsors have access to dragons. Lots of dragons."

Tal blanched at the thought of asking Bex's parents for anything more. "Do you think they'll want their dragons being studied? They run such a tight ship over there, I'd be surprised if their dragons have the time."

Nathan studied Tal. Pear had settled into a makeshift nest on the top shelf of Nathan's bookcase. It was lined with paper that looked suspiciously like it had been ripped out of books.

"Are you scared of asking them?"

"Not scared. Just cognizant of what they've already done for me."

"They're financing your studies. Don't you think they'd want those studies to be effective?"

Tal's desire to be honest with his mentor ground against his pride. The truth was that he didn't know what Bex's parents wanted. It couldn't be purely a display of gratitude. Tal had the keen sense that Theo and Marjory would want him on hand and on their side if things took a further bad turn with the dragons, given that he was the one person who could even hear the demands of rebelling dragons. He also knew that, regardless of their motives, more favors would come with more strings, and more strings meant more alignment with the people Bex hated most.

But he couldn't turn down Nathan, either.

"You win, as usual," Tal said, leaning his head back and staring up at the ceiling. "We can send a courier over to see when they're in the Thelspoint offices."

"I already sent one. Theo is there today."

"Have I ever told you that you're a remarkably efficient individual? And I do mean that in the worst possible way."

"One man's efficiency is another man's attempt to control a world that is inherently chaotic," Nathan said.

"I'd advise you stick to languageworking rather than philosophy."

As Tal turned to go, Nathan's voice echoed behind him. "Talarus, I hope you will be able to treat Theo as merely a partner and potential academic resource. Not as the father of someone you have a relationship with."

A snake of anger burrowed under Tal's skin. He seethed as he stood in the doorway. How did Nathan know about Bex? A strange thought followed that question. What if part of her parents' intentions in sending Tal to the university had been to get him away from Bex?

Tal paused for far too long. "I wouldn't worry about that. She doesn't like me anymore anyway."

Nathan's fatherly eyes showed nothing but concern for Tal's happiness. "You know you have someone to talk to whenever you need me, right?"

Part of Tal wanted to go back into the room and give Nathan a hug. Instead he said, "I'm fine, I swear."

THE SPIRE

A cold rain lashed down, sending Tal back to his dorm to collect his jacket and change into winter boots before heading west to the Heathermark Flight Group offices. The tallest buildings in the city clustered at the western edge of Thelspoint, on a collection of plateaus with steep stairs between them, and a winding road around the cliff's edge to accommodate vehicles. The Spire was the highest of these plateaus. It was really more a collection of spires, the five tallest buildings in Thelspoint all standing within a quarter mile of each other, pressing upwards as if in constant competition to see which could penetrate the farthest into the clouds. None of their tops was visible through the rain. Tal stopped at the Overlook, the public park that ran all along the Spire's edge. Floral plantings flanked the smooth walkway curving above a drop to the next plateau. The true appeal of the Overlook was not the carefully manicured flowers, or the stately progression of plateaus, but rather the view of the ocean. From here, high on the cliff, visitors were treated to a dramatic view down the seawall. If there was ever any question that stoneworkings were required to keep the city standing, those questions were rendered ludicrous here, as the cliff became impossibly steep just below the third plateau, its slope almost concave, making the entire western portion of the city feel like it was about to slide off into the sea. Waves crashed below. The wind tore up the slope. Tucked into the cliff were dozens of military fortifications, where soldiers were ready to dive down to protect the city on wyverns or one of the larger hovercrafts that required four mages performing simultaneous windworkings to operate.

On clear days one could see all the way across the Scythe, but today Tal couldn't see more than a few hundred feet into the sea. Even the persistent presence of Hammer Top was only a suggestion against the haze over the bay. Tal hadn't been here in a long time, and regretted that his return hadn't come on a clear day. He would've liked to take Bex here, remembering their night atop the greenhouse. He quickly put this painful thought out of his mind.

The headquarters for Heathermark Flight Group was, of course, one of the five towers of the Spire. Two others were financial firms responsible for the majority of the gold in Thelspoint—and by extension the majority of the gold in Thelanel at large—one belonged to the mage-run construction firm that built most of the improbable buildings in the city, and the last held the offices for dozens of different companies, including newspapers, successful visual artists, and the largest book publishers. These industries were prestigious enough for the Spire, but not lucrative enough to have their own tower.

Heathermark Flight Group, on the other hand, was certainly lucrative enough to have its own tower. Everything about the tower brought the word *lucrative* to mind. From the shimmering fountains in the plaza out front, to the portico the size of three whole buildings anywhere else in the city, to the view up the tower, which revealed the building to be constructed out of what appeared to be a single blue-green sheet of rock, the money poured into this place continuously suggested: *Look at this, we don't even* need *all of this.*

The cavernous lobby was filled with the echoes of employees moving around the high atrium and across the marble lobby floor. Two dragon skeletons stood in the center. One of these skeletons sported the newest design of Heathermark's flight cabins, a curved, aerodynamic windshield giving way to wide, tinted windows at the side. The macabre display of a prototype on the skeleton seemed to state that, even in death, the airline could still find a way to profit off the dragons.

A petite woman with blonde hair cut into a smooth sphere approached him, heels clopping against the floor. Her robe was inlaid with an intricate pattern showing a dragon in flight. All the employees wore similar robes, with the shield-shaped Heathermark Flight Group logo on one shoulder.

"Talarus, thank you for coming," the woman said. "I'm Hanne."

"Oh, yes, nice to meet you."

She gave him a polished, patronizing smile. Between the smile and her imposingly straight posture, Tal felt himself unconsciously unslouching his own shoulders.

"If you'll come with me, Theo is expecting you."

Hanne led the way up a winding staircase around the edge of the atrium. The stairs were marble, with several workings on them, so that each step not only left a faint glowing footprint behind, but also pushed subtly upward. Hanne had no problem with the stairs, but Tal stumbled several times over the steps that refused to stay in one place.

"You've created quite a stir around here," Hanne said. Though she had obviously noticed his struggles, she had the decency not to comment.

"It was entirely by accident, I assure you," Tal replied.

"A likely story," Hanne said with a derisive laugh that somehow managed to still be polite.

"How do you know about me creating a stir, by the way? Have people been talking about me?"

"I'm Theo's assistant. I hear everything."

Tal paused to collect himself. They had climbed three floors, and vertigo from the whirling stairs was starting to set in.

"Everything, including how he's sticking his neck out by sponsoring a mage with no magic's place at the university." Hanne motioned, still politely, for him to continue up the stairs. The conversation fizzled after that.

Ten stories up, at the top of the atrium, they reached an imposing set of wooden doors, their rounded top encrusted with golden images of dragons in flight.

The doors swung open as Hanne walked toward them.

Calling this an office would mean implying that every other office in the country was in fact a broom closet. They had to walk through three separate sitting areas and past a bend where a cold blue fire roared in a fireplace just to see Theo's desk. For all the grandiosity of the rest of the room, the semicircular wooden table Theo sat behind was strikingly utilitarian, cut to form a comfortable work area with a box of parchment stacked neatly to one side.

Tal looked to Hanne for instructions, but she was already making her way back toward the door, the sound of her heels echoing off the cold office walls.

"Talarus, please have a seat," Theo said. He stood and made his way around the edge of the desk, toward the nearest sitting area, which consisted of a single couch that bent like a crescent moon. Its shape matched the rest of the furniture—everything was rounded edges and circles. Even the ornament in a basket on the round coffee table was a blown glass sphere.

Tal sat at one end of the couch, while Theo perched on the other, facing him. Tal hadn't yet seen Theo up close during daylight. His presence was commanding, not least because he wore an obviously expensive waistcoat and jacket that walked the line between gaudy and tastefully restrained. His beard was tightly trimmed, his neck without a hint of stubble, as if a barber had already stopped by that morning. He was unceasingly polite in both word and posture, yet Tal read a hard edge in him, as if all that outward civility masked something feral in his heart. The killer business instinct, Tal assumed. Something wolfish and brutally competitive.

"It pleases me greatly to have you stop by," Theo said. "I confess I am extremely eager to hear about your progress at the university. I hope you are settling in well?"

"I am, thank you," Tal said. "And thank you again for the opportunity."

Theo graciously waved off his thanks. "I know it's still early days, but have you made progress in your studies? Nathan assured me he set some of the brightest minds to the task."

"Some. As you said, it's early days. We're exploring a connection between fireworking and dragon speech. We haven't been able to substantiate anything yet, though."

"Fascinating." Theo sounded the opposite of fascinated. "Well, know that our support is unconditional. You don't need to prove yourself with new discoveries. You've earned as much time as you need."

Tal was taken aback at how kind this statement was. So taken aback that it took him a few moments to recognize what Theo had actually said. He could enjoy his time at the university regardless of what he actually accomplished. It was every mage's dream, at least in theory, to learn as much as they could about magic and not be accountable to some final demonstration of their grand discovery.

"I'm curious," Tal said, "were you the one who suggested this area of study? Dragon speech must be of special interest to anyone running a successful dragon airline."

"Not at all. I simply asked Nathan to point you in a direction where you could take advantage of your gifts, and could reasonably justify your presence at the university."

Tal reflected that these were all questions he probably should have asked before he accepted Theo's offer of sponsorship.

"On a somewhat unrelated note, I have something to run by you," Theo said. He pressed a button on the side of the coffee table. With a whirring sound, a panel on the wall snapped open. A bar cart rolled out on large wheels. It came to a stop at a section of the table that had obviously been indented for this purpose. With a pair of tongs, Theo dropped a single round ice cube into two tumblers, and poured a healthy amount of brown liquor on top. "Try this."

"Thank you," Tal said, accepting the proffered tumbler. He usually had no taste for liquor, but the whiskey had a lovely velvety bite to it.

Theo had been watching Tal's face as he sipped, and smiled with satisfaction before taking his own sip. "That's an eighty-year there, with a long-lasting bioworking that encourages a host of bacteria to continue improving the flavor over time."

"It's incredible," Tal admitted. "It must have cost a fortune."

"Fortunately for me, my grandfather and father were both more connoisseurs when it came to collecting than they were when it came to drinking. As a result, I have hundreds of bottles of the rarest vintage that they never even bothered to open."

"Nice kind of family to have," Tal said.

"Indeed." Theo took another small sip, appreciating every drop. "What I want to run by you is this. Here at Heathermark Flight Group, we are always looking for alternate ways of growing our brand. One of the demographics where we're lagging is the student population. Historically, dragon flight has been too expensive for most students. There is also a strong bias in students from outlying provinces toward taking a slow journey to the university via wagon or horse, as if such a romantic mode of transportation somehow improves one's studies."

Tal remembered his own trip by cart, the weeks of bumpy travel over uneven roads, the dip through the tunnels beneath Lodefall. He did still feel somewhat romantic about it. He'd been just a boy, leaving his family for the first time, off to start the adventure of becoming a mage. Dragon flight did have its own sort of romance to it, though, despite being far quicker.

Theo reached into the inner pocket of his jacket and pulled out three rolls of parchment. He opened them one by one on the coffee table.

"You'll have to sit for a portrait so we can get a better likeness, but for our first campaign we would do various sizes of these," Theo said.

As Tal stared down at the first scroll, he felt a burst of disassociation. His own face—remarkably well captured, regardless of what Theo said—stared back up at him. He wore mages' robes and stared heroically into the middle distance. An inscription below him read: *Preeminent Mages Fly Heathermark.*

"We'll have some lightworkings animate you as well, of course," Theo said. The other two advertisements read: *Scholars of Distinction Fly Heathermark* and *Trips as Fast as My Spellwork.*

Tal stared at the pieces of parchment in a mix of fascination and horror. Such flyers and posters were common around Thelspoint. Most, however, depicted well-known individuals like poets, playwrights, and the most powerful mages. His face on these pages just seemed *wrong.*

"You've . . . ah . . . really had the marketing department take a big swing at this already, I see," Tal said.

"Of the thirty-seven possible slogans we came up with, those three did the best with the focus groups."

"Sir, are you sure this is the best way to publicize your airline? I mean, I'm hardly a household name. I'm not even the Preeminent Mage anymore."

Theo scoffed. "Of course it is! Our target demographic is students, and every student in the university will have heard of your special arrangement. Nothing creates interest quite like a special case, does it? You will of course be well compensated for your participation on top of the existing sponsorship. You'd just have to sign a minor contract addendum, a morality clause and all that formal nonsense."

Tal tried not to think about what Bex would say if she saw him on a poster for her parents' airline.

Theo continued: "This stays between us, but our brand aspirations are not all about customers, either. We're experiencing an unprecedented level of regulatory scrutiny. We've worked hard to change the perception in the Assembly that our airline is purely profit-driven and caters only to the affluent. Assembly members love nothing more than their vision of Thelspoint as this center of learning and knowledge, where every industry is in service of the university and learning. Branding our airline as student-friendly will go a long way toward softening their perception of us."

Tal wondered why Theo put so much weight on the words "regulatory scrutiny." Nothing in this building or any of his other experiences with Heathermark suggested financial hardship.

"Can I think about it?" Tal asked.

"Of course. The contract is already drawn up, so feel free to take it with you and peruse at your leisure. Just send a courier with the signed copy once you've made up your mind." Theo had removed a fourth piece of paper from his inner pocket, and set it on the coffee table.

"Thank you, this is very generous."

The offer had thrown Tal into such a strange headspace that he almost forgot why he had come in the first place. His dread at the thought of asking for any more favors had only grown. Theo was giving him so much, some of it out of a sense of business opportunism, it was true, but without Theo he'd still be scraping by as a flight attendant in Upper Boden rather than back on track to becoming a mage. Now there was this further offer of a lucrative branding deal.

"I actually had something to run by you as well," Tal said, fingers drumming on the contract. He'd skimmed it far enough to see the monetary terms, and had to avert his gaze to avoid retching in response to how many zeroes they contained. "We've hit a bit of a snag in our research. We're missing a fairly key component I wondered if you'd be able to help us get."

"Of course, Talarus, anything you need," Theo said.

"If we're going to fully understand how dragon speech works, how it interacts with other areas of magic, we'll need access to an actual dragon. One we can observe as it speaks, maybe one we can run some noninvasive tests on. Otherwise, we're relying on poor substitutes with snapdragons."

Theo studied Tal carefully. "You are asking if you could use Heathermark's dragons for your research?"

"Exactly."

One of the posters had rolled itself back up. Theo picked it up and tapped the desk with it, his expression stern. His intelligent eyes passed over Tal, making him squirm. This man had the ability to disorient you with a simple silence.

Tal was too uncomfortable to allow the silence to continue. "It would really speed up the process. Don't you want results as quickly as possible, for the good of your business?"

Theo let the silence continue, the slight slant of his head managing to make it not feel rude, or as if he wasn't listening. It was still oppressive.

"I'll allow it's possible that speaking with dragons directly could speed along this process," Theo said. "What you are saying makes sense, and I completely hear you. However, the speed of this project is not of particular concern to me."

"May I ask what you mean by that?"

"I mean that I'm happy to continue my sponsorship for as long as the research takes. You don't need to rush. Be thorough. Enjoy your life as a student. Work hard, but not too hard. You have as long as you'd like." Theo tapped the desk again with the poster. "Heathermark does not currently see the ability to speak with dragons as a business priority. If we could create a reliable translation system that a designated employee could use without the interference of an intermediary device or translator, then perhaps we would adjust our mindset. Until then, we won't ask our dragons to participate in research that's not a business priority. We need to be respectful of their capacity, and of their time."

"Business priority?"

Tal hadn't meant to press Theo further, and worried that he'd overstepped. Theo just smiled and said, "Our primary business priority is charging people a fair rate to fly them from one point to another. Until understanding dragons is proven to help that goal, it doesn't make the cut."

"Understood." Tal felt his disappointment softened slightly by Theo's gentle, matter-of-fact tone. "If the company's position changes, let me know."

"Of course." Theo rose, and Tal understood that he was being dismissed. He finished his drink, thanked his benefactor again, and left the office. Hanne, the same woman who had led him up to the office, took him back down to the lobby, gently nudging him out into the continuing rain.

A Pair of Spectacles, Brandished in Anger, Produces a Profound Effect in a Former Preeminent Mage

Tal had immediately gone back to Nathan, who described the conversation with Theo simply as "bollocks." The aggravating part was, Theo had behaved perfectly reasonably—and in some ways more generously than he needed to—in his denial of the request. At least on the surface. When Tal considered what Heathermark's actual business priorities were, and whether their dragons would object to a few hours of research if they knew what it was for, he was less and less inspired by Theo's generosity. It was, however, certainly Theo's prerogative whether or not to allow him access to the dragons.

In need of a break from thoughts about research and airline moguls, Tal sought out Meret and Clem. They soon found themselves at one of the more refined student taverns, one typically frequented only by upperclassmen, or underclassmen showing off their mature tastes. They sat on the balcony overlooking the long bar area below. A single piano, spelled to play by itself, plunked out unobjectionable music, and iron chandeliers burned next to them.

Tal was interrupted from trying to hatch a scheme to talk with the dragons at Dragon Air—a bit of a longshot given the uncooperative nature of their management—by Meret asking him a question.

"What was that?"

"I asked, how far down do you think it goes?" Meret asked. The tavern was loud enough that Tal's distraction didn't provoke any annoyance.

They had been discussing the Runnel, a gorge that ran deep under Lodefall and was famous for occasionally producing terrifying monsters from its depths. Most of the time these were contained by a team of dedicated monster hunters who camped by the opening, but recently a wyrm the size of a city block had squeezed out, and it had taken days to contain it. The Lodefallians had ultimately had to build a fire of such heat that the wyrm dried out and, as all worms did in the heat, shriveled up.

"Are you asking if I support the theory that the depths of the Runnel are infinite?" Tal asked. "Because I think it would probably be a very inconvenient volcano if it went all the way down into the Earth's crust."

"Lodefall would definitely be a fair amount warmer if it were flooded with magma," Clem said.

"At least a few degrees," Tal said with a laugh. "I only spent a few days in Lodefall on my way to the university, and I mainly remember how cold it was. Even with all their forges, all that rock just sucks the heat from your body."

"Did you see the Runnel?" Clem asked, eyes bright. She and Meret were both from the west—she from the suburbs of Thelspoint and he from the city itself—and neither had occasion to visit the city under the mountain.

"I did, as every good tourist must. It's not much to look at from the outside, but we did take one of the elevators down into it. Not as far as the excavation site, where they're building the staircases to explore further, just to the observation post where you can see the depths for the first time."

What had most struck Tal about Lodefall was how the city embraced darkness. The people of Lodefall didn't mind the dark, as a rule, lighting only the areas they absolutely needed to. They trusted it not to contain the nightmares a surface-dweller like Tal might imagine. Yet as they descended into the Runnel, there was no darkness. Torches lined the walls as far down as Tal could see, as if only in this one place the dark might contain something too horrible to remain in the shadows.

"It's impressive. You can see thousands of feet down, all lit up. We could only see a hint of the excavation site. From up there, it does feel like it goes on forever, but I don't believe that just because something is too dark or deep for us to observe means that it never ends. I would guess there's a whole system of caves and caverns at unfathomable depths, and the things that come out of them don't have any agenda more malevolent than exploring a new passageway where the air smells sweeter."

"Or maybe they're drawn out by the light," Meret said.

"Most of them can't see," Tal said. "There's not much use for eyes in the dark."

"I personally think the Runnel goes all the way to the other side," Clem said.

"The other side of . . . ?" Tal began to ask.

"The world, of course."

This was a wild theory, one that to Tal's knowledge had never made it into the official list of hypotheses about the Runnel.

"It goes straight through to the land of wyrms and monsters."

It was always hard to tell if Clem was joking.

"Or maybe it's a portal to another dimension," Meret said, "one where monsters roam free and the people have no magic to defend themselves."

"Meret likes to make fun of me by coming up with the most outlandish theory he can," Clem said, "completely ignoring the fact that even my outlandish theories usually end up being right."

Tal smiled. "Like fireworking being involved in dragon speech? I think the jury's still out on that one."

"I will be vindicated!"

Meret rose from the table. "And I will be inebriated. That is, if I have one more glass of mead. Which is why I am going to get one more glass of mead—does anyone need anything?"

Meret left to get mead for himself and Tal. Clem, a consummate lightweight, had only managed about a quarter of hers. It was probably a good thing the sweet mead didn't have the carbonation of ale, because it surely would've gone flat by now.

Clem made a breathy sound as Meret departed. She cut the noise short, catching herself as Tal eyed her.

"Was that a sigh?" Tal asked.

"If it was, I'm sure it was a very thoughtful and academic sigh."

"More like wistful and tragic at seeing a certain talented languageworker depart."

The redness that bloomed across Clem's face made it look like she had finished three more glasses of mead at once. She was incapable of a response.

"I was joking!" Tal protested. "But I guess to some the cold flame of pure ambition could be considered . . . dreamy?"

Clem muttered something about using a fireworking to turn Tal into a pile of ash. As she collected herself, she said, "You're not the first person to see us together and assume that. The best languageworker, the best fireworker, it just makes sense, doesn't it?"

"In a reductive way that sounds exactly like everyone at this university, yeah."

Clem smiled. "The truth is, I have more of a forbidden crush situation, and it's not on Meret."

"You do? On whom?" He leaned across the table and, with mock seriousness, whispered, "Is it an immortal being you accidentally created out of a fireworking gone awry?"

Clem's laugh broke the tension enough for her face to return to its normal color.

"You can tell me," Tal continued, "I won't judge."

"It's not Meret or an immortal being, you fool." She took a second to compose herself. "It turns out I find a certain member of the fireworking faculty extremely, inconveniently attractive."

"Oh, dear Varai. Helena?" Tal put his head in his hands as Clem confirmed this with a forced smile. "A dragon would probably be less terrifying, and more available."

Clem looked miserable. So much so that Tal found himself desperate to change the subject. He reached into one of his inner pockets and pulled out the larger sphere that Enna had given him. He had held it each night, noticing the way it changed with his touch, its cloudy depths seeming to take on nearly discernible shapes. Each time, he dropped the sphere before the shapes could resolve, too scared of what they might tell him.

Clem watched curiously, anxiety still tinging her features, as Tal set the sphere on the table, careful to handle it only with his sleeve.

"I don't know exactly how this works," Tal said, "but I have a hunch it might tell you something about your magic."

He scooted his chair closer to Clem as she lifted it into her palm. Instantly the sphere glowed red, the swirling green replaced with swells that could only be fire. Tal feared it would become too hot to hold, but Clem didn't look away. She was enthralled. And as she stared, the fire bent and softened. Chaotic swirls settled themselves into gentle lines. Smoke that had billowed within the sphere now rose in soft plumes. In the center of it was a figure, hands outstretched, their will extending outward to tame the fire.

Tal leaned closer, his shoulder touching Clem's as they took in the image. Clem clearly liked what she saw there.

Clem's smile was interrupted by a cup of mead smashing down on the table. It wasn't Meret, or a dragon, or Helena.

It was Bex.

And her face was a color of rage Tal had never seen before as it tipped over from red into orange. Even the sphere looked scared, sinking into a smoky gray as it fell back onto the table.

"Bex, hi," Tal said, pulling his chair away from Clem with a haste that he only too late realized made him look guilty. He saw that behind Bex, somehow not looking remotely out of place despite sporting a leather jacket a color that matched Bex's face, was Claret the adventurer.

"Hi, *Talarus*." Bex's pronunciation of his full name dripped with scorn. "Looks like your new life at the university is treating you well. At least well enough to forget all about us."

Claret, whose hair today was one shade purpler than pure silver, waved at Tal and Clem. He waved back meekly as he said, "I wrote to you. You're the one who never wrote back."

"Seeing this, I'm glad I didn't. The minute I show up, I see you're on a date with this . . ." She surveyed Clem, who currently looked a bit like a caricaturist's depiction of a dragon who had suddenly forgotten how to fly while hundreds of feet in the air. "Well, with this very pleasant-looking and no doubt intelligent young woman, who is probably on the face of it a very good match, and makes a lot of sense both demographically and in terms of relative physical attractiveness."

Claret rolled her eyes deeply. "You forget the word 'bitch' again?"

"You should too," Bex replied. Clem's mead had sloshed onto the table in her surprise, and she moved to wipe it up with her napkin, her attention catching on the sphere as she did. "So? Do you have an explanation for this bullshit?"

"To start, it's not a date," Tal said. "Clem is my research partner. One of a few."

Somehow this managed both to offend Clem and not to placate Bex, who said, "This might sound like a crazy notion, but it is entirely possible to date one's research partner."

"I swear I'm not," Tal said.

"We discussed it, and I told him I've got my heart set on someone else," Clem said.

"You discussed it?" Bex had removed her glasses in order to wipe rage-infused sweat from her forehead. She reached across the table with her folded glasses, jabbing them painfully into Tal's chest. "Why, for Arren's sake, were you discussing it?"

"Because for some reason people at this university have nothing better to do than gossip," Tal said truthfully. "We're here with our other research partner, Meret."

"There are three mugs," Claret said, putting a hand on Bex's shoulder. "Three jackets on the backs of the chairs." All of their eyes turned toward Meret's sleek gray coat draped over the empty chair next to Tal. "Bex, unless you're suggesting there's some sort of menage-a-trois situation occurring here, I think you're barking up the wrong tree."

As if on cue, Meret appeared with two meads and slouched into his chair.

"Oh, are we yelling at Tal?" he said without missing a beat. "Can I go next?"

Meret's presence, for the first time since Tal had known the man, was an immediate salve. Only a fraction of Bex's anger had dissipated, but at least her immediate concern that Tal had already started dating another woman had been put to rest.

A small part of Tal, a part that was difficult to listen to given how agitated every organ in his body had become, recognized that Bex being this upset must mean she still cared, and hadn't written him off entirely. A dim hope, maybe, but still a hope.

"Can we talk?" Tal asked.

"Outside."

They took their mead with them. The tavern had an adjoining garden, which was empty now that the cold of fall had asserted itself. The furniture was tied up in one corner, chairs flipped upside down and placed on the tabletops, then covered. Though it rarely snowed in Thelspoint, the coverings would at least keep the furniture dry in the autumn rains. The door to the tavern closed heavily behind them, cutting off the rowdy sounds inside.

There were few places to sit in the dim garden. They settled for a rock wall abutting a flowerbed, which still bore the remains of what must have been an incredible spring and summer bloom. A camellia bush on each side had dropped flowers that slowly degraded into compost in the weedy dirt. With the cold rock against his backside, Tal wished he'd remembered to bring along his jacket.

"It's good to see you," Tal said. "Truly, I've missed you."

Bex sat at least four feet away from him. She was curled with her arms between her legs, her face almost covered by her hands. "Of course you missed me, asshole. I missed you too."

"You did get my letter?"

"That festival of bullshit contained in parchment form? Yes, I got that one."

"Apparently my honest apology counts as a bullshit festival. I'll take note of that."

"Don't be obtuse," Bex said. "You could've come back so easily to deliver the message yourself. I don't care about you leaving practically in the dark of night, but you've acted like as soon as you're back to being a mage, you're done with me."

"The whole point of sending the letter was that that's not true. I've gotten thrown into a million things here. I'm suddenly expected to lead this research, work with multiple departments, all while pretending I know what I'm doing. Lest it be forgotten, I still don't have my magic."

"Small blessing," Bex muttered. Tal forced himself to let that one go. "You're honestly going to tell me you couldn't have flown back on a weekend, or even taken an overnight trip? From what I hear, money is suddenly no object for you."

"I was trying to settle in here." Tal breathed. The truth was, a large part of the reason he hadn't flown back to see Bex wasn't logistical. It was mostly due to his assumption that she hated him. Somehow this assumption had brought that fact into reality. "But you're right, I should've made it work. I'm sorry."

Bex was suddenly crying. She took off her glasses again, angrily wiping tears away.

"Okay, so that's apology number one," she said through sniffles. "I'm going to need like six more. And that's before we even get to the biggest one."

"About me working with your parents." Tal had no desire to discuss this, but Bex deserved his directness, for him not to pretend what he'd done was okay.

"It's simply stunning how quickly you would sell out your own beliefs as soon as it meant you could get something you wanted. Or maybe they were never your beliefs, and you were just helping the dragons because you wanted to get with me."

"How could you say that?"

"Well, is it true?" Her voice was ice, and it chilled Tal deeply.

"I wanted to help because I cared about you. Because, despite myself, despite the fact that you made my life difficult in almost every conceivable way, I found that there's nothing you could want that I wouldn't also want."

This caused Bex to pause. Somewhere inside, a glass—or maybe four or five glasses—broke, followed by a roar of applause. A moment later, a flustered waiter opened the door and deposited a pile of broken glass in the trash bin outside. He glanced at them, gave Tal a grimace that said he'd rather be cleaning up broken glass than be in Tal's shoes, and went back inside.

"That's . . . sweet," Bex said. "And also a little unhealthy relationship-wise. Doesn't matter though, you abandoned all that when you decided to take my parents' offer."

"What would you have done in my shoes?"

"I've already spurned my parents' 'generosity' enough times to prove I would've stuck to my principles." She scooted close enough to stab him again with her glasses. This time Tal was ready for it, and turned just enough so they glanced off his shoulder. She had a surprisingly long reach when she decided to use her glasses as a weapon, almost enough to make one wonder how much practice she'd had jabbing people with them. "I don't change my mind like the breeze, the way you do."

"You know this wasn't about changing my mind."

Tal let that hang in the air. Bex knew exactly what he meant, but she wasn't going to respond. Tal was forced to continue.

"I have wanted to be a mage my entire life. I told you what I was able to achieve, the person I became at the peak of my magic. Bex, this is my life, right here, regardless of how I get it. Magic or not, I belong at the university. I belong among others with the same aspirations. I sure as hell don't belong on the back of a grumpy dragon, being kicked around by customers who have zero respect for me."

"This person, the Preeminent Mage person you were at the university," Bex began. Tal's stomach dropped as he recognized this was the first time she'd used the correct title. "I have two questions about him. First is, would he do anything to be the most powerful, the most revered? Even turn against his principles? And second, are you still that person?"

Tal's immediate reaction was to snap that, yes, of course he was still that person. And whatever was necessary to remain that person was worth it.

"I'm not the Preeminent Mage anymore," Tal said. "I'm kind of enjoying just being here. Being around magic, but not having everyone asking me to cook up a spell for them. I'm doing something important, and I can honestly say I don't care whether it's recognized. It's the work itself that matters."

Bex gave a sharp, mirthless laugh. "Dammit Tal. I really, really hate when you're honest."

Tal's laugh had more humor in it. "I often find it hard to be honest with myself, so I appreciate you making me figure out what I actually believe."

A chill wind tore through the garden, rattling the remaining leaves above them. A lantern creaked on its chain by the door. Tal had forgotten the cold, but now he had the sudden urge to pull Bex close, if only for the joint warmth of their bodies.

Bex remained at a distance, though.

"I have to admit, you did manage one thing in line with your principles," Bex said. "I never thought Dragon Air would allow us to use the device to speak with their dragons. Now, all of a sudden, they're letting me interview a couple a week. We're getting a gauge on what in the contracts need to be adjusted. If anything."

"I take it it's slow going?"

"You know what they say: six dragons, twelve opinions."

Tal had never heard anyone say that, but he let it slide.

"The dragons of Dragon Air have no collective consciousness," Bex said. "They see themselves as individuals who happen to be the same species and have the same job, so their concerns are largely individualized. Everyone has a unique situation, and wants a slightly different thing. It's maddening." She looked more pleased than maddened.

"I'm sure you can synthesize all of that into positive change," Tal said. "You know, find the outcome that serves the most dragons."

"What's been most interesting is hearing the rumors going around the dragons' networks. What happened at Braisecroft has everyone buzzing."

"And yet no one here is talking about it."

"No humans, at least," Bex said. "The dragons, they won't shut up about it. Some are even saying that the dragon was slipped dragonsbane, that he was justified in nearly burning my family's entire estate to the ground."

Tal recalled the rumors of dragonsbane that had been floating around the tavern back in Upper Boden. He hadn't believed them then, and the properties of dragonsbane hadn't changed. Yet the rumors persisted.

"Do you think other dragons will get ideas?" Tal asked.

"That's as much the dragons' fear as anything else. Dragons are powerful, but there aren't enough of them outside the Claglands, and they aren't organized enough, to prevent humans from killing them off if they become a threat. Humans are remarkably good at figuring out ways to kill creatures that they see as monsters."

"And yet there are some dragons still willing to instigate, to draw out those darker parts of human tendencies."

Bex shrugged. Though she hadn't softened entirely from their earlier conversation, some ease returned as they delved into the topic that had bonded them in the first place. "A vocal minority can cause plenty of damage without the will of all dragonkind behind them. Part of me thinks the contracts my parents created might be an ace in the hole against dragons stepping out of line. You know, use their coercive magic to force the dragons not to continue whatever chaos they're sowing. Stop any revolutionary tendencies in their tracks."

"It makes sense. If the dragons were to all be murdered by angry humans, or to suddenly fly off to their own utopia, either would mean the end of dragon airlines like Heathermark."

Bex paused, chewing her lip. She stopped and started a couple times before eventually saying, "I've actually been doing more than just listening when it comes to the contracts. Don't be mad at me . . ."

Tal couldn't possibly imagine what he would get mad about. He was mainly relieved Bex cared if he was.

She continued: "I've been scouting dragons who are considering employment with Heathermark. When I find them, I send Ronar to meet with them and discourage them from taking the contracts. We've only caught a few because he has to do it between his regular flights but, well, I couldn't just sit around and do nothing, you know?"

"Ronar agreed to that?"

"He cares more than you think. He might not care so much about his own employment situation, but he recognizes that having any dragon under Heathermark's control is an evil. Speaking of which . . ." Bex pulled a packet of parchment out of her coat pocket. It was instantly recognizable as the stolen contract. "What do you make of this?"

She had opened the packet to the very last page. There, underneath the signatures and notice about the contract being legally and magically binding, was a new section. An addendum, which didn't do anything more than define a couple terms.

"Again, I'm not an expert on this stuff," Tal said.

"Not the contents. This wasn't there before, and I didn't write it."

"Meaning . . ." Tal paused to consider. "Meaning the contract is somehow being rewritten from elsewhere."

"Claret thinks it's some kind of binding, that all of the contracts are bound to a master copy. Change the master copy, and you change every contract at once."

Bex's concern was warranted. From a single master copy, Heathermark was free to update the terms—magically enforceable terms—on every dragon in their employ. They had complete central control.

"Maybe it's not an insurance policy." Bex's soft voice faded into the muffled background noise of the tavern. "Maybe it's a weapon."

"We can't know that."

"What a surprise that you're defending your sponsors."

"I'm not defending them. I'm just saying, we have to be cautious, but we can't assume the worst."

As he said this, another thought needled Tal. The magic required for this kind of binding was incredibly powerful and persistent. He knew of only a few people in the university who studied it, and just one who had ever successfully put it into practice. This one person had a tenured position in the language-working faculty because of it, and an annoying habit of treating Tal like he still had magical potential long after he had shown otherwise.

Bex had been watching the progression of Tal's facial expressions, his inner thoughts laid bare under her sharp eyes. She did that. She opened him up, somehow. Yet it was not an unpleasant, prying opening. It was the feeling of fingers that had been holding on too hard being gently massaged apart.

"You know who the languageworker was," Bex said flatly.

"I can't imagine why Nathan would've done this."

"My guess is—and you're not going to believe this—they paid him *money*, and in exchange, he provided a *service* commensurate with said monies."

Tal didn't give her the satisfaction of acknowledging her joke. "Nathan wouldn't do that."

"A similar arrangement worked on his protégé."

Tal felt his expression darkening. Whatever softness he'd felt toward Bex was evaporating under her persistence. Her continued insistence on assuming the absolute worst of everyone. Including him.

"I don't care if you think your parents are monsters," Tal said, voice hot. "But I'm not going to listen to this about a man who's been like a father to me."

"He's lied to you. Just as my parents have."

Tal got up. He had longed for this reunion, hoped against hope that Bex would accept him back into her life. Now, though, he saw that the enmity he had expected her to feel towards him cut both ways. He cared for her, probably even loved her, but alongside that love was a fresh, deep wound.

"I'm done hearing about all of this secondhand," he said, already halfway across the slate patio on his way back inside the tavern. "I'm done making assumptions."

"You can't tell Nathan you know." Bex had gotten up too, and there was a note of panic in her voice. She grabbed Tal's arm. "We have only a few advantages, and this is one of them."

"Keep your advantages." Tal wrested his arm free and opened the door to the tavern.

THE PARTY LINE

There were probably better times to confront Nathan than near midnight, when Tal had already indulged in multiple mugs of mead and had a painful reunion with Bex. Sleep, however, was far from Tal's mind. He made his way to the dense cluster of faculty housing just outside the university proper. There was no one out at this hour. The world was hazy under the streetlights. Each faculty member had their own house, varying in size depending on whether they had a family. Nathan, whose wife had died close to twenty years ago now, lived in a comfortable two-bedroom home on a quiet street. A kitchen garden grew in neat rows behind the waist-high wooden fence in front of Nathan's home.

The quaintness of it only made Tal angrier. He barreled through the wooden gate and rapped on the door.

A light was already on behind the curtain in the living room. A shadow moved. Tal heard shuffling in the hallway inside, and suddenly an eye the size of a horse's opened in the wood above the knocker. The magical eye blinked at him, as if struggling to focus in the dark, then closed back into the wood. The door opened.

"Tal?"

As close as they were, Tal had only visited his professor's home a few times. Nathan preferred to keep his informal meetings at teashops or restaurants, many of which he frequented regularly and treated like an extension of his home.

"Is everything quite alright?" Nathan asked.

"Can I come in?" The walk over should have given Tal ample time to get his anger under control, but he found that seeing Nathan, who was wearing a cozy plaid bathrobe, slippers, and had damp hair as if he had just bathed, reignited it.

"Of course, of course. The water in the kettle is still hot, I'll make you a cup of chamomile."

Tal sat on the deep couch in Nathan's joint living room and kitchen. As Nathan steeped the tea, Tal flung out questions about his role in writing up the Heathermark contracts.

Nathan set Tal's teacup down on the coffee table, with exactly one sugar cube on its saucer. The tiniest splash of sweetness that Tal liked in his tea in the evening.

"I just don't understand how you could help them create something like that," Tal said. As Nathan's expression softened into shame, some of Tal's anger drained out of him.

The armchair made a soft huffing sound as Nathan sat. A side table, attached to the chair by a metal column on one side, swung around so his half-full tea was close to hand.

"You do realize that simply revealing facets of the contract could technically be considered a crime," Nathan said. "They were never meant to be public."

"Not surprising. Heathermark had plenty to hide. So, are you going to report me?"

Nathan smiled. "Of course not. I'm proud of you for even knowing about them. Actually, I'm proud of you just for caring."

"You haven't answered my question." Tal was reminded of the day when he had served Nathan tea at the Dragon Air landing pen, when Nathan had first realized the extent of Tal's lost magic. He regretted that the tea he had served that day had been far less fresh, and that he had only a wooden chair to offer his mentor. Tal stirred in the sugar cube, watching the grains disappear in the current his spoon left behind. Though he hadn't visited Nathan at home many times, he'd drunk tea with him more often than with any other person. In the taste, in the sensation of warmth on his hands, he felt a deep sense of home.

"They came to me not long after Tilda died," Nathan said. "Heathermark did. I'm sorry you never met Tilda. I think you would have liked her. She was a far gentler soul than I. A far better soul than I, I think."

You got that right, Tal almost said. He bit his tongue. Nathan may have been involved in creating the contracts, he may have obscured the truth, but even with the venom flowing inside him, Tal couldn't find it within himself to speak so horribly to a man who'd lost so much.

Nathan rarely spoke of his deceased wife. All Tal knew was that she was a plantworking lecturer at the university, and had been at least ten years Nathan's senior. She had no particular academic aspirations other than working her plant magic and teaching students how to do the same. She had somehow managed to teach at the university for close to twenty-five years without ever receiving tenure or publishing more than a few papers.

"After she died, every part of the university reminded me of Tilda," Nathan continued. "I would walk past a table we had shared in the dining hall, or the greenhouse where she taught, and find myself so distraught I couldn't teach my own classes. I managed to petition for a yearlong leave of absence—never mind the fact that I hadn't achieved tenure and didn't have enough savings to live off of. It didn't matter. I needed to be away, so I found a rundown apartment in Heathermark, far from the university.

"That's when they came to me with a proposition. Word had gotten around of my languageworking abilities, and in the past I had occasionally taken on minor jobs involving contracts. This one was different. Daring. Something that had never been done before. Within the abyss of my grief, it was something I could focus all of my energy on, that could wear me down enough that Tilda's face would no longer appear around every corner."

"I'm sorry about Tilda," Tal said. "I never knew you left the university. I'm surprised they let you."

Nathan nodded. "It wasn't an easy conversation. It was heavily implied that I wouldn't be allowed to return unless I proved through research or achievement that I deserved tenure. That's the other truth about my work with Heathermark. Because the work on the contracts was so unusual, Heathermark allowed me to publish a redacted report demonstrating how the binding worked. I knew that presenting this to the higher-ups in the university would ensure that I returned in good standing."

"Was it about distracting yourself from grief, or about the prestige?" The question felt callous, but so did Nathan's rational calculation about returning to the university.

"Why couldn't it be both?" Nathan took a long sip of his tea.

In the eyes staring back at him, in the spark of intention and intelligence there, Tal had the uncomfortable sensation of looking into a mirror spelled to show an older version of himself.

"Talarus," Nathan said, "I have always asked you to be true to yourself, and I hold myself to that same standard. I do not think we should lie about who we are so that others will like us more. So yes, part of my decision to work on the contracts was due to my ambition. That's true. What is also true is that I needed the work to process my grief, and that my grief did not allow me to think through the implications of what I was creating. They asked me for an insurance policy against dragons attacking humans." Exactly as Tal and Bex had speculated. "However, as you seem to understand, its true potential is so much greater than that."

"Do you know which use they actually intend?" Tal asked.

"That's the question that matters most. My honest answer, though, is that I don't know."

Tal stared into his tea. The calming effects of the chamomile—both the mundane ones, and those of the plantworking that added an additional soothing magical effect—were beginning to kick in. Either that, or Tal was remembering just how hard it was to stay mad at someone he cared for as much as Nathan.

"You should've at least asked the question before you agreed to work with them," Tal said.

"You know as well as I do how difficult it is to broaden your perspective when you're in the heat of magical discovery. It can feel that the research is all that matters, not the way the research actually fits into the world."

The truth of this cut through Tal. Nathan finished his cup of tea and swung the side table back to the other side of the armrest. He leaned forward, the top of his plaid robe opening like a puff pastry to reveal the undershirt beneath.

"I know you, Talarus," Nathan said. "I know what your return to the university means to you. I felt the same thing when I came back, after I went from a grieving outcast to a top candidate for tenure. I know what having this opportunity taken away from you would mean."

And there it was. Not a threat, but certainly a warning. Tal's position was tenuous, subject to the whims of Bex's parents. All he had to do was piss them off, and his return would be cut short. Piss them off by, for example, messing with the contracts they had created to keep absolute control over their dragons. Nathan might have advocated for him, but the power to continue or revoke his sponsorship lay solely with the sponsors themselves.

"What if their intentions aren't purely protective?" Tal's voice was so low, Nathan had to lean in to hear him. "What do we do? Can't we just burn all the contracts up?"

"The contracts are binding even if the master copy is destroyed. Only the designated parties who have power over the contracts can amend them. That's only Theo and the dragons' legal representation, which is sadly no one. All of that is unnecessary, though. Nearly twenty years have passed since I first drew up these contracts. They haven't done anything evil with them in that time. Why should they start now?"

"But if they did," Tal pressed, "would you help us stop them?"

Nathan looked unspeakably sad. "I have my own contract."

Tal sighed. That should have been obvious from the start. Despite his exposure to how Heathermark operated over the past several months, Tal still felt a stranger to this corporate world, this world of contracts and control. All he'd ever cared about was magic. The invisible strands of money puppeteering that magic were becoming horribly evident.

"You called me back to the university against my will," Tal said. "I believed that you were doing it for me, that you never lost sight of my potential. But maybe I was better off with the airline."

Nathan withered under Tal's glare. And then he smiled ruefully.

"I've had to live with my decisions," Nathan said finally. "I don't need or deserve your forgiveness. But know that I'm sorry."

Tal shook his head. "I didn't know the man who created those contracts. That powerful mage, lost in grief. I do know the man he became. That man never needs my forgiveness."

He stood and hugged his mentor. Nathan's bony arms clenched tightly around him.

Tal left Nathan's home that night far calmer than when he'd arrived. In some ways he felt even more strongly about his defense of his mentor, and angry at Bex for speaking ill of him. He also felt he owed Bex at least three more apologies.

Worry reigned over all of these feelings. The inherent evil of the contracts was nothing compared to what Theo could do if he decided to act on the power he already had.

FIRE IN A BOX

Bex left a note on the door of Tal's dorm room—he had no idea how she had gotten inside the building, since it was restricted to students—to let him know she was heading back to Upper Boden and asking him to forgive her for "disparaging your slightly corrupt, potentially well-meaning, but ultimately misguided mentor." A truly Bexian apology if he had ever seen one.

No matter the contents, the note was a lifeline.

For his part, Tal responded to his roiling anxiety the way he always did. The way Nathan had taught him. He plunged fully into his research, spending even more of his time at the library, and driving Meret and Clem crazy with questions about their respective fields. Soon his frenzied life began to look more like that of a student on academic probation preparing for a crucial exam than a researcher on an independent study with no set deadline.

A breakthrough came on the day Helena brought in a square box the size of a hat box. It was metal, with a circular hatch on top. Tal and Clem huddled around as Helena placed it on the table in her lab.

"What is it?" Clem asked, leaning over the box. Tal noted how Clem's movements hesitated ever so slightly when they brought her closer to Helena.

Helena gave her a look like this would have been an acceptable question if she'd just waited between seventeen and twenty-one seconds longer to ask it. She opened the hatch. Tal winced backward, but Clem was far more accustomed to the substance within.

Inside the box was fire.

"Is that . . ." Clem squinted into the swirling flames, which stayed contained within the four walls of the box. ". . . dragon fire?"

Tal was more worried about the fire somehow escaping from the box. He noted the nearest sheet of fireweave to throw over himself, just in case.

Helena nodded. "Pain in the ass to get it, too. I had the box already, but had to buy the actual fire off a merchant who travels the mountain passes in the Claglands and had an everflame device ten times this size. Exorbitantly priced. I'm charging this to your research budget, Tal."

"Of course," Tal said, too intrigued to consider whether or not he could actually afford to foot the bill for a box full of dragon fire. It wasn't just the sight of the fire that had caught his attention. As soon as the hatch had opened, a hissing sound had slithered its way into his head. It didn't take long to recognize that it wasn't sound at all. Rather, some property of the fire seemed to instantiate itself in his mind. He leaned forward, heedless of the heat on his face. Helena watched with satisfaction.

Tal resisted the urge to put his hand out to the fire. Instead, he stared into its depths. Dragon fire moved much slower than regular fire, rolling continuously over itself rather than flickering and dancing. The hissing grew louder.

"Can one of you perform a fireworking on this?" Tal asked.

"I've never . . ." Clem started.

"I can." Helena placed both hands on the table, craning her head over the box so she and Tal were almost nose to nose. She closed her eyes. Effort flashed over her face. For a second, nothing happened. Then, for the briefest instant, the fire stopped moving. It waited, poised, before beginning to turn in the opposite direction.

The sight was somehow more startling than watching a similar change in standard fire. The fireworking obviously took more of Helena's effort. As the blaze settled into its new orientation, Tal heard a sound like a sigh.

Then a single lonely word: *opposite.*

He could've been imagining it. Surely the fire wasn't speaking. Yet somewhere within the fire was the will of the dragon who had breathed it. The dragon's consciousness, at least a small part of it, was still there, still aware of its existence and the mage enacting her own will on it.

"That's it." Elation bolted through Tal. "I could *hear* it."

Clem clapped. Helena looked even more satisfied, as if she'd known all along that this would work.

"Try giving it more instructions," Tal said. "I want to be sure."

Over the next several minutes, Helena and Clem shaped the fire with fireworkings. Tal marveled at Clem's fireworking, which would have surely eclipsed his own even in his heyday. She had a natural comfort with the fire, as if it might burn others but could not harm her as long as she had any say in the matter. Helena played off Clem, mentor and mentee seemingly in perfect sync. Had he not had a job to do, Tal would have enjoyed just watching them bend the dragon fire. Their options were somewhat limited since they couldn't let it leave the box, but with each expert twist of the flame, Tal could hear the briefest word: *sphere, fast, separate.*

"Does this mean dragon fire is . . . speech?" Tal asked.

"I can't tell you exactly what it means," Helena said. "All I can tell you is that we are closer than ever to understanding how dragon speech is made."

Tal sat back, stunned. His practical side thought that, now that they knew fireworking was the central component, they could probably stop their fruitless study of bioworking.

"It is impossible for us to grasp the full mechanism without seeing an actual dragon speak and breathe fire. Have we made progress there?" Helena asked.

Tal shook his head. "I do have an idea, though."

They were too close now. Without a dragon, they could investigate as much fire as they liked and never discover the source of his translation abilities.

Dragon Air be damned, he was going to talk to Ronar.

Tal hadn't stepped outside Thelspoint's walls since his return to the university. The cramped buildings near the landing pen where he had almost crash-landed with Ronar so many times had a gentle familiarity to them. He had always resented the second-rate placement of Dragon Air's pens, but now it felt more quaint than insulting. The pens also seemed smaller, new wood surrounding an area almost unfathomably narrow to support a live dragon. He slipped under the gate—Dragon Air being too cheap to pay for one that went all the way to the ground—and inside, checking for airline personnel. It was a couple hours after Ronar's usual flight from Upper Boden, so the dragon should be in the stable adjoining the pen.

Ronar was not alone. Enna and Bex sat on the wooden bench just inside the door. Bex's expression became several degrees frostier when she saw Tal enter.

"I didn't know Ronar kept such a busy social calendar," Tal said.

"However busy it is, I'm sure it doesn't have much room for former coworkers who abandoned him," Bex said.

Tal's excitement had been building all the way out to the landing pen, and not even Bex's ire could dull it. "I need to speak to him. We've discovered something potentially significant about dragon communication. It appears to be tied to fireworking somehow. I want to ask for Ronar's help."

"That's wonderful," Enna said.

"Wonderful that he wants to continue exploiting dragons when it's advantageous to him and ignoring them when it's not?" This earned Bex a disapproving look from Enna. "Anyway, he's busy. A rep from Dragon Air is here talking to him with the translation device. He's about to get a raise, it seems like."

"A raise?" Tal asked.

"That's what they said."

Tal peered around the wall dividing the outer section of the stable from Ronar's sleeping area. He could just make out a gray uniform, the Dragon Air insignia on a sleeve. There were the noises of dragonish speech being turned into human language inside, although the device's sounds were muffled at this distance.

Tal's first thought was how good this was for Ronar, how his work should be rewarded. A second thought nagged behind the first.

"What did they say their name was?" Tal asked.

"They didn't. They just said they were from Dragon Air."

"Yes, from Dragon Air and offering a raise. Have you ever known Dragon Air to give a raise to anyone?"

Tal pushed into the stable, displacing swishing clouds of straw behind him. The new wooden floor creaked as Ronar turned to face him. The Dragon Air representative broke off midsentence, surprise morphing into guilt in an instant.

The woman in the Dragon Air flight suit was petite, with her hair tied back severely. Without her usual blond sphere of hair, the woman didn't look quite as obviously corporate and out of place in the uniform as she otherwise might have. Her high cheekbones and imperious posture, however, were unmistakable.

"Hanne, what are you doing here?" Tal asked.

Theo's assistant paused, her hand over the translation device as if she couldn't decide whether it would be more incriminating to remove it. She looked down at her uniform in distaste. Tal wondered how she had come by it, knowing that when Heathermark was involved, "they paid copious sums of money for it" was usually not too bad a guess.

"Hello Talarus, good to see you again." Hanne picked up the device and tossed it absentmindedly from hand to hand.

"What are you doing here?" Tal repeated. In Heathermark's headquarters, Tal had felt back on his heels, unsure how to conduct himself in his corporate surroundings. But here amid the straw and earthy stench of dragon, it was Hanne who was out of place. She asked Ronar to wait just a minute, before pulling Tal aside by a shoulder.

"Outside."

She yanked Tal past Bex and Enna, and back out to the landing strip. Bex looked concerned, though not quite concerned enough to step in if Tal happened to be in any danger. They marched into the center of the flight field.

"I came to offer Ronar a raise, like I told your friends," Hanne said, indicating Bex and Enna, who watched from the shadow of the doorway. "I may have shaded the truth somewhat when it came to which airline I represent."

"Deceiving him is a great place to start an employment relationship."

Hanne clasped her hands behind her back, cradling the device. "You have your own employment relationship to think about."

She said it as if with regret, her eyes down on the cracked mud of the landing pen. The scrape of dry earth against Tal's shoe was as familiar as any cobblestone in a university courtyard. Tal waited for Hanne to continue.

"Look, I know you've come here seeking access to dragons for your research," Hanne said.

"Access that's been denied by your company's business priorities."

"Access I can give you, if you cooperate." Hanne let that hang in the air. "Just not access to this dragon in particular."

Tal shook his head. "Why are you doing this? Leave Ronar out of your schemes. He doesn't deserve to be used like this."

"Your friend has already been using him," Hanne said. She circled Tal now, once again moving the device back and forth between her hands, which was more than a little impressive given that they were still behind her back. "She has him on some kind of publicity tour, sending him on all sorts of extra flights beyond his usual workload. We've simply offered him enough comforts to make it worth his while. Who cares if it's for a different airline than he thinks it is?"

Tal remembered Bex mentioning Ronar's attempts to talk dragons who were being recruited by Heathermark out of signing any contracts, that genuine attempt to make a difference that still didn't feel like nearly enough. It took all of him not to rip the device from the woman's hands. He was walking a delicate line. He had no doubt Hanne had almost as much say over what happened to him as Theo did.

"This is wrong."

"It's your choice," Hanne said. "Tell Ronar to accept our terms, and you can use the Heathermark dragons for your research. Anything else, and your sponsorship is at an end. You go back to your pathetic, magicless life."

Hanne tossed him the device, which he almost dropped. Its weight was always about half again more than he expected. She stalked back toward the stable, shooting a sneer over her shoulder: "You choose."

Bex and Enna reached him before he could put a single thread of thoughts together, much less formulate a response.

"What was that about?" Bex asked, face flushed.

"She's from Heathermark," Tal said.

With those simple words, he knew what his decision would be.

He explained everything to Bex and Enna, leaving nothing out. He should probably have left his options open, should have massaged the truth so it sounded like it would be reasonable for him to get Ronar to sign Hanne's agreement. Surely Hanne could tell Theo to end his sponsorship in a heartbeat, and by telling his friends about her deception, he had all but sealed that fate.

"Well, what are you going to do?" Bex asked. That she would even ask the question hurt Tal immensely. Yet within that hurt was the shred of himself he had lost, the man who might have hated every second of his job as a flight attendant, but had always done his best to make sure Ronar was taken care of, or that his passengers were able to climb down the ladder after their flight ended. The man who had conversations with Ronar over long hours flying together, even before he knew Ronar could communicate back.

"I don't doubt that you would put me in a headlock if I said I was going to go along with it," Tal said.

Bex gave a shrug, as if to say, *If I have to.*

"No headlocks required today," Tal said. "I already gave up everything coming back to the university. Looks like I'm gonna have to give all that up, too."

Bex's expression was difficult to read. She wore a flowing shawl today, which only under the full afternoon light could he now see had a minor lightworking on it, making the sun and stars pattern slowly rotate.

"You're really willing to give that up?" Bex asked.

"Ronar is my friend," was all Tal said. He didn't want to discuss it further, and as he turned away it became immediately apparent the discussion was going to be cut short anyway.

Hanne was nowhere in sight.

"Where'd she go?" Tal asked. "Not that it matters, I have the device."

There was a roar from inside the stable. A roar Tal had never heard before. The roar of a dragon being *forced* to roar.

Then the roof of the stable came off, and Ronar lifted into the air. He circled once around the landing pen. It was hard to tell, as Tal was occupied with doing his best to shelter Enna from flying debris, but he thought Ronar's eyes had a vacant look to them, as if all will had deserted him. He flew higher and higher, then disappeared from sight.

"I'm alright," Enna said, accepting Tal's hand to help her up, and refusing any closer inspection. Bex was already sprinting back toward the remains of the stable. By the time Tal was convinced of Enna's safety and had dashed back inside as well, Bex had Hanne in a headlock in the scratchy straw. Both were bleeding from where they had scraped against the splinters that Ronar had sprayed everywhere. Dragon Air was not going to be happy about what had just happened to their brand new stable.

And Hanne was laughing, a high, keening, almost manic sound.

"Bex, the damage is done," Tal said, heart sinking.

Bex drove her opponent's face further into the straw, eliciting a hiss of pain that only briefly stopped the laughter. "What did you do?"

Hanne pointed to something a few yards away from her, a glint of metal nestled in the straw. Bex let her go, after giving an extra painful yank on her arms. She picked up the object.

It was smaller than Nirza's translation device, but almost identical in every other way. It had the same slots on the sides where a rod could pop out, the same grooves, nearly as much weight.

"You didn't seriously think you were the only one who had a device that allowed you to talk to dragons," Hanne said, spitting blood from her cracked lip into the straw.

"Ronar would never have agreed to your terms," Tal said. "He would've known something was off."

"Oh, he did!" Hanne said. "That's the best part. He said he wasn't interested until he talked to you about it. The beauty of a translation device is that, as hard as they are to make, it's no more difficult to make one that intentionally mistranslates. And a verbal agreement is just as powerful as a written contract, if you put the right strictures in place."

Bex had returned to Tal, listlessly handing him the mistranslation device and steadying herself against him. "This . . . this is . . ." She couldn't find the words.

Bex was surely now reckoning with how much this explained. Tal had always wondered how Heathermark had managed to get so many dragons to sign their contracts. With devices like this available, they wouldn't have needed the dragons to agree to them at all.

Tal's thoughts swirled. As much as this revelation shocked him, his foremost concern was for the creature who had just burst out of the ceiling. Tal didn't have it in him to stop Hanne as she rose and made for the door of the stable.

Ronar, his closest friend and dragon companion, was now under the thrall of Heathermark Flight Group.

Flames Over Thelspoint

"Every time I think they can't do anything grosser, they find another way to surprise me," Bex said a half hour later, when they'd gathered at her room in the grungy hotel just south of central Thelspoint. Claret, who was staying in the hotel across the street, had followed Tal and Enna inside. Next door was a department store featuring seven different haberdashers locked in an intense competition to price their goods as low as possible. The result was clothes that could probably handle only a single use, if one was gentle. "It's almost like I was right about them this whole time."

"We're aware," Tal said. "Could we skip to the solution-oriented phase of this, or are we going to be stuck in the gloating phase for a while?"

"My, how you two flirt!" Claret said. Tal and Bex were perfectly coordinated in giving her a look that would've caused someone with a weaker constitution to wilt.

"Flirtation aside, I don't really know what we can do," Bex said. "We don't even know what my parents are planning."

"And we don't even really know if Ronar is part of the plan," Tal said. He was still feeling awkward enough around Bex that he wasn't comfortable sitting on the room's bed or chair, and was instead perched haphazardly on a dusty windowsill.

"Regardless, Tal has tipped his hand," Claret said. "I doubt they're going to wait around much longer to take action. We need to prepare."

Bex's eyes darted to Tal, then back to the floor. "It would be nice if we had a secret society of powerful mages at our disposal, in case things go south."

As the conversation drifted toward all the possibilities for how to stop Theo and Heathermark, Tal found himself wondering if it wouldn't have been better if the Completists had survived. Maybe if he had stayed, he could have salvaged the situation. Meret's issue was his leadership, not his magic or devotion to the group. If Tal had remained, perhaps the group could have continued. Tal couldn't follow this line of thinking too far. He'd spent his whole life in Upper Boden, his whole life as a flight attendant up until the point when he met Bex, living in a haze of hypotheticals. He needed to be done with hypotheticals.

Tal was pulled back to attention as Claret asked him whether there was anything within his sponsorship offer that would tell them what Heathermark was planning.

"I don't know," Tal said. "I'm guessing my contract would end up being just as restrictive as the dragons'. I'd end up as their pawn, just like Ronar."

"His face would've looked horrible on posters anyway," Bex said. Tal glared. "What? I'm just saying, it's a face you have to see in person to appreciate."

Tal found the closest object he had to hand, which was the large sphere Enna had given him after his last flight, and hurled it at Bex. He had meant to startle her more than actually hit her, and she caught it easily. Immediately the color inside the sphere clouded, turning from dull green to sharp purple. Enna watched the shape inside intently. Bex stared into its depths as it settled into two sections with a dividing line in the middle. They stared at it long enough to divine that it wasn't really two sections, but instead two baskets, arranged on either side of a central pole. They moved in harmony, so that one basket dropped as the other rose. Once one basket reached the bottom of the sphere, it began to ascend and both baskets switched directions. It looked like a scale in the process of weighing ingredients. Bex tossed the sphere back in Tal's direction, giving no indication that she'd seen anything of note.

Before any other image could appear in the sphere, there was a noise like a trumpeting elephant from outside. They rushed to the window, Tal slipping the sphere back into his pocket. The window looked out on an alley, and with four of them craning their necks to look out, they could see very little beyond the chimneys rising from the haberdashers next door. Then there was an unmistakable streak across the sky. A dragon was flying overhead, bellowing so loud it shook the windows. Another sound came, this one the terrible shriek of dragon fire.

Was this the same dragon splinter group, only escalating the chaos they had caused at the landing pens, and at Braisecroft? Tal exchanged a skeptical look with Bex.

"Come on, let's get outside," Tal said. The four of them made their way down to the street. More people than usual were out, looking up in fear at what the night sky held.

And with good reason. Above them, at least fifteen massive Cernoth dragons circled. They shot fire in the air in coordinated streams. They were moving inward, toward the statehouse and the guild halls at the center of Thelspoint, joined by still more dragons as they flew.

"What are they doing?" Enna asked.

"We don't have to wonder," Tal said. He looked over at Bex, who held the dragons' contract in her hands. On the last page, words were scrawling onto the blank paper as if by an unseen hand. "It's not the splinter group. Heathermark is fully in control of these dragons."

Rather than the legalese of the rest of the contract, there was no doubt about what these new additions said. Bex summarized as she read.

"They're being summoned to the center of the city. They're going to form up in a show of strength over the Assembly."

"The Assembly is in session tonight," Enna said. "Some vote on guild representation or some such."

The others looked at her.

"What, don't any of you read the news?"

Tal laughed mirthlessly. He hadn't given a single thought to the political situation of his own country in years. He'd probably been allowed to vote in Upper Boden, but hadn't seen the point, as any representative would likely be from Upper Boden, and therefore, categorically, not a candidate he had cared to support.

"Does it say anything about them attacking?" Tal asked.

"For now, no," Bex said, her eyes dancing over the paper.

Claret put it bluntly. "I hate to point out the obvious here, but your parents are currently in the process of staging a coup."

"Well, shit," Bex said. "I hate those."

They tried to convince Enna to stay behind, but she was having none of it. They needn't have worried about her ability to keep up, as Enna paused to do *something* to her feet. From their conversations about the spheres, Tal had known Enna must possess some magic, even if he didn't know what form it took. And what she'd done didn't come from any discipline taught at the university. Her working made her shoes slippery, allowing her to slide along cobblestone streets as if she were on skates. Unlike with skates, she remained in full control of her speed, her shoes obliging whenever she wanted to stop or speed up.

They had briefly considered heading the dragons off at the Assembly Hall, but if they were going to stop them, it wouldn't be by confronting the dragons directly. The only hope was to find the master contract that dictated all the others. In theory it could be anywhere—there was no geographical limit on such magic—however, Theo would likely want to be close enough to provide moment-by-moment instructions to his enthralled dragons. There was only one place in the city where he could do this from a secure location: Heathermark Tower.

As Enna slid along beside them, a stream of pedestrians ran past in every direction. No dragon had ever attacked Thelspoint. These had not truly attacked yet, but the mere suggestion of what a rain of fire and scaly claws could do to the city had sent people into a panic. There was no rhyme or reason to where people went. Some were making for the underground storage areas beneath the city, others ran toward the gates as if to escape the city on foot, while a few actually dove into the river that ran around the interior.

The party passed the university, and two familiar faces emerged from the crowd.

"Tal!" Meret yelled from behind a wall of determined students on their way toward the city center. They looked ready to confront the dragons, which, though brave, seemed less wise than just letting the firebreathers have whatever they wanted and not being burnt to a crisp. Clem appeared behind Meret.

"Is there anything we can do?" Clem asked.

"We're going to Heathermark Tower to try to cut this off at its source," Tal said. "I don't know what we'll find there. We could certainly use you two, whatever it is."

Bex nodded approvingly. Claret smiled, looking between each face and making no effort to hide her satisfaction as her questing party came together.

"Think of it as research," Clem said. "High stakes research. Helena would be proud."

The mention of the dragon scholar made Tal wonder if they should find her and Nathan before doing anything. There was no time. Tal had to admit to himself that if there was any authority on dragons, it was him. That fact wasn't comforting on its own, yet as he looked at the expectant expressions around him, he saw that the others trusted him, trusted his talents, and would lend theirs to whatever they were about to face.

"They always say, research is nothing without a practical application," Tal said. "Let's go stop some dragons!"

With a yell that he took a regrettable few seconds to realize sounded like a scream of terror, he plunged into the crowd, the others pushing past bodies to stay behind him.

A dragon streaked overhead as they made their way into the ordered stone of The City. It let out a plume of fire, sending a rain of warm steam over the crowd. Several more panicked people swan-dived into the canal. The dragon didn't attack, but its mere presence caused dozens of injuries, as terrified citizens trampled over one another. It flew off, sweeping in a wide circle over the city.

The party moved on, climbing the narrow steps leading up to the greenway along the cliffs. They had to battle through a swarm of people coming down. Enna's enchantment somehow allowed her to slide up the steps, as if gravity ran upward rather than downward just for her. Tal panted behind her, Bex taking the steps two at a time at his side. Then came Claret, Clem, and, far enough that they were worried about losing him, Meret. Tal seemed to remember one conversation where Meret had boasted about having his Physical Education requirement waived by the university so he could focus on more impactful work. He wondered how he felt about that decision now.

"There it is," Bex said as they regrouped at the top of the steps. The tower reared at the end of the row of skyscrapers, its grand entrance showing no sign of the chaos that had overtaken the rest of the city. Even as people streamed out of the other buildings, the opening of Heathermark Tower loomed eerily quiet.

As they neared, they saw why.

Two dragons were wrapped around the middle stories, their heads over the entryway.

"Ah, dragon guards," Claret said. "A classic villain strategy."

"Classic as in there are a lot of known ways of getting past them, or . . . ?" Bex asked.

"Classic as in it's a strategy for a reason, because it rarely fails," Claret replied.

"Best kind, really," Meret said.

As the de facto leader of this group, Tal thought it probably wouldn't be a good look to tell everyone to shut up, but this thought didn't do away with the impulse to do exactly that.

They approached as close as they could without coming into full view of the dragons, sheltering in the shade of the enormous, manicured bushes running around the inside of the building's plaza. The dragons were still, their snakelike eyes intent on the area in front of the door. They were not the large Cernoth variety, but rather more medium-sized Eitnoths like Ronar. Large or medium, they could squash, incinerate, or slash Tal into a puddle, a pile of ash, or three separate pieces, respectively.

"Does anyone have anything resembling a plan?" Bex asked. "I would usually suggest a back entrance, but I've been to this building enough times to know my parents won't stand for anyone coming in a door that's not overwhelmingly impressive."

"Are you sure? A back door might have a smaller dragon," Tal said.

"I was once an intern here," Bex said. "Believe me, I would've found a way to sneak out the back if there was one."

Tal was momentarily distracted by the image of Bex as an intern for her evil parents. He would be sure to give her shit for that if they happened to survive. Or if the dragons didn't outlaw speaking ill of members of Bex's family when they inevitably took over.

"The dragons haven't been attacking," Tal said. "Bex, does the contract give any specific instructions?"

Bex removed the increasingly battered parchment from her coat and scanned it.

"It says not to harm any humans, unless either a) the contract specifically orders them to in the future or b) they attempt to stop the dragons or otherwise disrupt the operation. Even then, there's some language about not killing anyone until 'such time as it is decided otherwise that such actions should become appropriate.'"

"Reassuring," Enna said. She breathed heavily, her magic clearly having cost her a great deal of energy. She hadn't once complained, however, and seemed just as determined as the others. "Kindly ask the dragons not to murder. Just don't leave murder completely off the table."

"Wouldn't be much good using dragons otherwise," Clem said.

"I wonder . . ." Tal scanned the dragons again. His heart pulsed in his ears as he thought through what he was about to do. "How about I go talk to them?"

Over a chorus of protests, Tal stepped out onto the plaza. Despite the persistence of panicked sounds from further in the city, an odd and oppressive silence fell over him. The dragons' eyes bored into him, following as he walked slowly toward them. They didn't bother turning their heads, which made the movement of their eyes all the more disconcerting.

"Hello there," Tal said. "May I please enter the building?"

No, the dragon on his right said. This one was green, with a jagged scar on the underside of its neck that indicated it had once been in a crash from a great height.

"I need to speak to Theo," Tal said.

You may not, the other dragon said. This one was a pale blue, almost chalky, its eyes a light green. If it hadn't been positioned to kill him, Tal might have thought him one of the prettiest dragons he'd ever seen.

"Why is that? Is he too busy trying to overthrow the government?"

The blue dragon bristled. It turned its head toward Tal for the first time. A strange sensation washed over Tal. It reminded him of the first time he'd inadvertently understood dragon speech, except the communication didn't resolve into any concrete meaning.

No, was all the blue dragon said.

Yet it had obviously meant to utter more. Its eyes were full of meaning, but with no vehicle to translate it. Something flickered behind those eyes, something that was so far from malice it pulled Tal up short. Whatever words the dragon had been unable to speak, there was *regret* in its eyes.

Not only did the dragon have to follow the orders in the contract, it was also clearly forbidden from speaking to him in a way that could be construed as working against Heathermark's ends.

"I know you can't help me," Tal said, "but maybe you could just take a brief rest for a minute. You know, a nap might help you keep watch better in the future."

We are not stupid, and neither is the contract, the green dragon said.

Tal ignored this, taking a few paces forward. The dragons each let out a roar of fire. The two streams converged to cover the entryway, joining into an impassable wall of flame. They continued until Tal stepped back two paces. The flames stopped.

"So they won't actively harm you, but they would let you run into their flames and burn yourself alive if you try to go in," Bex said, appearing at his shoulder. The rest followed tentatively behind her. The dragons looked on impassively, no more concerned by the presence of six humans than they had been by Tal alone.

Tal pulled Clem aside, whispering to her so the dragons couldn't hear. Despite her terrified expression, she nodded vigorously in agreement with his proposed plan.

"Okay everyone, let's get as close to the door as we can," Tal said. He didn't finish the thought: *and hope the dragons were only explicitly told to keep people out of the building, not to continue attacking even after intruders get inside.*

They stepped close, and the wall of flame burst to life once again. The dragons did not speak further. There was no argument that could win them over. Luckily, Tal's group didn't need an argument. They just needed a talented fireworker.

Clem stood in front, her eyes closed and sweat beading on her upper lip.

Working with dragon fire was far more difficult than other kinds of fire. The same volitional properties that allowed it to contain speech also made it resistant to human magic. But Clem was as gifted as any fireworking student, and their recent studies into the properties of dragon fire had given her more practice with the stuff than anyone else.

The others braced behind her. Something moved in the fire. A shape appeared, a glimmer like a small human walking through the flame. The shape glowed blue, hotter than the fire around it. The shape began to vibrate as it turned black as ash. Then it grew in a roughly circular pattern, forming a tunnel not more than five feet tall.

It was now or never. Tal tamped down his fear and bolted forward, bending almost to his knees as he slid through the tunnel. Flames licked overhead, yet strangely he could not feel their heat. Clem's fireworking had formed a wall that reflected heat outward. Fire reflecting fire. How was Clem not the Preeminent Mage?

The others followed, Clem coming up last. The tunnel zipped shut behind them. Tal felt immensely stupid as he crashed into the front door, which was shielded from the flames by a massive marble archway. They pressed up against him as he pushed with all his might.

"It's a pull," Bex said sweatily.

They bunched to one side and Meret pulled the door open. They were inside. They had survived the flames.

Through the glass doors, Tal could see that the fire had stopped. His hope had been right—the dragons had been ordered to keep people out, not pursue them if they got in. Literal as snapdragons. Still, he kept looking over his shoulder as they made their way across the empty foyer.

The silence was haunting compared to the orderly bustle of the last time he'd been here. No one greeted them, no one manned the large reception desks along the far wall, no one trudged to their next meeting around the ring of balconies running along the rotunda.

They stepped forward tentatively.

"They called an evacuation in advance," Claret said. "This was all planned so their employees wouldn't be in the building as the attack was happening."

"Lucky for us," Bex said.

A voice shattered the silence. It sounded like it was coming out of the walls, and was instantly recognizable.

"All unauthorized personnel are advised to leave the premises. There is no cause for alarm. Anyone remaining in the building will be subject to apprehension by security. This is for your own safety."

The voice belonged to Theo. It was just as calm as it had been in his office, but so much louder as it resonated around the rotunda.

"Evacuation order, or intruder detection?" Tal asked.

There was no opportunity to answer. Just as they passed the center of the room, by the massive dragon skeleton with the newest cabin design on its back, the tramping of boots echoed over the marble floor.

A score of security guards emerged from the security office at the rear of the foyer. Most held three-foot metal rods that glowed, likely with a metalworking that would cause them to stun on impact. Two guards, who appeared to be in charge, brandished massive scimitars. Claret's own sword was now in her hand. Tal looked on in astonishment as its blade changed color, flashing from yellow, to pale blue, to red as Claret adjusted a set of dials on its side. It was only then that Tal reflected that no one else in their party was armed. Meret was muttering under his breath, preparing a few emergency spells.

"You're not allowed here," said one of the captains. He wore a sleek black helmet with matching plate armor. A wicked sneer was visible through the gap in the helmet. "I confess, though, I'm happy you are. My men could use some practice beating the shit out of intruders."

This man was under no magical contract. He didn't need to be coerced into violence—it came naturally to him.

"I can't fight them all," Claret said. "I'm worth exactly eleven of these idiots, not twenty."

"Then don't fight alone," Enna said. Her voice was just as creaky, just as worn as it always had been. But there was a warmth within it. A twinkle of something mischievous. And dangerous. "Tal, if you please, could you give me a little push?"

Her feet made a buzzing noise as she invested them once again with magic.

"I can't push—"

Enna cut him off. "Just push, you lovely young man."

Tal did as instructed, giving Enna a shove that in any other circumstance would've felt like a horrifying amount of force to apply to an old woman. This was no ordinary old woman. She rocketed forward, sliding toward the right edge of the guards' flank. She turned as if on a curved track. A few of the guards swung at her with their sticks, but none was quick enough to connect as she slid by, stretching her hand out toward the attackers after dodging their swings.

Claret charged forward, focusing on the guards that Enna had passed. The reason became immediately evident. Each guard had one of Enna's workings on their feet. Rather than the controlled workings that Enna used to get around, some appeared to work in the opposite fashion, binding their feet to the floor. The worst off found one foot stuck to the floor, and the other without any traction whatsoever. Claret moved between them, her sword now on the yellow setting, which let out a burst of electricity as it met armor, batons, the exposed backs of legs. In a moment, half of the guards were down, including one of the captains.

Tal and the others rushed to any fallen batons they could find, doling out blows to the guards who had been expecting a single combatant, and were now flailing for footing. All the while Enna zipped around in a circle, flashes of light coming from beneath her feet and the boots of the newly very slippery or sticky guards. Wherever she went, a trail of chaos followed.

In a few more moments, every single guard save for the last captain had fallen. His sword glowed a fatal red as he stepped toward Claret. He had either warded away Enna's spellwork or his boots were resistant to it, because his steps were sure and unencumbered. The armor that had at first appeared black rippled to a deep gray as he moved. A lightworking wound its way through it, more visible but likely no less powerful than the ones on Claret's jacket. Enna had skidded to a halt on the far side of the room, catching her breath. Tal and Bex each brandished a baton, but Claret held out a hand for them to stay back.

There was no possibility that this was Claret's first one-on-one duel with the leader of an opposing group of fighters. That the captain was a foot taller than her, and dressed in thick armor to Claret's comparatively minor protection of a leather jacket and simple cloth breeches, seemed not to bother her.

"Just a moment," Claret said. She paused, stuck her sword two inches into a crack in the marble floor to free her hands, and removed her teal jacket. She tossed it to Tal, before turning back to her foe. "I would hate to get your intestines on it."

This threw the captain into a fury, echoed all around him by cries of frustration from his incapacitated men—at least those of whom were still conscious.

What followed was too fast for Tal to describe. Claret moved with a fluid grace that had to be magically augmented, her blade seeming to occupy two or three places at once, deflecting the captain's blows in the same moment as it clanged against his shin or breastplate. Despite her threat, Claret had refused to use her sword's lethal setting, and sparks flew with each strike.

A furious assault pushed Claret back, her feet sliding over sections of the floor still slick from Enna's magic. The captain's shoes appeared to dig into the slippery areas. He stepped forward, keeping up a steady barrage.

Claret backtracked until she met the plinth where the dragon skeleton was perched, then vaulted up onto it. Tal wondered if the high ground was somehow advantageous, but with each swing of the captain's sword, each of Claret's rapid parries, it was impossible to see any advantage.

That is, until the captain tried to leap up to join her.

He did so carefully, leaving himself enough space so Claret could not strike him in mid-air. Claret didn't attack him. Instead, she struck one of the struts holding the dragon's ribcage in place. The ribs swung outward, catching the captain just as he landed. To his credit, the ribs only knocked him briefly off balance, and he fell into an acrobatic stance back on the floor.

A section of floor still covered with Enna's spellwork.

One leg stuck, the other gave out, and that was enough. The dragon ribs had swung back toward Claret, who vaulted around them, spinning and bringing down the full force of her nonlethal blade. Without his balance, there was no chance of the captain blocking the strike cleanly. Two smacks later, and he was flat on his back, armor clanging impotently against the floor.

"Thanks, Tal," Claret said, taking her jacket back and shrugging into it.

"No intestines on it, I promise," Tal said.

Claret smiled grimly. "The dragons have been trying not to hurt us. I thought we should probably return the favor."

"More than these lot deserve," said Enna, limping back to them.

"Are you alright?" Tal asked, rushing to her. He had one eye on the captain, but the man hadn't moved. His sword had slid beneath a wastebin on the other side of the room.

"I do believe I've overdone it." Enna looked down at one of her knees, critically. "I'm going to have to have that replaced again, I think."

Clem, who had not had the opportunity to meet Enna before, looked aghast.

"She's kidding," Tal said with no idea whether or not this was actually true.

Claret was already removing an impressive amount of rope from her pack. "Enna and I will stay here and deal with these fine gentlemen. You go on. There probably aren't more than a couple guards left, and now you've got those handy batons."

Tal felt a little sick with the baton in his hand. He had dealt perhaps three blows with it, all of which had been glancing and received the majority of their power from the metalworking that gave them a stunning quality. He still hated every second. If there was one thing the university had taught him, it was that being a mage gave one the means to avoid violence rather than inflict it.

He had to stop himself. He looked at Clem, who could probably have torched their enemies if she had a flame handy, and at Meret, whose language-working would do nothing if they came up against another batch of guards. They had their similarities, yes, and he had certainly come to care for them as friends in his short time back at the university. Yet there was a separation between himself and these mages that he could no longer leave unacknowledged.

Whatever he was, he was no longer a mage.

Right now, he was just a young man with a stolen baton, who would do anything to stop someone from enslaving dragons. He looked over his shoulder. Bex was at his side, baton at the ready. Tal might be trying to stop Theo in order to prevent the bloodshed of a dragon uprising, or the overthrow of the government by a dragon airline, but he knew that his deepest reason for caring lay solely with Bex.

"If there are more guards, they should be scared," Tal said. "I think Meret smacked one so hard he thinks it's last Tuesday."

Meret, who had not made contact with anything other than the guards' batons and the floor, smiled ruefully. The evacuation message in Theo's voice echoed around them, playing on a loop every few minutes.

Their shrinking party made its way up the set of steps leading up the rear wall of the rotunda. Claret and Enna got to work, the adventurer handling most of the heavy lifting and rope-tying while Enna made slight adjustments to her workings to make the process easier, massaging her injured knee between alternately releasing and pinning guards back to the ground as Claret wrestled them into position.

The steps propelled them upward. Tal led the way toward Theo's office on the top floor resolutely, trying to take comfort in the weapon. That was what you were supposed to do, wasn't it? Feel girded by the strength of the deadly—or in this case at least stunny—force in your hand? If Tal felt girded by anything, it was his conviction that Theo had finally gone too far, that despite what he might have done for Tal, there was no amount of bribery that would make Tal see him for anything but what he truly was: exactly the person Bex had always described. It was freeing to reach this point. He only wished he had reached it sooner. Bex placed a hand on his back as she ran behind him, its pressure immensely reassuring.

Claret had been right about the lack of additional guards. Security was focused around the entrance, and they saw no one save a confused janitor who looked up as they ran past, before shrugging and continuing to polish a nameplate on one of the office doors.

They continued up and up. From the windows at each level they could look out over the city and catch a glimpse of what was happening by the Assembly Hall. Dragons circled above it, their formations orderly and threatening. In place of the half sun, half moon flag that usually flew over the hall, above the giant statue of Arren built into its façade, a giant white flag flapped instead. That at least meant the dragons wouldn't attack for now. Maybe less ideal that the entire government had given up with barely any resistance.

"They didn't bother to stand and fight," Bex said bitterly.

Even with the help of the stairs, the group was wheezing by the time they reached the closed doors of Theo's office. They were locked, no handle or hinge visible on the solid wood.

"There's no way there's not some kind of woodworking on this," Bex said. "We're not going to be able to knock it down."

Meret, who had been brandishing his baton unconvincingly, looked relieved that they weren't going to try. Bex pointed toward a black box on the wall to one side. It glowed softly from a recessed circle in its center.

"It's some kind of access mechanism," Bex said, her glasses slipping down her nose as she inspected it. She spoke into it: "*Open.*"

"*Access denied*," the box said.

"Smash it?" Bex asked.

"This is a languageworking." Meret curled around the box like an otter playing with an object in the water. "Let me figure out how it works."

Tal looked over at Bex, whose focused expression was tinted with anxiety.

"Are you okay?" Tal asked. "I know it's been a while since you talked to your father."

She bit her lip. "You know, I don't even really think of him as my father anymore. That might make this easier."

"Also, I betrayed him much more recently than you did."

"True, I doubt he'll put you on a poster now that you've tried to ruin his evil plot."

Tal scraped at his brow. "Really not happy that you know about the posters."

"It would only be embarrassing if you actually went along with it. Besides, it was such a handsome poster, with such inspiring slogans."

It took a few breaths for Tal to collect himself, and to stop thinking about how close he had come to accepting the offer. Everything before Bex had come to Thelspoint felt like a dream. Not a nightmare, exactly, but something unreal and difficult to reconcile with his current situation.

"I've got it." Meret's voice fell into the exact tone he used when he was called on in class to explain an obscure concept. "It's attuned to a specific voice. Only Theo's voice, or the voice of one other person—I'm guessing an assistant—can open it."

So we're stuck, was Tal's first thought.

"So are we stuck?" Meret asked with a rhetorical flourish. "You might think. But luckily you have one of the top languageworkers in the university on your side."

"And have I told you just how very much I value you as a colleague and research partner?" Tal asked.

Meret rolled his eyes. "We just have to wait until that recording plays again."

They waited for what felt like an interminable period of time, though it couldn't have been more than a couple minutes. When the walls resonated with Theo's voice again, Meret opened his mouth, his eyes rolling back in his head in truly alarming fashion.

The recording ended. Meret closed his mouth, his eyes flashing back to their usual position. He leaned down toward the box.

"You'd be surprised how little it takes to imitate someone's voice," Meret said. "Usually I can do it with two or three sentences. The recording should be plenty."

Then Meret did something just as startling as the eye-rolling. He opened his mouth, and Theo's voice came out.

"Open door." Meret's diction was so indistinguishable from Theo's that Bex recoiled.

There was a long pause. Then the box blinked green, and a crack appeared in the door's previously solid wood. The two sides parted, sliding open to reveal the office. Tal nodded his approval, Meret shrugging like he'd just performed first-year level magic.

"That was the spookiest thing I've ever seen," Tal said.

"Maybe, but I still like him a lot more than my actual father," Bex said.

A voice boomed across the room: "You do, do you?"

Theo had always been cool, in charge, and intimidating. Now he was almost glorious in his power. He sat alone in the sitting area nearest the door, opting for the comfortable couch rather than his stately office chair. In front of him was a glowing sheaf of parchment.

"Talarus," Theo said, "you should be aware that the morality clause in your sponsorship contract specifies that you not associate with disreputable characters. My daughter almost certainly falls into that category."

"It's a good thing I didn't sign it, then," Tal said. They stopped behind the other couch, opposite Theo.

"Don't go any further," Bex whispered.

It was soon obvious why she said this. While one of Theo's hands hung casually over the contract, the other hovered over an exposed button built into the armrest. Some type of security device, though there was no way of knowing exactly what horror it might unleash.

"There's still time to reconsider," Theo said. "Even under the new regime, our airline will need to varnish our reputation. It would be helpful to have an ambassador to the university."

"I've taken all the time I need," Tal said, having to restrain himself from lunging at Theo.

Theo's eyes darted between the others in the group. "It appears I have an opening. Any of you want to make a ludicrous amount of money?"

Clem bristled at the thought, while Meret took an unconscious step forward. He seemed to catch himself, and an unfriendly grin spread over his face. Meret might salivate over the clout of a sponsorship deal in principle, but not one that looked like Tal's table scraps. If Theo thought he was going to buy his way out of this, he had clearly misjudged his audience.

"Enough, Dad," Bex said. "We have to talk about this. About the dragons."

"Simply wonderful, aren't they?"

"This is a perversion of everything they are. You've taken noble, majestic, gentle creatures and reduced them to mere pawns."

A chill went through Tal in response to Theo's horrible smile. "And what powerful pawns they are. As if each and every one passed to the other side of the board and turned into a queen."

Bex inched forward. Theo pretended not to notice, rising from the couch. For a second it looked like there might be an opportunity to rush him, but with a *click* the security button unhooked from the couch. Theo twirled it absent-mindedly between his fingers as he strolled toward the window overlooking the circling dragons.

"In the next few minutes, I am going to escort the entire Assembly to a temporary holding area. A new Assembly will then be installed, with spots left open for those in the existing government who are willing to accept a new form of rule. Decreed by the dragons, no less." Theo stared over his shoulder at Tal. "Of course, the dragons' 'translator' is really just a Heathermark employee with a script. It's a shame. You could've been their official mouthpiece if it hadn't been so obvious that you had your own designs."

"Not being a fascist is a pretty reasonable design," Meret said, a hand on Tal's shoulder.

"You act as if I'm taking over the whole government. I'm simply installing some friendly members of the Assembly."

No one in the room, including Theo, really believed this.

"Dad, all we want is to make sure no one gets hurt," Bex said.

"And no one will. If they cooperate." Theo turned to her, the resentment gone from his face. "Don't you understand, Bex? This is for us. For our family. For you. The core of our business has been rotten for years. It's been almost eighteen months since we turned a profit, all because the Assembly's regulations prevent us from expanding to new routes and running flights at maximum capacity. We've had to take loans from three separate entities just to maintain our operating budget."

"What are you saying?" Bex asked.

"I'm saying that if we don't do this, Heathermark will be dead in the next two years. Probably sooner."

Genuine shock overtook Bex's face. For all of her conflicting emotions about her father, she clearly saw the airline itself, their family wealth, as a constant in her life.

"I understand," Bex said. She took a step forward. Theo eyed her, suddenly mistrustful, a finger over the security button. "I understand completely."

Clem mouthed something that looked very much like *what the fuck?* Tal didn't allow himself a reaction. They had to place their faith in Bex now.

"Obviously I don't like the way you're doing this, but I respect that you were desperate," Bex said. She took another step.

"Desperate and mad, you mean?" Theo asked with a laugh that could definitely have been saner.

"I didn't say that. Desperate and understandable."

Another step forward.

"When I left, I was in a really dark place," Bex said. "I thought you and Mom were being unreasonable, that all your demands that I get an education in business were just you being hard-headed. But I see now that you did it because you wanted me to be prepared to help."

"We wanted you to run the business one day. You're smart, Bex, smarter than I am."

"I don't know about that." Bex's laugh was cut short by the briefest start of a sob. "Maybe just smart enough to run the business."

Bex took another step forward, and Theo now faced her fully, his face riven with pain. Joy bubbled somewhere beneath its surface.

Bex continued: "When I left, I thought you and Mom didn't see me. You wanted me to go down a track I thought wasn't for me."

"I'm so sorry."

"It's so clear to me now," Bex said, moving deliberately toward her father. "You did all of this for us, and that's the greatest show of love I could've asked for. So let's do this together. I'll help you clean up this situation, put our new Assembly together, and get the business back on track. As a family."

The security device stayed slack in Theo's hand as Bex took the last few steps and embraced her father. Both had tears in their eyes. Meret and Clem looked dejected.

Tal considered if his trusting nature had once again gotten the better of him. Had he misunderstood Bex this whole time, failing to see that, beneath an idealistic façade, she was a lonely child who missed the affection of her parents?

The thought diminished as Tal considered the Bex he had actually come to know over the past several months, the Bex who was so militant about her own idealism that she imposed it on everyone around her, the Bex who insisted he be the most ethical version of himself.

Tal smiled, because he knew they had already won.

With a twist, Bex pulled away from her father, the security device twinkling in her hand. Tal leaped forward and grabbed the contract, noting the new lines that had appeared since they had last looked at its counterpart. There was no doubt this was the master copy.

Only slightly less quickly, Clem pulled the fire from a gas lamp on the wall, turning it into a ball that bounced rapidly up and down, creating a wall between Bex and Theo. Theo held a hand to his jaw as if Bex had slapped him.

"I love you, Dad," Bex said, wiping away tears, "but there is no way in Arren's name I can let you get away with this."

Theo snarled, hemmed in by the fire. "You were never my real daughter."

Bex guided one of her tears onto the frame of her glasses, and wiped it clean on her shirt. "I really, really wish that were true. Tal, could you please amend the contract?"

"Gladly," Tal said.

No sooner did the word leave his lips than a sound like a hurricane shook the windows. Then came a roar as a massive scaly head came into view. Each stroke of the dragon's wings rocked the entire room. Tal's heart fell. Ronar stared in at them, terrible intent in his eyes.

"One last contingency, of course," Theo said, sounding almost bored. He leaned against the window, which glinted with a strange dimness unlike the others. With a sound like a mirror being slowly picked apart piece by piece, the window began to morph. It almost seemed to melt as it wrapped itself around Theo's body, clinging to his clothes and working its way around his face. When it covered him completely, he stood still, suddenly reduced to a statue.

"Fireweave," Clem said. "He's protecting himself."

Tal recognized the protective fabric from the fireworking classroom. It was strong enough to stop all but the most sustained direct flame if it worked its way fully around a person . . . and there it went. Theo's feet became encased, and he pitched forward onto the floor, hitting the tile with a sound like a suit of armor tipping over.

"While we get roasted!" Meret screamed in panic. The office door slammed shut behind them. Ronar smashed his head against the other windows, shattering them into shards that shot across the room, sending Tal and his companions ducking for cover behind the chairs and couches.

Tal tried to reach out to Ronar, to find any semblance of language connecting them. There was nothing. Whatever instructions he'd been given, they must forbid him from speaking to Theo's enemies. Another window smashed.

Tal turned his attention to the contract, grabbing a fountain pen off the coffee table and writing furiously as he tried to think of any language that could save them.

As soon as the pen touched the paper, the ink disappeared.

Tal stared in horror. He checked the ink. He scratched the pen against the back of the couch, spraying ink everywhere. It wasn't the pen.

Bex grasped his hand. Both of their palms were clammy, and a sheen of nervous sweat laced her brow, alongside a half dozen tiny cuts from where the window's glass had struck her.

"It won't work," Bex said, trying the pen herself. "We're not signees on the contract, or the representatives of either party. It has to be changed by a dragon or someone acting on the dragons' behalf."

So they were dead. About to be incinerated by a dragon Tal had long called a friend. A dragon who, by some accounts, had been his *only* friend at the lowest point in his life. He squeezed Bex's hand. Then he held her close.

The furnace inside Ronar's belly filled with fire. Heat reached Tal's skin through the dragon's scales. Not even Clem's fireworking could possibly stand between them and the flames.

Ronar? Tal tried one last time. *Listen, I know you can't speak to me. But I happen to know something those Heathermark assholes don't about dragon speech.*

Ronar gave no sign of hearing his words.

Your fire allows you to communicate in a way I couldn't possibly equate to human speech, Tal continued. *That's the key, isn't it? The words are in the fire?*

Ronar roared and pressed himself against the window, pulled by an invisible force. It seemed to take all his effort to prevent himself—even temporarily—from acting out the contract's will and raining flame upon them.

I don't need you to say anything, Tal continued. *I just need you to breathe a little fire—not so much as to cook us, please and thank you—but just enough so you can authorize me as your official legal counsel. I know that sounds weird.*

The dragon's eyes narrowed. Tal thought he saw the same wry humor in them that he'd become accustomed to. Even held by magical constraints, Ronar found his obstinacy amusing.

Tal had no idea whether this would work. He didn't even know if Ronar could breathe fire without seriously hurting everyone in the room.

Tal stood up and looked his friend in the eye. *Please, Ro.*

Ronar's eyes darted, almost panicked as he grappled against the magical impulses that bound him. The pain on his face was enough to make Tal want to rush over and kick Theo. The man lay facedown, unmoving, his hardened lip a sneer against the clean floor of his office.

Tal braced for fire.

And fire came.

It came in a narrow stream, turned toward the far end of Theo's office. The fire melted windows and sent the massive desk up in a plume of smoke. Tal reached his mind inside that fire. It still didn't come as easily as speaking with Ronar directly, but there was something *there*.

Tal tugged at it. He used every method he'd practiced during his time researching at the university, prying into the core of the fire's intent.

He had no confidence in this. Yet he found he didn't need his own confidence as Bex stepped beside him and once again took his hand in her own.

Meaning unfurled from the fire. Tal could not have put it into human speech, but its intent was obvious. The fire, Ronar's fire, wished Tal to act on his behalf.

The parchment in Tal's other hand flashed. Bex released her grip and handed him the pen. He wrote furiously.

All he could come up with was: *Dragons will not breathe fire at or otherwise act in a manner that causes Talarus and his companions harm.*

A Dragon's Choice

Ronar did nothing for a long while. His slow wingbeats were the only sound. He watched Tal intently, then shrugged as if to say, *what now?*

They got to work. There were close to two pages of addenda in the contract, most of which they crossed out. They kept the orders not to harm innocent people, of course. Finally, they reached the rules forbidding the dragons from communicating with—and ordering them to thwart by any means necessary (including violence)—those who interfered with the overthrow of the Assembly. A light blinked out in Ronar's eyes. They were suddenly warm and filled with regret.

Tal, I am so sorry, Ronar said. *I may not be able to hurt him with fire, but I could certainly crush this small man.* A threatening claw edged toward Theo.

There's no need, friend, Tal said. *He's lost. The legal system will decide the punishment for what he's done. We are not the ones to decide his fate.*

These are wise words. Ronar sniffed derisively. *At least for a human.*

Tal laughed and strode forward. He embraced Ronar's snout, wrapping his arms tightly around the warm, slightly damp dragon nose.

The others had been watching, unable to understand their conversation. Seeing that it was now clearly safe, they inched forward, picking their way through shattered glass to stand by Tal. Tal introduced Meret and Clem to Ronar, who bowed his head respectfully and apologized so profusely that Tal eventually stopped translating.

Over Ronar's shoulder, Tal could make out the shapes of other dragons. They no longer flew in formation. Some roosted atop buildings, while others hovered listlessly above. They appeared unsure of exactly what to do with themselves as they came out of their magically-induced trance. The crowds in the streets below were still frantic.

The next few minutes were all business. Tal suggested that they immediately nullify the contract, but Bex insisted they wait. The chaos of going from complete control to zero might cause the first real bloodshed of the day. They needed to get down to the Assembly Hall before things could get further out of hand. With the contract in Bex's jacket pocket and Theo held between all four of them—the fireweave made him incredibly heavy—they made their way back down to the lobby. They stopped only to unhook the state-of-the-art cabin from the dragon skeleton where it was being displayed in the foyer.

Claret and a very tired but no less inquisitive Enna asked for every detail of their encounter with Theo as they dragged the saddle outside. Ronar was waiting for them in the courtyard, in intense conversation with the two dragons who'd been guarding the door. They both apologized. The sleek cabin could easily have fit twelve passengers once they strapped it onto Ronar's back. They all piled into it, Theo stuffed in a storage compartment in the back. His still fireweave-encased body clanged against the floor as they dropped him in.

They took flight, making their way toward the center of Thelspoint, the two dragons flanking them like flying guards.

It turned out they didn't have far to go before they met the others. A dozen of the largest dragons Tal had ever seen streaked toward them out of the smoky mist. Ronar pulled up short. Tal climbed forward to the pilot's seat. He looked over his shoulder as he made his way forward, and saw Bex beside him. She'd somehow slipped into a harness and attached herself to the same lead Tal was using to secure himself. The look on her face told Tal all he needed to know: It didn't matter that he was the one with pilot training, who was used to navigating a dragon's back without losing his balance, or even that he was the one who could speak to the creatures. She would be there for this last encounter.

Do not stand in our way, small one, the lead dragon said to Ronar. The folds above his eyes were tinted blue, carving harsh highlights below a golden brow that almost looked like a crown. *We have come to destroy Heathermark Flight Group.*

Still more dragons joined them. Soon more than twenty hovered before Ronar. Tal and Bex stood on either side of the pilot's chair, feeling small. If it came to a fight, there was no possibility that Ronar and the dragons who had come with them from Heathermark Tower could win. In fact, the other two were slowly inching away. Probably good sense more than cowardice.

It was not Ronar who responded, but Tal.

You have much to be angry about, Tal said. *What is your name, friend, that I can address you properly?*

If he had been speaking aloud, the wind would have whipped away Tal's words. But one of the curious properties of dragon speech was that even a small dragon—or human—could project their voice a great distance.

The blue-gold dragon looked around, confused. When he registered the source of the speech, he glared down at Tal, gliding closer. His chest inflated so he could float without flapping his wings.

I am the one they call Tolvandril. I have never been addressed by a human before, and confess that my patience grows no longer at being addressed by one now.

You are speaking with the human who saved you from Heathermark's evil workings, Ronar said. *You owe him thanks.*

Tal stroked Ronar's scales. He wondered how this conversation looked to Bex. Tal was too frightened by the stare of the blue-gold dragon to translate in real time.

You? The dragon flew still closer, until his golden eye was less than ten yards away. His eye was as tall as Tal was. When it blinked, it slithered shut with a sound that felt as if it might swallow Tal whole.

It comes as a surprise to me, too, Tal said with a nervous laugh.

But the contracts that hold us shackled are still in place, Tolvandril said.

I can nullify them now.

Then do it. Tal felt the dragon's impatience. Clearly the deal with Heathermark was a sore that had been allowed to fester for far too long. *And tell us where the demon spawn responsible for this travesty is.*

"What are they saying?" Bex finally asked.

"They're asking us to destroy the contracts. And to give up your dad."

Bex stared with pure resolve at the dragon before them. Aware that she could not understand the conversation, the blue-gold dragon had simply ignored her.

"We have him," Tal whispered. "If we have to, we could give him up."

"But?" Bex asked.

"But for everything he's done, I think he deserves to be punished and made to see his own shortsightedness, not executed."

Though Bex's eyes were forward, Tal knew her mind was on her father, stuck inside fireweave in the storage compartment behind the cabin. If she said they would give him up, he wouldn't fight her. This was her decision to make, her father, her messed up family.

She had once told Tal that she could never forgive her father. Forgiveness wasn't an easy thing for Bex. What Tal saw now in Bex's eyes was not the softness of forgiveness. It was a flinty thing, one that nonetheless held love, and pain, and hope. She shook her head.

"We won't give him up," Bex said. "He deserves a lot of things, but not that."

Tal turned his attention back to the dragon.

I will dissolve the contracts. On two conditions. A sense of disassociation washed over Tal. He was negotiating with a creature who could easily bite clear through Ronar's neck and eat all of them. Who was Tal to stand up to such a being?

Tolvandril stared with unblinking eyes.

The conditions are these: First, you will seek no revenge on Heathermark or its leadership. Theo will be prosecuted according to human laws, and punished as he deserves. Second, in the future if the dragons have any grievances, they will come to me first before taking any action. We will do our best to come to a peaceful agreement.

Ronar nodded in approval. Several faces were pressed to the glass at the front of the cabin.

How do I know I can trust you? Tolvandril asked.

Words had reached the end of their usefulness. He only had one other option, and it rested primarily on a hunch. He reached into his pocket and extracted the large sphere Enna had given him.

It burned green as it always did when Tal touched it. Tal had always removed his hands before the image could crystallize, but it now came into full view as he held it aloft. A simple shape appeared on a field of green. It was the outline of a dragon.

Tolvandril's sharp eyes took in the image, understanding ringing their golden irises.

"I believe this sphere shows a representation of one's true nature," Tal said. "I can't tell you what it means, but whatever has awakened in me leads to one conclusion. I am dragonkind."

Tolvandril stared at him hard. The scales on his neck crackled as they flexed, his head rearing back. Tal prepared for the dragon to spring forward and cleave his jaws through him, Ronar, and Bex. Instead, the dragon nodded.

Surely you must know that I do not speak for all dragons, Tolvandril said. *I can make no promises for my fellows' conduct.* There was a long, resentful pause. *But for myself and the others with me, we accept your terms. We will leave the reckoning to you, and look to make our new home, a dragon's haven outside the reach of humans.*

Every bundle of nerves that had been holding itself in tension relaxed within Tal. He wondered if Tolvandril would be so receptive if he knew that Theo was immobilized in the back of the cabin, or that his daughter had been right in front of him. But dragons were known to keep their word. They were safe for now.

Tal took his time climbing back to the cabin, negotiating his lead around Bex's line. The others swarmed excitedly around them. He put up his hand to stop the questions before they could begin.

"Claret, I believe you have the most experience with this sort of thing," he said as Bex handed him the contract. "Could you please advise me on language to end this contract?"

After a few focused minutes, Tal was back out in front of Tolvandril. He and Ronar were chatting amiably about their respective employment experiences with the airlines. Apparently Heathermark dragons had short rib whenever they wanted, which caused Ronar to lament his long tenure with Dragon Air. They stopped talking as Tal made his way back onto Ronar's neck.

"Here it is," Tal said aloud. "This contract is no longer binding. You are all free to do as you wish now. Would you two do the honors?"

With no further ceremony, Tal crunched the contract into a ball and flung it forward over Ronar's head. As the ball of parchment fell, Tolvandril turned with alarming speed and shot out a burst of fire. Ronar sent his own blast of flame to meet it. In the heat of their joint blaze, it was impossible to see that the parchment had even burned. It was simply gone.

The flame went out. Tolvandril beat his massive wings, sending a wave of turbulence around Ronar. *That's that, I suppose,* Tolvandril said. Then he returned to his battalion of dragons, and they flew off together, leaving Thelspoint, and their old lives, behind.

WHEN THE TEA COOLS

The rest of the evening after the incident with the dragons had an air of unreality to it. They had been debriefed by a room full of still frightened Assembly members, had handed off Theo's immobile body to the constabulary, and walked for hours around the city helping to put fires out.

At the end of it, it was finally just Tal and Bex.

"People seem to be taking their near-death experience in stride," Bex said, referring to the revelers who were using the day's events as an excuse to take to the streets. The taverns were overflowing.

"Should we . . ." Tal pointed toward the nearest and rowdiest tavern.

"After all this, honestly, what I want most is a cup of tea and a blanket."

They were close to the university. The tea shops were mostly closed at this hour, and few would provide you a blanket as part of their service. Tal felt every bit as audacious as he had facing down Tolvandril as he said: "You know, I think the kitchen in my dorm might have some spare tea. And I've got blankets galore—special perk of being a senior student."

Bex just looped her arm into the crook of his elbow, and together they made their way to Tal's dorm.

He brewed them each a cup of tea, which they drank sitting on the floor of his room. Bex draped the blanket over her shoulders, pulling it all the way around so not even her arm poked out. Tal laughed as he watched her try to drink tea using a hand that was still under the blanket.

"I have to say, the shock of the night goes to Enna's magic." Tal sat with his back against the bed, his feet outstretched and his thigh pressed flat against Bex's. "Watching her scoot around the floor like that was a sight to behold."

"I always knew she had it in her," Bex replied.

"It was a good thing, too. I don't think even Claret could've taken on all of those guards."

"Not with what you and Meret call 'helping,' that's for sure."

Tal smiled. "I make no apologies for living a pacifist's lifestyle. Though I do admit that being somewhat more adept at clubbing one's foes might come in handy on occasion."

"I'm just shocked you didn't club yourself."

"Hey!" Tal jabbed Bex's shoulder, jostling her tea.

Bex cackled. The evening had left them both exhausted, and somewhat silly. The sound of the citywide party reached an even higher roar outside.

"I shouldn't make fun of you guys," Bex said. "I used the manipulative power of a daughter's love on my dad, and it fucking worked." She shook her head in disgust.

"I was going to ask you about that."

"You were going to ask if it was real?"

Tal froze, surprised she had cut so easily to his most burning question. He nodded.

Bex repositioned herself, tucking against Tal's shoulder. He let his arm fall over her leg, not wanting to overstep by pulling her close, yet still leaning into her weight.

"The truth is, it was real," Bex said. "Not what I said about working with him. The overall sentiment. I do still love him. I do still care about him. That doesn't mean I need to forgive him."

Tal's hand made a gentle circle on the blanket, and on Bex's knee beneath it. "You've been thinking about forgiveness a lot, I can tell."

Bex's smile was a pang of warmth in Tal's center. "Are you sure it's not you who's been thinking about it, and you're just projecting it onto me?"

"Maybe. But this isn't the first time you've brought it up more or less unprompted."

Bex shook her head in mock annoyance so vigorously that her entire body moved against Tal. She used the opportunity to press closer.

"You know, you reach a point in your life where you start to see the patterns," Bex said. "You start to see the things you do wrong over and over again, despite your best efforts to do otherwise."

"Like me coming back here," Tal said. "I should've stayed in Upper Boden with you. I'm so, so sorry about that."

"If you didn't always have one eye toward the university, toward the next great discovery, you wouldn't be you. And I quite like you."

"I quite like you too, you know," Tal said.

Bex smiled. "I do know. And it's 'yes,' the answer to the question you've been too much of a coward to ask." The question of forgiveness. "I forgive you, Tal. I forgave you even before you looked my father's assistant in the eyes and told her you wouldn't betray your friend, although that was quite something to behold."

"Not that it mattered, they took Ronar anyway."

"Of course it mattered." Bex held his gaze for a period of time that would have been uncomfortable if she were anyone else. "No, I think I really forgave you the moment I realized that you'd rather stand up to the mentor who enabled my parents' bad behavior than do the easy thing, the thing I wanted you to do in the moment. You risked the most important relationship in your life because you believed in accountability. I should be willing to save one of the most important ones in mine for the same reason."

"I forgave Nathan," Tal said, his voice catching in his throat.

"Of course you did, because you have a beautiful heart, even if you try to hide it under a larger than average ego."

Tal's pulse thrummed. At this angle, it was hard to meet each other's eyes without bringing their faces close together. This did not turn out to be a problem, as a second after meeting each other's eyes they were locked in a kiss. There was relief in that kiss, relief that everything they'd been through was over, relief that whatever forces both practical and magical that had been working against them hadn't managed to pull them apart.

Then there was another kiss, and the relief turned into heat.

Their teacups lay forgotten on the floor. They waited half-drunk and cooling on the carpet while Tal and Bex made love for the first time. It felt as if whatever had been undone within them by the past few months—and probably longer—was slowly being reknit with each touch of their bodies against each other, each tingle of pleasure at the other's presence. At the end of it all they lay together in Tal's bed, limbs splayed and sweaty sheets kicked to the bottom of the bed.

"Have I told you how happy I am that I chose your shitty airline to protest?" Bex asked. Tal wasn't used to the brightness of her eyes without her glasses shielding them. Every part of him hoped he would have the chance to learn this face.

"However you define it, it seems like your protest was a success." Then he kissed her, and said in a whisper: "I'm glad you chose my shitty airline to protest too."

As Tal made his way from his dorm at Thelspoint University, down through the widening rings of the city and out toward the eastern gate, he thought about how much he had longed to be here. The city had almost seemed to taunt him when he would fly in from Upper Boden, greeting him with an aspect that was simultaneously tantalizing and dismissive. Now he was carrying his few belongings as he left the city behind, and there was no regret within him.

That night with Bex had been about a week ago. In Tal's mind, all of that stuff with the dragons had been largely secondary to drinking tea on the floor with Bex, and then forgetting about their tea altogether.

He wound his way to one of the old Heathermark landing pens, which now operated in a fashion that was nearly as chaotic as the night when the dragon insurgents had torched the outer pens and forced everyone to land there. In light of Theo's crimes and subsequent sentencing, Heathermark had been repossessed by the Thelspoint Assembly, many of its assets sold off or leased to other airlines, as the government operated the business at just enough capacity to cover the flight routes necessary to keep the Unified Coast running. An entire unit of the constabulary had been commissioned to seek out and destroy any remaining mistranslation devices either still owned by Heathermark or on the black market. Nirza herself had offered to assist, even if she was still unwilling to let the genuine version of the device go into common use without an exorbitant fee.

Bex's mother had not objected to the dissolution of Heathermark Flight Group, and it quickly came to light through the settlement proceedings that she had had her own magical contract preventing her from stopping her husband's scheme. As a result, she was allowed to retain a minority stake in the enterprise, and primarily remained at Braisecroft, where she kept an entire wing of the house ready for Bex's arrival at all times. It would remain empty for at least a while longer.

Bex met him at the gate, her own bag slung over her shoulder, sweat bunching strands of hair around the stems of her glasses. Tal couldn't imagine anyone looking more beautiful.

"You ready?" Bex asked, wrapping him in a hug that nearly unbalanced them both.

"I own exactly four items, three of which I'm wearing," Tal said.

"I could've been asking if you're emotionally ready, you know, to go talk to undomesticated dragons on their home turf," Bex said.

"Dragons are never really domesticated. You taught me that."

"Damn right." As she said this, Bex jabbed his forehead with a single finger. She somehow transitioned this to a stroke down his jaw, and pulled his face toward hers. Their kiss had none of the desperate passion of those they'd shared a week ago, when the weight of what they'd been through had seemed sufficient justification for melting into one another. This was a long, hopeful kiss. A kiss with a future. A kiss that bound them together rather than fearing they'd be torn apart.

"There will be plenty of time for that in the Claglands," said a voice from just inside the gate. Helena was watching them. It was unclear if the forced smile on her face was one of amusement or regret at having forced herself into such lengthy proximity with the two lovebirds. She would be accompanying them to the Claglands, where together they would undertake the seemingly impossible task of making a first true diplomatic connection with the dragons. Ever since their exploits with the Heathermark dragons, and since it had become public knowledge that Tal could communicate with them, a growing swell had pushed him toward serving as an emissary. Tal had not been blind to the fact that the university had been involved in this push, which he suspected was at least in part due to the fact that Tal's old sponsor had been disgraced, and that the university itself had done nothing to stop the dragon attack despite knowing of Tal's ability. A break from the public eye might do everyone good, in the interest of optics.

In truth, Tal didn't mind.

"You'd better get used to this," Bex said, pulling away.

Helena just shook her head as she led them inside the pen. Ronar had already been kitted out with a long-distance harness. A motley group of well-wishers had gathered to see them off—Clem having ducked out from one of her lectures, Enna who was using a cane and sporting a limp but otherwise smiling broadly,

Claret in a bright red leather jacket, and of course Nathan in his best professor's robe. There were goodbyes all around.

Meret had been watching Tal like he was betraying everything he believed in by not staying at the university. The look softened when Tal shook his hand.

"I've been thinking," Meret said. "You being back, it made me miss the Completists."

"You're going to restart our little secret society? How could that possibly end badly?"

Meret looked down at his boots. "Well, that's sort of what I was thinking about. I think I'm going to get rid of the secrecy stuff, the exclusivity. If we only have one mage from each discipline, surely we're losing something? Maybe there's something important in the perspectives of people who—and I shudder to say this—aren't the best in their discipline. Just a theory, probably an incorrect one."

Tal's laugh warmed the crisp morning air. "Who would've possibly thought that a society designed to bring together all different types of people could benefit from actually allowing all different types of people to join?"

"Seems ill-fated, I know."

They clasped hands and shared an awkward goodbye hug before Tal turned to Enna.

"No final sphere as a parting gift?" Tal asked Enna as he released her from a ginger hug.

"The spheres have more than served their purpose," Enna said with a cagey smile.

Tal knew what she meant.

The final goodbye was with Nathan, who made him promise to take detailed notes on all his interactions with the dragons, dispensing advice on study design and the necessity of approaching a demographically diverse group of dragons, rather than advising him on his safety as he went into potentially hostile dragon territory. Tal was glad he could still count on his mentor for his focus on scholarship above all else.

Finally, they climbed aboard and made sure all of their luggage was safely tied down. They had brought enough equipment that there were only three empty seats. Tal made his way to Ronar's head and the pilot's seat, waving to everyone on the ground as he did.

All right, buddy, Tal said. *How do you feel about one last flight together?*

You don't need to be up here, the dragon replied. *I know the way.*

I'm not here to steer. Tal patted his friend's scales. Ronar growled approvingly, then suddenly beat his wings twice. His chest filled with hot air, and they were airborne. They hovered over the pens long enough for Ronar to shoot a spout of steam over the pen and the party gathered below. Then he soared higher, until the individuals in the landing pen were indistinguishable from the houses around them.

Tal rose from the pilot's seat and made his way back toward the cabin. Through the glass, her image refracted ever so slightly by the imperfections in the material, he could see Bex sitting with one leg crossed over the other. She looked poised for a grand and immediate adventure rather than a long and hopefully boring trip that would likely take a few days of flying time. Next to her, cleared of equipment and with a cushion smoothed over it, was an empty seat. Tal smiled, walked around to the door at the back of the cabin, and went inside.

The End

ACKNOWLEDGEMENTS

All writing is an act of transmutation, of taking disparate threads from every book you've ever read, keeping the fragments that strike your fancy and throwing away those that you don't until you end up with this vague thing called an "idea." As such, I owe so much thanks to the authors who I've read and enjoyed, especially those who are creating something a bit different in the fantasy space.

A huge thank you to Rachel Williams for this book's beautiful cover art, which so perfectly captures its tone and overwhelming dragonishness. Thanks as well to Katie Bucklein for her skillful proofreading and ability to spot an anachronism.

As always, thank you to my supportive family and friends.

And of course, to Lauren for your constant companionship and support.

A massive thank you as well to you, the reader. When I set out to write this story I had no idea how personal it would end up being. Thank you for taking this flight with me.

About the Author

Ethan Peterson-New (writing as E.M. Peterson) is originally from Western Massachusetts. He lives in Brooklyn, and is a member of the Brooklyn Speculative Fiction Writers Workshop. He has three published novels spanning different age ranges within fantasy:

- *Of Earth and Sky*: Book one of the Young Adult *Terraltum Saga*, in which a found family of teenagers must band together to save us all, after a magical world in the sky reveals itself and sets the magical and non-magical worlds on a collision course.

- *Carnival of the Mind*: A New Adult standalone about a boy trapped in a dreamworld with no way out, who must discover his memories and the nature of his reality in order to escape.

- *Turbulent Magic*: The book you just read (hopefully). There are dragons, a former mage, and a decent amount of tea.

You can follow E.M. on Instagram (@empeterson_books), or join his newsletter for more personal updates at newsletter.em-peterson.com.